RISKING TRUST

PRIVATE PROTECTORS SERIES

ADRIENNE GIORDANO

ALG PUBLISHING

Edited by Gina Bernal

Copyedited by Elizabeth Neal

Cover Design by Lewellen Designs

Author Photo by Debora Giordano

Print Edition ISBN: 978-1-942504-55-9

Digital Edition ISBN: 978-1-942504-54-2

AUTHOR'S NOTE

Dear Reader,

When I first drafted *Risking Trust,* like the book's heroine, I'd recently lost my father. Creating Michael and Roxann's love story not only sparked the idea for the Private Protectors series, but it also helped me tackle the brutality known as the grieving process.

This book means more to me than I can ever express, and I'm thrilled to see it reissued with a snazzy new cover.

Whether you are a new reader or you've been with me from the beginning, thank you for allowing my work into your library!

Here it is, the book that launched my writing journey. I hope you receive as much pleasure from it as I have.

Adrienne Giordano

For my husband.
You've been with me from the start of this crazy, wonderful road.
Thank you and I love you.

RISKING TRUST

PRIVATE PROTECTORS SERIES

ADRIENNE GIORDANO

ALG PUBLISHING

1

"Mr. Taylor, do you want to make a statement?"

Michael remained still, his hands resting on his thighs, his shoulders back. He'd been in this Chicago P.D. interrogation room for the better part of an hour and hadn't said a word.

"Mr. Taylor," Detective Hollandsworth repeated, "your wife was murdered last night and you have nothing to say?"

Oh, he had a lot to say, the first being he didn't kill his wife, but if he'd learned anything running one of the nation's most elite private security companies, it was to keep his trap shut. "Not until my lawyer gets here."

An alien sensation settled on him. Shock? Disbelief? Maybe even sadness because a woman he had loved, a woman who had once been vibrant and fun and sexy, a woman who had grown into a greedy, unhappy wife was dead. Jesus. He may have wanted to end the nightmare of a marriage, but murder? No way.

In his worst bout of rage he wouldn't have done that to her. Sure they were finalizing a brutal—and costly—divorce, but money he had and if giving up some of it meant getting her out of his life, he'd do it. Simple arithmetic.

Right now, the only thing Michael knew was that these two detectives banged on his door at 8:00 a.m. to haul his ass in for questioning.

He flicked a glance to the two-way mirror behind Hollandsworth's head. The room's barren white walls and faded, sickening stench of fear-laced sweat made Michael's fingers twitch. He'd keep his hands hidden from view. No sense letting his nerves show.

The side door flew open and smacked against the wall with a *thwap*. Hollandsworth and his younger partner, Dowds, shifted to see Michael's lawyer storm in wearing a slick gray suit complete with pocket hanky.

Arnie Stark set his briefcase on the metal table. "Is he under arrest?"

"Not yet," Hollandsworth said.

"Do you have anything to hold him?" Arnie held up a hand and his diamond pinky ring flashed against the overhead light. "Wait. Let me rephrase. Do you have anything to hold him on that I won't shred in the next two hours?"

The room stayed quiet.

Arnie turned to Michael. "Have you said anything?"

"No."

The lawyer jerked his head without dislodging even one strand of his gelled gray hair. "Good. Let's go."

Thank you. Before Michael could move from his chair, Hollandsworth stood. "We're not done."

Arnie stopped in the doorway, spun around and said, "Charge him then."

Again the room went silent and Michael broke a sweat. The idea of being locked up scared the hell out of him.

Hollandsworth's face took on the tight look of a balloon about to burst and Michael let out a breath.

Arnie pointed to the door. "We're leaving."

Once outside the police station, the late March wind coming off Lake Michigan slammed into Michael and he sucked in air as if he'd been without it for months. "I didn't do it."

"I don't care," Arnie said. "I'm your lawyer, not your priest. You want someone to hold your hand, I'm not your guy. You want someone to keep you out of prison, that's me."

Not that Michael needed a babysitter, but hell, he'd appreciate his lawyer believing in his innocence. Then again, this particular lawyer was the best in the city. Anyone living in Chicago knew that because he seemed to be on the news every other week touting another win.

"Keep me out of prison. What now?"

"We go back to my office and you tell me every disgusting detail of your relationship with your wife."

"Ex-wife," Michael corrected.

"Not yet she wasn't."

"IT'S ON THE FOUR O'CLOCK NEWS," MRS. MACKEY SAID, pressing the button on the television remote.

Roxann tore her gaze from the declining numbers on the revenue reports and watched as the *Chicago Banner Herald*'s longtime executive assistant, her hair teased and sprayed into submission, switched the channel from CNN to the local news station.

As much as Michael Taylor had wronged her, Roxann couldn't imagine him a murderer. Or maybe she didn't *want* to imagine him a murderer. "Has he been charged?"

"He's only been questioned. I heard from the newsroom that his lawyer got him out before he said anything."

"What about an alibi?"

"He says he was home alone. His doorman saw him go up."

Buildings have back doors.

"I can't believe it. I'd heard they were fighting over money and couldn't agree on a divorce settlement, but still, to kill her?"

Mrs. Mackey shrugged. "I always knew he was no good."

"Eh-hem."

Her assistant whirled to the office door and her head snapped back. Michael Taylor, the man who at one time had filled Roxann with unrivaled happiness, stood in the doorway. Her body went rigid. Literally frozen.

Twelve years ago he ripped her in two, carved out a chunk of her soul and left her emotionally obliterated to the point where she'd made her life so orderly there'd be no room for devastation. Ever.

She had yet to mend that wound.

How much did he hear? She shot out of her chair, sending the blasted thing careening against the wall. He stepped into the office and a tingle surged up her neck.

Michael.

Here.

Now.

"Sorry to interrupt," he said. The sound of his voice, resonant and edgy, had stayed with her over the years. A warm blanket on the coldest January day.

Then she remembered she hated him, despised him with a fury that would level a city block. Her back stiffened, pulling her into immediate battle mode. What could he be doing here?

An explosion of something Roxann hadn't felt in a long time consumed her. She'd spent years preparing a speech that would reduce Michael to a sniveling lump of flesh. Now she had her chance. Twelve years of compartmentalizing. Twelve years of missing him. Twelve years of righteous anger. *Breathe. One, two, three. Stay calm.* Roxann imagined starting at her toes and rebuilding herself bit by tiny bit.

Michael continued to stare, his angular face resembling sculpted rock. She had loved that face. Not quite handsome, but rugged and intriguing. He wore his dark hair combed back and the style accentuated the few wrinkles around his eyes.

Mrs. Mackey glared at him. "How did *you* get up here? Did you even stop at the security desk for a visitor's pass?"

This man left Roxann with enough emotional ruin to fill Soldier Field and her assistant was worried about a visitor's pass? *Squeeze every muscle. More control. Tighter. Rebuild.*

She held up a hand. "He's here now. Let's not worry about the pass."

"I would have gotten a pass if the guard hadn't ignored me for ten minutes. What should really fry you is I made it up eight floors unimpeded."

"Should I have him escorted out?" Mrs. Mackey asked.

A little late for that. Roxann turned toward her desk. "No, but thank you. I'll handle this."

"But—"

Roxann eyed her. "I've got it. Thank you."

Mrs. Mackey offered Michael one last sneer before leaving. Any other time, Roxann would have laughed, but right now? Not so much. She ran a hand over the coil of hair tucked behind her head. Something told her this wouldn't be good.

"So," she said. "This is unexpected."

"That, it is."

The understatement of the century. If someone had told her Michael would be in her office today, she'd have stayed in bed. Sure she wanted the opportunity to skewer him for the destruction he'd inflicted upon her, but seeing him now, a successful businessman whose simple presence commanded the room, took her breath away. Yes, Michael had become better looking with age and according to the media, more dangerous.

She had wanted a life with him and over the years, as she watched from afar, the what-ifs tortured her. He had given himself to someone else, when all she'd ever wanted was for him to give himself to *her*.

For all the time spent obsessing over it, Roxann still couldn't determine why he had chosen Alicia over her.

In place of marriage, Roxann lived alone, worked like a demon and occasionally squeezed in dating men who never managed to capture her interest.

And Michael, the one man who had captured said interest was now suspected of killing his wife.

AFTER THE ROTTWEILER OF AN ASSISTANT LEFT—TWELVE years hadn't thawed *her* out—Michael remained standing.

The light blue silk blouse Roxann wore magnified the sparkle in her eyes, which shouldn't have been a surprise. She always did have a sense of style. Her blond hair was shorter now, but still long enough to tie back. He preferred it loose, not that his opinion mattered anymore.

"I heard about your father," he said. "I'm sorry."

Roxann had adored her old man and losing the belligerent bastard to a massive heart attack had to be rough.

It also left her in charge of the second largest daily newspaper in the state.

"I'm managing." She tapped her fingers on the desk, glanced at her chair and finally sat. "You're here, you might as well sit."

He gave the office a once over and what an office it was. No sharp corners—only a smooth cherry desk, a couple of matching guest chairs and a shiny table with a few cushioned chairs. The feminine version of a power office. Gone were the days of her being buried under stacks of newspapers in a cubicle the size of a matchbox.

On the walls hung a variety of framed newspaper front pages from all over the country. Two from *The Philadelphia Times* caught Michael's eye and his belly shrunk to the size of a pea. She'd gone to Philadelphia following their breakup. After he'd made the biggest mistake of his life.

Roxann studied him with those big eyes that weren't quite blue or green and had always seen right through him. After all these years, being face to face with her clawed at him, reminded him of the pitiful excuse of a man—namely him—who'd failed her. A lot had changed since then and countless times he'd thought about marching in here and telling her he'd screwed up. But he'd never done that and always went home to the wrong woman. The woman who, as of early this morning, was dead.

A knifing pain shot through his shoulders and he cracked his neck against the invasion. Toast already. What a goddamned day. He could sleep for a month.

"What can I do for you?" Roxann asked in that what-are-you-doing-here-and-when-are-you-leaving tone she did so well.

He ignored her and set his briefcase on the floor before sitting in one of the chairs in front of the desk. He didn't expect her to be happy to see him. Truth was, he owed her a twelve-year-old explanation, and he'd love to give it to her. *Not gonna happen though.* Telling her why he'd left all those years ago would only hurt her, and there had been enough of that between them already.

He glanced at the television where a local news reporter stood in front of Area Thirteen headquarters speaking into the camera about Alicia's murder.

"The victim was found in her North Side home," the reporter said.

The victim. And then a photo from three years ago of Michael and Alicia at some charity function flashed onto the screen, and he dug his fingers into his forehead. What a shit storm.

Roxann remained silent, but used the remote to turn off the television before leveling a paralyzing gaze on him. She should work for the government. He doubted any man could withstand the pressure of those eyes.

"I'm sorry about your wife."

"Ex-wife," he said.

She turned her hand palm up. "Does it matter?"

"Legally, she was my wife, but the relationship was over. Had been for two years. I didn't consider her my spouse and I did *not* kill her."

If that information made any impact at all, Roxann didn't show it. She simply stared at him.

"What do you want, Michael?"

"I have a deal for you."

"What kind?"

Now or never, Taylor. "The P.D. is only interested in hearing a confession. If I don't want to be charged with murder, I'm going to have to find out who killed Alicia. I want you to help me."

She sat forward, folded her hands on the desk. "That's what *you* want?"

"Yes."

"I could give you a list of things I want, but if memory serves, that doesn't necessarily matter."

Michael whistled, long and slow. Damn, he'd missed her. "I see your aim is still deadly."

"Don't start."

"Why not? You used to enjoy verbal combat."

It had, in fact, been their version of foreplay and almost always wound up with them finding a quiet spot, wherever they were, to bang the living hell out of each other. Back then, whether it be sex or arguing, Roxann always engaged. Always. Without a doubt, there'd been times when he'd manufactured verbal swordplay to get himself laid. As selfish as it was, he always made it worth her while.

She sighed. "Our history doesn't give you the right to expect things from me."

Expect things? He didn't expect squat from anyone, particularly her. The instant throbbing behind his eyes warned of his firing temper and he stood to release some energy. *You're blowing it, Taylor.* "Wait—"

"My days of waiting for you are over, Michael."

Verbal swordplay engaged. "This is business, Roxann, not personal."

She stood. "I don't want any part of either."

"Yes, you do, because you'll get an exclusive. I'll give the *Banner* total access to my life, good or bad."

That stopped her cold. A high-profile murder and an exclusive. A publisher's dream come true.

Roxann pursed her lips, probably thinking about it. "Why come to me with this deal? Why not the *Chronicle*?"

"I'm pissed at them."

For some reason, that made her laugh. "Why? Because they lambasted your company last year when your operative got caught in that civilian shooting in Afghanistan?"

"Yes. He was in the wrong place at the wrong time and was eventually cleared. *The Chronicle* never followed up on that detail and left the public thinking my guys were a bunch of heartless, murdering barbarians. The *Banner* at least got the story right."

"Yes we did. Thank you for saying that. I still don't want your deal though."

She headed toward the partially open door, pulled on it and peeked out to the reception area where the Rottweiler waited to attack.

Michael's head pounded a steady beat as his frustration mounted. This meeting hadn't gone as he'd planned. He'd expected her to jump at the exclusive. Should have known better. She didn't jump at anything. He picked up his briefcase, wandered to the door and stopped close enough to Roxann to get a whiff of her almost non-existent perfume. Was it that same fruity, kind of floral scent? He had to be imagining it. He closed his eyes and breathed it in again. Yep, the same. Good old predictable Roxann.

He opened his eyes, their gazes met and the magnetic charge pulled him closer. That deep wanting he'd never recovered from still existed.

But Rox wasn't having any of it and slid sideways to reclaim her personal space. Didn't matter. She felt the power between them. How could she not? Her eyes narrowed and he half expected her to whack him.

"Just think about it, Rox. Please." The please couldn't hurt. "You'll realize it's a good deal."

She shook her head no, but said, "I'll think about it."

Forward motion. Excellent.

"There's something else you should know."

"Can't wait," she cracked.

"As of last Friday, Taylor Security has acquired DSI, the *Banner*'s security company. You'll get a letter. Nothing in the agreement will change."

Her eyes opened a bit wider, but she remained quiet.

"The *Banner* is an important client. I wanted you to hear about the change from me."

After another long minute of staring at him like he'd stolen her life savings, she said, "Well, I appreciate that. It's a bit of a shock, but hopefully the good service we've been getting from DSI will continue."

Yeah, this conversation was awkward, but a good businessman didn't walk away from a solid deal because his ex-girlfriend would be a client.

"I'll set up a meeting with your facilities manager. We'll bring our key people over, do a walkthrough of the building and make sure your security is adequate."

Roxann grinned for the first time. "Given that you got up here, I think we both know the security isn't adequate."

She had that right. Any psycho could have stumbled into the newsroom and blown it away. "You'll need some minor upgrades."

"I'm sure we will."

Mrs. Mackey appeared just outside the doorway. "Now should I call security?"

"Unfortunately," Roxann said, "he *is* security."

MICHAEL PARKED HIS SUV AND JOGGED THE LAST HALF BLOCK to Gina's. Tightly packed cars and houses lined the narrow street and his new toy, a monster of a black Escalade, made parking miserable.

He stopped in front of the house and did a visual inspection. The porch needed a fresh coat of paint and the two bright red rockers looked lonely. Michael knew that's how his widowed sister often felt.

The screen door flew open and a five-foot-three bundle of mad sent him a scolding glare. *Here we go.* Gina's mane of curly hair had to be the biggest thing on her, but she knew how to give a mean look. "You're late."

He climbed the porch steps and held his hands in surrender. "I'm sorry."

He had spoken to her and his parents earlier in the day to calm their panic over his trip to the P.D., and she'd invited him for dinner. His baby sister didn't want him to be alone. Stepping into the house, he smelled the glory of a pot roast and took a deep breath. Gina had made him a home-cooked meal on the worst day of his life. That alone made him a lucky man.

Seven-year-old Lily came bounding into the homey living room. She took a running leap and Michael scooped her up, only to feel a twinge in his back. His niece was getting too big for their usual greeting and he couldn't deny the stab of disappointment.

"What's up, cutie?"

"Can I paint your nails?"

Michael grinned. "I draw the line at makeup and nail polish. Find something else and I'm on it."

Lily wiggled out of his arms and charged up the stairs in search of something she could torture him with. In truth, he never minded. She was a sweet kid and if playing with dolls was all she needed, he'd oblige.

"I've been calling you for hours," Gina said, a tinge of irritation littering her voice. "You're all over the news, and

Mom and Dad are freaking. Your assistant said you were out. What does that mean?"

Michael drew a deep breath and sat in Danny's battered lounger. He tried to imagine his brother-in-law sitting there, drinking his beer, but the memory had faded. *Fucking tragedy.*

"I was with my lawyer all day and then I had a meeting at the *Banner*."

"The Roxann Thorgesson *Banner?*"

Leave it to Gina to skip over the part about being with the lawyer. She always did like Roxann. Roxann, with the blue eyes and the blond hair and the legs that seemed to go on and on and on. Those legs could get a dead man moving. "The one and only."

"Why?"

He peeked down the hall to ensure no nosy kids were in earshot. "With the DSI acquisition, we're the *Banner*'s new security company. Plus, I'm trying to broker a deal. I give them an exclusive on Alicia's case and they help me prove I'm innocent."

"Oh." Gina's mouth formed a perfect O.

"Yeah. *Oh.* I need to clear my name."

"I can't believe she's dead. I mean, she was a bitch for sure, but she didn't deserve this."

Hearing his ex-wife referred to that way smacked him. "How about we not call her that? Whatever she was, I loved her once."

When he'd needed a distraction from the Roxann demons, Alicia's acerbic wit had made him laugh. He often wondered what had become of the fun-loving woman who'd gone skinny dipping in the lake on a hot summer night. The unselfish woman who'd allowed him to keep her up all night making love because sleep eluded him.

All those things had vanished in the later years of their marriage.

"Sorry," Gina said.

He waved it off. "If this morning is any indication, the P.D. is bent on me going to prison." He curled his fingers into a tight fist until his knuckles ached from the pressure.

"They're morons. Almost two years of contentious divorce proceedings and you wait until now to kill her? No offense, Mikey, but if you were going to kill her, you would have done it a lot earlier and the cops know it. They just don't care."

"Frightening, isn't it?"

"So, what did Roxann say? Is she going to do it? She has to help."

"She threw me out."

Gina curled her lip. "Ew."

"She'll think about it. As of this morning, my name sells and she's got a newspaper to run. When she gets beyond the emotional crap, she'll realize it's a good deal."

"What's next?"

Michael shrugged." We wait and see what the cops come up with. They're already tracking me via GPS."

"How do you know?"

He rolled his eyes. "Please. Think about what I do for a living. I had one of the guys check my car. They must have put it there when I was being questioned."

"Did you take it off?"

"My ass. I've got nothing to hide."

"Darn tootin'. Besides, where do they think you're going?"

They were expecting him to run. "They think I'm guilty. And I've got the means to establish a nice life on some remote island. That's why I went to see Roxann. I have to prove I'm innocent and, after last year, the *Chronicle* is out."

"Does Ma know about this?"

"No. Don't tell her. I'll do it when there's something to report." He put his palms up to his eyes and pressed hard. "Can you imagine what a nightmare that would be?"

Their parents had been on a tear for months about his catastrophe of a divorce. Not only did they hate divorce, they hated the never-ending battle over money. He couldn't imagine what kind of reaction the *Banner* reporting his problems would garner.

"Ma is going to nag you about airing your dirty laundry."

"Yeah, but they'll support me."

"You might hear about it for the next ten years, but they'll be with you and so will I." Gina pecked him on the cheek. "I'm so sorry. I know the marriage was long over, but it has to hurt on some level."

Michael leaned forward, flexed his fingers. "I don't know what I'm feeling."

"It's the shock. It'll wear off."

Yeah. His sister had learned all about that after a building fell on her firefighter husband and left her with three kids to raise. "Thanks, G."

Gina hugged him tight and a lump the size of a tennis ball swelled in his throat. She'd been through enough and didn't need to be worrying about him.

"They'll clear me."

She stood back and jerked her head. "I know."

A noise from the second floor drew Michael's attention. "Do the kids know?"

"I went over to school this morning and told the boys. I was afraid they'd hear something before I got to them. Lily doesn't know yet."

"How did the boys take it?"

She twisted her lips. "Not well, but they love you and know you wouldn't have hurt Alicia. Talk to them. That's what they're used to and if you don't, they'll notice."

No doubt he'd talk to them. That's what he'd done since their father died. "I'll go up now."

"By the way," Gina said, "Jake's science project made the finals. Make sure you say something."

"No kidding?" Jake was the ten-year-old Jimmy Neutron of the family. The kid could probably disarm a nuclear weapon.

"Yep. That's my boy."

A crash, followed by a howl, came from the second floor.

"Get off him," Gina yelled. Like all mothers, she had x-ray vision and could see through the ceiling.

Michael heard a thud that could have been someone's head splitting open. "Knock it off!"

The kids were generally a good bunch, but fifteen-year-old Matt was a ball breaker and harassed Jake incessantly, and as sweet as Lily was, she had a tendency to be hypersensitive about every damned thing. Girls were way too high maintenance.

Michael heard another crash from upstairs—*enough of this shit*—and took the steps two at a time.

"It never stops," Gina said, her voice carrying the weight of single parenting.

"I'm on it."

He stormed into the boys' room and found Matt on top of Jake shoving a beat-up sneaker in his face.

"Take a whiff, buddy," Matt said.

Michael, hands on his hips, shook his head. This kid would make him nuts. "Get off him before I kick your ass."

He hated to say that in front of Jake, but it was the only thing Matt responded to.

Matt smiled. Typical. "You'd better straighten up. Someone who's seen as much trouble as you shouldn't be smiling."

"Jeez."

Matt waved the sneaker over Jake's face before getting off him and Michael thought his head would blow off his shoulders. *Pain in the ass.* "Don't screw with me, kid."

Being a couple inches taller than his mom had given Matt the idea he was indestructible. They'd see about that. Gina could hold her own, but Matt needed someone to talk to him like his father would have. And Danny would have kicked some serious tail around here.

"Dinner is ready," Michael said, deciding to hold off on talking to them about Alicia's murder. "Do something useful with those toxic shoes and put them away. Be downstairs in five."

Matt jumped up, stood at attention and saluted. "Yes, *sir.*"

Michael gave him the death look. "That Xbox I gave you? Gone for a week. Keep pushing and you'll never get it back."

Matt stared back for a second, but wised up and retreated. Smart move for someone regularly grounded for talking back to his mother. Unfortunately, the grounding never worked and he'd sneak out his bedroom window, shimmy down the porch pole and take off.

The kid needed extra attention. Michael figured the weekend would be a good time to take him to the gym and let him work the heavy bag to get rid of some anger. Michael knew about anger and how it could nibble away at your insides until all that was left was a gaping hole.

Precisely why he wanted Roxann's help. These kids

needed him. And, if he was being honest, he needed them. He'd never be Danny, but he'd gotten used to being the adult male in their lives and didn't want to lose that.

Spending the rest of his life in prison was not an option, and he'd do whatever it took to stay a free man.

2

THE HARSH OVERHEAD LIGHT REFLECTED OFF THE SURFACE OF Roxann's computer and she tilted the monitor to reduce the glare. Mrs. Mackey perched on one of the leather guest chairs, pen and notepad in hand waiting for the following day's schedule. "Here it is. Schedule senior management at eight. I'll meet with the pressmen at ten—make that ten-thirty. Lunch with the sales rep from Franklin at noon, and I should be back by one-thirty. That will give me the afternoon to read the revenue reports. If anyone wants to see me, tell them I'm quarantined. Typhoid fever."

Mrs. Mackey offered her typical suffering sigh, but Roxann knew she'd keep the masses at bay. It took a brave soul to attempt a breach of any space Mrs. Mackey guarded.

"You'll run yourself ragged this way, Sassy."

Roxann scrunched her nose. Mrs. Mackey had been calling her Sassy since she was ten and it had been cute then, but at thirty-five she didn't think it was so adorable. Thankfully, Mrs. Mackey only called her Sassy in private. "I'm fine."

"No, you're not. Take a few days off."

"No time for a few days off. Working is better for me anyway." Roxann's presence in the building so soon after her father's death was vital to employee morale. They needed to know they had a leader, and she'd spent the past three weeks meeting with department heads and union representatives to prove it.

Mrs. Mackey let out a huff. "I'm worried about you, and Michael Taylor showing up today doesn't help. Are you going to tell me what that was about?"

Roxann sat back and surveyed Mrs. Mackey, who, with her endless observation skills, could run the *Banner* single-handedly. She deserved the truth. "Well, in addition to informing me Taylor Security now owns DSI, he offered the *Banner* an exclusive on his story."

"*Really?*"

"Yep. He's mad at the *Chronicle* for their poor coverage of that incident with one of his operatives."

Mrs. Mackey set her pad and pen on the desk. "What do you think about this exclusive?"

"I think he's manipulating me."

"How so?"

"He's trying to leverage our past relationship. He knows how I felt about him and he probably thinks it'll sway my decision to let him use the newspaper's resources. If my father were still here, I don't think Michael would ever have considered this." She stopped, steeled herself against the ache of missing her father, but the pinch between her shoulder blades remained. She still couldn't grasp being the boss.

"What did you tell him?" Mrs. Mackey asked.

"At first I said no. Then I said I'd think about it. Getting involved with him would equal driving my car into a brick wall. Nothing good can come of it. Besides, I have enough to deal with."

A few weeks ago, she'd had her friends, an orderly life and an exciting career with her father, a man she had cherished and depended on for counsel. Today, she still had the friends but her orderly life had disappeared and her father was dead.

Dead.

The word alone made her ache. Gone was better, but not much. Gone could mean at the store or out to lunch. Simply functioning wasn't a problem. If she engaged her mind, she'd be okay, but the sight of her father's coffee cup or his empty parking space made her weepy. Those were the hard times when she couldn't believe people survived losing a beloved parent. Right now, she assumed she'd never recover and would exist in a world of emotional torture.

Mrs. Mackey leaned forward. "You're getting emotional about a business decision. You need to think about what this means for the paper."

Roxann felt a twinge in her belly, that little ball of pressure that built up when she worried about making a mistake. "I have to get emotional. My mother and I own this place now. How will it look if I'm willing to risk the paper's reputation to help my old boyfriend?"

"What if you're looking at this upside down? It's a risk, but if he's innocent and you can prove it, the *Banner* will be helping to find a murderer. Those are the stories that win Pulitzers."

"*You* think we should do it?" Mrs. Mackey despised Michael as much as Dad had.

She held up a hand. "I'm giving you the other side. I don't think you have enough information yet. Chances are, the minute that man walked into your office the rational

Roxann vanished. After what he did, who could blame you?"

He married someone else.

"That's the problem. He stirs people up. The last thing I need is Michael Taylor agitating me, or the reporters. He'll think he can dictate how we should be handling the story. He'll try to take over. This idea is insane. *Insane.* Even if my father ever would have agreed, we can't put our crime reporter on this story full-time. The managing editor would be livid."

Not to mention her Uncle Max, Chicago's superintendent of police. Max would be furious with her for interfering with an active case.

Roxann stopped and took a breath. Michael expected her to risk personal relationships *and* the solid reputation of the *Banner* to help clear his name and that took nerve. If he was guilty of murder, it took *colossal* nerve.

What if he's innocent?

"Well," Mrs. Mackey said, "if you make this decision and the editors don't approve, too bad. You're the boss now. I know it hurts, but your father would tell you the same thing. He'd also tell you to move into his office, which I know you're avoiding."

Her assistant stared at her with penetrating hazel eyes that saw all her fears and Roxann, buckling under the scrutiny, spun her chair toward the window. Grief settled on her as she remembered her father lying on his office floor. A ripping sensation charged up her spine, gripping harder and harder until it reached her throat and caught. Had she been turned inside out? Every artery seemed exposed and vulnerable, but she wouldn't cry in her office. She'd never done that before and wouldn't start now. *Put yourself back together.* Start at the toes. *Control. Control. Control.*

"Sassy, he wanted you to have the newspaper and do the things you always talked about. He knew you could do it. Why do you think he sent you to work for that idiot in Philadelphia? Experience. He wanted to make sure no one would question your ability, and no one ever has. Except you."

Twelve years ago, Philadelphia had been Roxann's father's solution to her broken heart, and he'd gotten her a job at *The Times* as an assistant to the vice president of operations.

Hoping to reconcile with Michael, Roxann resisted the move, but after constant pressure from her parents, she'd taken the job. She spent two years in Philadelphia and loved the anonymity of a new place. She wasn't the boss's daughter, and it freed her from self-imposed standards.

She'd dated periodically and even had a relationship, but the man had fallen in love with her, creating more problems than she could handle. She didn't just *want* to love him, she *ached* for it, begged for it. It would mean she'd gotten over Michael. But that spark she'd had with Michael never materialized.

Joel deserved to be loved with the ferocious, all-consuming need she'd had for Michael. For Michael, she would have sacrificed everything. That's what love meant to her. She ended the relationship with Joel and came home with knowledge that would propel her to a management position at the *Banner*.

Roxann spun back to face Mrs. Mackey. "You were always more than an assistant to Dad. To us. I hope you know that."

She reached across and touched Roxann's hand. "I know and I love you for it. That's why I feel comfortable telling you that you can do this, but do it your way. Don't worry about what your father would have done."

Leave it to Mrs. Mackey to cut right through the flesh and hit bone. This emotional stuff made her crazy. She preferred her orderly way much better.

Mrs. Mackey had a point. Roxann needed to look ahead and not worry about everyone else.

Including Max.

"Max," Roxann said. "I need to ask him about the investigation."

She and her Uncle Max had a longstanding agreement when it came to utilizing each other's professions. She made sure to pass along any information the *Banner* received about unsolved crimes and, in return, Max gave her a periodic heads up when something big was about to break.

He wouldn't be able to relinquish much about the case, but he could give her an indication of where the investigation stood, and whether there was proof of Michael's guilt. She would then be able to make an informed decision regarding working with him.

The knots in Roxann's shoulders began to loosen. She didn't know what to hope for. If Max had a solid case, she'd decline Michael's offer and live with the fact that he was a murderer. Maybe then, she'd be able to get him out of her system and stop wondering what went wrong all those years ago.

What was she doing? The Michael she'd known, even with the emotional issues stemming from his military days, couldn't have murdered someone.

Or could he? After twelve years, how would she know?

However—big however—if Max seemed ambivalent about the evidence, she'd risk the consequences and chase the story.

"That's what I'll do. I'll talk to Max."

When Mrs. Mackey stood, Roxann circled the desk and met her halfway to the door. "Thank you. I don't know what I'd do without you."

"Good, because I'm not going anywhere. And you're welcome. Now go home and get some rest."

"I will. I need to clear some emails first."

Roxann dropped into her chair, opened her desk drawer and grabbed a handful of M&Ms—her version of painkillers —from the well stocked crystal bowl. She spun toward the window again and stared at the bank across the street, appreciating the intricate Art Deco scroll that gave it such character. Her building, with its plain cement corners, seemed boring in comparison.

Sometimes boring wasn't bad. Right now, she ached for boring and with Michael involved, that wouldn't happen. Still, this deal might be good for the newspaper. That would never be a bad thing. No matter what kind of personal turmoil it caused. She leaned back, grabbed her phone and dialed Max.

3

"MY FAVORITE PUBLISHER. GOOD TO SEE YOU," UNCLE MAX said, smiling as he approached the table where she sat. His dimples shaved ten years from his features. Not that Max looked old, but with fifty-eight looming, the wrinkles around his blue eyes seemed to change daily.

Roxann offered a grin, an odd sensation because she was sure she'd never get used to being referred to as publisher. She'd always imagined her father gradually slipping into retirement. Not dying in front of her on his office floor. The thought clogged her throat.

"I thought lunch with my uncle would be a welcome relief."

"Sorry I'm late."

"Not a problem. People-watching is always entertaining."

The Downtown Grill was the restaurant of choice when it came to servicing the city's leading business people. White tablecloths and linen napkins gave it an elegant feel, but the place served the best burger in town.

Max planted a kiss on Roxann's cheek, and did his

habitual scan of the dining room before slipping off his uniform jacket and slinging it over the back of the vacant chair next to him. Often times, the uniform and its large gold buttons and silver stars, was more recognizable than the man, but Max's powerful frame carried the flamboyant outfit with the ease of someone accustomed to authority. Next to the mayor, Max Hostetler was one of the most identifiable city officials in Chicago. And he wanted it that way.

"The usual, sir?" the waiter asked.

Max nodded, picked up his linen napkin and dropped it in his lap. "Thanks, Marty."

The waiter skittered off and Roxann focused on Max. "Thank you for the help these past weeks."

He shrugged. "We're family, Rox. My sister needs me now."

"I know, but a lot of people would go back to their daily routine. You've taken the time to be with Mom. I know it's keeping her going."

"What's keeping *you* going?"

Their eyes met and Roxann breathed in. "I'm all right. You know, I don't think I've ever really thanked you for always being there for me."

Max screwed up his lips. "That's what we do. We help each other."

"I just wanted you to know I appreciate it." She sat back, fiddled with her fork. "Anyway, what's new on the Taylor case?"

He smiled at her subject change. "Why?"

"Michael's company acquired DSI."

"Your security company?"

Roxann nodded. "It got me thinking about his wife's murder. I don't know how comfortable I am with the whole situation." Not a *total* lie.

"Off the record?" Max teased.

She held up two fingers. "Scout's honor."

He waited a beat. Deciding what to say? Not a good sign. "He did it, Rox. We don't have it locked yet, but we're confident."

"You're positive?"

"You sure you want to hear about this?"

No, but she needed a reason to risk her father's dream. He had nurtured the *Chicago Banner-Herald* from a miniscule weekly to the second largest daily in the state.

"I'm sure."

Max leaned forward and rested his elbows on the table. "There's motive," he said. "Plus, it was done by a pro. Snapped neck. The house was wiped clean, no forced entry. The killer either had a key or she let him in."

"Based on that, you think it was Michael?"

"It fits with his background."

Of course Max would say that. Michael, as an ex-Army Ranger, had seen and done horrible things during his stint with Special Forces, but she wasn't about to convict him of murder because of it. "I don't know, Max."

He drummed his fingers on the table. "Don't get caught up in this. Leave it to your newsroom."

She ignored his condescending tone. "Alicia Taylor was a social person. She knew a lot of people. Maybe she had a falling out with one of them. It seems too obvious to be Michael and, frankly, he's smarter than that. He'd know, based on their hostile divorce, he'd be the suspect."

"That's exactly why I think he did it. *I* think he'd had enough of the bullshit fighting. He went to talk her into settling their divorce, they argued, it got heated and he killed her. Happens all the time, Rox."

Roxann clenched her teeth so hard she thought they'd

crack. She didn't mind Max disagreeing with her. Heck, that happened all the time, but treating her like an infant was unacceptable. She wanted to smack him on his buzz cut head.

"I know it happens, but they'd been doing battle for almost two years. If he intended to kill her, why would he wait so long? It doesn't make sense."

Max waved at a passing patron. "People do things when they're enraged."

"Enraged people don't take the time to wipe fingerprints."

The waiter appeared and they sat silently as their food was served. After the normal, ground pepper-parmesan-let-me-know-if-you-need-anything-else routine, Roxann went to work on her salad. She wanted Max to say they had other suspects and weren't railroading Michael, but knew he wouldn't.

Michael was right. The police had their own theory and were sticking with it. Max had unintentionally confirmed it. Her palms began to itch, the sure-fire tell something was up. She'd have to figure it out on her own though, because Max wouldn't help. She never was one to balk at a challenge.

ROXANN STOOD AT THE COAT CHECK WAITING FOR HER JACKET when the city's mayor walked through the restaurant's front entrance.

"Good afternoon, Mr. Mayor," Max said to his boss.

Running into Douglas Richmond was always an event, whether it would be good or bad remained the question.

At fifty-five, the mayor was one of the most enigmatic public figures the city had known. He'd been in office ten years and with those ten years came a spotless city and, thanks in large part to Max's top-notch police force, a dropping crime rate.

Still, people loved and hated the mayor's outspoken ways. For months, the *Banner* had been running editorials on corruption rumors within the administration and it put the mayor at odds with the paper.

Roxann couldn't help it if the *Banner* had a steady stream of information regarding someone on the mayor's staff doing favors for some distant relative or friend. Even bribery allegations. Just her luck to run into the mayor the day after the paper ran a corruption story involving a streets and sanitation worker using city equipment to patch holes in his neighbor's driveway.

She took the high road and offered her hand in greeting. "Mr. Mayor."

"Roxann, I'm sorry about your father. We never agreed, but I respected him."

"Thank you, sir." That was something at least.

"You and Carl should set up a meeting to discuss your coverage of my office. Don't know where that newsroom of yours gets this crap, but they'd better get their facts straight."

Roxann pursed her lips to hide what would have turned into a face splitting smile. This was the mayor she knew.

"We can certainly set up a meeting, sir, but I can't guarantee anything will change." She pulled her hand from the mayor's grasp. "Freedom of the press and all that."

The mayor turned to his top aide, Carl Biehl. "She always was tough, Carl."

"Do I need to jump in and protect my niece's honor?"

Roxann slid Max a sideways glance. She didn't need him playing white knight.

The hostess appeared. "Mr. Mayor, your table is ready."

"Yes, thank you." The mayor turned to Roxann. "Call my office to set up that meeting."

Not a request, but an order. No use shaking hands after *that* exchange. "Have a good lunch."

She watched the mayor make his grand entrance, stopping at tables, kissing cheeks, slapping backs. "He is the master glad-hander," she said to Max.

"It works for him. He doesn't seem too happy with you."

"He's mad because we quoted him when he called the mayor of Milwaukee a cheese head."

Her uncle let out a blast of laughter. "That was priceless."

"I don't know what we'd do without him. It'd be boring around here."

"You're right on that one." Max sobered and touched her shoulder. "Set up that meeting. You don't want him pissed at you all the time."

She rolled her eyes. "We're a newspaper. He's the mayor. It's normal for a politician to be mad at the media. Besides, if he didn't give us so many opportunities to quote him, we'd lay off. He brings it on himself, and he does it intentionally. He enjoys us talking about him, Max, whether it's good or bad."

"It's your ass, honey. I hope you know what you're doing."

Roxann agreed with him on the ass part, but wasn't at all sure she knew what she was doing. Particularly because she was about to call the man who almost destroyed her life and make a deal that might destroy her newspaper.

4

—————

Michael sat in his office analyzing his company's latest profit and loss statement and decided the increased P and the decreased L would never be a disappointment. It had been a tough fight, but the past few years had been fruitful and keeping things on the upswing took managing.

He sat back, took in the shiny chrome of his office, and let out a long breath. He'd paid that thief of a decorator a small fortune to do her magic and she'd achieved the right balance of functionality and form. He did have to replace the all glass desk that lasted one day before he sent it back for one with drawers. Who the hell could run a company without drawers? And he wasn't talking about pants. The new desk, an inky, glass-topped, six drawer unit served him better.

A sleek leather sofa sat against the far wall with two bright red armchairs anchoring the sides. The decorator said the blast of color, in an otherwise black and chrome setting, fit his temperament. He tried to be insulted, but what was the point, considering he agreed with her.

Michael glanced at the neat stacks of files sitting on the

desk. Nice and tidy. Security people needed to be tidy. If you couldn't keep your workspace organized, how could you get some VIP from point A to point B without them getting shot?

The speakerphone came to life, tearing him from his thoughts.

"Roxann Thorgesson for you on line one," his assistant said.

"Who?" Michael asked, not believing what he'd heard.

"ROX-ANN THOR-GES-SON," the assistant repeated as if he'd suddenly gone deaf. He figured he deserved it, but still found it irritating.

"Put her through."

The phone rang. What if it wasn't good news? He snatched the handset before the call went to voice mail.

"Michael Taylor."

"It's Roxann. We should talk."

The business voice. The voice that told him anything else would be off limits. Too bad.

Michael stared at his office door and realized she was about to agree to work with him. Why else would she want to talk?

"I'm all yours," he said, keeping his tone casual.

"The police aren't looking at anyone else for your wife's murder."

Michael collapsed back into his chair and a sharp, no nonsense throbbing began behind his right eye. He pressed the palm of his hand against the pain and wondered if he'd ever be free of Alicia. Or her death.

"She was not my wife."

There was a brief pause and Michael imagined the famous eye roll. Roxann could roll her eyes so far up she nearly tipped herself backward.

"Regardless, I think there's a story here."

"You'll give me access to your reporters?"

A long sigh came through the phone line.

"You've got Phil Dawson—as long as newspapers fly off the racks. I'll pull him the minute I see fit though."

"What about you?" he asked, hoping to throw her off-balance for even a second.

"What about me?"

"Do I get access to you?"

She laughed the sarcastic laugh of a woman only mildly amused. "Not on your life. And before I turn you over to Phil, I want to set some ground rules."

He hated rules.

"Okay," Michael said. "But you have to let me buy you dinner."

"Why would I do that?"

"If we're working together, we should be civil. Simple logic."

"Nothing is ever simple in this business."

Tough cookie.

"You used to be fun, Roxann."

"I used to be a lot of things. You can buy me dinner only because I want to hear what you have on this story before I get anyone else involved."

Okay then. A start. Michael reached for his cell phone. "How's tomorrow night?"

"I can make it work. Seven o'clock at Cassatta's. See you then."

He hung up, punched her name into his phone along with Cassatta's. Figures she'd pick the restaurant owned by her closest friend's father. She'd feel comfortable there. Safe maybe? He didn't want to think Roxann could be afraid of him, not after what they'd had together, but with his current status of murder suspect, he wouldn't blame her.

He propped his feet on the desk and focused on working with Roxann. She loved a challenge and her instincts were always dead-on. If she thought there was a story to be written, she'd find it. She always had drive. Or was it a need for the truth that made her such a refreshing part of a sadistic world? Either way, he missed it.

"What are you doing?" Vic Andrews asked as he entered the office.

His partner wore khakis and a blue golf shirt and, in Michael's opinion, took business casual to the boundaries of too casual. Plus, his normally scruffy hair looked exceptionally rumpled and Michael wondered about the fine line between fashion and a mess. Vic had recently started with the day-old beard look that had the women in the office going nuts. This company didn't need its already over-stimulated vice president becoming the sexual fantasy of half the female employees. What a shit storm that would be.

"You golfing today?" Michael asked.

Vic waved him off and dropped into one of the two guest chairs. Vic wasn't big on rules either. "I asked you a question first."

Michael pointed to his phone. "*That* was Roxann."

"Ahhhh, the lovely Roxann with the most amazing legs you've ever seen." Vic made a low growling sound.

Michael laughed. "No shit."

And wouldn't it be nice to have them wrapped around him. *Whoa. Down boy.* No sense getting Mr. Happy worked up. *Must be the fatigue.*

Still, the legs got him every time. The first time he'd spotted them, he'd been twenty-seven years old, sitting on a folding chair in the miniscule backyard of a friend of a friend at a fourth of July party he hadn't wanted to go to. Four weeks fresh out of the army, he'd been dealing with undiagnosed PTSD that left him exhausted and supremely strung-out. Between the lack of sleep and the nightmares, when he did manage rest, he hadn't had a lot firing in the mental agility category.

But he'd gone to that party because he felt like crap and needed to get laid. A piss poor motivating factor, but the physical release would clear his mind.

On that summer night, the sky was clear, the air cooler than normal and filled with a mix of music and chattering voices from the crowd packed into the tiny backyard. He sat alone nursing his beer when the long-legged blonde entered the yard. She wore shorts and a sweater tank top that clung to her lean form. The sleeves of the cardigan tied around her shoulders hung over her chest, but he saw enough to know he'd like to get his hands there. Her long hair, streaked with sun-drenched highlights, fell loose around her face and she tossed one side over her shoulder, exposing a softly sculpted cheek that he immediately wanted to run his fingers over.

Perfection.

Suddenly, his world didn't seem such a fucked-up place. Michael breathed in. *She's the one.* What that meant in his horny-as-ever state, he wasn't sure and didn't necessarily care. He knew he had to have her.

A group of people huddled in front of him, blocking his view, and he shifted a little. The blonde stepped to the picnic table not ten feet from him and parked her trim ass next to five women.

Thirty minutes later he still sat there, watching and waiting, damn near mesmerized by her. She hadn't so much as glanced his way, but she hadn't glanced anyone else's way either. He couldn't call her aloof. Not with the way she laughed and yapped with her friends, but she had a quality to her he couldn't define. Elegant maybe. He didn't know, but it worked. Hard.

A few people stopped to say hello to him, but his attention stayed on the blonde. If she moved from that group, he'd be on her. No doubt.

The break came when the two women closest to her got up and left. She wasn't alone, but the three remaining women were deep into their own conversation. *Take the shot.*

He made his way to her, squeezing through the crowd that had once again gathered in his path. He stepped up to the table and set his beer down. She glanced at the beer, then brought her gaze, a blue-green that nearly stopped his heart, to his face.

"Hi," she said.

"How do you feel about love at first sight?"

The corner of her mouth quirked. "I'm not sure."

"Well," he said, "I'm suddenly a believer."

She rolled those amazing eyes and laughed at him. For a few seconds, Michael let himself forget about being a miserable bastard and soaked up the sound of her soft laughter.

She gestured to the seat across from her. "It's too soon to tell, but you can have a seat and maybe I'll let you know in awhile."

Score.

He dropped onto the bench and she propped her chin in her hand. "As opening lines go, I have to say, that one got my attention."

He grinned. "It was a maiden voyage. And just so you know who it is that's fallen in love with you, I'm Michael Taylor."

"Hi, Michael Taylor, I'm Roxann."

And damn those blue eyes glittered. So incredibly gorgeous. To Michael's disappointment, Brian, the guy hosting the party, appeared. "Hey, Rox."

Roxann-the-beautiful shifted to face him. "Hi, Brian. How are you?"

"Thanks for coming. Haven't seen you since you got back from the Olympics."

"You went to the Olympics?" Michael asked.

Brian snorted. "She was *in* the Olympics. Won a gold in the four-hundred relay. You grabbed a silver too, right?"

She smiled and the glow could have lit the darkened yard. "Yep. In the two-hundred."

Beautiful, athletic and a competitor. God help him. Fried already and he hadn't laid a hand on her.

Someone called Brian away—*thank you*—and he high-tailed it.

"The Olympics. That's amazing. Do you still compete?"

She twisted her lips. "For fun. Now I have a big girl job."

"What do you do?"

"I work at the *Banner-Herald*"

To Michael, who was working a laborer job while he figured out how to use the skills acquired as an Army Ranger, the newspaper gig sounded pretty cool. "Are you a reporter?"

"No."

"What do you do?"

"Whatever my father tells me to."

"Your dad is your boss?"

She laughed. "My dad is everyone's boss. He owns the paper."

Michael's euphoric high plummeted. Gone. That fast. *Fuck me.* This girl was so far above him he might as well quit now. If that didn't suck the mother lode, he wasn't sure what did. He laughed his derision, slapped his hands on the table and stood. "Enough said. I'm leaving. I'm glad we met though."

He started to turn away, but she grabbed his arm. "This from the man who just proclaimed his love?"

Could he possibly have a shot with this girl? "Honey, I'm a kid from the neighborhood. You're so far out of my league I've got no business being on your planet."

"Why do you get to decide I'm out of your league? I'll make my own decision. Why not stay and see what happens?"

It made enough sense that he sat again and spent the next two hours hearing about the Olympics, her doubling up on classes to graduate on time and taking the job at the newspaper. When the party began to fizzle, he and Roxann moved to a 24-hour coffee shop two blocks away where they talked until six in the morning.

He finally walked her to her apartment and, as much as he wanted to, didn't try to worm his way in. After all night together, he'd hoped he'd get his shot another time. A fast lay wouldn't suit. That he could get anywhere. He'd wait it out. The beautiful Roxann Thorgesson was not a girl to disrespect. On any level.

Controlling the I-need-to-get-laid beast, he kissed her goodbye with a quick peck on the lips, waited for her to get into the house and walked home knowing he'd met the love of his life.

And now, sitting in his office, thinking about her long legs, he was surrounded by his hard-fought wealth and wreck of a life, and it made his chest ache.

"Mike?" Vic said.

Michael shook his head. "Yeah, sorry."

"Does she still run?"

"I see her on the lakefront occasionally." *When I'm standing on my balcony watching for her.*

"She never wanted to coach?"

"Sure she did, but she was the heir apparent and her father expected her to work for the newspaper."

"Sucks."

"Yep."

Michael linked his hands together and placed them on top of his head. Serving in Special Forces together had forged a bond between Michael and Vic and very little went on that the other didn't know about. When two people watched men die together, perspectives on life changed. Maybe they didn't talk about it, but they both understood it, and talking to Vic about Roxann brought Michael a sense of calm. It had been years since he'd spoken of her freely.

Hadn't that always been the way with her? From that first night, her acceptance of a man who flinched at the sound of doors slamming gave him hope. Back then, any banging noise sent him ducking for cover, but she always took it in stride and never made him feel weak or less of a man for it.

"So, are you two doing the horizontal mambo?" Vic asked, his face a cross between amusement and curiosity.

Ball-busting. Great. Roxann had been special and Vic knew that. Michael sat up and put his feet on the floor. "I should knock you out."

Vic put up two hands. "Whoa, boss. Chill."

"She's a responsible and savvy businesswoman. She has the chops to help me clear my name. That's it. Got it?"

Vic grinned like the asshole he was. Michael had been played. The son of a bitch knew what buttons to push.

"Why are you here?" Michael asked.

"Crazy Tiffany. Mike, this chick is nuts."

"Don't I know it?"

Michael sat back while he waited for the latest gossip on Tiffany Limone, a twenty-four-year-old rising star they provided security for. A former pop singer trying to break into acting, she was a royal pain in the ass. As if he didn't have enough to worry about with a murder hanging over him.

"What's her problem now?"

"She wants another guy on her."

"Jesus. She's got three already. Who wants to kill her so bad they'd fight off three guys?"

"She wants Toby off. Personality conflict."

"Who gives a shit? He has to keep her alive, not like her. Tell her everyone else is assigned."

Vic held up a hand. "I talked to Toby. Miss Crazy got hammered one night and wanted our boy to slip her the hot salami. He told her no can do. She got pissed and called me with this personality conflict crap. I had to beat it out of Toby. He's all business and scared shitless of her now. Thinks she's gonna attack him after she belts back a few."

Michael shook his head. People. Someone always screwed up. After years of busting his ass to build his business from one guy doing personal security to a multi-faceted company, he was still a well-paid babysitter. He shifted to his computer and pulled up his personnel roster. And then reality sucker punched him. He leaned forward and propped his elbows on the desk before he ruined his best friend's day. This would suck.

"Listen, if things go bad for me, are you gonna be able to take over here?"

Vic snorted. "Don't be stupid. You're not going anywhere."

Vic hated being confined to an office for any length of

time. Michael understood this because he preferred the action in the office versus anything he'd find in a war torn country. That's what worked about their partnership. Vic handled the government contracts that sent their employees overseas to guard diplomats or other high-ranking officials, and Michael handled the private security. Perfect partnership.

"We should be prepared," Michael said. "If you don't want to do it, I need to find someone else. Who that would be, not a fucking clue."

Vic huffed out a breath. "I'll do it, but it's not going to be a problem. Let's move on."

He didn't want to discuss it. Fair enough. They'd established he'd take over if Michael went to prison and that's all Michael needed to know. They could get to the particulars later.

"One more thing—"

"Ah, Christ, Mike, give it a rest."

Michael held up his hands. "My sister will need help. Not financially. I wouldn't put that on you. The kids though. Sometimes she needs a man to straighten things out. Mostly Matt. The other two are easy. Can you do that for me?"

"Yeah, but I'm telling you, it won't be an issue. Can we get back to my problem with Tiffany-the-hot-salami-slut?"

Michael busted out a laugh and clicked through his personnel spreadsheet. "Steve's in L.A. Put him on her. He's so big and ugly, she won't look twice."

"Gotta love these high maintenance clients."

Michael picked up an invoice his assistant had placed on his desk and perused it. "At least she's moved on from me."

"Huh?"

"Why do you think I moved her to *your* client roster?" Michael said.

Vic's mouth dropped open. "Am I the only one she doesn't want to get busy with? Did you thrash her?"

Michael curled his lip. "Please. She's a client and nothing screws up a business arrangement more than sex. Remember that."

He made a mental note to remember his own decree when it came to his dealings with Roxann.

Good luck there, pal.

5

Stood-up.

Michael scanned the crowded bar of Cassatta's. *Nope. Not here.* Multiple sets of eyes from around the room glared at him—accusers—and he drew air through his nose and slowly let it out his mouth before meeting the stares. The inquisitive patrons flicked their glances away, probably not wanting to enrage the murderer.

Where the hell was Roxann? Of course, it would have been easy to miss her because the place had been renovated in the years since he'd been here and a wall, probably to cut down on the noise for those wanting a quiet meal, now separated the bar from the dining room. The dark walls had been replaced with a lighter shade of gray and swirly hanging light fixtures offered enough light to accommodate a romantic dinner or a business meeting.

Michael had brought Roxann here early on in their relationship using borrowed money because his measly construction salary barely bought them a meal at the diner, never mind Cassatta's.

After they'd broken up, he'd never come back.

Alicia had begged him for a meal at Cassatta's, but he had refused. He suddenly wondered if it had been fair. He thought about it, and decided he'd made the right decision. This was Roxann's territory and, out of respect for her, he'd stayed clear. Too many memories and regrets. Why torture himself wondering what could have been? Particularly when trying to concentrate on his wife and making their marriage work.

There was also the fact that Roxann's best friend's family owned Cassatta's and he never wanted to risk running into Janie. He wasn't afraid of many things, but Janie gave him the willies. That woman, with her acerbic tongue, could make the toughest of men bawl.

Unfortunately for him, it wasn't a mystery why Roxann picked this restaurant for dinner. She'd be acquainted with everyone in the place and would feel comfortable.

Safe.

That frosted him, but he couldn't hold it against her. Half the city thought he was a murderer—some of those people were in this room. The other half of the city hadn't seen the news or were members of his family. Either way, he was grateful for that half.

What if he were found guilty?

Jesus.

His intestines were shredding. He couldn't spend the rest of his life in jail. His family depended on him. And what about someday having kids of his own? If he were locked in a cell, he'd never get the chance to teach his son how to swing a bat or take his daughter to a father-daughter dance. Yep, horrific territory.

Having a successful business had served him well, but family was what mattered. Too bad it took the death of his brother-in-law to make him realize his marriage was a disaster.

Rather than ruin his evening, Michael put away thoughts of prison and traitors and turned toward the entrance to see Roxann chatting with the hostess. She smiled the smile he saw in his dreams and he held his breath for a second, absorbing the pleasure.

Would wanting to see that smile on a regular basis be selfish? Did he deserve it? Were they even compatible anymore? Maybe not, but if he got out of this mess, he'd damn sure try to find out.

ROXANN GREETED A FEW REGULARS AS SHE CROSSED THE BAR toward Michael. He wore navy dress slacks and a gray sport coat that hugged his shoulders and indicated there'd be nothing soft underneath. Relaxed elegance at its best. Michael never was one to wear a tie unless the occasion, without question, demanded it.

"Sorry I'm late." She hated being late and still wondered how she had gotten so behind. She'd arrived home in plenty of time, but after showering couldn't decide on what to wear and spent thirty minutes rifling through suits and dresses, finally opting for the black sheath.

Even her hair, typically a no-brainer, caused strife. She'd done a French twist. Too fancy. She settled on her normal low ponytail with a side part, adding a rhinestone clip to hold it in place. This was so typical. Michael Taylor, Mr. Chaos. A simple business meeting with him had already disrupted her routine.

Michael did a slow, thorough visual exploration of her and her stomach pitched with an unusual bout of insecurity. The snap of a memory flashed to the first time they'd made love and she walked out of her bathroom wearing sheer lace. He'd worn that same look back then. In it she'd seen physical hunger, but also a raw vulnerability that made her stomach quiver the same way it did now. At the time, her unexpressed love for him blew her soul open and she imagined a life with kids, maybe a dog or two and soccer games where parents became too competitive.

Back *then*, when he looked at her this way, her excitement over the future had surged. Now, it left her with regrets. They could have had it all and he'd married someone else.

She shooed the thought away. "I've suddenly turned into a disorganized fashion victim."

Michael smiled. "That's okay. You're stunning."

Her cheeks grew hot from the compliment and she gave herself a mental head-slap. *Twit.* "Thank you. Our table is ready." Making small talk could lead to something personal and she needed this meeting to be all business.

Ignoring the distant stares and hushed voices as they were led to their table turned out to be a challenge Roxann hadn't anticipated. Being alone with him was out of the question, for a variety of reasons, but maybe meeting in such a public place hadn't been a stellar idea either. They should have met in her office. During business hours.

What were all these gawkers thinking? Yes, he was a suspected murderer, she the publisher of a large newspaper and they were having dinner together.

She had to be insane. She didn't know this man at all anymore. He could have murdered his wife. And yet, somehow, she didn't want to believe it. When had she become so foolish? Battling her doubts, she glanced at Michael who appeared unaffected. Impossible.

The hostess led them to a corner table away from prying

eyes and ears—*thank you*—and Michael held a chair for her. After seating them, the hostess went on her way.

Frank Sinatra crooned from an overhead speaker while Roxann waited for Michael to say something. Maybe *she* should say something. She smoothed an invisible crease on the spotless white tablecloth and he smiled. She stopped smoothing. He'd always thought that little nervous habit was cute.

He held up his menu. "Let's decide on dinner and get to work."

A waiter, wearing a white jacket and bow tie, appeared and Michael ordered a bottle of wine.

"Opus," she said. "Are we celebrating something?"

"You need to celebrate something to enjoy good wine?"

"Apparently not." Roxann went back to pretending to read her menu. She ate the same meal every time. Right down to the wine. Except for tonight. Tonight they were having *Opus*.

"How are you holding up?" he asked after the waiter finished with them.

She assumed he was curious about the status of the newspaper. He wouldn't want to partner with a failing company. She went with her best make-the-board-members-happy speech.

"I won't make any immediate changes. We have a good senior staff so there's no need for anything drastic."

"I wasn't talking about the *Banner*."

"Oh, well." His fingertips were suddenly resting on her hand and she snatched it back because, after all, they were in a crowded restaurant and he was suspected of killing his wife. Again she wondered where her good sense had disappeared to when she agreed to this dinner.

Dammit. Why did he have to touch her? Let her feel the

warmth of that big hand on her skin? She bit her lip to distract herself from the pounding in her ears and focused on his question. She could lie and tell him she was fine. Or she could be honest and say she was miserable. Every inch of her slowly being torn away, piece by piece.

She settled on a compromise because laying it out there would be too much for her, and dismissing it would be a travesty.

"It's overwhelming. I can't get used to him not being down the hall."

Michael's gaze met hers. Knowing her father wouldn't approve caused the emotions she'd been containing since walking into the restaurant to collide and batter her head. *Don't think about it. Rebuild. Start at the toes.*

The past couple of weeks had taught her that grief was unmerciful. It would snag her by the throat until her lungs wanted to burst. It had forced her to her knees more than once, and she had no desire to fall apart in front of Michael.

She reached for her water glass and sipped. *Okay. Feels good.* Ice cold water. *One, two, three...deep breath...you can do this.* Her heartbeat slowed. Good. Back to work. She pulled her digital recorder from her purse and discreetly held it out. "Do you mind? Taking notes distracts me."

Michael shrugged and she pushed the record button before setting the gadget behind the small table vase. "What do you think happened to your wife?"

"Alicia," he corrected.

Roxann hesitated. What could have broken down his marriage to the point where he refused to acknowledge the woman he had chosen as his wife? "Alicia. Got it."

"I don't know who killed her. She was no angel though." He sat forward so he wouldn't be overheard. "She had no problem screwing married men."

"Do you know who?"

He made a *pfft* noise. "With the war we were in? Of course I know. I had someone on her for almost three years. She and the boyfriend weren't too discreet. He'd go in the front door for Christ sakes."

Michael waved a hand in frustration. Was his anger based on someone he loved betraying him or the recklessness of the act?

"Who was he?" she asked, getting back to Alicia's lover.

Michael stared at her for a moment. Stalling? No way. "We agreed you'd tell me everything. Spill it or this deal is off."

"Carl Biehl."

Before she could stop herself, Roxann groaned. She now understood Michael's hesitation, but when the waiter approached with their food, she held her response and smiled.

Outside of work, Roxann didn't know much about Carl Biehl, but hadn't he and his wife attended her father's funeral holding hands? Marriage was a screwy thing. Now she knew why she'd never been married. She couldn't deal with all the complications.

The waiter disappeared and Roxann leaned forward. "You *cannot* be serious? The mayor's top aide was openly having an affair?"

"You own a newspaper and didn't know about it."

She should jab the fork into his eye for that comment. *Deep breath.* "Did you come to me because you thought my uncle, who also happens to work for the mayor, told me about the affair? Assuming he even knows." She kept her voice low, the tension within her escalating until it became a taught wire about to snap.

"I came to you because the *Chronicle* pissed me off and I

knew you'd do a good job of reporting the facts. Your uncle working for the mayor is a side benefit. You know as well as I do, if there is anything to this story it'll work for both of us."

She shot him a castigating look and he sat back. "That look might bring most men to heel, but not me, babe. My life is on the line."

Roxann held out a hand for him to continue. "Go on, but please don't tell me you think he did it."

Michael shook his head. "I don't know."

"You said you had someone following her? Did he see anyone go into the house the night Alicia was killed?"

"He didn't see anything. Whoever killed her must have gone in the back. The few times Billy saw Carl go in; he used the front door."

She thought back a few nights. "Carl was at the policemen's ball. I saw him."

"Are you sure it was that night?"

"I'm positive. It was only three nights ago and I heard about the murder in an editorial meeting the morning after."

And you can bet I remember that.

"I don't know that Biehl is even involved, but it's too convenient to dismiss." He hesitated and lowered his voice. "Hell, it could have been his wife."

Forgetting her good breeding, Roxann propped her elbow on the table and rested her chin in her hand. "She was at the fundraiser with Carl. Maybe she hired someone?"

"Maybe Carl hired someone. Alicia could have been putting pressure on him by threatening to tell his wife. She'd do that if it got her what she wanted."

Roxann closed her eyes. "I can't believe this."

"Rox, if you want out, say it now, but this story is happening. If the cops continue with their witch hunt, you'll be running my mug shot on your front page. I'm not going down for this. I didn't do it."

Michael was a puzzle with missing pieces. He seemed relaxed, yet his words hit her like a furnace blast. "I'm not backing out. It's a lot to take in, that's all."

"No kidding." *Damn right it's a lot to take in,* he thought. Did she think this was fun? A nice dinner, a good bottle of wine and talking about his ex-wife's murder.

Fun would have been talking about what Roxann had been doing for the last twelve years and whether or not she'd let him spend an extended period of time in her bed.

Now *that* would be fun.

Unlikely, but a guy could dream.

And here he was, ignoring his own rule about mixing sex and business. Did it really count if he only *thought* about mixing sex and business?

Semantics.

Semantics sucked.

Michael knew he wanted to sleep with her. Fighting it was the challenge. He'd never lost that itch, but he'd kept it locked inside for so long he'd learned to ignore it. By his way of thinking, good husbands didn't fantasize about old girlfriends. Early in his marriage, he'd tried hard to be overly attentive, generous to a fault and understanding when Alicia had her first affair. He chalked her betrayal up to a one-time thing and forgave her.

Now, long after his marriage had fallen apart, despite Alicia's death, Roxann captured too much of his attention for him to feel guilt. And why the hell did she wear her hair back all the time? She used to wear it up only when she ran. He remembered it falling over her shoulders, remembered running his hands through those long blond strands. Now she had ice queen hair and he hated it. Maybe he'd reach across, pop the clip open and watch all that hair go free.

Roxann snapped her fingers in front of his face. "*Hello? Are you in there?*"

He cleared his throat and sat up. "Sorry. Thinking."

She rolled her eyes. "You were *gone*."

He grinned. "I was mesmerized by your hair."

If only she knew how true that statement was.

She snorted. "Oh, shut up."

He did an imitation of her eye roll. "A minute ago you were yelling at me for not talking. Since when are you fickle?"

"Excuse me? I am probably the unficklest—if that's even a word—of all females. There's not a fickle bone in my body."

Michael grabbed his wine glass and held it up. "Which is why I came to you. I knew you'd think this to death and if you agreed to it, maybe I'd be able to clear myself. You have amazing instincts. Always have."

She threw her shoulders back. *Here we go*. He complimented her. Big deal. Did she have to get tense about it?

"Let's hope my instincts are right this time."

"They are. You can trust me on this one."

Roxann's gaze burned into his. "I'd love to trust you, but I don't even know you anymore. Smart women don't put their trust in men they haven't seen in twelve years. Men who left them without an explanation. Don't you agree?"

And there it is. The eight-hundred-pound gorilla finally out to play. It came as no surprise, but he didn't have one decent response. He shrugged. "It's reasonable."

"Well, thank you for that." She fiddled with the tablecloth again. "I'm seeing an opportunity here that might benefit all parties, but believe me, if I start feeling this won't work, I'll pull the *Banner* out of this. The newspaper is my priority. Don't disappoint me."

"Again?"

"What does that mean?"

"What you wanted to say was don't disappoint me *again*."

Michael's cell phone vibrated, but he ignored it. Whoever it was could wait. He had to gain her trust and dumping her for a phone call wouldn't fly. Plus, it would be damned rude.

Roxann stuck her chin in the air. "If that's what I meant, I would have said it."

"Okay, are we arguing? It feels like we're arguing."

"We're having a discussion."

"Good. I don't want to fight with you, and I don't want us sniping either. You're still pissed at me for what happened twelve years ago. I get that, but let's put it behind us."

The waiter, of course, stepped up to offer dessert. Did waiters receive special training on the worst possible moment to approach?

Roxann ordered a decaf, double something or other.

"I'll have coffee."

"Espresso or cappuccino?" the waiter asked.

Jesus H. Christ. Michael shot him a look. "Just a plain cup of Joe. No fancy stuff."

The waiter huffed off. "You didn't need to get nasty," Roxann said, but Michael swore she might have been hiding a smile.

"I wasn't nasty. I said I wanted coffee. Can't a guy just get a cup of Maxwell House? Why does it have to be double damned lattes all the time?"

She rolled her eyes. He hated that irritating habit of

hers, but somehow found it settling. Like returning home after a long absence.

"Anyway," she said, her voice not packing such an edge this time, "I don't think discussing our past relationship will help this situation. We're business partners and that's how it should stay."

Business partners? Was she kidding? There was enough of a charge between them to light up the entire city. "Please. We both know, no matter what we call it, there's a lot between us, good and bad, and if we don't deal with it soon, one of us will go off."

The waiter stepped up and handed him a message. Someone was looking for him in a bad way. He read the note and the immediate punch of having ignored the first call blasted him. "I'm sorry. I have to call my sister. I'll be right back."

Gina tracking him down at a restaurant brought on a not-so-distant memory of his baby sister screaming into the telephone that her husband was dead, and Michael quickened his steps while he dialed.

ROXANN TAP-TAP-TAPPED HER SPOON WHILE SHE WAITED FOR Michael to return. The sick, twisted part of her that loved verbal combat had enjoyed their sparring session and the rush streaming through her couldn't be denied. She hated a man she could push around and Michael never allowed himself to be pushed.

She reached for her wine glass and caught the woman at the next table staring. All evening she'd been dealing with people eyeing them. Even if she couldn't catch them doing it, from somewhere deep inside, she knew it and found it atrocious. She'd sat alone in restaurants hundreds, thousands of times, but never had the feeling of being stripped naked. Not that she'd put up with it. She made eye contact with the woman, who immediately shifted away.

Nosy.

Michael slid into his chair; his short hair rumpled with the evidence of fingers plowing through it. "Sorry."

"Everything all right?"

He sat back. Took a breath. "I'm sorry, I need to cut our evening short. Gina and Matt had a fight and he took off."

"Is she okay?"

Michael pulled his wallet to pay the check. "She's upset. It's late, he's fifteen and looking to blow off steam."

The waiter cruised by and grabbed the credit card and check. Michael turned to her. "Can we finish this another night?"

She nodded. "We were almost done anyway. Don't worry about it. You need to find Mattie."

"Matt. He wants to be called Matt now."

She had to smile. She understood how the kid felt. She'd tried for years to get those close to her to stop calling her Roxi and finally gave up. She'd learned to accept it as an endearment, but only from certain people. "I'll remember that. Are you going to look for him?"

Michael signed the sales slip and nodded. "He has some hot spots I'll check out. This isn't the first time he's taken off. Matt's an angry young man. Can't say I blame him after his father got crushed under ten tons of concrete." He set the pen down and gazed at it for a moment. "You wanna ride along? We can finish our conversation and I'll bring you back here later for your car."

She should say no. The devil Roxann urged her on, but the angel insisted she beg off.

Devil: they'd talk business while he searched for his nephew.

Angel: she'd be alone in a car with a man suspected of killing his wife.

Devil: she had loved him once.

Angel: she never got over him.

Back and forth it went until Michael waved a hand in front of her face.

"It's late," she said. "I should go home. Unless you need help."

He flashed the smile. The one that always slayed her. "I could tell you I need help, but with Vic already out looking, that'd be a lie. I just want you around."

Roxann held her breath and let the words settle. As much as she wanted to give in to that girly part of her that loved hearing an attractive male enjoyed her company, she wouldn't. Not after the damage this man had inflicted. "Knock it off."

"Crossed a line?"

I think so. "Yes. Anyway, I should head home."

He rose from his chair. "Whatever you want, Rox."

If only she knew what that was.

THEY STOOD IN FRONT OF THE RESTAURANT WAITING FOR THE valet to bring his car. The late March wind had forced the temperature down a notch. Michael slid Roxann's wrap over her shoulders and wondered how he called Chicago home and still couldn't adjust to temperatures that dropped forty degrees by nightfall.

"What's next on the case?" he asked.

"I'll talk to Phil Dawson tomorrow and see what he has. I'll have him ask around the P.D. He has a source there."

"How reliable of a source?"

"Rock solid reliable. To his consternation, Max doesn't even know who it is. Phil's sources are his business. He's old school and doesn't reveal them."

The perfect answer. "Let me know what he needs from me."

"I will."

"Tell him not to take too long. I'm a hunted man here."

The wind knocked a strand of her hair loose and, ignoring the urge to resist, he tucked it behind her ear. Touching her again, feeling her so close, sent a jolt of heat through him and before he could pull his hand away, she shocked the hell out of him and tilted her head into his hand. The movement, so small anyone would have missed it, might have been the best thing that had happened to him in years. His phone vibrated and Roxann snapped her head up, reminding him that maybe he should fucking concentrate on Matt being missing. He pulled the phone from his belt and glanced at the screen. Vic. He punched the button. "What's up?"

"I found him."

"Where is he?" The valet pulled up and the second attendant held the passenger door open for Roxann.

"No," Michael said to the kid, but Roxann held up her hand.

"I changed my mind."

She slid into the car and he stepped up before the valet closed the door. "You sure?" He kept his eyes locked on hers, hoping he'd hear the answer he wanted.

"No, but it's okay. In some ways I'm sure and that's what I'm going with."

The strength in those words gave him a boost. Maybe

she didn't trust him completely, but she'd get into a car alone with him. Progress.

He shut the door and went back to Vic. "Is he okay?"

"Yeah," Vic said. "He's skateboarding at that old freight yard off Fullerton."

"The freight yard? He's begging to get rolled."

"The stupid shit," Vic said.

"You found him fast."

"He was in the office last week and told me some kids put together a makeshift skate park down here. Figured I'd take a shot, and here he is. He doesn't know I'm here. You want me to grab him?"

"No. Watch him. I'll talk to him when I get there."

"Roger that."

Michael jumped into the driver's side, threw the phone on the dashboard and a curling mass of relief and outrage settled in his neck. Matt didn't have a fucking clue what kind of degenerate drug dealers and thieves would be hanging around a freight yard at night. Michael should kick his ass for being stupid.

At least Michael was around to take care of this stuff because his own father wouldn't be any good at it. Frank had grown too old and cranky to deal with his fifteen-year-old grandson and the reality of that gave Michael pause. If he went to jail, Vic would be the one helping with the kids.

"He found him?" Roxann asked.

Michael turned to her, stared a sec. Somehow, he'd forgotten she was beside him. "He's okay. At least until I get my hands on him."

"SON OF A GUN," MICHAEL SAID AS THEY PULLED INTO THE abandoned freight yard and parked next to Vic's Tahoe.

Roxann stared out the windshield wondering how long Matt had been in this darkened freight yard with its old, broken down trains and stacked cargo containers. The useless, sporadically placed lamp posts threw hardly enough light for anyone, much less a fifteen-year-old, to be skateboarding on homemade steel ramps. Only a teenager would be naïve enough to feel safe here.

An urgent need to check the door locks flooded Roxann. "This is quite a place."

Vic got out of his car, jumped into the backseat of Michael's.

"Hey, Roxann," he said as if her presence was normal.

Michael glanced at Vic in the rearview. "If you were a woman, I'd kiss you."

Seeing the opportunity for some levity, she perked up. "You want me to kiss him?"

Vic shoved his adorable, albeit scruffy, face between the bucket seats and puckered up, only to receive a shove from Michael. At least she'd gotten Michael to laugh. He'd spent the last fifteen minutes in a brooding silence that left her guessing if he were mad, worried or both. She realized now it had been worry.

Vic gestured toward Matt. "He spotted me right after I called you, but he hasn't come over."

"He was probably crapping his pants until he realized it was you. I can't believe kids are hanging out here." Michael rested his head on the steering wheel. "Did I just say that? When the hell did I become a grown up? And I forgot to call Gina."

He dialed the phone and muttered to himself about being a moron.

"Hey, G. We found him...I won't...Right...I *won't* yell at him." He punched a button and tossed the phone onto the dash. "Lunatic." He tapped his fingers on the steering wheel and watched his nephew for a moment. "I'll be back."

"I gotta ask you," Vic said after Michael got out of the car, "have you ever seen such a nutty bunch? I mean these people are postal. And I've seen postal." Before Roxann could respond, he said, "Watch this."

She turned to him. "I guess you've done this before?"

"Yeah, I'm part of the hunting party. We're getting good at it. We rendezvous at Mike's parents' house afterward. His ma usually had a good meal ready. It's late now though. This is the first nighttime run the kid has tried. He's getting brave."

Michael leaned on the front of the car. "What's he waiting for?"

"Matt'll come over. He knows he's busted."

But Matt was busy doing board tricks and seemed unfazed by his uncle's presence. The boy wore tattered jeans that hung to his knees, a phenomenon she would never understand, and a long-sleeved T-shirt. No jacket. *Must be freezing.* He'd gotten tall since Roxann had seen him last, over four years ago.

She couldn't see his features in the dark, but he had his father's broad build. His dead father. The agonizing squeeze of loss settled in her chest. This boy had been eleven when his father died. She was thirty-five and couldn't figure out how to deal with the grief. How was a teenager supposed to do it?

She watched as Michael stood, hands in pockets, waiting for Matt to come to him.

"I'm just not believing this."

The old Michael would have stomped over, grabbed Matt by the shirt and thrown him into the car regardless of the humiliation he'd have inflicted.

"It's the kinder, gentler Mike Taylor," Vic cracked. "Don't tell anybody."

Eventually, with all the enthusiasm of a man going to the electric chair, Matt made his way over. Michael talked. No yelling. No arms flapping or veins bulging. Amazing. Matt listened, said something, shuffled his feet, then turned away and wiped his eyes. Crying. Poor kid.

Roxann thought for sure her heart would snap when Michael reached out, threw an arm over Matt's shoulder and pulled him close. They spoke briefly again, but then Matt was climbing into the car, looking at her and she held up her hand.

"What's shakin' bacon?" Vic said and they did some crazy hand thing that lasted a solid minute. Didn't teenagers just shake hands anymore?

"Matt," Michael said, "this is Roxann."

"Hi, Matt."

But his eyes, slightly narrowed, remained fixed on her and she realized he had his father's long, nose and full lips. How must it feel to Gina to have a constant reminder of her husband?

"I remember you."

Michael glanced at Matt via the rearview. "How? You were three years old when Roxann and I...uh...knew each other."

Matt held her gaze, taking in the features of her face. Remembering. "From the lake. You used to run in the morning."

"Yes," she said. "You'd ride your bike when your dad ran."

Matt drew his eyebrows together. "Is Mom pissed?" he asked Michael.

"Watch your mouth. Mixed company."

"Sorry. Is Mom mad?"

"She's worried. I'll take you home and we'll talk about it. You can bet on being grounded though."

"I figured."

Roxann shot a sideways glance at Michael, who drummed the fingers of his right hand on the center console. He had a constant nervous energy that bubbled just below the surface and she reached to still him.

When he turned his hand palm up and squeezed her fingers, she let the heat spill through her until her brain guided her body to a rigid state. Probably the angel going into defense mode. She shouldn't have touched him. It sent a wrong signal. She needed to stay emotionally detached. That's how it had to be. Detached. Very.

Except she'd gotten into this car with him.

But really, asked the devil, how could she continue to resent Michael when he'd gone tearing off to find his nephew? *Don't go there,* the angel warned, and Roxann shook her head to quiet the madness.

Too late. The devil pulled ahead. A part of her had simply crumbled when she saw Michael, a man with no children of his own, taking on the role of stand-in father for a rebellious teenager. Could there be a more unselfish thing when he had major issues of his own?

She didn't think so. And that was a problem because it touched her in the deepest part of her soul. The part that knew how important it was to have love in one's life.

So much for emotional detachment.

6
_____

PHIL DAWSON ENTERED ROXANN'S OFFICE LIKE A THIRD grader who'd been sent to the principal. She had only summoned him to corporate a few times and, on each occasion, he seemed more nervous.

This, she surmised, came from his insecurity over not having a blockbuster story since she'd lured him from the *Philadelphia Inquirer* two years earlier. There had been plenty to report on, but Phil wanted an award-worthy story. The kind that made investigative journalists drool.

He ran his stubby fingers over his tie as he approached the desk. He'd lost weight recently, but was too cheap to buy new clothes until he lost the last twenty pounds.

"Hey, Phil." She held a hand toward one of the guest chairs and he plopped into it.

"Is there a problem with one of my pieces?"

Yep. Nervous. "Not at all. I have a lead for you, but it requires discretion."

"Great." He opened his ever-present note pad. "Shoot."

She leaned back in her chair and took a breath. Helping Michael was about to become real. "It's the Taylor murder. A source told me Alicia Taylor had an affair with a married man."

Phil's bottom lip shot out as he wrote, and he paused to shove his horn-rimmed glasses up. "Do we know who the affair was with?"

We sure do. "It's Carl Biehl."

"The mayor's Carl Biehl?"

She nodded. "Easy, boy."

"Yes, ma'am, but that's a pretty big dime to drop on someone. Do the cops know?"

"I don't know. See what you can come up with."

Phil jotted a note. "My P.D. source might be able to confirm it. Is that it?"

"For now. I'm going to check around a little myself. Don't be surprised if I call you with something. I'll clear it with your editor, but for the time being, I want you concentrating on this. If you have a workload issue, we'll get something reassigned."

"I'm good, but if anything comes up, I'll let you know." He stood. "You'll be popular in the editorial meetings."

No kidding. Under her father's rule, the newsroom ran autonomously. Mitch, Phil's editor and general newsroom grouch, would have a fit about her interference, but he would have to adjust to the change at the helm. Particularly because she suspected Carl Biehl had something to do with Alicia's murder and Phil, being a die-hard journalist, would help her confirm it.

"It's my problem," Roxann said. "If it goes anywhere the editors and lawyers will have to review everything anyway."

Phil smacked his notepad against his thigh. "Thanks, Roxann. I've been working this story, but nothing is popping."

"This might be the story I brought you here for."

He left the office, his steps quicker now. She knew he'd been chasing dead-end leads and she'd given him something to work with. It was only a morsel, but sometimes the biggest story started from scraps.

THE FOLLOWING MORNING, ROXANN ENTERED HER OFFICE AT the *Banner* and dumped her notepad on what used to be her organized workspace. The gorgeous cherry desk had morphed into an eruption of piles and piles of manila folders.

Banker's boxes, stacked three high, sat in one corner of the office—her father's files. All she needed to do was find a place for them. Good luck with that.

A sliver of panic shot up her arms. Control freaks couldn't function in messy spaces. This office needed to be firebombed.

A knock sounded on her door. "Morning, Rox."

"Hey, Phil." She motioned him to a chair—one of the only surfaces not covered with folders or notebooks—unbuttoned her suit jacket and sat behind her desk. "What's up?"

"Something went on with Alicia Taylor and Carl Biehl, but nobody will go on record that it was an affair. I didn't get anything from Mrs. Biehl. She didn't deny it though."

Roxann rested her head against the back of her chair. She needed an aspirin, maybe ten, for the dull throb that had grown into a raging headache. Fatigue did that to her. Was this the right time to make an important decision? Would there ever be a good time to run this story?

"What did your P.D. source say?"

"He wouldn't confirm the affair, but said a friend of the

Taylors saw them—Alicia and Biehl—in a restaurant one night. The friend said Biehl seemed nervous." He leaned forward and pushed up his glasses. "Also, a neighbor said he saw Biehl leaving Alicia's two days before the murder."

"They certainly weren't shy."

"Nope."

Roxann ran the options. Running the story would mean scandal for Carl Biehl. The mayor would go ballistic and Max would be right there with him because she'd messed around in an active case. On a personal level, if her uncle set his mind to it, he could create dissention between Roxann and her mother during a time when they needed each other. She didn't want her mother feeling additional emotional upheavals because Max was in a snit. But would his anger be fierce enough to drag her mother into it? Roxann hoped not.

She sat silently, turned over the options, ran the scenarios. Would it be worth the backlash? Her palms began to itch—the itch hadn't failed her yet—but this decision carried personal and business implications. Breaking it down to its simplest form, this was a newspaper and the mayor's chief of staff having an affair with a murder victim was news.

Roxann leaned forward. "Can you combine this with other new details about the murder? You can add the Biehl information, but don't say it was an affair. Call it a close friendship. Whatever."

Phil nodded. "Sure. My source gave me some stuff on the crime scene."

"Good. I'll talk to Mitch about it. He and the lawyers will have to check for libel issues. I want to see a final before it goes to print. We'll see what else is running tomorrow before we make a placement decision, but we'll get it close to the front."

Phil whistled. "Thanks, Rox."

He rose from his chair and she held up a hand. "Michael Taylor is my source. Obviously, that's not for disclosure."

A slow, satisfied smile spread across Phil's face. "This is a *really* good day."

Roxann crawled into bed, her body feeling as if it had been plastered by a wrecking ball. When morning came, the Alicia Taylor story would break and create an avalanche of speculation. She burrowed farther into the supple, pink sheets and drew comfort from them. Sometimes a well-made bed was all she needed. Wouldn't it be great if a well-made bed could cure all her problems?

She gazed up at the ceiling, painted the palest of peach to add warmth. She'd need all the warmth she could get because come morning, Max would be furious. Should she call him with a heads-up about the story? The sickening swell of bile in her throat made her rethink the idea. Part of her was too chicken to tell him. The other part couldn't summon the energy to deal with the fit he'd throw.

The digital clock on the bedside table showed eleven thirty-five, late for an early riser who kept to a regimented schedule, but nothing unusual lately. She flipped the lamp off and snuggled into her pillow. Thirty seconds later, her brain still buzzing, she sat up, turned the lamp on and whipped off the covers.

Damn.

She snatched her phone from the charger and scrolled through her contacts for Michael's number.

"Taylor."

His voice carried the fog of sleep and she closed her eyes while her insides melted. It had been a long time since she'd heard that just-woken-up-I'm-so-sexy voice. *Don't go there.* She cleared her throat.

"It's Roxann. Sorry to wake you."

"I'm used to it. Why're you up?"

She tugged at a loose string on the comforter. *Need to fix that.* "We're running the story on Carl and Alicia tomorrow. I didn't want you to be blindsided."

She heard a *ffftttt* and wondered if he'd tossed the covers and gotten out of bed. She hoped so. Talking to him while he lounged in bed unnerved her. Particularly if he still slept naked. She imagined his tall, solid frame wearing only his lightning quick smile and it stirred up a whole lot of memories. She squeezed her eyes shut again. *Don't go there.*

"Phil's been busy," Michael said, but nothing in his tone revealed pleasure.

His reaction wasn't a surprise. After all, some of the seedy details of his failed marriage were about to be splashed across the front page of her newspaper.

"That was it," she said. "So, goodnight."

"You okay?"

"Sure. My editors hate my management style, but other than that, doing just fine."

Where did that come from? Wow.

"Fine generally means *not* fine."

She couldn't help but laugh. "You're so astute."

"I'm in my sensitive phase. What's on your mind, Rox?"

She gripped the phone tighter, reluctant to hang up, but also terrified of sharing the intricacies of her life with him. And yet, here they were, both executives at large companies.

He would understand it from a business angle. Yes, back to the *business* arrangement. *Focus.* "My father's only been gone a few weeks. I'm trying to get through it and working is the best way, but my managing editor is mad at me, which is nothing new, but it's annoying. Another little thing to deal with." *What am I doing?* "I'm sorry. You don't need my problems added to your stack. I should go."

"Rox, us working together is...odd."

"I'll say."

"Anyway, thanks. For everything." He hesitated. "I can't go to jail. You saw why the other night with Matt. He's having a tough time. The poor kid wants to have sex in the worst way."

"Oh. How does Gina deal with that?"

Michael snorted. "*Gina*? She's not going near that one."

"*You* talk to him about sex?"

This revelation nearly put her over the edge. Michael discussing the birds and the bees. Frightening. He had always been more of a let's-get-a-hooker-in-here-to-give-the-kid-his-first-lesson type of guy.

"Somebody's got to," he said. "My sister wants to lock him up somewhere. He's fifteen and hormonally challenged. I feel for him."

"It's nice they have you."

"I need to stay around."

There it was. The anxiety. His attitude toward people's suspicions of him was generally casual. Nothing seemed to penetrate the armor, except a discussion about a young boy going through puberty.

"Look, Rox, Alicia and I were at each other, but I wouldn't have done that to her. Never. The money isn't worth it."

A sudden burst of heat saturated Roxann's cheeks and

she tugged on the loose string again. Minutes ago she had fantasized about his sexy voice and now he was proclaiming innocence to his wife's murder. A woman he'd married instead of her. Complicated.

"As you said, it's a good business deal. I don't know what will come of it, but we'll both benefit."

"I hope so," he said.

Roxann flattened the loose string for the last time and sat on her hand. "I should go now, but I guess we'll talk tomorrow. Goodnight."

She hung up and stared at the wall and the framed front page of the *Banner* from the day she was born. She had stored thirty-five newspapers, one from each of her birthdays, and could immediately pick the year she'd celebrated with Michael. As much as she would deny it, a late- night phone call with him was nice. It sent her spiraling back to the time when she waited for his calls and the anticipation that came when the phone finally rang.

That's what she felt now. That silly burst of hope for something more, not knowing what that something was. Yes, she could try and control it, but she wasn't having much luck in that department. And worse, it involved a man suspected of murder.

AT EIGHT IN THE MORNING, WITH HER HEAD HIGH AND wearing her favorite red suit for moral support, Roxann strode through the *Banner*'s executive suite carrying a copy of the morning paper.

After her morning run had eased the tension of a sleepless night, she appeared confident and pulled together. The competitor in her refused to let the stress win.

She slid past Mrs. Mackey's desk where the computer

hummed and messages were already stacked. The aroma of fresh brewed coffee assaulted Roxann's senses and she looked toward the galley area where Mrs. Mackey stood pouring her a cup. A saint.

Half of the office doors remained closed, but it was early. Most of the senior staff made it in by eight fifteen because two years ago she'd implemented a company-wide rule that any chronic late comers be spoken to. She understood being late every now and again, but if employees did it repeatedly with impunity, it would lead to a total loss of control.

The senior staff needed to set the example for the rest of the employees. If their leaders couldn't arrive on time, why should the followers be expected to?

The phone rang as Roxann entered her office. Not a surprise given the story in the day's newspaper. She let it go to voice mail.

She shrugged off her trench coat, hung it behind her door and got to her desk to find the red message light flashing. Some nasty messages probably waited for her, but they'd wait a little longer.

She located the Alicia Taylor story on the bottom of page three. The final draft had been approved, but she needed to read it again to make sure Phil's editor hadn't made any late changes.

As usual, Phil had given them excellent reporting. She retrieved a legal pad from her drawer and made detailed notes because, if her instincts served her, the day would offer a battle with the mayor of Chicago and every tiny detail mattered.

Mrs. Mackey knocked once on the open door and entered with the steaming coffee and a stack of pink message slips. "You're popular today. Three calls from the mayor, one from Carl Biehl, two from Max and one from your mother. I have no idea what's on your voice mail, but your phone has been ringing nonstop since seven-thirty."

After a deep breath, Roxann punched the voice mail button. "Let's see what we've got."

She was greeted by a cheery voice announcing her mailbox was full. Good Lord.

Mrs. Mackey hit the disconnect button. "Let me go through them and summarize. I've probably already given you most of them."

"You just earned yourself a bonus."

"Ooooh, I hope it's that condo in the Alps. I was upset I didn't get that *last* year."

She strolled out leaving Roxann smiling for the first time all morning. Mrs. Mackey skiing. Ha.

A minute later the phone buzzed and Mrs. Mackey's voice boomed through the speaker. "You have the pressmen in ten and the mayor is holding. What should I tell him?"

Roxann slumped back in her chair and the bowling ball lodged in her intestines grew. She should avoid the call and take a few more minutes to prepare for the skewering.

Coward.

Perhaps she'd slip into her armored suit, cross her fingers and get it over with. Put it behind her so she could go about her day. She had to be sharp for the pressmen and didn't need to be distracted by an impending bashing from the mayor.

"Put him through. Thank you."

Roxann closed her eyes, imagined herself on a warm toasty beach and picked up her ringing phone. "Mr. Mayor, I was just about to call you. How can I help you?"

"You can start by issuing a retraction. Have you people lost your minds? I thought your father was bad, but even he wouldn't have signed off on this. Prepare yourself for a libel suit, missy."

She winced. Missy? Of course, the mayor would go for the jugular by implying she wasn't living up to her father's standards.

She squared her shoulders, allowed the competitor in her to take over. "Sir, there is nothing libelous in the story and my father most certainly would have run it."

"Goddammit, Roxann. Do you have any idea what this is doing to Carl's family?"

"He should have thought about that before he carried on —whatever his *relationship* was—with Alicia Taylor."

The mayor huffed, "I don't disagree, but for God's sake, this is a man's family. And his career."

"Not to mention bringing embarrassment to your office."

"Listen, *honey.*"

A honey and a missy in one conversation. *Stay calm, Keep it in check. Start at the toes, tighten every muscle.*

"My name is Roxann."

"*Roxann,* you just put your tits in a vise."

A sudden and mind freezing anger shot through her. So much for calm. The limit on what she could take from this sexist maniac had just been reached. "*Mister* Mayor, this conversation is over."

She slammed the phone down, jumped from her chair and stormed around her office. "Pig!"

The nerve. Could she bring a sexual harassment suit against the mayor of Chicago? Maybe he needed his *balls* put in a vise.

Mrs. Mackey appeared in the doorway, her face carrying the blanched look of someone who had just witnessed a bombing. "Are you okay?"

Roxann stopped pacing, counted to ten and rolled her

shoulders. "I'm fine. No more calls from the mayor today. He needs to work off that mad. Besides, I just hung up on him."

"You hung up on him?"

"He deserved it."

"That's my girl. The pressmen are waiting for you."

"Perfect. Let's get all the negativity out of the way first thing."

7

ROXANN SUCKED IN THE MISTY DAWN AIR. THE RHYTHMIC *thump, thump, thump* of her feet hitting the path settled her and brought peace to her tortured mind.

Her forty miles per week goal had gone astray lately and the effects dragged on her. Working off the stress wasn't the only concern. The M&M component had to be recognized. She was single-handedly keeping the Mars Company's stock price up and her butt had the squishy feeling of a life raft equipped to hold twenty people. New territory for a girl who'd been a size six for twenty years.

The dawn sky stretched to a brilliant orange that could have been hand-painted. Sunrises truly were a miracle. Cold this morning though. Spring in Chicago was a fool's bet, but Chicagoans were a hardy bunch and adapted easily. It would take more than a cold spring morning to keep her, and the smattering of other runners, inside. To ward off the morning chill, Roxann wore second skin running tights, a T-shirt and a zipped jacket. If the temperature climbed, she could strip off her jacket.

At six miles in, she reached her cruising altitude where

her breathing and heart rate leveled. The challenge came with pushing past the point where she wanted to stop. If she kept moving, her body would eventually find its rhythm and perform better than expected. That was her joy in running.

At the Starbucks, her mile marker nine, the sun now blazing, she slowed to her cool down jog and felt the blissful ache of a healthy and de-stressed body.

Someone muttered something from a bench she had just cruised by and she snuck a peak behind her.

Michael.

What was he up to? Had she not been so focused on completing her run, she would have recognized his voice.

Narrowing her eyes, she retreated the few feet to the bench where he looked better than a bowl of M&Ms. Casual today, faded jeans and a white T-shirt under a black fleece pullover. He held two coffees and a brown paper bag.

"Kind of cold for an early morning picnic with yourself, isn't it?" she panted, her breathing not yet regulated.

He scooted over on the bench and patted the spot beside him. "I wasn't intending on eating alone. Have a seat."

She stopped her in-place jog, pursed her lips and, taking the coffee he held out, sat down. Her hamstrings begged for a stretch and, still holding the cup, she obliged by extending her legs and folding her upper body forward. "What brings you out here?"

He peered at her over the top of his sunglasses. "I needed coffee. Figured I'd have it out here and maybe I'd see you."

"How'd you know I'd be out here?"

That got a laugh out of him. "You've been doing this route for years." He shoved the brown bag at her. "Got you a muffin."

Roxann peeked into the bag, inhaled the warm, tangy

scent of a fresh cranberry-orange muffin. He remembered her love of all things citrus. *Big trouble.* "Good memory. Thank you."

She held up the muffin and imagined herself drooling. Her stomach had been growling for three miles. She leaned back on the bench, bit into her breakfast and groaned as the flavor seized her mouth.

Michael stared.

"What?" she asked, wiping her mouth.

"You and the muffin." He wiggled his eyebrows. "It's sexy."

"Easy, big boy. It's all about the food."

"How you wound me."

"You'll bounce back."

Michael shifted toward her. "Coffee okay?"

After a sip that scorched her tongue, she held the cup up. "Black, no sugar. Perfect."

One of the regular runners ran past and waved to her.

Michael studied the guy. "Friend of yours?"

She shrugged. "I see him out here."

"He likes looking at you."

A chunk of muffin caught in her throat and she coughed, nearly spitting crumbs everywhere. Her mother would be mortified. "Pardon?"

"He spotted you a block down and didn't take his eyes off you. You need to be careful out here."

Was he kidding? She'd managed just fine without him for the last twelve years and didn't need him lecturing her. "All of a sudden you're my bodyguard?"

"Just saying."

"Well, don't."

"News flash, Rox. You look good in that getup and if I'm

thinkin' it," he swooped his index finger toward the other runners. "They're thinkin' it."

Oh please. She set the muffin on top of the bag and held up two hands. "Whatever."

Her hamstrings still whined and she stood for a full stretch. Irritating man. Not only was he condescending, but he was probably right. *Shoot.* She hated giving him the satisfaction. In the years she'd been running along the lakefront, she had allowed herself to get complacent and ignore the possible dangers around her. For a smart girl, that was dumb.

Michael's intense study set her comfort level at zero and she shook out her legs before moving on to her next set of stretches. The man had a way of looking at people that made them want to curl up in his lap. Or, maybe that was just her.

Stretch. Think about the stretch. By the time she'd finished her quads, the angst had cooled. Minimally.

She sat beside him, retrieved her muffin and coffee. "I was going to call you today."

"Lucky me."

She smiled. "Don't say that until you hear what it's about."

He groaned.

"Exactly," she said. "The other night you mentioned you had someone following Alicia."

Michael shifted to face the lake and stared out. "You want to see what I have on her."

No sense hedging around it. They needed to see those files and compare it with the information Phil had. "Phil wants to look."

Michael remained quiet, gazing out over the lake for a

minute. Maybe two. "There's information in there that would hurt people."

Seriously? "It didn't seem to bother you when we used what you told us about Carl."

He glanced over at her. "Alicia's parents don't deserve to see photos of their daughter giving someone a blow-job behind a building."

Roxann reeled back against the bench, tried to imagine how it would feel to see her spouse doing such a thing. Her stomach turned sour and she stared at Michael whose cheeks had hollowed. If she pulled his sunglasses off, what would she see in those dark eyes? Exhaustion? Regret? Hurt? Maybe all of the above.

She breathed out. "I'm sorry."

He turned toward her again. "I got over it a long time ago, but her parents are good people. They shouldn't have to see it. Whatever Alicia had become, she used to be my wife and she didn't deserve to die. If you want to see the files, I'll let you look at them. Just you."

"But Phil—"

"Rox, *you* know what will be important in those files. You've got an eye for that. Plus, you have a yearning to do the right thing. Always have. You decide what's relevant, and we'll see if it gets passed to Phil. That's the deal."

Could she argue this? What choice did she have? They needed to see those files and although she'd rather brand her own skin than look through pictures of Michael's wife... "I'll do it."

He nodded. "Thank you. I know it's a lot to ask."

"It's fine."

A runner went by and Michael again studied the person. What was he always looking for?

They sat for a moment and the sounds of gently lapping

waves and cars whooshing along Lake Shore Drive caught her attention. Roxann glanced at her watch. She needed to get moving, but stayed anchored to the bench, that devil inside her enjoying the early morning company. She could stall a few minutes. Hadn't she cleared her morning schedule so she could catch up on phone calls?

"So, I think we should talk about a couple of things," she said.

Michael shook his head. "No."

"You don't know what I'm going to say."

"With a lead-in like that, it can't be good."

He laughed and the sound glided through her. She sent her elbow his way and connected with his arm. "I just want to be clear about our arrangement. This is business. No funny stuff."

He turned toward her, smiling the smile that heated her up.

"Hey," she said. "I don't need people thinking we ran the story about Alicia and Carl because—well—you know."

He leaned in close. "Because they'll think we're lovers?"

The warmth of his breath skittered over her cheek and she angled away. "Exactly."

"You worry about crazy shit."

"Maybe so, but it's how I feel."

He watched two joggers run by. "Whatever you say, Rox."

"You're humoring me?"

"Absolutely."

"You are so irritating." Irritating and sexy and cute all at the same time.

"My mother says that all the time. She doesn't mean it."

"Yes. She does. Trust me."

"I do trust you, just not about my mother. Anyway, I'd

love to stay out here with you, but I have to change for work."

Roxann walked over and tossed the cups in the garbage can. "Me too."

Michael stood. "I guess I shouldn't kiss you goodbye then?"

"Ha, ha."

They walked a short distance to the concrete pedestrian bridge that stretched over Lake Shore Drive. "This is my stop." He snapped his fingers. "We have to talk about your lobby desk situation. You should reassign those guards. Let us put a couple of our guys there."

She rolled her eyes. "I know, I know. Vic has been bugging me about it. I'll get to it."

"Well, tick tock. Don't wait too long."

"Blah, blah, blah. I said I'd get to it."

Michael grinned and tugged a loose tendril of her hair. "Those files you want to see are locked in a safe in my office. If you want to come by after work, I'll let you go through them."

"Okay. I'll call you later."

She watched him jog up the steps and couldn't help noticing his great butt. With that, she let out a sigh. *This is just not good.*

Traffic on the Drive had picked up, the cars speeding by for another busy day in the city. Another five minutes and it would be a rush hour parking lot. Roxann gazed up at the thirty-story building Michael called home, its gold tinted windows drenched with sunlight. A condo on the famed Gold Coast. He'd done well for himself. Over the years, she'd seen or heard him mentioned in various places and his wealth had surprised her. Twelve years ago, he'd just gotten out of the military, was dealing with wicked post traumatic stress and simply wanted to survive.

After all he'd been through, how far would he go to protect his hard-fought wealth?

She thought about it on her jog home, but—her tortured mind be damned—didn't have one decent answer for herself. She'd have to see where this story led her and then decide. She strode through the back door of her childhood home, locked it and snatched the cordless phone from the kitchen counter. Voice mail. Not even eight o'clock. The people in her life knew her too well. She propped the phone at her ear, grabbed a bottle of water from the fridge and sat at the table.

"Hi, Roxann. It's your mother calling." As if she wouldn't know her mother's voice. "I just spoke to Max and he's upset. Call me, dear."

She grunted, hit the delete button and waited for the next message. As predicted, Max had moved out of the bullying phase and into the silent treatment. Of course, the silent treatment had been directed toward Roxann because, rather than deal with her, he'd chosen to complain to Mom. Brat.

"Hey, girlfriend." Janie's raspy voice popped through. "Just checking in. My dad has two waitresses out with the flu and needs me to help tonight. I'll be at Cassatta's after five if you need me. Love you."

Roxann hit the delete button. She'd call Janie back—chatting with her friend would be a nice distraction. First, she had to deal with Max and that would be a task. She glanced at the clock, dialed Mrs. Mackey's direct line at the office and left a message that she'd be making calls from home and would be late. Nothing compared to breaking her own rule about being on time. Blame it on Michael for distracting her. She took a much-needed gulp of water, set the bottle on the table and dialed her mother. When voice mail picked up, Roxann pasted on a smile hoping it would inspire her to be cheerful.

"Hi. It's me. Got your message. I'm going to call Max myself and take care of this. Please don't worry about it. Call me if you need anything. I'll see you soon. I love you."

She clicked off and dialed Max's cell.

"What is it, Rox?"

Her head snapped back at the toxic tone. "And good morning to you." Why not take a shot at cheerful?

"I'm working."

Okay, he didn't deserve bright and cheery. "If you're so busy you could have saved yourself time this morning by calling me, rather than my mother, to complain."

"I didn't call to complain—"

"She told me—"

"Don't interrupt me. I called to check on my recently widowed sister. She asked me if I knew anything about Carl's relationship with Alicia Taylor. Did you want me to ignore her?"

Roxann's gaze fell to the table and, using her free hand, she drew imaginary circles. Burying Max with guilt backfired on her and left her feeling the fool.

"I apologize. A little jumpy, I guess. I thought you were mad about the story."

"I am. We're working this case hard and I don't understand why you're doing this, but you're a big girl with big responsibilities. I don't need to remind you, of all people, about libel, obstruction of justice, impeding an investigation. You know the drill."

Obstruction of justice was a new one. "I have to pursue this, Max." Roxann stood and paced the kitchen, wanting nothing more than to work off the negative energy filling her. "I know this is an active investigation, and I respect that, but it's news. Carl Biehl was involved with a murder victim and if he wasn't the mayor's aide the public would already know about it."

"We were aware of his association with her and cleared him early on. Why release information that's not going anywhere?"

"Carl may have been cleared, but what about all the people that work for him or are related to him?"

"Are you a detective now?"

Her heart hammered from the frigid tone in Max's voice. Anger always made him distant and unaffected, but she'd experienced this with him when he didn't agree with the *Banner*'s coverage. And, as before, he'd get over it because she wouldn't give in. "Absolutely not. I'm not accusing Carl of murder, but I think his relationship with Alicia warrants him being looked at. His involvement with her might lead to something. I'd love to tell you we'll drop this, but until these questions are answered, we're following this story."

"Do what you need to, Roxann."

Max had shut down. Done talking. Silent treatment mode would continue. "I *will* do what I need to and I hope you and I will come out okay. I don't want you mad at me."

He stayed silent for a long moment and she wondered if he'd hung up.

The silence dragged on. A battle of wills. Time for a subject change.

"How about lunch one day this week?" Maybe if she could see him they'd make nice. Losing her father had been devastating enough without the added stress of Max being absent from her life.

"Okay," he finally said. "Call my assistant and set something up."

She clicked the phone off, slid into a chair, threw her head down on the table and rolled her forehead over the cool surface. Max being mad was a mine field. You never knew when you'd step in the wrong place and get blown to bits.

8

"JUST SO YOU KNOW," ROXANN SAID WHEN SHE STROLLED INTO Michael's office dressed in a black pants suit that made her legs look five miles long, "your lobby guards barely stopped me. Haven't you been nagging me about beefing up my security?"

Michael tossed his pen on the desk and sat back in his chair. "The difference is I told them you were coming and to send you right up."

She stopped, scrunched her nose and said, "Oh."

He laughed. "Yeah. *Oh.*"

That got him an eye roll, which, right now, could have been a badge of honor in the Roxann-verbal-sword-play challenge. Damn, he'd missed the banter.

He waved her to a chair. "Have a seat."

"So," she said, folding those long legs and taking a look around. "This is your office."

"Yep."

"My office used to be this neat. I'm working on getting it that way again."

Small talk. He shrugged. "Transition is always tough. Then again, you could be Vic. His office is a war zone."

"I can't work that way. Too much clutter."

"Rox?"

She took a huge breath, let it out. "Yes?"

"Are you sure you want to do this?"

In the span of three seconds, her gaze darted to the window, came back to him and went to the window again.

"I *don't* want to do this. Not for one second. Not even out of curiosity. But I'm going to. There are plenty more reasons to do it than there are not to."

He stood, circled the desk and leaned on the edge just to her right. "No one outside of the photographer, Alicia, the judge and our divorce attorneys has seen these photos. I have not turned them over to the P.D. My attorney advised me to hang on to them for the time being. I can deal with that. Oddly enough, it doesn't seem fair to let the city Alicia loved see her like this."

It had taken a long time to deaden his nerves to the sight of the woman he had married with other men, but he still wasn't willing to let the public glimpse into their life. The downside was too big.

"Michael, it would take a lot of pressure off you to turn the information over."

"Or, it could get worse. All that bad behavior? People will think I finally snapped."

Roxann bit her lip. "Didn't think of that."

He shrugged. "Listen, if it helps at all, I'll let you look through the photos alone. I'll stay at my desk and you can work at the table."

She glanced to her left at the small conference table with four chairs. He'd already pulled the two boxes of files from his safe—Vic called it the vault—and stacked them beside the table. The idea of Roxann going through the photos made his chest ache. Two women he'd loved in different ways and now, the one he'd never completely let go, had to study the evidence of his colossal fuck up of a marriage.

"Those are the boxes?"

"Yep. Two-and-a-half years of Alicia Taylor's life."

She rose from her chair and moved to the table. "Wow."

"You probably don't want to tackle it all in one sitting."

She didn't answer. Only stared at the boxes. After a minute, she pulled her suit jacket off and draped it over one of the chairs. Ready to dig in.

Michael boosted himself away from the desk and returned to his chair. This wouldn't be any easier on him than it would be on her. Did humiliation ever sit well with anyone? He doubted it. But then, Roxann had always accepted him without passing judgment. For that alone, he'd adored her. Hopefully, she still had a little of that left in her. "Have you eaten?"

"Not yet."

"I'll order something. We'll probably be here awhile."

After flagging several items to be looked at again, Roxann closed the file marked April and pushed it to the side. Each folder had to be over an inch thick and she would have to read through all of them. Two-and-a-half year's worth. It would take days. She rolled her aching shoulders.

She glanced at Michael, still at his desk, shirt sleeves rolled while he dealt with something on his laptop. His five o'clock shadow had come in and she suddenly remembered his need to shave twice a day if he were going out for the evening. The memory of scraping her fingers across his beard stubble roared back as if it had only been a day ago. How many times had she curled into his lap and dragged her hand over his cheek just to feel the texture? At twenty-three it had made her feel she'd had a real man by her side. One who would protect and take care of her. One who would stand by her when things got rough. He'd done neither by walking away and eventually marrying the woman in these photos.

Michael must have sensed her study of him. "You okay?"

Maybe she should ask him how he could have looked through these files. His *wife* had carried on blatant sexual affairs with prominent men and there were photos—explicit ones—to prove it.

Roxann blew out a breath. "Have you seen all of these?"

He didn't answer, but wandered to the table, sat and pawed through one of the boxes until he found a specific folder. After setting it on the table, he propped his chin in his hand, but continued to stare at the folder.

"This one is the worst," he said. "We'd been separated a few months when these were taken. She'd already started in on accusing *me* of all sorts of crap—adultery, emotional abuse, alienation of affection—you name it. None of which I ever did. Well, alienation of affection maybe. By the time we'd separated I could barely look at her, much less touch her. I'd decided to put someone on her to protect myself. And my money."

"Probably smart on your part."

He tapped the folder. "This was when I knew how vindictive she could be. Any good feelings I had left got blown to hell when I saw this folder."

Yikes. Morbid curiosity forced Roxann's gaze to the folder. In comparison to what she'd already seen, what could be that bad?

Michael put his hand flat on top of the folder. "I'll give you a few minutes to look through it and then, if you want to discuss it, fine. If not, we'll let it go."

What was with all the cloak and dagger stuff? "Should I be prepared for something here?"

He shrugged. "These are photos of Alicia with a man you know. I'm not sure how much that man matters to you."

Right off, she could eliminate her father and Max because Michael knew what her relationship was with them. Those would be two men she'd have a whopper of a time understanding having any involvement with Alicia Taylor. They simply wouldn't do that to her.

Roxann reached for the folder. Might as well get it over with.

"Do you want me to leave?"

"You're fine," she said, because whatever was in this folder couldn't be that bad. There just hadn't been any men in her life over the last few years that meant that much. At least there hadn't been anyone she'd completely given herself over to, taken a risk on. No, her personal life was pretty much one big safe zone. The past twelve years had been about order and control and becoming a good publisher. It was easier than dealing with her feelings for the man in front of her.

Truth of it was, she had enough baggage floating around to accommodate four divas on a shopping spree. She just never wanted to admit it to herself.

She flipped the folder open and saw the first photo of Alicia, dressed in a low-cut and exceedingly tight black cocktail dress, her long blond hair falling over her shoulders in fat waves. An absolutely stunning woman. The glammed-up look wasn't quite to Roxann's taste, but there was no denying why men had been attracted to her. In the photo,

Alicia spoke with a man and a woman. The man wore a suit and the woman a sequined dress. Clearly some type of event. Roxann checked the date. June. Almost two years earlier. She flipped to the next photo.

There he was.

Senator Neil Findley. Roxann had dated Neil for six months, but eventually found herself to be more eye candy, a political trophy, than someone Neil actually cared for. After all, what senator wouldn't aspire to be involved with the associate publisher of a major daily newspaper? All in all, Roxann wasn't feeling the pull of attraction for Neil and ended the relationship.

She checked the date on the photo again and did the math. At that point, she'd been seeing Neil a couple of months.

Roxann spread the next few photos in front of her and dared not look at Michael. She knew his eyes were on her though, gauging her reaction. The photos looked harmless enough, except for the last one where Neil was bent low listening to something Alicia said into his ear. An immediate pulsing started under her skin and Roxann shifted in her seat.

The next photo, taken the following day, showed Neil standing on the front porch of a brownstone. Next photo: Alicia Taylor opening the front door. Next photo: Neil going into the house. Next photo: Neil leaving the house. The time stamp revealed he'd been there an hour.

"He is such a weasel."

"That's one way to put it."

She flipped the folder shut. "He was sleeping with your wife while he was seeing me?"

"Appears so. If it matters at all, it didn't last long. It was a few times and then he doesn't show up again. At least my investigator didn't catch him."

"That son of a bitch."

Not that she'd loved him, but she'd thought they'd had an exclusive relationship. And to have broken that trust with Michael's wife? Sickness pooled inside Roxann. She'd had sex with the man after he'd been with Alicia Taylor.

Could Neil have known about the connection to Michael? She'd certainly never told him, but he could have learned it from one of his aides when they'd vetted her.

But Alicia. She had to know. Roxann turned to Michael. "Did she know about us?"

He scoffed, "That was the point. When I saw these photos, I knew her resentment had consumed her."

"But why? She had wealth, status, all the things someone like her would want."

Including the man I wanted.

Michael looked up at her, his gaze steady. *Please don't let him say something that will make me crazy.*

"Yeah," he said, "but her husband wanted you."

No. No way, bucko. Roxann pushed her chair back, shot out of it and paced the room. No, no, no. She didn't want to hear this. Not after all these years. Not when she'd wasted so much time wondering. Not when her emotional state was already being tested with her father's death. "Don't do this to me. *You* married *her*."

Michael stayed seated, his eyes tracking her as she paced the room trying to get rid of the anger and hurt devouring her. She could use a good long run about now. And could he please stop staring at her?

"Rox, I know I was the one that left, but you were in my system. I tried to hide it, but she knew. We saw you and Janie in a restaurant one night. It was after you'd gotten back from Philadelphia and I couldn't stop looking at you. You were right there. I couldn't help myself. It was the longest hour of my life. I could have walked over to you and begged forgiveness, or I could have stayed with Alicia, who, at the time, had been good for me. I was finally faced with choosing. Then she asked me who you were and I told her your name. I didn't give her the details, but she found out. She asked around, I guess. We were engaged by then. She wasn't stupid and knew from that night in the restaurant I hadn't gotten over you. But I'd made a commitment to her. Regardless, I don't think she ever shook the feeling of being my second choice. After we got married, things were good for awhile, but everything started coming apart. When she drank, her need for male attention worsened and that's when I knew she was on the prowl."

Roxann could not believe it. "She knew I was seeing Neil and having an affair with him was what, revenge? Against *me*?"

Michael lifted a shoulder. "Mostly, it was for my benefit. She was punishing me for missing you. She wanted me to know that Findley had you and now he'd had her. The fact that it might hurt you was a bonus."

"A bonus," Roxann said, her voice thick with trapped tension.

He held up his hands. "By that time, she'd turned into someone I didn't know."

She threw her hands in the air. "And you married this woman?"

Instead of me.

She wouldn't dare say it though. Never. He'd made his choice and now he had to live with it. This woman had been his *wife*. The person he'd chosen to share his life with had humiliated him. Taken other men to their bed.

He leaned forward, rested his elbows on his knees and stared at the floor. Uncomfortable. Well, too bad.

"She was different when we first met. Bold and adventurous. Always on the edge."

I'm not any of those things.

He looked up at her again and she stopped moving. "At the time, if I couldn't have you, I thought she would be what I needed."

What the hell did that mean? "And what? She was the *anti*-Roxann? That's what you're telling me?"

He nodded. "I wouldn't call it that, but yes, she was different and I didn't have any reminders. In the beginning, we had fun. The fun ended when we got into the day-to-day of marriage. I was working a lot. She wanted me, but I wanted to build my business. So, in that sense, maybe I wasn't attentive enough. Three years in, she had her first one-night stand. She marched in at dawn and informed me she'd fucked—her word, not mine—some guy from the benefit she'd attended."

"Good God."

Michael shook his head. "Yeah. That's when things went south. I forgave her though. I believed she was lonely and took it as an act of rebellion. I tried spending more time at home, was attentive to the point where it physically drained me and it still wasn't enough. There was no making her happy at that point."

A knock sounded on the door. Michael answered it and came away with two bags. Dinner. Fabulous. As if she could eat. He brought the food to the table and set it in a corner.

"I screwed up. I'm thirty-nine years old and—" he pointed to the folder, "—that's what my marriage became. The only reason I showed it to you was because I didn't want you to get slammed. I wanted to at least try and explain it. Be pissed if you want, but that's the goddamned truth."

He hadn't wanted to blindside her. She couldn't be mad about that. Even the photos... None of it was his fault. Other than marrying the anti-Roxann.

What am I doing? She'd made this deal with him to get an exclusive for the newspaper. She wanted the big story. To prove herself as a publisher. That's what she needed to stick to.

Wasn't this all old news anyway? What was the point of rehashing it? They needed to move forward. Get back to business. If they got back to business, Roxann could bury the emotional carnage.

She blew air through her lips. "Let's focus on our task here. I'm only part way through the first box and I think it's safe to say we can add a few people to the suspect list. And just for kicks, I'll have Phil call Senator Findley and ask him about his affair with Alicia Taylor. If nothing else, it'll make him squirm. Bastard."

Michael stood, held his hands out. "That's it? We're back to Phil and the story?"

"Yes."

"Unbelievable."

She glared at him. "Not really. The *story* is the only thing keeping me sane right now. You came to me with the idea of teaming up to find Alicia's killer. I never imagined I would have to sit here, in your office, looking through boxes that detailed your *wife's* transgressions. A woman who shared your bed night after night while I was left to wonder what made you marry her and not me."

"It wasn't—"

But Roxann blew right past that. "And you know what? I'm still wondering." She grabbed the file off the table and smacked him in the chest with it. "We could have had it all and this is who you gave up on us for. I simply do not understand."

Michael snatched the folder away. "She had nothing to do with it. Not until I came home and found out you had moved to Philly, but I'm not getting into that tonight."

Typical. "Great, Michael. Be honest about the things you want to be honest about and keep the rest to yourself. Nothing has changed."

He tossed the folder on the table, sending a few of the photos scattering. "A lot has changed."

"Feel free to share because I'm not seeing it."

"Here's what I know. If I could go back, I'd have never married her and that's not easy to say. I threw away years of my life and not one good thing came out of it. I now know I should have pounded on your door and talked you into taking me back. I should have fought for you. That's what strong men do. They fight for what they want. Seeing the woman you've become, the fierce businesswoman who only wants to do what's right, I know it would have been damn good to have you by my side. I'll always regret not fighting for you. That's what's changed."

Her head caved in. Just *bam*. Damn him for that little speech and making her once again yearn for what might have been. Well, that was long gone now. Besides, he could be playing her. Pushing her buttons to get her cooperation. Would he be that manipulative?

She didn't think so. Something in the way he stood so tall in contrast to his puffy, tired eyes made her think that this time he'd given her all the truth he could manage for one night. For whatever reason.

She glanced at the bags of food and wondered if a bite to eat would give them a distraction. Something needed to. "I don't want to fight over this anymore. If we're going to work together, I can't do this emotional chaos. I have too much of that with my father being gone and running the newspaper. Let's just call a truce on this subject and move forward so we can find a murderer. Can we do that?"

Michael nodded. "Yeah. We can do that. But eventually, I want to settle it. For good. You don't trust me. I don't blame you. I had my reasons for leaving twelve years ago, and I know I made a mistake, but I can't change that. I'm sorry I hurt you. And I'd like a shot at making it up to you."

What was he talking about? "Make it up to me? How are you going to do that?"

He held up a finger. "Glad you asked. The way I see it, we've got two choices. You can tell me for the hundredth time our relationship will be strictly business. Or we can say screw that and see what might happen between us. I'm sick of dancing around twelve years of bullshit."

He just didn't get it. "Michael, think about this, your wife—"

"Ex-wife."

"—was just murdered and I happen to own a newspaper large enough to convince the masses you didn't do it. Forgive me if I don't think it's wise to become sexually involved with you."

Michael stepped forward and his gaze wandered over her face. She shifted her eyes away. *Not* good. A spiraling panic swirled in her chest. This must be what the electric chair felt like just before they threw the switch.

Time to be honest. "You hurt me. It's going to take more than a couple of weeks to undo it and you need to understand that. If you can't, then we have nothing to hope for."

"I can be patient, but you need to give me a fair shot. Don't keep making me serve my penance for hurting you. I won't do it. If we're going to have a chance, we need to start over. I understand if you don't want to be out in public with me, but I want to spend time with you."

She stared at him. After all this time, he wanted to court her. And darn it if she didn't like that idea. Her mind wandered back to laughter-filled walks on the lakefront, nighttime picnics on the beach where they would lay side by side staring at the sky discussing their hopes for the future. Back then, he knew he wanted his own business, but didn't know what it would be. *She* dreamed of watching him conquer his demons and succeed. It seemed so simple and yet she'd never gotten it.

"Well?" he prompted.

She cleared her throat. "Dinner at my house."

He grinned.

"No gloating. We still have a twelve-year-old mess to clean up." She strode to the table and their cold food.

"Dinner at your place is good."

She smirked. Later, she'd probably realize getting involved with a man who is a person of interest in a murder would be emotional suicide.

9

JOHN CALLAHAN, THE *BANNER*'S ASSOCIATE PUBLISHER, knocked twice and entered Roxann's office.

"Morning. I got a coupla things for you."

She halted her inspection of the morning newspaper. "Hi. You're in early."

She gave cheerful a solid try, but knew she didn't pull it off. She'd spent a sleepless night thinking about work and Michael and whether she'd lost her mind. Her early run helped clear her head, but she should have skipped it to conserve energy. Plus, she had hoped Michael would show up with coffee and muffins again and it didn't happen. What a miserable feeling, this wanting him there and being disappointed. How had she allowed him to wind her up in such a short time?

John, looking dapper in a navy pinstripe suit, stopped. "Should I come back?"

"Nah, you're here. What's up?"

He took a seat in one of the two chairs in front of the desk.

"First, the proof copies of *Progress* just came off, they look good."

He handed her one of the copies of the newly printed section. Mental head slap. She had forgotten they were pre-printing the largest section of the year that morning. She unfolded and perused it.

The annual *Progress* edition had been Roxann's baby. Touted as a business section, *Progress* had once been a cash cow in terms of advertising revenue, but over the past few years advertiser interest had dwindled. Roxann volunteered to lead the overhaul effort and, after working with the editorial staff and polling some of her business contacts, *Progress* was given a makeover and had become the largest section of the year. Digital might be on the rise, but people clearly still had faith in newspapers.

Flipping through the pages, Roxann smiled. *Progress* would be a success and she had a part in it. "This looks great."

"It's a damn nice section."

Mrs. Mackey appeared in the doorway. "Sorry to interrupt, but Craig is calling from the pressroom. Also, Max called."

"Put Craig through. I'll call Max later."

Roxann reached for the phone and tried to ignore the tingling on the back of her neck. A call from the production manager during the print run of the largest section of the year couldn't be good.

"Craig, what's up? Okay...Do I need to come down? Let me know...Thanks."

Returning the phone to its cradle, she sat back in her chair while her chest seized. "There's a problem with the press. They're working on it."

"How big of a problem?"

"It's down."

John's face nearly slid to the floor. She couldn't blame him. When was the last time the entire press went down?

"Shouldn't we go?"

It took most of her self-restraint to stay put, but she needed to allow the supervisors to do their jobs. "Let's let them have at it. If they don't call in fifteen minutes we'll go down."

Mrs. Mackey appeared again. "Pressroom. Line two."

"Too fast. Not good." Roxann jabbed the speaker button, allowing her office to fill with frenzied, muffled voices from the other end. She and John exchanged a discouraged look.

"What's happening, Craig?"

"You'd better come down. The blanket bar came off."

"Off?" John said, his voice carrying the weight of disbelief.

"Yeah, it must have come loose."

The blankets held the images to be printed and the blanket bar secured the blankets to each of the press units. Without one of the bars, the entire press would be down. A knot ripped into Roxann's shoulders.

Hadn't anyone checked the bar to make sure it was secure? Was it wedged in the press? How long would it take to replace the damaged parts? Would they be able to print *Progress* before Saturday night to ensure its inclusion in Sunday's paper?

A cold panic shot up Roxann's spine. "I'm assuming you called maintenance."

"They're here now," Craig said.

"We'll be right down." She punched the button and retrieved her suit jacket from the back of her door. "Here we go. Buckle up."

Nothing disturbed a newspaper publisher more than

staring at a quiet three-story press when there should have been the glorious *pfft-pfft-pfft* of churning machinery. The city-block-long room buzzed with the activity of twenty pressmen huddled around the back of one unit of the enormous twenty-four-unit press.

The pressmen on the lower landing, stared at the catwalk overhead as Craig and two others reviewed the situation. Roxann, cursing herself for wearing a skirt, took a breath and marched up the stairs. Lovely. Giving a room full of men a free show would be great for negotiations. How humiliating. She couldn't worry about it now. With one hand, she pulled the skirt taught and ascended the stairs, her shoes clickety-clacking against the metal. A woman in a man's world.

Craig Rawlins, who had been with the newspaper a long time and knew how to run his pressroom, stood on the catwalk wearing his fifty years like a hundred. His thinning hair and extra forty pounds added to the layer of stress.

"Hey, Rox. Sorry about the call, but the bar is wedged between the blanket and plate cylinders. Maintenance says we have to replace the cylinders. They're making calls to locate the parts."

She glanced down. Thanks to the plank on the catwalk, the pressmen muddled below could not see up her skirt. She let go of it.

"How far into the run were we?"

Craig rocked back on his heels. "Maybe ten percent."

Damn.

She did a quick calculation and turned to Craig. "If we get this fixed today, can *Progress* be off press before we need to print tomorrow's paper?"

"If we're up by noon. If not, we print *Progress* after we

run tomorrow's paper. Then we'll do Sunday's. The presses will be running all day tomorrow. It'll cost us overtime."

"I'm not worried about the overtime. We need to get *Progress* into Sunday's paper."

"What's your gut on this, Craig?" John asked.

An anguished frown gave John his answer. She imagined her father whispering in her ear. *Stay calm and work this problem, Rox. You know what to do.*

"Okay," she said. "I'm going to call the manufacturer and see what they can do. I'll be in my office."

Figuring out how to get the damn paper printed.

Her mind moved fast. Presses down. Overtime. *Progress* in jeopardy. Could they get the next day's paper printed in time? She counted off ten to quiet the madness in her head. *Focus. Go to worst case scenario. Work backwards from there. Plan B.* She could handle this.

Pushing through the glass double doors leading to corporate, she spotted Mrs. Mackey, already springing from her chair, notepad in hand. Roxann cruised by her and the assistant fell into step behind.

"Get me Gil Collins at the *Chronicle*. Please. And no one comes in for ten minutes."

She closed her office door, sped toward the desk and dropped into the chair before throwing her head between her legs. Still, the sickness rolled in her stomach and her thundering head drowned out the ringing phone. *Focus. Focus. Focus. Get the paper printed.* Even her father had never dealt with an incapacitated press.

She waited for the panic to subside, took a deep breath.

She could do this. She *had* to do this. She'd been around the newspaper industry her entire life; she had a good staff. They'd get the presses running again. She simply had to get through the repair issues. One step at a time. And if the repairs couldn't be done today, she'd lease press time elsewhere. If that didn't work, she'd put all the damned content on the website. The faithful newspaper readers would go crazy, but it would be better than nothing.

Mrs. Mackey's voice came through the speaker phone. "Gil Collins. Line one."

Deep breath. She picked up the phone, punched line one and said, "Gil, Roxann Thorgesson. Thanks for taking my call. I'm in a jam here and would like to lease press time."

Five minutes later, Mrs. Mackey opened the office door to alert her of John Callahan's presence. Roxann waved him in.

"I just finished with Gil Collins."

John dropped into the seat he'd vacated earlier. "You think that's necessary?"

He was obviously not happy about using the rival *Chronicle*'s presses, but options were few. A reciprocal agreement had been in place stating that, in an emergency, each newspaper would allow the other to utilize their presses. The agreement had been made years earlier between Roxann's father and the former owner of the *Chronicle*.

When the *Chronicle*'s owner sold to a newspaper conglomerate, the relationship between the rival newspapers soured due to the *Chronicle*'s continual criticism of the *Banner*'s stance on everything from politics to little league.

"We don't want to be hunting down press time at three o'clock."

"You're right. Sorry."

"We're all tense. What's happening down there?"

He shrugged. "They're working on it. What did Gil say?"

She picked up a pen, tossed it down again and sat back. "He's doubling our costs." *Thief that he is.*

"Double?"

She held up a hand. "I know, but the agreement is loose. There is nothing regarding lease rates. I guess, at the time, they figured they'd work it out if necessary. Obviously, my father didn't expect the *Chronicle* to be sold or he assumed the agreement would be rewritten." How her father could have missed this, she'd never know.

"Jesus." John rubbed his hand over his forehead. "What about the inserts?"

"Hopefully, we'll be running by then because the papers would have to be shipped back here to be stuffed. A logistical nightmare. We'll also have to go on press before the *Chronicle*, which means—"

"Earlier deadlines," John said. "Our news will be old before it even gets in-home. Son of a bitch. What about trying the suburban papers?"

"The only one big enough is sixty miles away. The transportation time alone would kill us."

"We're fucked."

"If we don't get our presses running, we are indeed."

SATURDAY MORNING THE NEWSPAPERS WERE WHERE THEY WERE supposed to be. Roxann stared at the navy blazer she'd tossed across the arm of her office sofa. Most of the employees were off, so she'd opted for the more casual mode of tan dress slacks, a white shirt and the blazer.

Wearing business clothes on Saturday had to be a crime, but wearing jeans wouldn't do when trying to prove her leadership skills to the men on her staff. She wondered what they thought of their lady publisher right now. The good ole boy network still existed at the *Banner* and the older staff members had moments when they all but snickered at her. They'd have to adjust.

The phone buzzed. "The rep from the press company is here," Mrs. Mackey said. "And Phil is looking for you. He said to call him on his cell."

"Got it. I need to talk to him anyway. Send the Franklin Press guy in and please ask John to join us. Did I say thank you for coming in on your day off?"

"Three times," Mrs. Mackey said. "Now get back to work."

The presses had been down twenty-four hours. The production staff, after a mind- boggling day, built the pages and electronically transferred them over to the *Chronicle* for printing. All in all, the transfer went smoothly.

Roxann had gone home at midnight after receiving the call that the pressrun had been completed. She was back by 6:00 a.m. to monitor activity on the customer service lines. By six-thirty, they were getting slammed with complaint calls because they'd missed the late scores and news from the previous night.

Anticipating that, she'd made sure the website had been updated, but the non-internet users didn't want to hear it. She stood to retrieve her jacket and silently asked for a bone to be thrown her way.

A young geeky guy, maybe late twenties, dressed in an oversized business suit entered the office and introduced himself as Charlie Rhodes.

John came in behind Charlie and Roxann motioned for them to sit. "What do you have for us, Charlie? Can we get running today?"

Charlie pushed his sandy blond hair from his eyes and cleared his throat. Did she detect a bit of squirming? That meant trouble.

"No ma'am. Not today."

She snapped her jaw shut. *Control.* She needed it. *Start at the toes, tighten, tighten.*

"What the hell happened down there?" John wanted to know. "Maintenance said they checked the bar day before yesterday and it was good to go."

Charlie stretched his neck. "It appears someone loosened it."

The jolt of his words forced the air from Roxann's lungs and she let out a whooshing breath. Why didn't he just shoot her between the eyes and end the misery? "Someone deliberately did this?"

"Appears so," he said.

John looked whiter than a snowy day. "How? When? *Who?*"

"We'll get to that later," she said, understanding his outrage. She turned back to Charlie. "How quickly can the parts be replaced?"

He squirmed again.

"That's a problem."

"Why?"

"The presses are over thirty years old. As you know, we're in the process of building you new ones, but they're not nearly ready."

Roxann pressed a fingertip to her throbbing forehead. Had her body been sawed down the middle? One side in shock and the other bubbling with anger? "I know that. What does it have to do with replacement parts?"

The room went silent and, after a moment, John spoke up. "They don't have the parts." He turned to Charlie. "Am I right?"

"We don't keep a large inventory of older parts. We have some, but not enough to fix your press. We'll have to locate the additional parts."

Roxann leaned forward, aghast at what she was hearing. "How long will that take?"

"Hopefully, not long."

Blood rushed to her head, the pressure building behind her eyes. "What kind of answer is that? We have half a million newspapers that need to be printed today."

Charlie retreated farther into his chair. "We're working on the extra parts."

On another occasion, she'd have felt sorry for him. He

was obviously too inexperienced to be dealing with a situation of this magnitude. His boss would get an earful for sending in a rookie and wasting her time. Not to mention throwing this poor kid into a snake pit.

"I suggest you dial fast," she said.

"Mrs. Mackey!" Roxann hollered after Charlie left. "Get me the president of Franklin Press." She turned to John. "They *don't* have the parts? What is that?"

"I read about this in one of the trade magazines. The manufacturers don't stock old parts because of the expense."

"And what? They hope nothing goes wrong with old presses? *Ridiculous.*"

"Yep."

She drummed her fingers on the desk. "One of the pressmen had to have done this. They're angry that the contract negotiations aren't going their way."

John did a yes-no thing with his head. "We don't know that."

"Not yet we don't, but I want their union representative in here this morning. Someone is going to jail for this."

He stared at the floor a moment then brought his eyes back to her. He'd obviously made the correct decision this was not the day to argue with her.

"I'll get the union people in here." He stood to leave.

"John, we *have* to know who did this. They jeopardized the livelihoods of every one of our employees."

When he didn't answer, she assumed he got the message. There would be no shrinking away from this. She contemplated the kind of destruction an angry employee could inflict on a newspaper and disturbing flashes of computer viruses and destroyed machinery settled on her like a lead vest. No, she had to come on strong with this act of sabotage.

"Let's bring in the security people and put cameras around the building. Just in case."

"On it, Rox."

John left and she dialed Phil's cell number to return his call. She needed to give him the information she'd collected from Michael's surveillance photos anyway. "Hi, Phil."

"Yeah, hi, Rox. My P.D. source called me awhile ago. Mike Taylor is being questioned again."

MICHAEL PUSHED THROUGH THE EXIT OF POLICE headquarters with his Doberman of a lawyer in tow. "That wasn't bad," Arnie said.

Easy for him to say. He wasn't the one taking a polygraph. "You think?"

"You're a convenient suspect. They're busting your balls. Probably also going through all your insurance policies and finances. If they had something, they'd get a warrant and be tearing through your house and office."

Yet another comforting thought. Michael's cell rang and he snatched it from his belt. Vic. "Hey."

"I've been calling for half an hour. Where are you?"

"I had my phone off. The P.D. hauled me in for a polygraph. They don't believe I was home alone the night Alicia died."

"Shit," Vic said.

Michael glanced at Arnie who stood waiting for his driver to scoop him up. "My lawyer tells me I don't have to worry about it."

Arnie's Lincoln pulled to the curb. "Your lawyer," he said, "has things to do. I'll let you know if I hear anything."

"Thanks." Michael waited a beat until Arnie was tucked

into his car. "Vic, this guy is a maniac. I think he might be nuts."

"But he's a good lawyer. Wasn't he the one who got that serial killer off on a technicality?"

Michael headed for the parking garage across the street. "Should that make me feel better?"

"He's a good lawyer, that's all."

"He just told me they're probably going through my finances."

"You got anything to hide?"

"Not that I'm aware of."

But major companies had been brought down by employees violating laws and the boss never even knew. Michael liked to think he was relentless when it came to running his company, but he couldn't possibly watch every transaction.

"Then don't get nuts. Deal with what you can."

"Yeah, but you need to be prepared if they arrest me."

"Mike, I told you, I'm on it. In fact, I'm on my way to the *Banner*. They need us over there ASAP. There's a problem with the presses."

On a Saturday? Odd that he hadn't heard anything from Roxann on this. Then again, his phone had been off and he hadn't checked his voice mail yet. "Did Roxann call you?"

"No. The guy that works for her. John."

The associate publisher. "Right. I'll be there in fifteen minutes."

What the hell could this be now?

11

ROXANN ENTERED THE EXECUTIVE BOARD ROOM WITH HER head high. No sense letting the boys see their lady publisher sweat. The men around the table stood to greet her, and she took her seat at the end. Her gaze went straight to Michael, who hadn't bothered to return her phone call regarding his trip to the police department. That, she had to admit, irritated her but he sat looking perfectly at ease at her conference table. Michael in the *Banner*'s board room. Her father would have been furious. She certainly never imagined it and wasn't sure what to think. Time for that later. Work needed to be done. "Hello, gentlemen."

The room, as familiar to her as her own living room, had held countless meetings and, as a result, her father had furnished it for comfort. The shades were drawn, probably to block the midday sun bouncing off the adjacent building.

Seated in the deep cushioned, leather chairs were John Callahan, Jeff Morgan, Michael—she stopped at Michael and nodded. Vic, in his Sunday best of a suit and tie, sat to her right.

Jeff Morgan cleared his throat. "Uh, Roxann, you know Michael Taylor, correct?"

Oh, she knew him. She knew he used to like dozing with his head resting on her lap when they were supposed to be watching the Cubs. She knew he liked long showers, not necessarily alone. She *knew* he liked waking up with searing early morning sex. Then again, that had been twelve years ago. "We're acquainted."

Vic—all Mr. Professional—leaned across the table to shake her hand. "Nice to see you again, Roxann."

"Thank you for getting here so fast. I trust we've done all the introductions, so let's get started. John, have you told Michael and Vic why they're here?"

"Not yet, I was waiting for you."

Michael sat forward, opened his portfolio and gave his pen a click. The sound carried and everyone turned toward him but, as usual, he remained unfazed.

Roxann stared at him for a moment. She would have to tell him about the pressroom. Admitting it to a stranger would have been easier. A stranger wouldn't understand how this would affect her emotionally. How it would tear into her soul because she faced a major problem and needed to make her father proud. She folded her arms to fight off the exposed, vulnerable feeling raging inside her.

"Someone," she began, "apparently within our organization, has tampered with our presses, causing it to become incapacitated. In short, we are a newspaper without working presses and it appears we'll be that way for some time."

Michael looked up from the notes he jotted, his dark eyes narrowing. Trying to read her. She couldn't take the intensity and turned to Vic. "The entire building needs to be scrutinized and suggestions made on upgrading security. Obviously, I'll need it done fast."

"How do you know it came from inside?" Vic asked.

"Someone loosened the blanket bar." Vic shook his head indicating he hadn't a clue what that meant. "If the bar is loose, the press will only run for fifteen to thirty minutes. It eventually comes off. The bar became wedged in the plate cylinders and stopped the press. The bar was checked two days ago and it was tight. Someone loosened it before we began yesterday's run."

"We'll need a tour of the building," Michael said. "Inside and out."

She glanced back at him and their eyes met. "Jeff will take care of that. He'll be your contact once the upgrades are made." She turned to Jeff. "Why don't you do the tour now and we can reconvene after."

The men stood and began filing out, but she stayed seated. "Michael, I need to speak with you."

Vic turned to Michael and raised his eyebrows. "We'll get started."

Roxann gestured for Michael to sit in the chair to her left. With her face so pale, she wore the look of a worn sheet that had been stretched across too many beds.

"I called you earlier," she said.

"I had my phone off. The P.D. dragged me in for a polygraph. I was on my way here when your message came through."

"A polygraph?"

He shrugged. "Arnie says they're trying to rattle me." He leaned forward, propped his elbows on the table and dug the palms of his hands into his eye sockets. *Damned pressure.* "They're doing a good job."

"Arnie Stark is brilliant. If he says there's nothing to worry about, I'd believe him."

"Still, I'm not sitting around and waiting for the P.D. to figure out who killed Alicia. I've been paying her bills. Court ordered until the divorce was final. I asked Arnie to leverage that to get me copies of her phone bills."

"Will that work?"

"I don't know." He blew a breath out. Time to focus on her problems. Nothing he could do about his right now. "What do you think happened in that pressroom?"

"My guess is one of the pressmen did it."

"Because of the contract negotiations?"

"How do you know about the contract?"

"The *Chronicle's* been hammering you on it. Not that I read that newspaper, but I hear things. Besides, your sports are better."

She half smiled. "Thank you, but last night our coverage stunk. I want this building secured. I don't care what it costs. Someone obviously wants to put us out of business, and I have twenty-five hundred employees to protect."

Her eyes sparked and her face became a glossy red. The Roxann version of a temper tantrum. Her determination to preserve not only her family's legacy, but her employees' income multiplied his respect for her. This was the woman he wanted. Right here. He reached to touch her arm. "I'll take care of the security."

She gazed down at his hand, her head tilted sideways and he thought about pulling back, but, nah, he'd wait her out. Slowly, she slid her arm free and patted his fingers. Good enough. For now.

"Thank you for not saying I told you so."

What did that mean? Michael held his hands out in question.

"You told me to change the guards at the desk. I've been dragging my feet."

She thought this was *her* fault? She had to be the sharpest woman he knew and she didn't deserve this. He wouldn't mind getting his hands on the son of a bitch responsible.

"Rox, you couldn't have prevented this. Switching the lobby guys wouldn't have mattered if it was an employee. They'd have been in the building anyway."

She stared up at him, thought about it and shrugged. "Which is why I want cameras everywhere."

"And you'll get them."

"It'll be a prison in here."

Michael felt the slap of her words. Prison. A word he'd become intimately involved with over the past week. She turned to him, realized what she had said and buried her face in her hands.

"What an idiot. I can't believe I said that."

"Forget it. You got bigger things to deal with."

She tugged her hands over her cheeks. Damn, she looked beat. By his way of thinking, he should just wrap her in a hug, but she'd kill him if he tried. Comfort wasn't what Roxann needed. Strong-willed people, himself included, didn't allow themselves to show vulnerability. Coddling would piss her off. Still, the thought of her in his arms turned his body to steel. *Take it easy, Taylor.* "You okay?"

She nodded and glanced toward the window. Not looking at him.

Rising from her chair, she walked to the window, opened one of the blinds. "It's the fatigue. This pressroom thing threw me. My uncle being a brat isn't helping."

"He rip into you again?"

She turned back to him and leaned against the window

sill. With the light hitting her face, the shadows under her eyes became evident. A few strands of hair had broken free from her hair clip and he itched to tuck them behind her ear. But the way he was feeling right now, if he touched her, he'd want more and still more and there'd never be an end to his want.

He flexed his fingers. Sitting around and listening wasn't his way. He really wanted to pummel Max for making this strong, knowledgeable woman feel insecure and childish. More than that, he needed to accept responsibility for getting her involved in his mess. Had he not gone to her, the *Banner* would have covered this story as any other and she most likely wouldn't have been dealing with her uncle's pissy moods.

"Sorry about Max," he said.

"He wouldn't have reacted that way if we weren't onto something. This is typical of his behavior. He's trying to bully me off the story."

"Nice guy."

"Generally, he is. He just doesn't want me getting into his investigations. Having his boss's chief of staff involved makes him tense. He must be getting pressure from the mayor." She checked her watch and fiddled with it for a moment before heading toward him. "I have to hunt down parts for my press."

Michael stood. On instinct, he reached out a hand, palm up, hoping she'd lay hers on top of it. What the hell. Why not? They were friends. Hopefully more than that.

"Anything I can do?"

She stared at his hand, clearly understanding his intention and—after hesitating—moved her hand over his.

Whoosh. The sound of breaking waves ran through his head. He'd been holding his breath, hoping she wouldn't ignore the gesture. Hoping she wouldn't *reject* him. And she hadn't. *Easy, Taylor. Don't scare her off.*

She stared at their hands for a moment then gazed up at him, her eyes clear and focused and oh-so-aware of what he wanted.

"You can let me know about the security," she said.

He squeezed her hand and held it for another minute. "That I can do."

12

STANDING ON THE BRICK STOOP, ROXANN MANEUVERED THREE briefcases stuffed with files from her father's office, and attempted to shove her key into the front door lock. On the third try, the briefcases forced her off balance and the key missed its mark.

She blew out a heavy breath and eyeballed the lock. "Don't do this to me." All she wanted was some semblance of a meal and to get off her feet. Not a lot to ask.

Dumping the briefcases would have been a good idea, but even that seemed hard. She'd only have to pick them up again. Bad enough they were a reminder she'd put in a fourteen-hour day, on a Saturday no less, and still had to start reading her father's old files.

Saturday. She missed the Cubs game. Wasn't that just great? The only thing offering any pleasure was the looming start of baseball season and she couldn't even manage to watch a pre-season game.

The pinch of keys against her straining fingers drew her attention and she uncurled her hands, watching the keys fall to the ground. Now she had to pick them up. Damned door. She gave it a solid kick and a knifing pain pierced her big toe.

"Ouch."

Standing tall, she stared at the lock for a second before retrieving her keys from the stoop. "You can do this, Rox. Just get the key in the lock."

She tried again. The key hit its mark, the lock tumbled and the weight of a relieved sigh settled in her throat. She opened the door, dragged the briefcases behind her and gave the door a backward kick. Teetering on one foot, her body swayed too far left and—*crash*—she landed in a heap on the hardwood floor, the pain from the impact shooting into her hip and down her leg.

"Ouch. *Dammit*." She slammed her hand on the floor and the sting shot up her arm.

Tears threatened and she held her breath because— absolutely not—she would not cry over briefcases. Maybe she'd cry over her father's death and a newspaper in crisis, but not over three damned briefcases. Not today. Not ever. She counted to ten and set her mind to the task ahead.

Her left foot had somehow gotten wrapped in the straps of two of her cases. Okay. No problem. She reached to untangle herself, but the twisted straps kept her hostage. *Just relax a minute and try again.*

She reached for one of the briefcases. Stopped. No. Can't do it. She opened her mouth and the motion triggered something. Something primal and urgent and frightening and she began an ear-splitting, someone-is-cutting-off-my-hands screaming that makes the neighbors want to call 9-1-1. And it kept coming. Yes, a volcano of screams had erupted and she couldn't stop them. *Please stop, please stop, please stop.* Fat tears darted down her face and plopped onto the dreaded briefcases. She rocked back and forth, back and forth, back and forth feeling her arteries pump until she was sure her body would split from the pressure.

"He was there," she howled, fists balled, nails biting into her palms. "And then he was gone. That was it. No goodbye. Nothing. I had things to tell him and I'll never be able to."

What was this insanity? The control freak in her tsked-tsked, while the grieving daughter assured her it was okay, that she wasn't having a nervous breakdown.

Either way, she had to pull herself together. Only crazy people carried on this way.

Her throat and lungs ached from the screaming fit and she slumped to the side and rested her head at the base of the stairs. Heaving breaths rocked her body and she concentrated on taking air in and blowing it out.

White flag time.

She gazed at the well-lit living room and praised automatic timers. At least she wasn't on the floor in the dark trying to free herself. She gave one of the briefcases a shove with her free foot.

The thing she needed at this moment was a run. She'd simply run until all feeling drained from her body and she collapsed. Only, she didn't have it in her to get off the floor, much less go for a run. The grind of the last weeks had finally caught up to her and the physical and emotional exhaustion kept her body a step behind her brain. She needed sleep. The glorious, non-medicated sleep she'd enjoyed before her father dropped dead in front of her.

When did her life become this living hell? She sat up, pulled her knees into her chest dragging the cases, her own personal ball and chain, with her.

Trapped. In her own life. She pushed the thought aside. *No. Settle down.* The fatigue was too much. *I need sleep.*

She stayed on the floor, her foot still tangled, while the

quiet of the house seeped into her. How could she have allowed it to get this bad? Even if her father was dead, his presses destroyed and the mayor maligning the *Banner* at every opportunity, she shouldn't melt down this way.

The phone rang. Great. Roxann stared at the cordless sitting on the end table. Instead of crawling over to it, she reached for one of her shoes and sent it sailing toward the phone. The world could just buzz off because she needed a damned minute.

A second later, someone pounded on her door and she sucked in a breath from the shock.

"Roxann!"

Her insides congealed and she tried to straighten up. Oh no. Not now. "Michael?"

The door flew open and crashed against the wall sending a whoosh of air by her. Not to mention nearly knocking her daffy.

Michael hovered in the doorway, his dark eyes glancing left, then right before zeroing in on her with such menacing focus he made Charles Manson look like a boy scout.

What a nightmare.

"What's wrong?" he asked.

"Where should I begin?"

Michael scanned the room for an unknown predator, but finding nothing askew, he looked down at Roxann and his heart thumped. She sat on the floor, her legs bound in the straps of three briefcases—*three?*—and wet tears ran down her face leaving a trail of some funky colored eye makeup. Chunks of hair jutted from her hairclip and she was missing a shoe. *Missing a shoe?* What was up with that?

She, in no way, resembled the put together executive he'd seen that morning. What the hell happened here?

"Are you hurt? You scared the shit out of me."

He'd parked two doors down and decided to call and let her know he was coming. When he reached the walkway, he heard the screaming. Insane thoughts of some armed intruder doing hideous things to her flashed through his head and he went crazy. Completely flipping insane.

He squatted down, ran his hands up and down her legs feeling for broken limbs. Nothing bruised, everything in place. She was safe. *Thank you.* Walking in on her being beaten or raped would have turned him into a madman.

Placing his index finger under her chin, he tilted her head up. "You look beat, Rox."

He held out a hand, she reached for it, shifted to get up, but collapsed back to the floor.

"I can't move. I've got nothing left. He's been gone four-and-a-half weeks and everything's a wreck."

He wrapped his arms around her, was mildly shocked when she didn't pull away, and tried to think of something, anything that would comfort her. Nothing. *Useless.* "Rox, it's not you. It would have happened if your father were here. Bad timing."

Michael had seen grief before and despised its power. When she didn't move, the caretaker in him kicked in. He unhooked the straps on each of the briefcases, unraveled them and, after setting them aside, scooped her up and deposited her on the sofa. He ran a hand over her hair. "Stay there, I'll be right back."

He hadn't been in Roxann's childhood home in twelve years. He'd known she'd taken over the house when her parents moved to a bigger home in the suburbs. He surveyed the room to get his bearings. Big changes. Sofa, two chairs, large ottoman that doubled as a coffee table, dining room on one side, hallway on the other. Kitchen in the back. He headed down the corridor. Jackpot.

He pawed through cabinets, shoving the freakishly lined cans—*Jeez-us*—and packages aside until he found the jumbo bag of M&Ms he knew would be stashed somewhere.

The leftover Chinese food in the fridge got tossed into a bowl and nuked until a spicy aroma filled the air. If he could smell it, it was hot.

Roxann was still sitting where he'd left her, but she had wiped her face dry and fixed her hair. The calm, in control Roxann had returned and his heart did that flip-flop thing because he'd helped. He handed her the bowl and a fork.

"Food first. M&Ms later."

She smiled halfway. He'd take that. It was better than the destruction he'd walked in on.

"Thank you," she said.

He sat across from her on the dark brown ottoman that matched the wing back chair and watched her eat. His heartbeat had resumed its normal pace and he decided he was way too old for this shit.

After a few more swallows, she set the bowl down. "What are you doing here?"

"I've got our recommendations ready and when I called the newspaper, the lobby guard said you'd already left. I figured I'd go over them with you and we'd jump on it tomorrow."

"Your guys work on Sunday?"

"When they need to."

"What service." She ran her hands over her face. "Do you mind if I get cleaned up? I'm a mess."

"No problem." Michael stood as she walked toward the stairs. She used her foot to sweep the briefcases aside, saw the portfolio and blueprints he'd dropped by the door and picked them up.

"Thank you," she said, handing him his things.

Roxann soaked for ten minutes in a shower that left her skin warm and pink. The extreme heat helped to ease the tension that had settled into a tight ball between her shoulder blades. Her body felt bull-dozed.

And Michael had witnessed it.

Yeesh.

How humiliating having the man she once loved watch her crumble in defeat.

She pulled her wet hair into a knot behind her head, slipped on her favorite jeans and a white T-shirt and made her way downstairs.

Michael sat at the kitchen table; the sleeves of his Notre Dame sweatshirt pushed up to his elbows while he reviewed his notes. He shifted toward her, hesitated and then smiled. She wasn't the only one uncomfortable.

Reclaiming the bowl of Chinese food he'd brought into the kitchen for her, she sat across from him. The bag of M&Ms sat open in the middle of the table.

After sliding his things over, Michael moved next to her and sat close enough that his denim clad leg brushed her thigh. A zing of heat whipped through her and she cursed her body for the betrayal. *Way too needy tonight.*

She turned her attention to the blueprints of the *Banner*.

"We suggest you install cameras throughout the building, inside and out." He used his pen to point to different areas of the building. "Fixed cameras on the doorways and pan-and-tilt throughout the interior rooms."

"Pan-and-tilt?" Roxann asked, chomping on an M&M.

"They constantly sweep back and forth throughout the room and when motion is detected they begin recording. We can also set them to record constantly. It's all digital."

"Right. Is there an area where we'll have monitors? Can the guards see what the cameras are taping?"

"You can set up monitors at the existing desk in the lobby or in a less conspicuous place, but you'll still have to have a guard in both places at all times." He jerked a shoulder. "It's up to you."

She tilted her head sideways. The lobby would indeed be a prison entry. All they were missing were strip searches.

He put a hand on her shoulder. "I know it's a lot."

No kidding. Here she was, a woman who'd rather take a sharp stick in the eye over a loss of routine, being forced to endure huge adjustments, some life altering, one right after another. She drummed her hands on the table. "Keep going."

She could handle this. It might kill her, but she'd deal with it.

"You also need card-reader access—"

"That's the key card thing?"

"Yes. Card-readers on all exterior doors and probably some interior ones. You'll have to tell us which interior doors. The only unlocked exterior door would be the lobby so visitors can access the building. The employee entrance would have card-reader access."

"We'll always know which employees are in the building?" she asked.

"Yes, but it's not foolproof. Someone could piggyback— walk in with another employee who already swept their own card—or someone could use another employee's card. The card readers would be wired to computers allowing management to generate a report of who came and went."

"That's a good idea."

"It's important. I have them in our building. Also, all windows would be armed with glass break. If someone breaks a window, the alarm will sound."

Michael flipped to the next page of the blueprints.

"Additional cameras would also be installed in the parking garage behind the building as well as the warehouse. The warehouse should have key-pad entry and an alarm system. Bottom line, no one enters any part of the building without being seen."

"You did all this in one day?"

"You said fast."

Twelve years ago this man had been emotionally devastated and lost. The military had tested him in a way that left him unable to decide what to have for lunch. Watching him now, discussing security for a major corporation, she felt a pang of remorse that she'd never gotten the chance to see him become *this* Michael Taylor. She popped another M&M in her mouth while analyzing the blueprints. "I'm wondering if it's too much. I don't want innocent employees thinking we're spying."

"After what happened in your pressroom, it should be a non-issue."

She folded her arms, forced herself to not chew on her lip. He was right. Those responsible for the pressroom situation needed to know she wouldn't allow equipment to be destroyed. She had to protect the employees by making sure this never happened again. Prove to them their jobs and livelihoods were safe.

"What do I need to sign?"

"Nothing now, I'll get you a contract outlining everything. We'll start first thing tomorrow. Let your people know to expect us."

She let out a breath. The added security meant drastic changes from the casual way her father had done things. Under his reign anyone could have walked into the building and vandalized it.

"It's what you need to do, Roxann. It should have been done long ago."

Now Michael was a mind reader?

"I know, but it's hard."

He turned toward her, sat back a little. "Sure it is. And after what you've been through, most people would have collapsed by now. You're handling it. You should be proud of yourself."

Proud of herself. Not yet she wasn't. She blinked a few times and drew a breath of thick, suffocating air. So blasted tired.

"Let's deal with the lobby desk situation," he said, obviously picking up on the tension. "You need to make a change there. An eighty-year-old blind woman can get by those guys."

Her shoulders tightened and she ground her teeth until they ached. She was a reasonable manager, but she would not blame the security staff for the pressroom incident.

"I won't fire them. If we'd had adequate security cameras this might have been avoided."

"I didn't say you needed to ax them. Add people for the lobby and reassign the ones you have."

"Fine. I'll take it under advisement," she said.

Michael put up two hands. "Don't get pissy with me. You asked what I thought and I told you."

He began rolling the blueprints. Irritated. Roxann dropped her head into her hands. "I'm sorry. I didn't mean to snap at you."

She could make excuses—tired, grieving and just plain

mad—but she wouldn't. Excuses didn't give her permission to lash out, especially when he went out of his way to be helpful.

"No big deal."

It was a big deal, but she was too tired to worry about it. She reached out and touched his arm. "Thank you for understanding."

He secured the blueprints with a rubber band and turned toward her with a grin. "I told you, I'm in my sensitive phase right now."

Lucky her.

"I'm assuming you'll bill us for this. I think I'm afraid to see that bill."

Michael draped his arm over her shoulder and gave an affectionate squeeze. "You're getting a what-a-deal. Call it the old-friend discount. It'll still hurt though."

A ripple shot up her spine and she found herself wishing he wouldn't touch her. His touch clogged her already harassed brain and made her want to curl into him. Not good in her current state.

"Thanks for the what-a-deal."

They stood, ran into each other and stopped. Her gaze fixed on his throat as his warm breath tickled her cheek. *Please back up. Please.* He remained still. Of course he did. She knew she should step back, willed herself to do it, but her body refused.

Michael reached up, ran a finger down her cheek. "Bang."

She jerked to attention. "Bang?"

"It was the sound of your head exploding. You think *way* too much."

"And this is news to you? Of all people?"

"I like it. It gets you all uptight. Sooner or later you'll

need to decompress. I have to time it so I'm around. If my memory serves, I'm good at helping you decompress." He wiggled his eyebrows.

She laughed. Really laughed.

"Good luck with *that*."

She'd missed this easy banter between them. The joking and verbal combat. Michael brought out the silly in her and not many people had accomplished such a feat. The only problem was he could roll her into a heap of heartbreak.

"THE MAYOR WENT OFF AT HIS PRESS CONFERENCE TODAY," Michael said as they walked to the door. He'd tried to avoid the Carl Biehl article, but wanted to make sure Roxann knew he understood the backlash she faced. The risks she'd taken by making this deal with him.

"I heard he lambasted us on the early news. He's been calling me every day since the story ran. He thinks I'm vulnerable. He *thinks* if he keeps harassing me, I'll give in."

Michael snorted. "Moron."

"Yep. I took great satisfaction in giving the approval for a follow-up article on Alicia and Carl. Apparently, they were seen together quite often leading up to her death. Phil's source told him Carl was questioned the morning after the murder. None of that was released. I also gave Phil the list of leads we came up with from your surveillance folder."

"Thanks."

"It's a story," she said. "That's what we do."

"Not many people would stand up to the mayor of Chicago. You've got guts, Rox."

"I should thank you too. You came over to discuss business and I pulled you into my emotional swamp."

He shrugged. "I'm used to it. I should have drowned in Gina's swamp by now. Her only luck is bad."

The mention of Gina and her dead husband brought silence, and Roxann rocked back and forth on her toes— probably his cue to leave. He pulled the door open, shut it again and turned back to her. "You okay? I can stay awhile. Talk if you want, not talk, whatever."

She gazed up at him, those big blue eyes hesitant. What was she thinking? A clanging erupted in his ears and he imagined himself going over a cliff in slow motion. The ride over the edge might be exhilarating, but it would hurt like hell when he landed.

"I'll be fine," she said. "Besides, you've done plenty. I'll get some sleep and be ready to fight again tomorrow."

Something in her tone tore him up. He wasn't sure if it was sadness, exhaustion or the weight of her responsibilities, but he knew she'd never give up. The competitor in her wouldn't allow it.

Years earlier, when Roxann tried to help him, he'd been too stubborn to let her. Maybe if he had, their lives would have gone differently and they'd have a few kids running around by now.

Without thinking, he leaned in and let his lips glide softly over hers. She stiffened.

Shit. *Big mistake, Taylor.*

He stood motionless, waiting for her to push him away as the citrus scent of her soap surrounded him, made him crazy enough to kiss her again. She didn't move. Nice. When the stiffness left her and she began kissing him back, his heart hammered and he felt sure the world could hear it. All these years, he'd thought about this, the way her body, with those long, long legs, curved against his. He pulled her closer and settled in, let himself enjoy the moment because the memory of kissing the unequalled Roxann had never left him.

Suddenly, the room became hot. Boiling. Explosive.

And he had a woody.

She must have noticed that bad boy because she slapped her hand over the back of his neck, sending sparks roaring through him. She hauled him closer, kissing him harder and harder still, her tongue darting in and out until his mind nearly disintegrated. *So good.* The moment became a battle of lips and grunts and bodies pressed hard, and he swept his tongue along her bottom lip and nipped her. *Too damn good.*

When she slid her hands under his sweatshirt—*thank you!*—he dropped the portfolio he held in one hand and it hit the floor with a smack. Roxann jumped out of his reach.

Nuh-uh. No way.

She stood inches from him, her chest hitching with each breath and her gaze darting over his face. "We shouldn't do this, Michael."

Sure they should.

He stepped forward, wrapped an arm around her waist to keep her from retreating again. "Why not?"

With her hands against his biceps, she pushed back. "Call it self-preservation on my part. I've had a rotten day and I'm needy tonight. It would be for all the wrong reasons."

Michael dipped his head lower and grinned. "It might be a lot of things, but wrong isn't one of them."

She shoved him a little. "Reckless, then."

On a sigh, he stepped back. He could charm her into giving in and they'd have a hot night ahead of them, which would be pretty damn great. Or he could give her space, which would be boring as hell, but it would earn her trust.

Trust had to be the goal, and manipulating her into the sack wouldn't do it.

He opted for boring as hell. The spark between them obviously still existed. He could take it slow. Work on her a little at a time until she realized they'd be good together. Maybe even great.

This from the guy with the iron clad rule about not mixing business with pleasure. He'd already blown that sucker out of the water.

Besides, even horny as hell, he'd come to believe she was right about destroying the integrity of a story with rumors about the publisher sleeping with the suspect. In fact, he'd put Vic in charge of her security. Michael would stay as far away from the *Banner* as he could. Problem solved.

He took one step back and smiled.

"I'm not giving up." He picked up the blueprints and portfolio, pulled open the door and walked out of the house.

Halfway down the walk he angled back, saw her standing in the doorway, her mouth partway open. Perplexed? Mad? Either way, he had to snap her out of it.

He laughed. "I'll come back in, *if* you beg me."

From his distance, he could see her jaw tighten. *Atta girl,* he thought. The warrior returns.

"We'll see who begs," she fumed and slammed the door so hard he swore the house shook. He stood on the walkway grinning. This would be fun.

13

Early morning talk radio jolted Roxann from a restless sleep.

With a swipe of her hand, her ancient clock radio sailed through the air only to be jerked back when the cord caught. The blasted thing was still making noise.

Had a jackhammer gone through her right eye? She pressed a finger to it. There would be no way she could run today. The first time in years, barring illness, she'd missed her normal run, but she was too damned tired after staying up half the night to work.

After bracing one foot on the floor, Roxann rolled out of bed, crawled to the insidious alarm and smacked the snooze button. She curled her bare legs—hadn't she put on the bottoms of her pajamas?—into a ball and figured she could hit snooze at least three more times until she absolutely had to get up.

After the third snooze, she rolled to her back and was never happier she opted for the double thick padding under the carpet. The only bright spot was that the follow-up story on Alicia and Carl would be in the paper today.

At least she had warned Michael so he'd be prepared for the embarrassment.

Who was she kidding? Michael had yet to experience an embarrassing moment. A crisis turned him into a building that refused to implode. She supposed it came from his military training.

"Enough," she said. "Stop analyzing. Pretend he's not involved. This is a regular story. Let Phil handle it."

Forty minutes later, after three ibuprofens and a hot shower, she slipped into in her most comfortable slacks—the beige ones that matched her mood—and headed downstairs to her office to collect her laptop and briefcase. Sundays were just not meant to be spent at work.

She stepped through the office doorway and her low heels dipped into the carpet. A faint, musky smell caught her attention and, on instinct, she spun and jerked the door away from the wall. A relieved whoosh of air escaped her straining lungs.

She sniffed again, but didn't detect anything. Did exhaustion make people paranoid? It had to be the headache. She sat at her desk to pack her laptop and froze. The gold pen had been moved. She stared at it while her veins turned to icicles. She always—always—placed the pen in the holder with the *Banner Herald* logo facing out. All she saw now was glinting gold and no logo.

She took inventory of the office. Nothing else appeared out of place. Well, the stacks of folders on her desk shouldn't be there, but that was her own fault. The pen though, that was something else entirely. She'd been distracted lately. Maybe she wasn't paying attention when she put it back? Again she surmised it could be exhaustion inflicted paranoia.

If someone *had* been there, it was while she slept. A

fierce panic blasted her. She didn't want to contemplate all that could have happened.

A burglar would have snatched her laptop and Blackberry, but both of those items were still on the desk. By the time she'd gotten done making all these assumptions, she had almost talked herself out of the intruder theory.

To ease her mind, she charged up to the bedroom and rifled through her dresser, checking all the places she kept her jewelry. Part of the joy of being anal retentive was knowing where she kept everything. All accounted for. Excellent. She continued her quick tour of the house, but nothing looked disturbed and all the doors and windows were intact.

Okay, she was losing it. She thought about calling Max and telling him about the incident, but nixed the idea. What could she tell him that would warrant a police report? An odd smell and a wayward pen? Didn't sound like much of a crime scene and Max would say the same. He'd probably laugh at her.

Thirty minutes later, Roxann strode into the corporate suite at the *Banner* and found Mrs. Mackey at her desk. A good woman to come in on a Sunday when her boss hadn't even asked. She wore a red and white floral dress way too busy for Roxann's reeling head. "Good morning. You do remember Illinois has a law that requires employees to have one day of rest for every seven they work, right?"

"Are you going to tell?" Mrs. Mackey asked.

Roxann forced a smile, grabbed her messages and read the first few until she felt her laser sharp assistant studying her.

"You feeling okay, Sassy?"

"I'm a little off, nothing to worry about. Would you get me Vic Andrews at Taylor Security please? And find Phil

Dawson? Otherwise, hold my calls. Thank you for coming in. I so appreciate what you do for me."

Roxann took the remaining messages into her office, tossed them on the desk with the stacks and stacks of folders. With a tired sigh, she hung her suit jacket behind the door.

A few moments later her phone buzzed and she scooped it up to silence it. "Vic?"

"At your service, *Miz* Thorgesson."

"Good morning."

"What's happenin'?"

She loved his easy, happy style, so different from Michael's. Brooding worked for Michael. Vic belonged on a surf board somewhere.

She pasted a smile on her face hoping it would lighten her mood and make her sound casual. "I'm thinking about putting a security system in my home."

"Sure. What happened?"

That question certainly squashed her trying-to-sound-casual theory. Roxann tapped her pen on the desk. "Just precaution."

"Okay, let me check the schedule, see when we can get there."

"I was hoping to do it today." As if *that* wasn't a red flag.

"Today?" he said. "Come on, Roxann, what's up?"

The tap-tap-tapping of her pen continued as she contemplated her next statement.

"I'm not sure what's up. I could be paranoid, but it can't hurt to have a security system, right?" Didn't her father always say the best defense was a good offense?

"Yeah, but what's your hurry? I've seen you at least eight times in the past week and you've never mentioned it. Now you want it installed on a weekend. No dice."

Darn. She had purposely called him instead of Michael because she didn't want to be questioned. Thinking on it, it was probably easier to tell Vic than Michael anyway. Vic could at least stay impartial.

"I think someone was in my house last night, but I could be making the whole thing up because I'm so brain-fried. I don't know what I'm doing. How's *that* for a reason?"

He half laughed. "Not bad. Are you okay?"

"I'm fine. I'm not even sure someone broke in, but why take a chance?"

"Absolutely. I'll get someone there today. What time can you meet us?"

She sat back and closed her eyes. The little ball of nausea that had plagued her since stepping into her home office that morning unwound itself. "Thank you. I'll work around your schedule. Just tell me when."

"I'll call you back."

Roxann picked up the advertising revenue reports sitting on her desk. She hoped the numbers were good because they were going to need all available cash to get through the next few weeks.

The *Chronicle*'s exorbitant leasing fees would severely cut into the already sinking bottom line. First thing tomorrow morning she needed to check on the repair of the presses. All but one of the parts had been acquired so the repair should be imminent. She hoped.

Otherwise, she needed to come up with a cash flow plan to get them through. Advertising revenue would be key. Subscribers were important to a newspaper, but the big money came from major retailers and airlines that spent tens of millions of dollars peddling their services. The *Banner* would need to keep said retailers happy, not an easy task.

An hour later, Mrs. Mackey knocked on the open office door wearing her bulldog look. "Michael Taylor has called twice."

Roxann, distracted by the email she'd been reading, went back to her computer. "What about?"

"He said it was personal. He must think you have nothing better to do all day than chit-chat."

"If he calls again, ask him if I can call him back." She had to get through these emails.

Roxann swore a trail of dust kicked up as Mrs. Mackey stormed out.

Ten minutes later the assistant hovered in the doorway again. "Remember when I said Michael Taylor called?"

Dammit. The stupid headache had Roxann's skull throbbing and the pattern on Mrs. Mackey's dress wasn't helping. Could it be getting bigger? And moving? She placed both hands on her head. "I'll call him back."

Undeterred, Mrs. Mackey entered the office. "Mr. Hot-Shot is downstairs and wants to see you. Can I get rid of him?"

Between the two of them, Roxann was out-muscled. "Let him in, Stonewall." When Mrs. Mackey got this way, *she* could have been the one holding the line at Bull Run. "Something has crawled up his butt and the sooner I know what it is, the sooner I can get my work done."

Mrs. Mackey turned and started for the door.

"And I'll handle him." Roxann didn't want the pair of them having it out in the middle of the office.

She pulled her mirror and did a quick hair and lipstick check. What a mess. Nothing could help her pale, puffy appearance, but she pulled her lipstick from the drawer and slicked some on. Couldn't hurt.

Michael stepped into the office just as she finished

putting her makeup away. He shut the door and when he turned to look at her, she couldn't move. He wore gray dress slacks, a black v-neck sweater and that dangerous, brooding look that was so much a part of him. She sat mesmerized by the force of him. So amazingly hot.

Don't go there.

The first time she'd seen that look was early in their dating when he'd gotten mad at her for running alone at night. Even then he'd brought a quiet energy that immediately put her on edge. After that, she never ran alone in the dark.

"What's wrong?" she asked.

Michael planted his hands on the desk and leaned in. She scooted back an inch. She didn't appreciate people, men in particular, in her personal space. Even if he was sexy.

"Why didn't you call me this morning?"

"Pardon?"

"You called *Vic* instead of *me*. Why?"

It took a minute to register. The pulsing in her head flared and she counted to ten. Now he thought he could come into her office and demand answers? Wrong.

She got to her feet and mirrored his stance. "*Vic* has been here day and night, why wouldn't I call him?"

"*I* could have helped you."

They stared at each other for a long moment until Michael finally gave in and dropped into one of the guest chairs. *That's better.*

Roxann nodded, then sat. "I'm sure you could have, but Vic's been in charge around here and I thought he should be my first stop. If I was mistaken, I apologize. He should have told me. Besides, I wanted to keep it between us."

Michael's hand shot up, his voice still holding a bit of frustration. "He didn't squeal. Tell him something and it stays there. The scheduling manager came to me because Vic pulled two of our best techs off a commercial job that was paying double for a weekend install. He thought Vic was smokin' crack."

She smiled, her disappointment in being betrayed diminishing. "I don't think he was stoned. He was doing me a favor."

"What the hell happened?"

MICHAEL LISTENED—QUIETLY—UNTIL ROXANN FINISHED. It took great effort to not bombard her with questions and he tried to stop tapping his foot, but the more she talked, the higher his frustration climbed and the faster his foot moved.

Why the hell didn't she call him with this?

He should have been her first phone call. No matter how much Vic had been around. Did she not think he'd help her? The sound of her voice broke into his thoughts and he focused on her words, ignoring the roaring chaos in his brain. *You got her into this.*

"So nothing was missing?" he asked.

"Nothing. The pen was the only thing disturbed. I'm not even sure anyone was there."

"You're sure."

She gave him a puzzled look. "I am?"

"You know your house. No broken windows?"

"No," she said. "Locks are intact. If I reported it, my uncle would tell me there's no proof. I'm putting in a security system to make sure it doesn't happen again."

"Who do you think it was?"

"My guess is, one of the pressmen. I had to put them on furlough until we get the presses repaired. Plus, with the ongoing contract negotiations, maybe they're trying to scare me."

"No. If they wanted to scare you, they would have tossed your underwear all over the place."

Her head jerked back and he knew he'd gotten his point across. Between running alone, sometimes at night, and working late, she took too many chances. It was incomprehensible that she didn't have a security system.

"Maybe they were looking for something that wasn't there."

He let out a sarcastic grunt. "Think about it. You pissed people off by running that story about Biehl and Alicia."

She gave him one of her famous, irritating eye rolls and he jabbed his finger at her. "Don't give me that. It's possible."

"You honestly believe someone broke into my house to see if I have Phil's notes?"

"Don't you?"

She was way too predictable not to have brought Phil's notes home to read. She probably didn't have time during the day and, as he would do, brought memos and reports home.

She opened her desk drawer, pulled out a small bowl of M&Ms and offered him some. They wouldn't cure her problems.

He waved off the candy and she glared at him. "I haven't had lunch; I've got a massive headache and Vic hasn't called me back."

"He's not going to. I told him I'd handle this. Knowing him, he'll call you later for a temperature check. He hates being in trouble with women."

Roxann looked skeptical.

"Believe it." Michael stood. "Now, get your stuff."

"Why?"

"You want an alarm on your house?"

"We're going now?"

"Yeah. I've got two of my best guys sitting on ice. They'll meet us at your place and you tell them what you want."

Roxann's eyes, so big and blue and definitely unsure, leveled on him. "You put two of your best employees at my disposal?"

"It's important to you and I want you safe. If getting you an alarm will do that, it's a no-brainer."

"I don't know what to say."

"Say you'll get your ass moving because my well-paid employees are waiting for you."

She laughed as she circled the desk to grab her purse from the chair where she'd thrown it. She stopped in front of him.

"What?" he asked.

"I'm...overwhelmed. You didn't have to do this, but you did it anyway. I'm not used to people putting me at the top of the list. It's...well...nice. So, thank you."

Score one for me. Even if I did drag you into my hell hole. "I'll even buy you a sandwich on the way."

"What a guy."

He pulled her suit jacket off the back of her door and held it for her. "You have no idea, babe."

An hour later, Steve and Sammy walked through the house mapping out locations for window sensors, motion detectors, and keypads while Michael sat with Roxann at the kitchen table finishing beef sandwiches from Portillo's.

She swallowed her last bite of the huge sandwich. For such a skinny girl, she could put it away.

"I haven't had a beef sandwich in a long time."

"You used to love them."

"I still do. I just don't eat them anymore."

Beef sandwiches were a staple for Michael. He couldn't figure out if he loved the messy layers of roast beef and mozzarella or the memories the sandwich brought back. They had shared many late-night munchie attacks over Portillo's beef sandwiches.

He polished off his sandwich and crumpled the wrapper. "Phil did a nice job with today's article."

"He's a pro."

Roxann carried the wrappers to the garbage and, while over there, shot a look toward the living room where the guys worked. She motioned Michael to follow her and headed toward the back bedroom. Back bedroom?

Oh, baby.

Who was he kidding? Roxann pulling a nooner with two strangers in the house? Not to mention with him. Yeah, that's dreaming.

She swung the door open and invited him into what used to be a bedroom, but was now an office. The walls were a dark, dark green and floor to ceiling bookshelves lined the inside wall. The oversized desk sat buried under stacks of paperwork and folders. The office, despite the messy desk, was all her. Style and class.

After she closed the door behind them, he sat on the sofa and enjoyed the softness of good leather while Roxann curled her legs under her in the armchair to his left.

"I've been thinking about the night Alicia was murdered. There hasn't been much said about where she was. Phil told me she had an early dinner with friends."

Michael shrugged. "I have no idea. We communicated through our lawyers. It had been that way since we split up."

Roxann shifted a little and tapped her hand on the arm of the chair. "What would she consider an early dinner?"

"Anything before seven o'clock. Another thing we disagreed on. I like to eat by six."

She tilted her head, waited a beat. "Okay. Going with an early dinner, would she have gone straight home?"

Hello? Hadn't he just said he didn't know? "I can't answer that."

"Remember I said I went to a PBA fundraiser that night?"

"And?"

"If she were having an affair with Carl, would she have the nerve to attend a function where he would be with his wife?"

Oh, yeah. Michael scooted to the edge of the sofa. "Absolutely. She thrived on the rush of being somewhere she didn't belong. And if she had a plan, she'd have done anything to make sure she got what she wanted. We should check it out. Do you have any contacts at the P.D.? Anyone who could tell us who bought tickets to that event?"

"Sure, but I've become persona non grata since the first article on Carl and Alicia ran."

"Where was the event?"

"The Legends Ballroom."

No way. Could he get that damned lucky? Michael pulled his phone from his pocket with one hand and held a finger to Rox with the other. "Hang on."

"What?" she asked.

"I'll tell you in a minute." He waited for someone in the Taylor Security call center to pick up. "Jackie, this is Mike Taylor. Will you check something for me?"

"Sure," Jackie said.

"I think the Legends Ballroom is on the DSI client list. I need you to confirm that and then see if we have the security tapes from the last few weeks."

He heard the clack-clack of a keyboard.

"Yep. We have the last twelve months."

Yes. He fisted his hand and pumped it. "Perfect. Thanks."

Roxann leaned forward. "Does perfect mean you have them?"

"You can bet that beautiful behind of yours we've got 'em." He stood. "I need my laptop out of the car."

"Why?"

"Because I'm going to log into our system and pull up those security tapes."

"It'll be hours of tape."

He grinned. "Not if we use facial recognition software."

"Okay," she said. "Now we're getting somewhere, but if she went to that fundraiser, wouldn't the P.D. know? Or maybe they know and they're not telling the media."

Michael shrugged. "All valid points. I know they haven't asked for the security tapes yet. Those requests go through me. Let's start with the tapes and see what we find."

He hauled ass to his car, got his laptop and went back to Rox's office while she grabbed them a couple of pops from the fridge. He sat in the guest chair and set the laptop on the edge of the desk. A ginger ale landed on a coaster in front of him and Roxann stepped back to look over his shoulder.

"How does this software work?"

Damn she was standing close. That fruity scent she wore jabbed right into him and he closed his eyes, let the idea of her being so close settle in. Her outer thigh brushed his arm and he imagined those long legs wrapped around him. *Woody.* God, he wanted her. *Stay focused.* What kind of a rotten son-of-a-bitch could he be that all he could think about was getting into Roxann's pants when he was supposed to be finding Alicia's killer?

Ass.

"Michael?"

He looked up and saw her staring down at him. "What?"

She smacked his shoulder. "The software. How does it work?"

"We add Alicia's picture to the database and the software scans the images to see if there's a match."

Turning back to the laptop, he went into the folder marked divorce where all those telling photographs of his wife fucking other men were stored—yes, he had electronic files just in case the hard copies disappeared. He found a close-up of her full face. Bingo. He added the photo to the database and clicked back to the security tapes from the night of the fundraiser.

"Wow," Roxann said, "all those links are the images we need to scan?"

"Each link is a different camera." He clicked the first link and ran the software. Images flew across the screen and he waited. Would it be too much to hope that they'd find Alicia? Even if they did, what did it prove? Unless she appeared to be arguing with someone. Then this long-shot might pay off.

"I can't believe it scans that fast."

Roxann leaned forward for a closer look and her jacket brushed his shoulder. He angled away. He already had a raging hard-on and what was the point of torturing himself. A man could only take so much.

"This software is in development. One of our guys created it. There are other facial recognition systems out there, but we wanted to add some different features."

She touched his shoulder to get his attention. Did she have to do that?

"So you develop your own software?"

Michael stayed focused on the laptop. No chance he

could look at her right now. Not with the slugger he was sporting. "Not me, but my people do. Why not? I hire the best. Most of my people have been trained by the military or a federal agency and if they can come up with a way to improve on something, you'd better know I'll support it."

"That's actually quite brilliant."

Brilliant. Now he had to look at her. No man alive could resist a hot woman telling him he was brilliant. He wiggled his eyebrows. "I can be brilliant in other ways."

She rolled her eyes. "I'm sure."

A beep sounded from the laptop.

"Saved by the bell," she quipped. "No match. Darn it."

He shifted front, tapped more keys. "That's only one camera. We have all these other files."

The images began to scroll again. "Hey, there's Max giving his speech. He's great at mesmerizing a crowd." Roxann leaned forward again and her hip bumped the chair.

Dammit. That's it. Time out. Break. Take five. Michael gripped the arms of his chair and moved it left. "Rox, honey, you have *got* to step back." He pushed his hands in front of him. "Or move that way."

She tilted her head. "Is something wrong?"

"I'm trying to work here and you're close, way too close, making me want things I shouldn't want when searching for my ex-wife's murderer. Between the perfume and the brushing against me, it's sexual torture." *Just step away from me and my woody.*

A wicked half-smile dripped across her face and Michael knew he was dead. Screwed. This woman challenged him in ways he didn't want to admit and he was damned glad for it.

"Well," she said, still smiling at him, but stepping back, "I wouldn't want to give you any *discomfort*."

Cooked. He stood, and before she could move, he took three steps forward, grabbed her around the waist and kissed her so hard he thought she'd slug him. Just crack him one good.

But he held on with one arm, keeping her against him while he put his tongue to work in her mouth. After five seconds of resistance, she gave in and kissed him back, but he pulled away, licked along her jaw and down her neck—the magic spot he remembered all too well—until she groaned. *That's my girl.* He moved his hands over her breasts and she hissed at him, but ground her crotch against his hard-on.

Oh, yeah. No more waiting. He shoved her blazer off her shoulders and she wiggled out of it while he kissed every available spot of exposed skin. Finally. He'd have a taste of Roxann again.

Then she tugged his shirt out of his pants and he had a mind-melt. Totally gone. Her fingers traveled across his belly and her touch was so friggin' hot he didn't know what to do with all the heat.

"I must be crazy," she said, her lips moving against his neck.

Game on. He reached for his fly. All these years of fantasizing and he'd get his wish. He stepped back, reached up to touch her cheeks and grunted. "Totally destroying me."

The computer dinged and Rox jumped backward, her chest rising and falling as she stared at him with narrowed eyes, so blue and focused. He could see the want in her stance, in the way she flexed and unflexed her hands at her side. Predatory. Hungry.

Something told him it had been a long time since

Roxann had let loose on a man. And wouldn't he love to be her next victim?

Another ping sounded from the laptop and she glanced at it. "No match."

Fucking thing. "Yes," he said, "but we have other opportunities."

WHAT COULD SHE POSSIBLY BE THINKING?

Roxann shook her head. This man had the ability to turn her body into a vat of pure, hormone-induced, burning lust. Sure he'd taken hours out of his day to supervise the installation of her security system, but did she have to turn into a sappy school-girl? All because he wanted her to be safe?

The answer was yes. Heaven help her. Every part of her felt scorched and needy and her cheeks burned with the embarrassment. If the computer hadn't dinged, she probably would have had sex with him right in this room, with two of his employees working on her second floor.

No sense. But—*Lord*—it had felt good. All that lust and madness tearing around inside. The wanting. Fabulous. How had she lived without it for so long?

She blew out a breath. "So, wow. Pretty darn amazing."

Michael grunted and stepped toward her for round two. Could she even take anymore?

Probably not without completing the mission. And would that be so horrible? To let go? To enjoy a man's passion for nothing but the sheer pleasure of it?

A knock sounded on the door.

Michael laughed and Roxann threw her hands over her cheeks. "The computer is dinging; someone is knocking and

I'm freaking out. I think the message is we should wait on this endeavor."

"I can change the message. I'm brilliant at that too."

The knock came again. "Mike?"

Michael groaned. "Sometimes brilliance isn't everything." He spun to the door. "Yeah. Come on in."

Yes, Roxann thought, *come in and save me from myself.*

Sammy poked his head through the door and nodded at both of them. "We're all set upstairs. Can we get in here to finish up?"

"Sure," she said. "We'll move to the kitchen."

Where it's safe.

By the time the techs were done in her office, Michael and Roxann had finished reviewing the tapes.

"Not one darn match," she said. *Totally unacceptable.* "How accurate is this software?"

Michael curled his lip. "That's the thing. It's 3-D technology, but if the security camera only caught Alicia's profile, the software doesn't have a full-face print to analyze. It's plausible that she was there, but the system didn't pick her up."

Roxann spread her fingers wide in front of her. "Okay then. We'll just go through the tapes manually. Can you email me the camera footage?"

"Yeah. But, Rox, you said yourself it'll be hours of tape. Plus, we'll have to keep pausing it so we can study each image. It could take days. We're not even sure she was there."

Yes, originally the idea of going through hours' worth of tape hadn't appealed to her. It still didn't, but she refused to take a defeatist attitude. And she wouldn't let him do it either. Not when the possibility existed that his dead ex-wife could be on those tapes. "Would you rather go to prison? You'd have plenty of time then."

"Hey," he shot. "I'll give all the time necessary."

"Good. Then send me the tapes. You'd recognize her better than I would so maybe we can set up our laptops next to each other. You work on one set of tapes; I'll work on another. If I see someone I think might be a match. I'll ask you to confirm." Roxann snapped her fingers. "I also need to continue going through your investigator's files. Bring those when we review the tapes. If you trust me to keep the boxes, I'll go through them at home. How's that?"

Would he trust her? Did she even have the right to ask considering she'd been upfront about her tentative faith in him? But hadn't she let him inside her home? And left him alone the night before while she showered? She would never have done that if she didn't trust him. At least on some level.

And she wasn't seeing a whole lot of evidence from the police that proved Michael was a murderer. Maybe he was just convenient. A way to take the pressure off someone who might or might not work for the mayor.

"I'm in if you're in," Michael said. "You know I trust you. I wouldn't have let you see any of this stuff if I didn't."

14

"HE'LL SEE YOU NOW, MS. THORGESSON," THE DESK SERGEANT at police headquarters said.

"Thank you. I know the way."

Heading toward Max's office, Roxann noted the smell of fresh paint and new carpeting. Though recently remodeled, the walls were a dull gray, the carpets even duller, but she supposed a police station wasn't meant to be a day at the spa.

The corridor stretched with each step and she wondered if Max chose the last office so he could check in with his subordinates along the way. Given that it was the weekend, most of the offices sat empty. Except for Max's. He worked constantly.

"Knock, knock," she said when she reached her uncle's office.

The dark beige walls—out of the cold into warmth—held various photos of Max with high ranking city and state officials, and Roxann spotted a few shots of Max and the mayor at various functions. So complicated.

He swung around his desk, the knot in his tie sagging

and the top button of his shirt open, but his salt and pepper hair remained neatly combed. He kissed her on the cheek, gave her one of his infectious smiles and the strain between them momentarily vanished. *If only it could stay this way.*

"What brings you here?"

Admission time. She could tell the truth and risk him thinking she was crazy, or she could give him a hypothetical situation. This *situation* would include a friend who thought she'd had a break-in and, Roxann, being a great gal-pal, wanted to see what Max thought.

Yeesh.

Dumbest idea ever.

She cleared her throat. "I think someone broke into my house."

Max focused on her with such intensity, she burrowed further into her chair. "You think? Someone did or didn't, Rox, which is it?"

"I don't know. Nothing was stolen. There were certain things out of place and I know I didn't move them."

"You're sure?"

"Positive."

"Do you want to file a report?"

"Doesn't seem worth it. Other than to put it on record. I wanted to talk it over."

Max scooped up his pen and made a note. "I'll have someone get over there and dust for prints. Who do you think broke in?"

"I'm not sure. All the windows and doors are intact."

"Who has keys to the house?"

"Janie, my mother and you."

"That's it?"

"Yes."

"Then someone copied your key. Who has access to your key ring? Have you valet parked or had your car serviced?"

She rolled her eyes. "Please. Growing up around you, you think I'd be crazy enough to leave my house key with a stranger?"

Max smiled. "Good girl. What about the office. Who has access to your keys at the office?"

The thought had been nagging her all day. "Anyone in the corporate suite has access, but I don't think it was any of them. Someone from outside of corporate must have snuck in and grabbed my keys. If Mrs. Mackey were away from her desk, it would be easy for someone to do."

"After your pressroom vandalism, do you think it was someone from there?"

Roxann shrugged. "Possibly, but they're all on furlough. The pressmen have friends in the production department. One of the production people could have copied my keys and handed them off."

Max held up a hand. "What would they be looking for?"

"Information regarding a new contract. Maybe they wanted to be prepared."

He had his cop face on. The serious, mentally-reviewing-every-detail face where he squinted his eyes and tapped his forefinger against his lips.

"That's crap," he said. "You're already having the paper printed elsewhere. What's the rush on a contract while the men are on furlough? And why risk jail time for a preview of your latest offer?"

She hadn't thought about that. She was too busy being paranoid. "Then I'm stumped."

Max propped his feet on the desk. "How about your friend Mike Taylor?"

Just great. "You think *Michael* broke into my house?"

Max closed his eyes, shook his head in that way that inferred she was an imbecile.

"Maybe he thought he could find some information on his case. He's facing life in prison. He'd probably risk jail for a breaking and entering charge."

Despite the lunacy, she considered the idea. Michael certainly had opportunities to grab her keys and copy them. He'd been in her office and in her house. She kept a spare on a hook inside one of the cabinets. He could have taken the key, made a copy and replaced it before she'd noticed it missing. A torrent of disappointment forced her to drop her head forward. No. She would *not* do this. He'd been nothing but kind to her.

He couldn't have.

Could he?

"It makes sense," Max said.

Roxann raised her head and saw smug all over him. *So not giving in to smug.* "It also makes sense that someone other than Michael—*Carl* perhaps—wanted information on the case."

"Michael Taylor has connections."

She knew where this was going and wasn't it typical of Max to bring it up? "Meaning Jerry Foyle? They were friends in high school. So what? Janie and I were friends in high school."

"Janie's not associated with organized crime. Foyle is."

Roxann sighed. The Jerry Foyle argument wasn't a surprise. She had assumed Max would use it at some point and, unfortunately for her, she had no worthy response. Jerry Foyle *was* linked to criminals and he and Michael *were* friends. A plus B didn't necessarily equal C, but it was a fair assumption.

"I'll take it under advisement," she said, not wanting to believe Michael would break into her home.

Max sat back. "For now, put in a security system like I've been telling you."

"I've already done that." She hoped Max wouldn't pursue it, but she should have known better.

"Don't tell me *he* installed it."

The sarcasm in Max's voice swarmed and Roxann squared her shoulders. "His people did. Yes."

Her uncle leaned over his desk. Mad face. *Exceedingly* mad face. "He's in nice and tight, huh?"

"Max—"

"Change the goddamned code as soon as you get home. It won't stop him if he wants to get in. He'll know how to bypass his own system. Where the hell is your head at?"

The question of the month. She didn't know where her head was anymore. All she had wanted was a great story for the newspaper, but she'd let herself savor someone wanting to relieve her pressure. Between the grief, managing the pressroom situation and being at war with the mayor, why not? Michael seemed to be the only person willing to help. Why shouldn't she accept it? She had thought his motives were pure. Now she wasn't so sure.

Would he have done this to her? She pushed herself out of the chair and balanced on shaky legs. "I—I need to go."

Max hurried toward her and grabbed her arm. "Rox, I didn't mean to yell, but you need to get smart about this guy."

"I don't know what I have to do. I'm confused. Everyone has an agenda. Including you." He released her arm. "You can't possibly deny it. Your connection to City Hall makes you want me off the Alicia Taylor story. I appreciate your opinions, but I don't think Michael killed her. And it has nothing to do with our personal history. This is business. It's about justice for a murdered woman."

Max strode to the door. Held it open. "Business. Right. We'll see."

If ever there was an I'm-done-with-you look, Max wore it. She'd had enough of him trying to push her around. When had she ever let any man do that? Never. She marched past him. "Thanks for the advice."

Still, his concerns were plausible and she wanted answers. Fortunately for her, she knew the person who had those answers.

MICHAEL STOOD IN FRONT OF HIS REFRIGERATOR, SWEAT pouring off him by the truckload after hauling ass up thirteen flights of stairs for the extra cardio push. He grabbed a bottled water and chugged half.

His house phone rang and he checked the caller ID. Doorman.

"Hey, Hal."

"Evening, Mr. Taylor. I have Roxann Thorgesson down here to see you."

Michael clucked his tongue. The night just got better. "Send her up."

He looked down at his smelly, soaked through T-shirt. Nice. He'd let her in and go shower, but what the hell was she doing here? Those damned manners of hers always prompted a call before visiting.

He opened the entry door and waited for the ding of the elevator. When she stepped out, the frigid glare she gave him made him sweat for other reasons. Jeez, he couldn't keep up. One minute she wanted to get screwed stupid and the next he was three-day-old bread.

She took a few steps in, stopped, scoped out the living room and whirled on him.

"Did you make a copy of my house key and go through my stuff?"

The accusation seared him, and his empty water bottle slipped from his fingers and bounced off the entryway tile. "Excuse me?"

"Are you avoiding the question?"

Huh? What the hell? He ran a hand over his face. *Settle down. Don't blow your stack.* "I'm going to give you five seconds to tell me why you think I would do that. I can guess who put that crap into your head."

She turned away from him, traipsed down the three steps leading to the living room and went to the sliding glass doors that lined the far wall.

"Your five seconds is up. I don't deserve this, Roxann. I put myself and two of my best guys at your goddamned disposal today and you come in here and accuse me of breaking into your house?"

He slapped the door shut and strode over to where she stood. She continued to stare at the lake, but her shoulders hunched an inch.

"Yeah, now you're quiet," he said, the hurt from her accusation still smarting.

Without turning from the window she held out her hands. "I don't know who to believe anymore."

"So, you believe the last guy you talked to? That sucks for me, doesn't it?"

He left her by the door and stalked down a short corridor into the kitchen for another bottle of water. Maybe he'd dump the thing over his head to cool off before he said something stupid.

She still didn't trust him. He'd known she had doubts,

but he also thought they'd made progress. He must have been kidding himself. *Schmuck*. How were they supposed to get anything done—business or personal—if she didn't believe in him?

He leaned against the counter, looked past the breakfast bar and dining area to where Roxann waited.

Should he give her a break? She'd been through some nasty crap, but it didn't give her the right to accuse him of breaking into her house when he wanted to help her. Nope. He'd stay pissed awhile.

She finally turned from the window and glanced around the living room. "Your home is lovely."

There it is. The olive branch. She'd never had a taste for modern furniture, but she knew quality and he had plenty of that. He set the water bottle on the counter and spread his hands across the granite. Maybe the cold from the surface would soak through him.

After a moment of clearing his head, he walked back to the living room and dropped into his favorite chair. Screw the sopping wet T-shirt and the noxious fumes.

She stared down at the steel gray sofa. "Can I sit?"

"As long as you don't accuse me of stealing the couch," he muttered. Yeah, he was being an ass, but he wasn't hearing any apologies. She remained standing, a testament to her will, or was it good breeding? He wasn't sure, but he knew she wouldn't sit unless invited. "Sit, Roxann."

She lowered herself onto the sofa, crossed her long legs and ran both hands up her forehead. "I'm sorry. I let my imagination go wild. There's no excuse. Not after you helped me today."

"Apology accepted. This time. But if we're going to work together you have to be prepared for Max to come at you. I don't know what he said and I don't care, but I know he manipulated you."

She shook that off. "He didn't manipulate me. After talking to him, my brain went haywire."

Michael held up a hand. "I know he's your uncle and is probably concerned, I get that, but he's also trying to close a homicide. He'll do what it takes to make that happen."

"He just wants it over. The P.D. is getting a lot of attention. You, of all people, know that."

"I want it over too, but I'm not willing to convict an innocent man. That's the difference between him and me. You either trust me or you don't. Pretty simple, Rox." He sat back and waited, because as much as he wanted to see where things between them might go, he wouldn't be her fool.

"You certainly know how to get a girl's attention."

"The truth always seems to work."

She stared at her shoe. "Everything Max said touched a nerve. For the first time in my thought-out life I made a rash decision and rushed over here." She abandoned the shoe and turned to him. "I can't even be mad at Max. I let him convince me and I'm sorry. It won't happen again."

Her accusation hurt like hell, but he didn't want to argue. He'd let it go. The silence between them grew, but he refused to move. He'd wait. Opening his trap now would end up bad.

Roxann shifted toward the windows. "I'd love this view. Amazing." She stood, walked to the doors again. "Do you mind if I go out?"

"Be my guest. How about a drink? I'm having a bourbon."

Maybe ten.

She nodded. "That sounds good."

A few minutes later he joined her on the balcony with

two glasses and the sweatshirt he had grabbed from his bedroom. Why freeze his ass off in shorts and a sweat-soaked T-shirt?

"If I lived here, I'd be in this spot every night. What a perfect way to unwind."

Michael gazed out over the lake. He'd grown used to the view and took for granted the slashes of orange and blue sky that meant sunset.

"Mornings are spectacular. When it's warm enough, I have breakfast out here."

She placed the glass on the table, sat in one of the two cushioned chairs and took in his soaked shirt as he slid the sweatshirt on.

"Did I interrupt your workout?"

"I just got home. Sorry if I stink."

"You don't stink. Or maybe the athlete in me doesn't notice it anymore." She turned to him. "Do you see me running in the morning?"

He nodded, but didn't look at her. "Most days. Sometimes you play Saturday loose, which is unlike you." He grinned. "Not that I ever noticed."

Talk about giving her a stalker alert.

"You were watching me while *I* was wondering what *you* were doing. I knew you lived here, but I didn't know what floor."

This information was the equivalent of being tattooed by an express train. Every coherent thought evaporated. Now who was speechless?

She shifted to him, propped an elbow on the arm of the chair. "We should talk about it."

"What?" He knew.

Coward.

"Let's talk about it and get it over with."

He slouched into the chair, took a slug of his drink. "Not a good idea."

"It's been twelve years. Another twenty could come and go and I still won't know why you left me."

"I didn't leave you."

"Please," she mocked. "You got into your car, which was loaded with your belongings, and you drove away. You didn't tell me where you were going—"

"I didn't know."

"You didn't tell me when you'd be back or when I'd hear from you. I'd say that constitutes leaving someone."

Cornered. *Son of a bitch.* Maybe he'd jump over the railing. He rose from his chair and wandered there. "I was screwed up. You deserved more than waking up to my screaming nightmares. Every time I closed my eyes, somebody was getting a body part blown to hell."

She walked to where he stood and her ram-rod posture indicated she wasn't feeling sympathetic.

"I never asked you for anything. I tried to help. I was proud of you. You just didn't see it."

She had been proud of him. He'd known that. From the start she'd accepted him. She'd told him, but thinking back on it, rather than helping him, it somehow added to the pressure. His immature and selfish mind hadn't let him see her help as a gift from someone who cared. He'd taken it as pity. Yep. She was right. He'd been a world-class dick back then.

"How is talking about this going to help anything? Let's move on."

"Move *on*?"

"We're already arguing. Why argue over something that happened years ago?"

Her mouth opened quick, but millimeter by millimeter

closed again. He'd wait on her.

"I guess," she said, "move on is the modern version of getting into your car and driving away? You're still avoiding me?"

Blood plowed through his head, the pressure unbelievable, and he rubbed his temples. No good. "I'm not."

She stepped away from the rail. "I'm not doing this. You asked me to give you a second chance, and I agreed, but I expect you to clean up the mess you made the first time. If you're unwilling to do that, I'm out."

"Hold on a sec. Jesus, you're moving at warp speed."

He had to do something. And putting his head through the door wouldn't count. He could tell her the truth and be done with it. It would certainly ease him of the burden, but at what price? The truth would filet her and he couldn't live with that. He grabbed her arm, gave it a light squeeze.

"Don't ask me to do this, Roxann. Please, for both our sakes."

She brought her hand up and wrapped it around his forearm. "I don't understand why you won't talk to me."

"I will. It's not the right time now."

"When then?"

"I don't know," he said.

"That's not good enough. If you can't be honest with me, we're no further along than we were twelve years ago and I'm too old to settle for that."

She stepped back.

"Rox, hang on—"

"Are you going to talk to me?"

He should say something. That he knew. For sure. But he stood there, his mind whirling with indecision. *Come on, get in the game here.*

"I guess I have my answer," she said and walked out.

15

Boom, boom, boom. The pavement jarred Roxann's aching knees and she lightened her steps. Continuing with this angered stomping would give her an injury and who needed that after yet another restless night.

What was with Michael's secrecy? Was he stringing her along? Her brain said yes, but her heart had seen the anguish in his eyes. The man was tortured by whatever caused him to leave her twelve years ago. She sensed it, but he wouldn't admit it.

She ran past Michael's building and glanced up to see him standing on the balcony. She held up a hand to acknowledge him, but snatched it back fast. *Still mad, bucko. Deal with it.*

Did he always stand there in the mornings? She, oddly enough, had never noticed him. The footsteps of another runner approaching sounded from behind her and she scooted over to give way.

"Drop this story, Roxann."

The unfamiliar voice jolted her from her thoughts and

she halted. A man, maybe an inch or two shorter than her, came to a stop beside her. A baseball cap hid most of his short blond hair and wraparound sunglasses shielded his eyes. He appeared to be in his late twenties. Perhaps he worked at the newspaper.

No.

On closer inspection, she realized she didn't know him.

A stinging sensation shot up her arms. Not good. Max's safety lectures came rushing back.

Focus.

Pay attention to identifying features. A couple of runners and a biker behind her. Not alone. Good. And Michael was on the balcony. She glanced up. Gone. Where the heck did he go?

She brought her attention back to the man in front of her. "Do I know you?"

"I know you," the stranger said.

The bad B movie dialogue startled her for a moment, but the security of other runners on the path bumped her flight instinct to fight mode. The phone clipped at her waist chirped. Maybe it was Michael. She tilted her head up, saw him on the balcony again. *Can't talk now.*

Back to the stranger. "Do you think not telling me your name will preclude me from identifying you when I press charges for whatever threat you're about to make? If so, you are mistaken."

She had the urge to knock this jerk's baseball cap off. He had the nerve to approach her, yet he hid behind a hat and glasses. He smiled in that slithering way men do when they want to get over on a woman. *Creep.* She took note of a crooked front tooth. Burned the image into her memory. Gotcha, crooked-tooth boy.

"No threats, just a word of caution to a journalist in over her head."

For added effect he perused her legs and an icy burn went through her. *Creep!*

She folded her arms because, at the moment, it was her only protection. She glanced around again to reassure herself she wasn't alone. A biker cruised by. Fine. Good. Back to the stranger. She could outrun him. No doubt. But no. She'd never give in to the fear. *Harness it. Make it work.*

"I don't know whether you work for Carl Biehl or the mayor," she said, "but you can tell your boss this little episode assures me someone is nervous, and we need to find out who it is. You've screwed with the wrong woman." She spun away from him. "I have a run to finish."

After the first few steps, she yearned to look back. Was he still there? *Don't look.* Stay focused. Listen. No sound from behind. Maybe he gave up.

After two minutes, she couldn't stand it and looked back. Only a few other runners. Crooked-tooth boy must have gone the other direction. A wave of relief rushed at her and she drew a hard breath of cold air that stung her throat.

Uh-oh. Fuzzy, moving ground. The spinning. Vertigo. She stopped, bent at the waist and rested her hands on her thighs. *Deep breath. One, two, three. Control.* Once the ground stopped spinning, she straightened and unclipped her phone.

Missed call from Michael. *Knew it.* She headed back toward his building.

BY THE TIME ROXANN CAME ACROSS THE PEDESTRIAN BRIDGE, Michael's breaths were coming fast and short and he forced himself to take deep, diaphragmatic inhalations. Had he forgotten everything the military had taught him about controlling his emotions?

He charged up the stairs to meet her at the top. "Are you okay?"

"I'm fine."

"What happened? Did you know that guy?"

She leaned against the railing as cars whooshed under them. "No, I don't know him, but he said to drop the story so I'm guessing he works for Carl."

"Are you sure he meant that story? Did he say it specifically?"

"Yes and no," she said, answering both of his rapid-fire questions.

"What did he say?"

"I did most of the talking."

"Why doesn't *that* surprise me?"

And hello? Hadn't he warned her about running alone? *You put her in this situation. You could ruin her life, dummy.*

Roxann gave him a nasty look. "I wanted to make sure he was talking about the Biehl story, so I brought up Carl and the mayor. He didn't flinch."

After she recounted every word of the conversation, Michael waited a solid minute before opening his trap. Some asshole accosts her and she antagonizes him?

"First thing," he began, "threatening the mayor might not have been the best thing to do, but I'm gonna let that go because you were probably on an adrenaline high."

"I'll say. I wanted to tear him to pieces."

Roxann fisted her hands and he reached for them. "Don't get worked up. Would you recognize him if you saw him again?"

"You bet I would." She tapped on one of her front teeth.

"Crooked front tooth. He had on sunglasses and a hat, but I'd recognize that tooth."

As usual, she'd been good under pressure. Damn, she was hard not to admire. She'd had the presence of mind to find an identifying feature. "Nice."

Michael stroked his unshaven cheek with the backs of his fingers and realized he'd thrown shorts and a T-shirt on to have breakfast, but didn't bother to brush his hair.

"What are you thinking?" she asked.

"Besides the fact that I want to throw myself into this traffic for putting you in danger, I'm thinking I've got bedhead and you need to pay a visit to Carl's office today. See if anyone on his staff has a crooked front tooth."

Roxann rolled her eyes. "He can't be that dumb. Sending someone from his office? It'd be too easy to get caught."

"Carl's not a rocket scientist. You never know, it might shake something loose."

"Maybe you've forgotten, but I have a business to run, a business in *crisis*, and I don't have time to be playing detective."

Michael folded his arms. "Humor me. Besides, with all the security at City Hall you'll be safe going there during the day."

A long moment passed with the two of them squared off in a brutal stare. She finally gave in. "Fine. If it'll get you to shut up about it, I'll do it."

"Thank you."

She wasn't mad. She just had to act put out. Roxann didn't have it in her to give up tracking this guy so easily. Not after he'd gotten in her face.

"Whatever," she replied.

She dropped into a cross-legged position on the bridge. *O-kay.* He sat next to her and couldn't help noticing the sparkle in her blue eyes. Adrenaline still flowing.

"You're not running alone anymore."

She leaned back, stretched her legs in front of her. "I'm not giving up running."

"You don't have to. All I said was you're not doing it alone."

After huffing a breath she stood. Michael fought a smile. Typical of her to take a position of power by looking down at him.

She wanted a fight and he'd give it to her. Up he went. "Don't be ignorant about this. Any number of things could have happened this morning. You could have been dragged to a waiting car. Sure, there are people around, but do you know how easy it is to grab someone, toss them in a car and be off? It happens quick, especially if they get you off guard."

"You alpha males fracture me. You're inflexible and bossy. I decide where I run, Michael, not you."

"I didn't say you couldn't decide where to run—"

She waved him away with both hands and whipped around to face the lake. "Give it a rest."

Staring at her back, he crossed his arms, mentally ran some options. Why should he waste his time arguing with her? The conflict only charged her battery. He knew that well enough.

"I'll drive you home," he said. "It's getting late and you were close to being done with your run anyway."

Roxann offered up the squinty eyed stare. "That's it? No argument?"

"Nope. I have a busy day today and it won't get us anywhere. If you want me to drive you home, we need to go now."

"I'd appreciate that. I'm already twenty minutes behind."

"Heaven forbid."

"You can make fun, but twenty minutes is a lot these days. Especially if I have to go over to City Hall and play detective this afternoon."

16

Roxann stood outside the door leading into the administrative offices of Mayor Douglas Richmond. She pressed her palm over her forehead and took a deep breath. This playing detective thing was a nerve shredder. Michael's instructions were plastered into her brain: look around, don't be obvious, and make sure you see everyone in or around Carl's office.

Don't be obvious about it? Was he kidding? There had to be forty people in Carl's office.

Bad enough she had to come here, but she got stuck on line at security, then her shoes set the metal detector off. At least now she knew her Blahniks didn't have any bombs hidden in them. Good to know.

Who had time for this when the newspaper's bottom line was sinking?

A drop of sweat dribbled down her shoulder blades and she ordered herself to be calm. The door suddenly opened and a young woman, moving at a clip, smacked into her, sending Roxann's tote to the floor.

They both laughed, but Roxann wondered if all these

impediments were somehow a warning to get the heck out of there.

"I'm here to see Carl Biehl."

"His assistant is at her desk. Just check with her." The woman handed Roxann her tote bag and went on her way.

Roxann closed the suite door behind her, found herself alone in the corridor and took the liberty of popping her head into two open offices.

Nothing.

The next office held three people—no crooked-front-tooth boy—and she made up a story about trying to find Carl's assistant. She knew perfectly well who Carl's assistant was, but they didn't know that.

The remainder of the offices were empty or had closed doors.

Shoot.

Carl's assistant sat dutifully outside his office typing faster than a jack hammer and, without stopping, told Roxann to go right in.

"Sorry I'm late. Hang up at security." Roxann sat in one of the two wing-backed chairs. An adjoining door to the mayor's office stood open and she experienced an unexpected thrill over sitting just yards from the most powerful man in the city. Sure, he'd been an ass to her, but still, how many people got to come here?

Carl closed the door. So much for that.

"Let me guess," he joked. "Your shoes went off."

"Yep."

He sat on the sofa directly across from her and smiled, but it was the weak smile of a man stuck in places he shouldn't be stuck. Still, the mayor wanted this meeting so she'd let Carl squirm. Particularly if he'd sent a goon to scare the hell out of her.

"We both know why you're here," he said.

Maybe, maybe not.

"I didn't have an affair with Alicia Taylor," Carl continued. "I had a friendship with her. When she was murdered, I went to the police myself and told them about our relationship. They felt there was no need to release the information."

"You went to Max?"

Carl nodded. "Yes. We may share the same boss, but he won't protect me from a murder charge or, at the very least, obstruction. You know that better than anyone."

Yes, she did know. "You're right, but Michael Taylor has been vilified and it appears the police haven't looked any further for potential suspects. The public has a right to know there were extenuating circumstances in Alicia's murder."

"Extenuating circumstances?"

Roxann's temples began to hammer. "With all due respect, Carl, maybe you didn't murder Alicia, but someone around you could have."

Carl rested his elbows on his knees. He suddenly appeared every inch of his fifty years. His once dark hair had gone completely gray and the creases by his eyes had become canyons.

"Roxann, I'm angry over the *Banner's* coverage of this case. My family has been needlessly humiliated, but I'm sensible enough to know how it must look. My visits with Alicia had nothing to do with sex."

"So, what was it?"

"I can't say."

Of course he'd say that, but she had to give it a shot. "Are we going to get anywhere with this meeting?"

He shrugged. "The mayor would appreciate any relief

you can give us on the *Banner*'s coverage of our office. Your newspaper is hard on this administration."

"With good reason. I'm not saying it's the mayor's fault, but he's in charge and there's corruption here. Until the mayor cleans house, we'll continue to pursue it."

"We're working on it. It's a large staff."

"I realize that."

He stared at her for a long moment and then smiled. "I always admired your spunk, Roxann. No nonsense."

"We're both too busy for nonsense, but the mayor requested I come here and I wanted to make the effort."

"Right. Now I can tell him you and I have talked, and the *Banner* will continue to do its best when reporting on City Hall."

She stood. "Sounds good to me."

Carl opened the door. "You know your way out?"

She sure did.

On the way, she stopped and asked Carl's assistant for directions to the ladies' room. The assistant pointed down the hall, but made no movement from her chair. Perfect. Roxann could roam the office unaccompanied for a few moments in search of the mystery man, then slip out the main door.

For show, she stopped briefly in the bathroom and then headed toward the front of the suite, stopping every few feet to peek into open offices.

Maybe she had a knack for this Colombo stuff.

"Can I help you?" A not so friendly middle-aged man asked.

She jumped. *Forget the Colombo stuff.* "I just finished a meeting with Carl, and after a stop in the ladies' room, I'm all turned around. I thought if I looked out the window, I could get my bearings."

Yeesh. Could she come up with anything lamer? Hopefully the guy was dumb enough to buy that load of garbage. She gave him her best blonde-girl smile.

He eyed her. "I'll walk you out."

Maybe he didn't buy the load of garbage, but he didn't challenge her. Throwing Carl's name out there probably hadn't hurt. She knew this staffer didn't want to be the one to cause a problem for Carl's guest.

After being led out, Roxann punched the elevator button. This excursion was a total bust. Why didn't she just stand her ground and talk Michael out of it? Carl wouldn't be stupid enough to send someone from his office after her, but in the spirit of her partnership with Michael, she gave it a try. It turned out to be a waste of time. And she didn't need him wasting her time.

AT DAYBREAK THE NEXT MORNING, DRESSED IN RUNNING tights and a long-sleeved shirt, Roxann peeped out her front window and saw exactly what she expected to see. Michael. Waiting for her on the sidewalk. Wearing running clothes. He'd given up the fight too soon for her to believe he wasn't planning an alternate strike. As much as she wanted to moan about the loss of her alone time and her independence being compromised, something about the sight of him on that sidewalk gave her a feather light feeling in her belly. Wasn't this the way he'd settled her not running alone at night twelve years ago? No matter how tired he'd been, he'd always run with her at night.

The man's protective instincts ran hot and deep and, for once, she found herself open to it. For years she'd been the one in charge and a quiet relief settled inside her because she didn't need to be that person around him. Still, she wouldn't totally give in. *Nah*. He'd be disappointed with that. He loved the sparring as much as she did. She'd go out the back, sneak down the alley and surprise him. Let him know she could have gotten away if she wanted to.

She went to the back door, opened it and heard the chirp of a phone followed by a familiar male voice.

"She's coming out the back."

Vic. *Shoot*. She turned, pepper spray in hand, mad enough to squirt him because he'd foiled her plan, but she quickly backed off when she saw his lopsided grin and the bright pink T-shirt that read Tough Guys Wear Pink. These men. Too damn much. Michael came tearing around the side of the house before she'd even stepped off the porch.

"Ha," he said. "Nice try, babe. How stupid do you think I am?"

She jogged down the steps. "That's a loaded question."

Unperturbed, he continued, "You are so busted. Here's the deal. Vic's doing the first five with you and I'm doing the last five. No reason we should exhaust ourselves," he turned to Vic. "Right, buddy?"

Vic grinned. "Roger that."

They were having fun? Good for them. She'd still pretend to be irritated. Why not? She'd play. "Glad you two are enjoying yourselves." She scooted past them. "Try to keep up. I'm not slowing down for you."

"You got it, darlin'," Vic said.

"Ho," Michael said, his hands wide. "What's with the darlin' crap?"

Vic did the who-me look and she rolled her eyes.

Michael jabbed his index finger. "Roxann is a client and you don't call her *darlin'*. She's an educated woman running a two-hundred-million-dollar company. Don't you think she might get offended by you calling her *darlin'*?"

Vic shrugged. "She doesn't look offended."

"*I'm* offended."

Vic held up two hands. "Jeez. Sorry." He turned to Roxann and jerked his head toward Michael. "*Someone* is crabby today."

"I'm not crabby. You need to be respectful."

"I am respectful! Rox, you're not offended, are you?"

"You know what?" she said, half laughing at them. "You girls can fight while I go for my run. I need some semblance of normalcy and listening to the pair of you bicker is not part of my routine."

Even if it was fun.

17

ROXANN STOOD IN HER KITCHEN STARING DOWN AT THE TWO boxes filled with copies of Michael's notes on his wife's filthy behavior. The task would be daunting, but she'd do it and most likely wind up thoroughly hating the woman. Did that make her a horrible person? Probably. She just didn't know what to do about it. After all, this woman landed the love of Roxann's life and then, years later, had the nerve to sleep with her boyfriend.

She glanced across the table where Michael logged into his laptop. "I ordered us a pizza. Not a five-star dinner, but it'll do."

Without looking at her, he said, "I don't need five-star. I need to stay out of prison."

He had a point there. Setting one of the boxes on a chair, she pulled it open. Battered manila folders had been sorted by date and she ran a hand over them before pulling one out. February. She returned the folder and searched the remaining boxes for March. To do this right she needed to go back to the night Alicia died.

Second box. Pay dirt.

She pulled the March folder and set it in front of her on the table. When she was younger, she'd sit in this same spot ruminating over her homework while her father sat across from her reading reports from the office. She glanced up and stared at Michael, who now sat in that chair. Her father wouldn't approve. For many reasons. She couldn't dwell on it. Not after Michael had managed to crack open a bit of her hardened heart.

"March folder," she said.

Inside the folder she found several pages of hand-written notes and copies of photos of Alicia at various social functions. Roxann stared down at Alicia Taylor's stunning face and an unexpected ball of jealousy clogged her throat. The woman was dead. How could she feel jealous? The idea of it sickened her. She should be feeling sorry for her, not envious because she'd shared a bed with Michael for years.

Onward. The March folder had nothing but a recap of Alicia's activities before her death. Nothing about her relationship with Carl or whether she attended the PBA fundraiser.

Roxann reached behind her to the drawer to retrieve a note pad and pen. Most people kept linens and utensils in their kitchen drawers. She kept legal pads.

Something in these notes begged to be found. She was sure of it.

The police had nothing.

No problems with the polygraph.

No witnesses.

No prints.

With each day, she became more confident they couldn't build a case. Michael would be declared innocent. He had to be.

"Something has to be here," she said. "We just haven't found it yet."

The doorbell rang. Pizza. She moved to answer, but Michael waved her off and did it himself. Having someone around definitely had its merits.

Five minutes later, they sat at the table, an open pizza box in front of them.

"I've been reading everything from the month of the murder, and I know I'm missing something." She pumped her palm against her head. "It's so frustrating."

"Yeah, well, digging through these tapes will take a month. Too many damned people. All the images are running together."

Roxann nodded. "There must have been five-hundred people at that event. I met one kid, he worked for Carl as an intern. He was cute. It was his first—" she made imaginary quote marks with her fingers, "—official function. He was so excited."

She thought back on her visit with Carl the previous day and realized she hadn't seen the young man. She should have asked if he still worked there. It had been fun to meet someone that young and revved about his job.

The slice of pizza she held slid from her fingers and landed with a splat in front of her.

Michael jerked his head back. "Rox?"

"That intern was Carl's assistant. He might know something."

Her mind worked like water rushing over a fall and she shot off her chair, knocking it backward. She ignored it and grabbed the phone off the counter.

"How do we find him?" Michael asked.

"I'm calling Phil."

A rush of relief and anticipation surged when Phil answered. "It's Roxann."

"Hey, Rox."

"Where are you?"

"Working a stabbing on the west side. It's good and savage."

Phil got excited over the most gruesome things, but that came with years on the job. "I was hoping you were at the office. Can you talk a minute?"

"Yeah, but I might have to dump you. Shuman's writing the story as we speak."

Roxann understood the life of a reporter on deadline.

"That's fine. What do you know about a kid who works in Carl's office as an intern?"

"There are lots of interns. Got a name?"

She paced the length of the kitchen, tried to ignore Michael's eyes tracking her. "I can't remember, something with a B. Brian maybe. I don't know, but he worked directly for Carl."

Phil hesitated, probably jotting notes.

"Okay. I'll check it out first thing in the morning. What's up with this kid?"

How to explain this one? She had no idea what was up with him, but it would be worth a conversation to see if he knew about Carl's relationship with Alicia.

"I'm not sure. Maybe he overheard something. I've got a hunch."

"Hunches work. I'll let you know."

"PHIL'S HERE FOR YOU," MRS. MACKEY ANNOUNCED VIA speakerphone. Roxann abandoned the circulation reports she'd been studying since noon. A break. *Thank you.*

Phil entered the office and dropped into the chair in front of her desk.

"Did you find the intern?" It had been less than twenty-four hours, but she could hope.

He flipped open his notepad and gave his pen a click. "Bryce Cooper, twenty-one-year-old junior at Northwestern. Nice kid, responsible, preppy. Started working for Carl in January for a semester long internship. He quit the internship last week."

Phil closed the notepad.

"Did you get an address?"

"Yep. Apartment near campus."

"And?"

"Moved. No forwarding address. I checked with my source at the phone company, but there's nothing current."

She cocked her head. "A source at the phone company. Love it."

"It didn't get us anything. If he has a cell phone, he may not have a land line in his house or he could have a room-mate and the phone is in their name."

Roxann tapped her lip. "Let's check one more thing."

She dialed Michael's office, only to be told by his assistant that he was in a meeting. Roxann left a message saying they needed to locate Bryce Cooper.

"Let's see if they can come up with anything," she said. "Michael and Vic have a lot of contacts. As a last resort, I know some people at Northwestern who might be able to help. Seems odd this guy is gone, doesn't it? Why did he leave his job before the end of the semester? And then move? I lived in the same apartment the whole time I was in school. Even when I went to the Olympics, I kept my apartment."

"Something rattled him."

A murder perhaps? "I agree." She glanced down at the circulation reports on her desk. "The single copy numbers were up last week starting with the day the Taylor story ran. Nice work, Phil."

He nodded. "Thanks. Maybe we can pull something together on this intern angle and run a follow-up."

"Sorry to interrupt," Mrs. Mackey said from the doorway. "The pressmen representatives are here."

"Thank you. Please put them in the conference room."

Mrs. Mackey nodded and turned from the door.

"Sorry, Phil, I have to run. I'll let you know if Michael comes up with anything."

She grabbed her notepad and followed him out, hoping this meeting wouldn't run long because she had her dinner date with Michael tonight and wanted to take her time getting ready.

Not that she'd be cooking, but she still had to order the food and make the table look nice. That had to count for something. And she had to decide what to wear, take a shower, all that stuff girls do when getting ready for a date. Warmth spread through her neck and face and she hated it. Michael had once pummeled her emotionally and her brain wasn't ready for her heart to give in to him.

She knew she wouldn't be changing the sheets on her bed. That would be the last line of resistance for her. Taking a man, this man, to bed on non-laundered sheets would never happen.

Ever.

MICHAEL RANG THE DOORBELL AT SEVEN O'CLOCK ON THE nose and stood on the porch waiting for Roxann to answer. He rocked forward on his toes and gripped the bottle of wine a little tighter before it slipped out of his sweaty hand. *Any time now, Rox.*

"Hi," she finally yelled through the door.

What the hell? "Are you going to open the door?"

"I'm not dressed yet. I'll unlock the door, but give me a minute to get upstairs and then come in. Okay?"

He laughed. "*You're* late?"

"Don't start. Just give me a minute to get upstairs."

The lock on the door clicked, but he did as he was told by counting off a minute before entering the house.

"Have a seat," she yelled from the second floor when he closed the front door behind him. "I'll be right down."

Not wanting to make himself too welcome, he cooled his heels in one of the big wing back chairs in the living room while he waited for Rox. The wine and gift bag he'd brought with him bounced on his lap with each tap of his foot and he set them on the ottoman before they both crashed to the floor. Damn but his nerves were firing. Rightly so. This date had been twelve years in the making. A sudden layer of guilt landed on him. He'd always loved Roxann, had that deep yearning for her and it hadn't been fair to Alicia. Even if she had turned out to be a horrible wife, she still deserved her husband's love.

But then he heard Roxann pattering around just above him. Her bedroom?

And didn't that get him thinking about wandering up those stairs? What would he find up there? A king-sized bed, he hoped. Maybe bold prints in red? Was she into red these days? He had a lot to re-learn and it put a smile on his face.

"What's funny?" Roxann said when she came down the stairs wearing jeans and what had to be a cashmere sweater. Casual but elegant.

The blue in the sweater enhanced her eyes and it carved right into him. Made him want to see those eyes sparking at him every day. He stood and cleared his throat. "Nothing."

There would be no way he'd own up to his thoughts.

"I don't know what gets into me when I'm supposed to meet you," she said. "I'm always late and that never happens."

"It's my fault you're late?"

"No, I'll take responsibility."

He held up the gift bag and swung it from one finger. "These are for you."

A wide smile curved her lips and she rubbed her hands together. "Can I open it?"

No oh-you-shouldn't-have, just an excited gush of anticipation over having received a silly gift. She might be the perfect woman.

"Sure."

She stuck her hand in the bag and burst out laughing. "You brought me M&Ms?"

Michael nodded. "The jumbo bag."

"Are you trying to tell me something? Am I going to need these M&Ms tonight?"

He shook his head. "I hope not. I've already gone a few rounds with Vic today. I don't think I could take any more."

She stared at him, which was just fine because he'd stare right back and maybe they could stay that way for the next, oh twenty or thirty years. She finally took a step toward him, went up on tip toes and kissed his cheek. His hands, as a precaution, went into his pockets.

"Thank you. This is a great gift."

"You're welcome. Figured I couldn't go wrong with M&Ms." He reached for the bottle of wine. "We should put this wine on ice."

"Right. Come in the kitchen, dinner is in the oven."

"You *cooked?*"

That drew a searing glare from her. He remembered a lot about Roxann from twelve years ago, and the night she tried to poison him by serving half raw chicken stayed right there in that memory bank. That one would never leave his mind.

"Seriously?" she said. "You're bringing up the chicken?"

"Not me."

"Besides, I *could* have cooked. You probably wouldn't have survived it, but I could have done it."

"Atta girl."

He sat at the kitchen table and absorbed the pleasure of being in Roxann's space. He'd felt it the other night too. Even when they were immersed in work, there had been an ease to it. A familiarity. Not much in his life had been easy or familiar lately.

She slid a tray of antipasto, bursting with salami, peppers and cheese in front of him and the pungent smell of parmesan made his mouth water.

"We can go in the other room if you'd like," she said.

"The kitchen is good."

She pulled two wine glasses from the cabinet and went back to the fridge for a cold bottle.

"Oh." He reached into his pocket, pulled out a slip of paper. "I found your intern. Here's his address."

Roxann rushed back to the table, handed him the wine and an opener and snatched the paper. "How did you find him?"

"Cell phone bill. We've got a specialist on staff."

She stared hard. "A specialist?"

He shrugged.

"Did you obtain this legally?"

"Please." He batted his lashes. "I'm not the kiss and tell type."

"Please." She batted her lashes. "You are so the kiss and tell type."

Got me there.

Roxann held up the note. "This is great. I'll check it out tomorrow."

"No you won't."

The frosty look she gave him said it all. Not that he cared. She wouldn't go chasing after this kid alone. Not when he could be involved in a murder.

"Someone has to do it," she said. "I've met him before so it should be me."

Oh, hello. That's not flying. "You can't go alone. You don't know why this kid suddenly disappeared. I'll go with you."

She rolled her eyes. "Your picture has been all over the news. Bryce dropped off the radar for a reason and seeing you at his doorstep will only make him nervous."

Had to give her that one. "Fine. We'll bring Vic and I'll stay in the car."

She waved him off. "Great. Whatever. Let's not talk about this now or I'll have to bust open the M&Ms."

That made him laugh. "Speaking of Vic, I'm sorry about the darlin' thing this morning. He gets a little carried away. I talked to him and it won't happen again."

After checking on dinner she slid into the seat across from him. "He doesn't mean anything by it."

"It's inappropriate."

"It wasn't a big deal. He and I are pals. He's been a huge help with the security at the paper."

Pals. They were *pals*. What did *that* mean? "He's a good guy."

I'm going to break his fucking face, but he's a good guy. He watched her pick up a cube of cheese and pop it in her mouth. Her jaw worked as she chewed and when she licked her lips...uh-oh, wrong thought pattern. He shifted in his seat.

"Are you okay?" she asked. "You seem...uncomfortable."

Uncomfortable. Right. He wanted to tear her clothes off and get rid of the bulge in his pants, but otherwise, he was good.

He couldn't do this.

He couldn't sit here and pretend this was a casual first date. Not with their history.

"I'm not okay."

Her eyebrows came together. "What is it?"

"It's just...a guy thing...I guess. I can't concentrate."

She pondered him. *Yes, every one of my brain cells has died and might spill onto your tiled floor.*

"I don't understand."

He forced out a breath. Rubbed his hand over his eyes. His mouth was drier than Arizona. *Take it easy, Taylor, just talk to her.* "The grown up, responsible part of me is saying I should take this slow, this thing with you and me. After all these years, we're finally, well, not together, but at least talking and I don't want to blow that, but every inch of me wants to forget slow. And after what happened here in your office the other day..." He stopped. *Don't get nuts here.* "We're beyond slow, don't you think? How do we start over? We can't. And the truth is I want to have sex with you." He held up two hands before she hammered away at him. "Romantic, I know. But think about it. I could tell you how beautiful and smart you are. How much I respect you as a businesswoman, but you probably hear that all the time from guys trying to get laid. I guess, in a way, I'm one of those guys.

Hell, I like getting laid." He laughed and shook his head. "But *I* know what moves you, Rox."

She raised her chin an inch and her quirking lips couldn't hide the smile. "Do tell."

Rolling now. Michael sat forward. "You don't need compliments. You need to experience them. You're working in a male dominated industry and you're ordering those males around all day. When work is done, you don't want to be in charge. You don't want a guy you can beat up or that's threatened by you. You want a guy that'll listen, but not try to fix everything because you're capable of fixing it yourself. You want to be treated like a woman, but not feel patronized."

Now she gave him a full-on smile. *Jackpot.* "And I suppose you're the guy that can do that for me?"

"Of course, I am. Otherwise, I wouldn't be bothering with this little speech."

Silence. Nothing. Nada. Suddenly, the limited confidence he'd felt a few seconds earlier went right out the window. *Right* out the window.

Might as well keep talking. "So, here we are. We got the wine and the dinner. I know what I'd normally do, and—I'm not being cocky here, just honest—we'd probably wind up in the sack, but this is not normal. Way not normal."

He shut up and waited for her to say something. Then she did it. She bit down on the edge of her lip and it destroyed him because it was the look she used to give him when she wanted some smoking-hot sex. Lots of it. The buried beast inside had dug himself up and Michael wiped his sweaty palms on his jeans. "That's what I'm talking about, that biting your lip thing. Don't do that. It makes me want to...just...please, don't do anything with your lips."

What the hell was wrong with him? Had he never

seduced a woman before? Or maybe it was that he'd never *not* seduced a woman.

"Nothing with my lips huh?"

"I'm serious."

Before he had a minute to think, she bolted out of her chair, hauled him up by his shirt and kissed him. With plenty of tongue.

His body coiled into knotted steel and he balled his fingers to keep his hands from wandering. Hadn't he been clear about her not doing anything with her lips? This definitely included use of the lips. Big league unfair. This is what trying to be a nice guy got him. She was taking advantage. Not that he'd complain. What was to complain about? He'd wanted this for a long time and it would be so-oh-oh easy to give in. He reminded himself they were taking it slow. He backed up.

"This is a problem because I'm not going to slow this down. Are we clear on what's happening?"

There was a moment of hesitation but then she gave him that wicked half smile from the other day in her office and he lost his fucking mind.

"Are we clear?" he asked. *Please let it be clear.*

Roxann leaned forward until they were nose to nose. "I'll race you upstairs."

HE CHASED HER UPSTAIRS AND ROXANN'S BODY TINGLED because finally, finally, finally the in-control Roxann was going to let herself go, just unload and have some amazing, mind-melting, body paralyzing sex. *Don't think, don't think.* Over analyzing it would totally kill the mood. So what if Michael equaled skipping through an emotional hurricane?

She stopped short in front of her bedroom, every muscle

tensing from the horror flooding her. He plowed into the back of her, nearly knocking her over.

She hadn't changed the sheets. Her last defense. "We can't."

Michael laced his hands in front of his face, squeezing so tight his knuckles swelled. "Please don't do this to me."

"Wait." She turned toward the guest room. "In here. These sheets are clean."

"Huh?"

"Never mind," she shrieked and yanked off her sweater before she even got to the bed. "Get naked, dammit!"

She cracked up at herself because, for the love of any dignity, what was she doing? Michael grunted, spun her around and kissed her while trying to kick out of his pants. *Wow.* He could kiss. All soft and warm and wet.

"Wait. The oven."

"Fuck the oven. I'll buy you a new one."

She had to laugh. "Not *the* oven. The food *in* the oven."

"I'll order something."

She pushed his shirt up and he tossed it away as she toed off her shoes. In an explosion of moving arms and kicking legs he unbuttoned her jeans and shoved them off of her. His big hands skimmed down her legs and the air in her lungs disappeared. Gone. *Breathe.* She wanted this. So badly.

They should slow down. *Too fast, too fast.* This wasn't what she'd imagined. Her dreams of making love to him were always torturously slow. Never this frenzied rush. She should slow him down. Their first time together again should be what she'd wished for, cherishing every second.

But then he pushed her back on the bed and suddenly slow didn't seem so important. She sucked in a breath because what she wanted was fast and primal and hot. All the things she hadn't had in so long because in-control Roxann had become boring—B.O.R.I.N.G.—and never allowed herself the freedom.

"Bang," he said. "You're head just exploded again. Stop thinking."

He stood at the foot of the bed, naked and fully aroused —*oh, baby, come to mama*—yet waiting, making sure she knew they could stop the whole thing.

She let her gaze travel over his long frame, his solid chest and shoulders until she got to his face, where their eyes met and held. Decision time brought a hissing in her ears.

"Forget slow," she said. "There's time."

She hoped.

He moved over her. "You're sure?"

What was his problem? Didn't she just say it was okay? "Shut up already and screw me."

Within seconds, he moved inside her and her breath caught. *Yes.* The feel of his body against hers, so familiar and yet so new, the way his hair glided under her hands, became something that twelve years couldn't take away. After the military his body had been lean with wired muscles. He was heavier now, different than what had been embedded—sealed—in her mind. Age had filled him out and this solid Michael offered so much more to enjoy. And that was trouble.

Right now trouble seemed pretty darn good.

Michael shifted and she moaned.

"Someone's happy," he whispered.

"Please." And suddenly her pride vanished. She knew what she wanted.

He slowed his pace and her system fired. *Not yet, not yet, not yet.* She slammed her eyes shut. It felt too good to end, but a wild rumbling in her core drowned out all thought. *Not yet. Please.*

Then he kissed her, their lips coming together so gently that all sound drifted away and she allowed herself these moments of having this man back, loving him after all the years.

It can't be a mistake. Not when it's this good.

He stopped moving, pulled back from the kiss and propped himself on his elbows. He looked into her eyes while their bodies remained pressed together, skin to skin.

"What?" she asked.

"I don't want it to stop. Is that nuts?"

He felt it. That wanting to explore each other. To linger in the moment. She trailed her fingers through his hair. "But we have all night."

He shot off one of his all-teeth smiles. "Just what I wanted to hear."

Minutes later, she knew for sure that nothing beat a Michael-inflicted orgasm. Nothing.

Roxann ran her hands over his trembling back, felt the light moisture from sweat and eased out a breath. Reluctantly, she peeled her legs from around him.

"Am I expected to move?" he asked, his voice muffled by the pillow he'd buried his face in.

"Only if you want to."

He pushed himself up and smacked a kiss on her cheek. "You're gonna have a long night."

"I hope so."

Snorting a laugh, he rolled off, slid an arm under her and pulled her to him. "How do you think it's going so far?"

"Not bad for a first date." With any luck, they'd improve with practice.

He waved his free hand toward the door. "Do I want to

ask about the bedroom switch thing? What the hell was that?"

Roxann pressed her cheek into his chest and the warmth found there. "I didn't change the sheets on my bed. I thought it would keep me from...well...doing what we just did."

"Lucky for me you have a guest room."

"With clean sheets."

"Of course."

She burrowed farther into him and hooked her leg around his. "I have to take that food out of the oven or it'll be ruined."

He rolled out of bed, slipped on his underwear. "I'll do it. You stay here."

No argument there. If that's the way it was going to be, she could get used to having him around. "Bring the wine back with you. And the antipasto."

He stuck his head back into the bedroom. "Anything else?"

She made a humming noise. "Nope. I'm *fairly* satisfied at the moment."

"Oh, that is so wrong."

He still laughed though.

With Michael's absence came a feeling of being overexposed and she pulled the sheet up. Her hair clip had disappeared—where the heck did it go?—and she shoved her hair away from her face. She didn't remember undoing the clip, but, then again, she'd been occupied.

At some point, her arms and legs turned into tree trunks that sank deeper into the bed and she closed her eyes for a moment. She needed rest. Maybe the orgasm had thrown her into this languid state, but whatever the reason for her exhaustion, she'd be a heck of a bad date if she fell asleep.

Michael entered the room carrying wine, two glasses and the antipasto. He placed the glasses on the side table and poured while she sat up. He glanced at the sheet covering her. "Shy all of a sudden?"

"A little, I guess."

He tucked himself under the sheet with her. "You look like you need a nap,"

"A three day one. Don't take it personally."

He nodded and ran his hand through her hair. "You're on a wild ride these days. You're entitled."

He held out the tray of food and she plucked a piece of cheese from it.

"That's the problem. I never sleep anymore. I sleep for an hour, wake up for two, sleep for another hour and by then I'm so frustrated I give up."

"I know that feeling." He turned to her, wiggled his eyebrows. "You need to come up with other things to do in bed."

She stuck her hand under the sheet and moved it along his hip. "Probably."

He grabbed her hand before she got to her intended target. "You're calling my bluff?"

"Gotcha."

"Smart ass."

Freeing her hand from his grasp, Roxann reached for the wine she'd placed on the side table.

"If I could get something to settle down at the office maybe I'd sleep a little, but I don't think that'll happen anytime soon. Max called today and told me they have nothing on the pressroom vandalism. They have no idea who tampered with the press. I also met with the pressmen and got nowhere. I'm out of patience. They destroy my pressroom and then they want more time off. As if I'm an idiot."

"Are you sure it was them?"

She shot him a look. "Are you and my associate publisher comparing notes?"

"Nope."

"I *was* sure it was them. Now I don't know. I guess it could have been another employee. Or maybe a freak accident. Anyway, the pressmen will probably strike when their contract ends next week. Not that it matters since they're on furlough, but I want to avoid a strike. They're working on a counter-offer, but we're so far apart it'll take a minor miracle to work out an agreement."

"What then?"

She shrugged. "After the press is fixed, we might have to continue leasing press time from the *Chronicle*. I don't know how we'll stay afloat. Our numbers are down, other than the spike in single copy on the day we ran the Taylor story—" She stopped talking. Oh boy, did she really say the Taylor story? How completely insensitive. She glanced up at him. "Sorry. That's what we call the story at the office."

"I knew what you meant, Rox." He leaned back into his pillow and propped a hand behind his head. "Why don't you get some capital to keep you afloat? Can't you dip into your credit line?"

"It's maxed out. My father, unbeknownst to me, used it to pay for the new presses that won't be ready until next year."

"He used the whole thing?"

Michael hadn't bothered to mask his surprise. She couldn't blame him. She'd had the same reaction when the bank informed her there was no available credit.

"The whole thing."

He shook his head, but stayed silent.

"I've thought about trying to find outside investors, but I'm not ready yet. I have some other ideas." Going without a salary was one. By industry standards her salary was low, but it would be enough to save a few clerk positions.

"You could always reduce your workforce."

"Absolutely not. Some of those people have been at the *Banner* for twenty years. I'll figure something out."

Michael shifted to his side and ran a hand over her hip. Taking pleasure in his hands being on her, she realized she had fantasized about this—relaxing in bed, ruminating over day to day life—and here they were. Talking business.

Somehow, it seemed right. Not many people understood her work issues. She could complain to Janie, but Janie had no frame of reference. Talking to her staff would be catastrophic. She didn't need the male executives thinking the lady publisher couldn't handle the job. And Max, he'd just lecture her.

Roxann lounged back into her pillow and smiled. Despite her grief and stress, her battered mind enjoyed this reprieve and she gave herself permission to savor it. No analyzing every word or touch. Just a conversation that eased her burdens.

She glanced at the mostly naked Michael as he studied the olives.

"What?" he asked.

"You're cute."

"Men don't want to be cute, Rox."

But he was, and this whole episode brought her shameless joy. What a concept. She didn't believe in happily ever after. Not anymore. No relationship could survive all the roadblocks they would face. She'd enjoy it while she could though.

Michael tugged on a strand of her hair. "How about I have a couple of my guys look into your pressroom problem? See if they can come up with anything."

"Look into it how?"

He pushed his hand through her hair, and then did it again. "I can't promise anything, but some people don't like talking to cops. I, unfortunately, have experience with that and sometimes it blows."

She knew he'd been questioned by the police again and assumed they were keeping tabs on him. She didn't want to acknowledge the idea that the police knew he was with her at this very moment.

"Are they harassing you?"

"Let's not talk about it. I'm in a good mood."

She understood. "Is my hair a mess? You keep playing with it."

He shrugged. "It's a good mess. Wicked sexy. I hate that you wear it back all the time."

That got her attention. She used to only wear her hair back when she ran. That changed twelve years ago when she became a neurotic control freak who needed everything in its proper place.

"It's easier. Plus, I'm surrounded by men all day and I want them looking at me like a publisher, not a wicked sexy blonde."

"So, maybe outside the office you could wear it down once in awhile?"

There was a thought she hadn't entertained in years. Now that he'd posed the question, she'd have to decide if she'd do it simply because he requested it. Was she ready to change her habits because he'd asked her to?

Absolutely not.

"Maybe," she replied, knowing she was a complete fool

who would surely give in because this was Michael, her Michael, and heaven help her, she got a thrill every damn time he came around.

ROXANN SLEPT. MICHAEL WATCHED HER CHEST RISE AND FALL with each quiet breath and thought maybe he could sleep too, right here next to her.

A few hours earlier, he'd have never guessed the night would end with the two of them in bed. So much for taking it slow, but he'd be damned if he'd complain. In the past, emotional ups and downs got his engines fired, but after his crappy marriage and his responsibilities to his family, he wanted peace of mind. Why couldn't his life ever be bland?

She snuggled closer and he rested his cheek on her head. He could do this every day. No problem. Whether or not he deserved it, he didn't care. He wanted this. His gut told him Roxann wanted it too, but she'd fight it. He'd have to convince her and that might take some time. Time he didn't have.

They had to find that intern and fast. The kid might know something that could point the cops in the right direction. His family and friends didn't deserve the scrutiny that went with him being a murder suspect. And hell, he wanted his freedom and a shot at a life with Roxann. If she'd have him.

Why the hell had he married Alicia? He knew the anti-Roxann theory had become the driving force behind the relationship. Not that it had been fair on his part, but it made sense at the time.

Alicia had yearned for Roxann's class and style, but didn't have the heart to pull it off. Sure, he'd been enthralled with Alicia's wit and adventurous spirit, but marrying her had been a mistake. She proved to be too high-maintenance and constantly needed attention. In the end, she'd turned to other men to satisfy her cravings for male interest and he'd stopped caring. A wasted marriage.

Roxann's hand moved across his chest and he glanced at her.

"Go to sleep, Michael. Whatever it is, it'll wait until tomorrow."

She'd known he was awake, thinking too much, and he smiled. Yeah, sleep sounded good. He scooted down, snuggled closer to her and closed his eyes.

Tomorrow they'd search for Bryce Cooper.

18

—————

"RISE AND SHINE, GORGEOUS. WE GOT AN INTERN TO TRACK."

Roxann opened her eyes and the sun peeking through the drapes framed Michael's wet hair. Morning. Already. He must have taken a shower. "What?"

The sheet came flying off.

"Let's go, Mary Sunshine. Vic is meeting us in half an hour and I need to stop home for clean clothes."

She pulled the sheet up. "What time is it?"

"Eight o'clock."

Eight o'clock. She shot up to a sitting position bringing the sheet with her. "I missed my run."

Michael pulled his watch off the bedside table and strapped it on. "You were sleeping."

She flopped back into the pillows. "I'm still sleeping." She'd already missed her run, she might as well sleep. Call it a sick day. She did own the place. And hadn't Mrs. Mackey been bugging her to take a day off? Well, that's what she'd do. Call it orgasm exhaustion.

He leaned over, braced his hands by her hips. "Honey, I almost woke you up the way I used to, but I took pity because you were so tired. I promise, if we find this intern and he's got something, I'll let you sleep for a month." The sheet was gone again. "Now, get up."

An hour later, Roxann knocked on Bryce Cooper's door while Vic stood behind her with his stupid I-know-what-you-did-last-night grin. She imagined spinning on him and kicking him in the shins. Just letting him have it.

"No one's home," she said when the front door remained closed.

Vic laughed. "No shit, Sherlock."

He backed up a few steps, gave the house a once over. Roxann did the same.

The two-story duplex sat on a tree-lined street located in Harwood Heights, a suburb northwest of the city. The house, similar to the others on the block, needed fresh paint and new screens, but the yards were tidy and the neighborhood appeared safe. Quiet too. Roxann marveled at the lack of traffic on the street.

She turned to Vic. "What're you thinking?"

"I'm thinkin' I'm gonna go in and have a look."

Her throat swelled. "*What?*"

"Chill, sister."

MICHAEL DROVE AROUND THE BLOCK TO SCOPE OUT THE BACK of the house. Vic sat next to him, his gaze darting along the opposite side of the street.

"You cannot break into that house." Roxann's voice carried the quiver of strained nerves. "What if we were followed? How do you know the police aren't watching?"

"We weren't followed. We'll just look around."

"Besides," Vic added. "We're not *breaking* in." He held up a small tool. "We're unlocking the door without the key."

Roxann stuck her face between the front bucket seats. "It's daylight. You'll get caught. What then? Especially given your current circumstances."

Vic snorted. "You don't think it's a good idea for us to get caught when Mike's up to his nuts with people thinkin' he killed his ex?"

She smacked him on the back of the head. "It's not funny."

"Ouch. Fuck." He turned and speared her with a look. "That hurt."

"Well—"

"Quiet down," Michael said between gritted teeth. "Let me think a minute."

How was a man supposed to think with all the damned chatter? He did a U-turn at the end of the block, cruised by the back of the house one more time and turned right, moving in the opposite direction. He needed to find a busy place to park so they didn't attract any nosy people. And stupid ass that he was, they should have taken Vic's car because of that damned GPS the P.D. planted. Busy place to park. That's what he needed. Then he and Vic would walk back to Bryce's.

"Thank God," Roxann said, but her relief was thwarted when Michael pulled into a McDonald's parking lot around the corner.

"Okay, Rox," he said. "You wait with the car."

He jerked his head toward Vic and got the hell out before she could argue.

"Wait." She climbed over the console into the front seat. "How long will you be? What if you get caught?"

Michael leaned one arm over the doorframe. They'd never been caught. Those words weren't in their vocabulary. "Give us thirty minutes and then go home."

"Go *home*?"

"If we get busted no one will know you were here. It'll be on me and Vic." He stepped back and shut the door before she could respond. Because surely she would respond.

Go home.

Roxann understood Michael trying to keep her out of it, but going home while they were carted to jail didn't seem right.

"What am I doing here?" What a nightmare.

Michael Taylor, Mr. Chaos. So much for her boring life. Here she was riding shotgun on a B&E. Max would love this. Her nerves were already fried *and* she might have to drive Michael's tank of a car. She'd never driven anything bigger than her four-door BMW, but she'd manage. Even if it meant bouncing the SUV off parked cars, or anything else that crossed her path, she'd get it done.

She opened the window halfway and turned the engine off. No sense wasting gas and the crisp, fresh air would calm her down.

Part of her couldn't help being revved up. A solid lead. All they had to do was find Bryce Cooper.

It had been an interesting twenty-four hours: Bedlam at the newspaper, sex with the long-lost love of her life, *and* aiding in her first criminal act. Not bad for a girl whose most recent adventure had been a trip to the hair salon.

Roxann waited an intolerable ten minutes, yearning for a cup of coffee, but too chicken to leave the car. What if they came tearing back with someone giving chase and she was in Mickey D's getting coffee? Sorry, hon. Needed my caffeine fix.

The clock on her phone clicked off another six minutes

and, blowing out a breath, she closed her eyes. Four more minutes and she had instructions to leave. Maybe she'd give them another five just to be sure.

Thunk.

What the heck? She turned to look over her left shoulder. A policeman, all of twelve-years-old, parked behind her and stepped up to the driver's side door.

They got caught. Suddenly she had to pee. Quite badly.

Keep it together, Rox.

Play dumb.

She counted to ten and took a breath. "Hi, Officer—" she glanced at his name tag, "—Bramble. Is there a problem?"

The cop smiled. "Your gas cap was open."

Whoosh. She eased a breath out. Michael, in a rush to gas up that morning, had forgotten to close the gas cap door. Roxann laughed and smacked her palm against her head.

"Dope," she said, making the cop laugh.

He peeked through the half open window into the back seat. "Everything okay?"

"Fine. I'm, uh, waiting for someone." Not a lie.

Bramble's gaze roamed along her body and Roxann instinctively folded her hands over her crotch. Ick. She swallowed hard. How incredibly rude of this cop, on duty, in full uniform, to put the moves on her. And worse, Michael and Vic would be strolling up at any second.

The cop smiled that oily smile again. "How about I buy you a cup of coffee while you wait?"

Roxann checked the rearview mirror. "Oh, well, thank you, but my friend should be here any time."

Where were they and did she really want them walking up to the car with a cop standing here?

The cop leaned against the car. *Great, now he's getting comfortable.*

"Your friend can look inside for you."

Okay, creepy man, time to go.

Not waiting for her answer, he reached for the door. *Dammit.* Now she'd have to get mean about it. A loud hammering began in her head and she grabbed for the door, but too late, he had it open, waiting for her to step out.

"What the hell?" Michael asked, grabbing Vic's arm and bringing him to a halt. They had just crossed the four-lane roadway heading back to the car when he spotted the cop opening Roxann's door.

"Holy shit."

The blood rush hit as Michael mentally fired off scenarios. Maybe she knew the guy? Maybe the cop recognized the car and thought Michael was in it? Maybe it was a friend of Max's? Maybe...maybe he had no fucking idea, other than it had nothing to do with what he and Vic had just done or they'd be in handcuffs.

He hustled toward the car, slowing down before he got too close. Who needed to get shot by a startled cop?

He stepped up to the car, saw a crazy-eyed Roxann—jeez, she looked freaked—or maybe pissed. Not sure. "Hey, Rox. Sorry, we're late."

Michael, forcing himself to stay calm, turned to the cop. "What's up?"

Popping out of the car, Roxann pecked Michael on the lips, but her eyes were wide open, silently begging him to focus on her.

"We were chatting," she said. "*I* left the gas cap door open and the officer closed it for me."

Nerves had carved a tightness into her face and he squeezed her hand. *Stay cool, Rox.* "Goofball."

Fwak. Vic smacked his hands together. "Hey, I'm starved. Who's ready to eat? Officer, can we buy you some breakfast?"

Vic worked the Mr. Congeniality angle to get rid of this cop, but the guy took a lingering look at Roxann and, like a gut punch, Michael got that this fucker was hitting on her.

"No, thanks," the cop said. "I'm just getting coffee."

"Coffee it is then. I'm buying." Vic took off toward the restaurant and dragged the cop with him.

Michael hung back. "We'll meet you in there."

Roxann collapsed into the driver's seat and smacked his arm. "You left the gas cap open. How could you do that? Do you know how nervous I was?"

What's with the smacking? He backed up a step in case she decided to hit him again. "I'm sorry."

"Yeah, no kidding. At first, I thought you got caught and then I realized that creep was trying to pick me up. Ew."

"I should crack that guy's skull."

"Hey," she said, "focus. You're here now and I want to leave. I'm so creeped out I need another shower." She shuddered. "I wish he were Chicago P.D. I'd have his butt in a sling for using his uniform to pressure women."

Michael took a breath, tried not to think about that asshole's hands on Roxann. What the hell was wrong with him? Bad enough he'd gotten her wrapped up in Alicia's murder to the point where she was taking fire from all sides. He'd have to work harder to keep her insulated. The selfish part of him loved having her back in his life and he didn't want to lose that.

He leaned into the car, ran his fingers along her chin. "I'm sorry about this. I never thought..." He shook his head. "Forget it. I'm sorry. Slide over while I get Mr. Hospitality back here." He pulled out his phone. "You want anything?"

Roxann climbed over the console into the passenger's seat. "Only for you to tell me you found something."

"It's his place. Looks like he's got a couple of roommates. He's working at a Jewel not far from here. We'll go see if he's there."

"How do you know he's working at the Jewel?"

"Vic found some paperwork in his desk."

Roxann flopped her bottom lip out. "He went from the mayor's office to a supermarket? That's a little odd."

"Jewel has a lot of employees," Michael said. "Easy to get lost."

It seemed getting lost was exactly what Bryce Cooper wanted to do. They just needed to find out why.

19

MICHAEL FOUND A SPACE AT THE END OF THE JEWEL PARKING lot. The place was a madhouse and even if they found the kid, with the store this busy, he probably wouldn't be able to talk.

"What's the plan?" Roxann asked.

Michael cut the engine. He had no right to drag Rox along on this, but she was the only one who'd recognize Bryce.

Plus, he had to agree with her that he couldn't be the one to approach this kid. Michael's picture had been all over the news and nobody would willingly discuss his dead ex-wife with him.

"You and Vic go in. See if he's around. I'll wait here."

She bobbed her head and reached for the door handle, but Michael grabbed her hand and wound their fingers together. "Relax. It might be nothing."

She squeezed his hand. "It might be something."

Michael grinned. "Let's hope."

"Hey, lovebirds, can we move along here?"

. . .

AFTER A BRIEF WAIT IN FRONT OF THE CUSTOMER SERVICE
desk, Roxann spotted Bryce coming around an aisle end-
cap. He was not the same kid she'd met a couple of weeks
earlier. His confident stance had morphed to a slump and
his neat, sandy hair was a tangled mop. What happened?

Her shivering from the frigid temperature in the supermarket—at least that's what she told herself—increased and
she rubbed her hands over her bare arms.

"This is him," she said to Vic.

"Showtime."

When Bryce saw Roxann, he hesitated and she imagined
him combing through his memory to place her.

Her palms started to itch.

Yep, they were on to something. Her fear melted away
and they stepped up to Bryce, introduced themselves and
explained what they wanted.

"What would I be doing at the Jewel if I worked in the
mayor's office?" he asked.

"Look," Vic said, his six-foot-five frame looming over
Bryce. "We know you worked in the mayor's office, so stop
dickin' around. All we want is information."

Roxann wasn't sure scaring the you-know-what out of
Bryce was the way to go, but she supposed Vic had more
experience with this type of thing. She laid a hand on Vic's
arm to quiet him.

"The *Banner* is doing a story on the mayor and we need
some corroboration. Can I ask you a few questions?"

Bryce looked at Vic then back to her. "I don't know
anything."

"You don't know what we want yet," Vic said.

The kid turned to Vic, who outweighed him by an easy
sixty pounds. "Fuck you."

Wow. All righty then. Roxann slid in front of Vic before

he made ground meat out of Bryce. She did her best desperate blonde girl routine, widening her eyes, silently pleading with him to talk to her.

"Bryce, please, I won't use your name."

He thought about it. Glanced around. "I have to get back to work. I need this job."

"I own a newspaper. I can give you a job. A better one than stocking shelves."

That got his attention.

He angled back toward the courtesy desk where the middle-aged woman standing behind it eyeballed them with the energy of a gossip columnist at a celebrity DUI hearing.

"Hold on a sec."

Bryce dragged himself to the wannabe gossip columnist and Roxann turned to Vic. "No man can resist a begging blonde. You all think with the wrong body part."

He laughed. "You're a witch."

"Yeah, but I got it done."

"I'm on break," Bryce said to Roxann without even a glance at Vic.

"Great, we'll buy you a pop."

The three of them sat at a small bistro table in the market's café. Vic, off to the side, straddled his chair and appeared relaxed, but Roxann knew he'd be dissecting every word.

"There's not much I can tell you. My internship was up and I left."

"Why did you leave before the end of the semester?"

Bryce shrugged. "I wasn't into it anymore."

"Really? You seemed excited about the job when I met you at the PBA fundraiser. Did something happen?"

Bryce stole a glance at Vic, who was doing a fine job of

looking completely uninterested. "The place is fucking weird."

"Watch your language."

This from a guy who considered it his personal mission to find a good use for the F-word.

"Sorry."

She cleared her throat, shot Vic a scathing look. "Bryce, I know you don't want to be involved in this, so let me tell you what we have and all you need to do is agree or disagree. I only need a second source."

She didn't have a *first* source, but Bryce didn't know that and, after Vic's admonition, he seemed ready to wet himself.

He scanned the café. "Okay."

"I assume you've heard about the Alicia Taylor murder?"

The vein at Bryce's temple began to throb and Roxann cut her eyes to Vic, but he either didn't notice it, or he wanted her to feign not noticing.

"I read about it."

Leaning in, she focused on him. "I think you more than read about it. I think you know something about the relationship between Carl Biehl and Alicia Taylor. *I* think you know why Alicia was murdered."

Bryce shook his head so hard it should have flown off.

Vic held a hand out. "Calm down, kid. Nothing's gonna happen to you. Tell us what you know and we're outta here."

"I don't know anything."

Vic sat straighter. "Do I look like a schmo?"

Bryce slumped in his chair and Roxann had a vision of something very large and criminal weighing him down. Maybe her crazy hunch was about to pay off because a burst of energy slammed her. She folded her shaking hands on the table. Part of her wanted to wrap this obviously terrified young man in a hug. The other part wanted to get on with it and catch a murderer.

"Bryce, I can help you. I have connections in the city. If you tell me, I'll get you whatever help you need."

After a deep breath burst free, Bryce dug his fingers into his forehead.

Come on. Crawl out on a limb with me.

"The night before that lady got killed," he said, and Roxann nearly levitated from her chair. *This was it.* "It was late, everyone had gone home. I was working on a project for Mr. Biehl at his assistant's desk."

"Was Carl there?" she asked.

"Yeah, but he was in the john. His cell phone rang. Then he got a text. Right after that, his *private* line rang. I figured it was his wife or something, maybe an emergency, so I picked it up. I mean, it seemed like someone really wanted to get him. It was a woman and I asked her name so I could tell him. They always told us to ask who it was and, I didn't want to get in trouble for picking up his private line in the first place."

"Who was it?" Roxann pressed, trying to keep him on track.

"She said her name was Alicia."

Hot damn. "No last name?"

"Just Alicia. I put her on hold until Mr. Biehl came back. I didn't know who she was, but I figured she was someone important because she had his private number. He tore me a new one for picking up his line, shut his office door and took the call."

"That was it?" Roxann asked. "Did you hear the conversation?"

She wanted to take notes, but feared any movement

would break the momentum and she hoped Vic could fill in anything she might forget.

"I heard him yelling. I couldn't hear all that much, but he was pissed. I'd never heard him yell that way and I was curious. I went into the office next door to see if I could hear anything. Figured it wouldn't hurt. I wish I'd stayed away."

"What was he saying?" Vic asked, his voice soft as if he'd morphed into an understanding guy.

"I heard him tell her she was trash. He said some really nasty stuff. I'm not real comfortable repeating it."

Roxann nodded. "I understand, but it's okay."

Bryce hesitated, looked at Vic and then Roxann again. "Um...well, he was just telling her she was a whore and um...well, something about letting herself be used."

Roxann heard Vic shift, but dared not look at him. Why bother? She knew what thoughts plagued him. She had the same ones and dreaded Michael's reaction to them. But still, this was a breakthrough. A big one.

She pushed past the sickness swirling inside her, needing to hear this. "Did he say who used her?"

"No. But they were going at it. He told her to never call him again and not to contact the mayor."

"The mayor? What did he have to do with it?"

Bryce shook his head. "I don't know, but after Mr. Biehl hung up, he must have called someone else because I went back to the desk and saw his private line lit up again. I went into the office to see if I could hear anything because, dudes, this is the stuff you see on TV. I should have been smarter and left. Anyway, Mr. Biehl was telling the person that Alicia was putting pressure on him about the Wingate thing."

Roxann, ever-so-calmly, shifted to Vic. "The Wingate thing?"

He shrugged.

"That's all I heard," Bryce said. "Anyway, the next day was when that lady got killed. I guess Mr. Biehl figured I'd overheard the call because he came to me a few days later and said he'd told the police about her calling the office that night. He said they might want to talk to me."

"What else did he say?"

"Just that he'd cared about her, that they were friends and had a fight. He didn't want me to think he'd ever hurt her. It didn't sound like he cared about her that night on the phone. The next day I was offered a job in the mayor's office."

Roxann's legs went numb. "*Really.*"

"Yeah, a Poly Sci major in his junior year getting offered a job as one of the assistants to the mayor's chief of staff. You know what it would take for me to get that job? A lot more than bustin' my ass as a free intern. It didn't seem right, so I got out of there. Mr. Biehl called me once after that to see if the police had contacted me and it freaked me out."

"Did the police contact you?"

He shook his head. "No."

No surprise. To protect the mayor from further scandal, Max would have made sure no one called Bryce.

"Are you wondering if Carl and the mayor had something to do with the murder?" Vic asked.

Bryce shifted to Vic; his mouth slightly open. "Wouldn't you?"

WHAT THE HELL WAS TAKING SO LONG? MICHAEL, TIRED OF waiting, opened the car door, but didn't need to go anywhere because Vic and Roxann rushed out of the store. Neither of them spoke and he took that as a bad sign.

Shit.

He pulled the car up, Roxann hopped in front and Vic in back.

"Bingo," Vic said

Michael pulled into traffic. "Bingo what?"

Roxann reached over and squeezed his arm. "Alicia called Carl's office the night before she was killed and they argued."

Something akin to a two by four hit him in the gut and a rush of air escaped. "Wait. I need to pull over."

He pulled into a gas station and parked. Instinctively, he knew parts of this conversation would be painful and he didn't want to risk Roxann and Vic's lives because he couldn't concentrate on his driving.

He listened as Roxann relayed Bryce's story with Vic filling in the parts she'd missed. He'd been faithful to Alicia until the day they'd separated and hearing about her exploits humiliated him, but now he had a solid lead. A sliver of something—hope maybe—solidified inside him. "We need to get on this Wingate thing."

Roxann already had her phone in hand. "I'm calling Phil."

Michael turned to Vic. "You believe this kid?"

"Yeah. He was crappin' his pants. He knows he's in some shit, but he doesn't know what it is. He's broke and scared."

Broke and scared. Michael had encountered that scenario before and it still haunted him. This kid had some bullshit luck. All he wanted was experience and he wound up in the middle of a murder.

Maybe Michael could do something about that.

WHILE MICHAEL MERGED INTO TRAFFIC, ROXANN RELAYED the conversation to Phil via speakerphone so she could jot notes and talk at the same time. *Don't miss anything. Get it all down.* Could her brain actually hold anymore? She just wasn't sure.

"I have to stop at the cash machine," Michael said, hooking a right into a bank parking lot on the corner. He got out and walked to the machine.

Roxann hung up with Phil and waved her phone in Michael's direction. "He's stopping for money now? What's that about?"

He took the money from the slot, grabbed a deposit envelope from the stack on the machine and stuck the cash into it. He wrote something on the envelope, put it in his back pocket and returned to the car.

"Mikey, Mikey, Mikey, what're ya doin'?" Vic asked.

"Shut up."

At that moment, Roxann may have been the only English speaking person in a foreign country. She became more confused when Michael pulled onto Bryce Cooper's street.

"We don't know jack about this kid," Vic said.

"You just said you believed him."

"He could be a good liar."

"Then you're losing your edge."

What were they *talking* about?

Michael parked in front of the house, walked to the door and stuffed the envelope under Bryce's door.

Roxann turned to Vic. "Did he just do what I think he did?"

"Yeah. Christmas came early, I guess. Don't say anything, he'll pop a vein."

"Why would he do that?"

"Pop a vein?"

"The money!" *Idiot.*

"Oh. Probably because someone gave him a foot up once."

Michael had given a stranger a handful of cash. She had no idea how much it was, but it didn't matter. The idea that he wanted to help this young man, despite how much it must have hurt to hear about Alicia's actions, filled Roxann with a sense of wonder. She shouldn't have been surprised. He'd always been generous with material things. It was the emotional stuff he got stingy with.

Michael jumped back into the car.

"You didn't need to do that."

He shrugged, put the car in gear and hit the gas. Clearly, he didn't want to discuss it. Well, that was fine.

His phone rang and he glanced at the ID. "This should be good." He hit the button and held the phone to his ear. "Hey, Arnie...Now?...Could they give me a little goddamn notice?...Right...I'll meet you there."

After clicking off, he tossed the phone onto the dash. "He got a call from Hollandsworth. They want to see me." He slammed his open hand against the steering wheel. "Son of a bitch."

"What do they want?"

"I don't know. Arnie says they have follow-up questions from the polygraph."

"What the fuck?" Vic said. "I thought you passed."

Michael glanced into the rearview. "According to Arnie I passed. He said if I didn't, they would have immediately started interrogating me. The cops aren't going to tell me that though."

"They probably just want to press you," Roxann said, hoping she was right. *It had to be a ploy. Had to be.* She dialed Phil. "I'm calling Phil back to see if his source can give him anything. If that doesn't work, I'll call Max."

Michael snorted. "Rox, you think he's going to tell you anything?"

"I have no idea, but I'm going to ask him. It beats wondering."

He checked the rearview again to get Vic's attention. "If I get jammed up—"

"It's not gonna happen."

"Right. But if it does—"

"I'm on it."

"What," she said, "are you two talking about?" She held up a finger when Phil's voice mail beeped. "It's Roxann. Call me back A.S.A.P."

Michael stopped at a red light and turned to her, held her gaze. "They might arrest me."

That snapped it. She didn't want to hear that from him. Despite their history, she was sliding headfirst into taking his side over Max's and risking the reputation of the *Banner*.

Max hadn't offered any solid proof that Michael was a murderer. And that constituted news. "They have nothing. What could they possibly hold you on?"

Vic grunted. "How about the two of you shut the hell up until he gets down there and sees what they want? They might be busting his balls and you two are having a coronary over it."

"He's right," Michael said.

More than likely, he just didn't want to discuss it any longer. Her phone rang.

"Saved by Phil," Vic cracked.

She waved her hand at him and punched the button. "Hi. Michael just got called in for more questioning. Can you check with your source and see what's up?"

"Call you back." Phil hung up.

Roxann breathed deep and counted off ten. *Relax. Start at the toes. Tighten.* "He'll call back."

Three minutes later he did just that. "What's up?"

"There's a witness."

"A *witness*?"

Michael swiveled his head in her direction.

"Whoa," Vic yelled because they nearly rear-ended another car. "Pull over, Mike. I'm driving."

Roxann snapped her fingers toward the side of the road and went back to Phil. "What did the witness see? Wait, hang on. Let me put you on speaker."

Mike and Vic changed places, and Roxann hit the speaker button. "Okay, Phil."

"A tall man went into the back door of Alicia Taylor's house the night of the murder."

"That's it?"

"Yep."

Vic made a face. "You got this, Mike. It's nothing."

Ten minutes later, they pulled in front of police head-quarters where a group of reporters stood huddled around Arnie Stark.

"So," she said, "clearly they've leaked you'd be here."

Michael dialed his phone. "Let me get Arnie in here. We'll go for a ride and tell him about this witness before we go in."

When Arnie climbed into the backseat, Michael intro-duced him to Vic and Roxann and they pulled from the curb at a leisurely pace.

Arnie gawked at Roxann. "*You're* the publisher of the *Banner*? Christ, they don't build publishers like they used to."

The moment of levity shattered the tension inside her and she laughed. She immediately liked Arnie Stark.

"Here's what we know," Michael said. "Rox's reporter has a P.D. source that told him the witness saw a tall guy going in the back door of the house the night of the murder."

"Do we know what time?"

"He didn't say," Roxann said.

Michael snapped his fingers. "Hold up here. If it was dark, the witness couldn't have gotten a good look at the guy. When Alicia and I were together, we never used that door and rarely turned the light on. I'd be shocked if that light was on."

Arnie jerked his head. "This is easy to check out. I'll get my investigator on it. Meanwhile, when we get in there, you keep your mouth shut. Let's go have some fun."

MICHAEL MARCHED INTO THE SAME SMALL, CAUSTIC ROOM where he'd originally been questioned. Once again, he forced his heart rate down, breathed deep without making a show of it and prayed for a break here. Arnie tossed his briefcase on the table and got the loud bang he was hoping for. "What's this about, gentlemen?"

Hollandsworth gestured to the chairs. "Have a seat."

Sure. Why not? Considering Michael's knees were shaking so badly he could barely hold himself up. Arnie scraped a chair back and dropped with a huff. Nothing but a bother, this being summoned.

For the first time since this mess started, Michael relaxed a fraction. Not only was Arnie Stark a top-notch attorney, he was a ball breaker to the nth and Michael knew he'd go to war for him.

"Mr. Taylor, a witness has come forward—"

Arnie lowered his head and stared at the detective over

the rim of his glasses. "A witness? Where's this witness been hiding all week?"

"Keep your shorts on, counselor," Dowds said.

Hollandsworth held up his hand. "The witness saw a man, about Mr. Taylor's height walking in the back door of Mrs. Taylor's home."

"What time was this?"

"Around 11:30 p.m."

Arnie stood and tossed his notepad in his briefcase. "Let's go, Mike."

"Maybe your client wants to make a statement?"

"Please, detective. It'll take three minutes for me to have my investigator confirm Mrs. Taylor's porch light was not on. And you got a witness that says they saw a man, in the pitch black, about Mr. Taylor's height—" He turned to Michael. "Let's throw these boys a bone. How tall are you?"

"Six-one," Michael said.

Arnie stuck out his bottom lip. "Huh, my brother is six-one. My neighbor is six-one. My *son* is six-one." He held a finger up. "I have an idea. Let's round up a bunch of guys who are six-one and put 'em in a lineup. With the lights off."

The detectives stared at Arnie as if he were dog shit that somehow landed on their shoes. Despite the rampaging energy consuming him, Michael remained motionless. Not an inch of movement. He was way over his head and until Arnie told him to speak, he'd keep his mouth shut.

Arnie, from his standing position, did the over-the-glasses stare and swung his head from Dowds back to Hollandsworth. "You got anything besides this witness who saw a man who could have been half the men in this city?"

The detectives stayed silent and Arnie scooped up his briefcase.

"Let's go, Mike."

No problem, boss. "Gentlemen," he said, nodding to the detectives on his way out the door.

THE INTERNET CARRIED THREE THOUSAND REFERENCES TO THE name Wingate and Roxann didn't have enough time to go through each hit. Sure, she could go through and narrow the search, but the chances of her missing something important increased with each link she eliminated.

Damn.

She stood to stretch. Everything ached—her shoulders, her butt, her head. All of it. She glanced around her home office, growled at the files on top of her desk and decided tonight would not be the night to tackle them.

Good news—sort of—came earlier when Michael phoned to give her the details about his visit with the detectives. Still, it seemed they were grasping for something and right now, Max had shut her out. She'd have to rely on Phil's source for any information.

The laptop chimed the arrival of an email and she stooped to check it. The pressmen had sent their response to her latest offer. Well, good for them because she hadn't expected it until the following morning.

After the hectic day with Michael, did she really want to read this email? Who was she kidding? She could moan about the craziness with Michael and Vic, but it gave her a rush. That duo had a frenetic energy about them and it brought her alive again.

As much as she told herself not to fall for Michael, she'd done it and in a ridiculously limited amount of time.

She'd become a failure to control freaks worldwide.

Roxann sighed. Maybe those control freaks should try resisting a man who gave a struggling college student a stack of cash, or who managed to look movie-star handsome while pounding out a five mile run. He could *sweat* sexy. Incredibly irritating.

And what about the splintered heart he'd left her with? She still didn't have any answers from him and that was unacceptable. In fact, no more sex until he 'fessed up to why he left. She could do it. She could hold out. Just because she'd given in last night didn't mean she was a shoo-in.

She couldn't allow him to put her off on this subject. She deserved answers. No matter what his reasons were, even if it hurt her all these years later, she had to know. Not knowing had been easier with him out of her life. Now that he'd come back, those buried emotions needed to be freed.

She stared at the email from the pressmen. It would be a counteroffer or she'd have received a call telling her they had agreed to *hers*.

With her mood in the tank, she might as well read the email. Sitting down at her desk, she highlighted the important parts. Four ten-hour days a week *and* a pay increase. Ridiculous. She ran a *daily* newspaper. They needed to work all seven, otherwise, she'd have to *hire* more to rotate in on the fifth, sixth and seventh days. The *Banner* would lose money across the board. No can do, boys.

The email had come from Rick Turnbull's office. Rick was a decent union representative, but if she gave a little he'd take more. She dialed his number.

Voice mail.

It didn't stop her from telling him she was rejecting their proposal. She'd given them a fair offer, one she had busted her butt on, and she'd had enough.

Could this be it? The final act that would make the dreaded strike a reality? Somehow, all the worrying that had gotten her here didn't seem worth it. Weren't they getting a newspaper out without presses? Weren't they managing?

She sat back in her chair and, oddly enough, smiled.

She could do this.

"I FOUND WINGATE," PHIL DAWSON SAID AND ROXANN nearly kissed him full on the mouth.

It had been three days since she'd given Phil the Wingate tip and she'd begun to worry it was a dead end.

Excitement energized her and, amazed at the steadiness of her hand, she motioned for Phil to sit. "What is it?"

"*It's* a *he*. Leland Wingate. He owns a construction company on the west side. I knew the name sounded familiar, but I couldn't remember. I searched the *Banner's* database and found an obit for Wingate's father. The obit mentioned he was the founder of L&L Contracting."

"Tell me they've done work for the mayor?"

"The city. They have a contract with streets and sanitation. Also, his son is rumored to be involved in racketeering. I called L&L, but the office manager is new and doesn't know anything." Phil held up a finger. "I did find the last office manager and—get this—she's filing a sexual harassment suit against Leland Wingate."

"Why does that matter?"

"She hates her old boss and gave me the name of an ex-foreman to talk to." Phil flashed his teeth. "He's the magic bullet. He won't go on record, but Wingate is greasing the director of streets and sanitation by way of a hundred grand a year for the renewal of the contract. Plus, they're short-pouring the concrete—paid for by our fine city—on the sidewalks and using the extra for side jobs."

"He's making money on city funds?"

"Yep."

"How does he know about the bribery?"

Phil scoffed, "He once made a delivery of ten grand in cash. That's why he won't go on record. He's afraid he'll be prosecuted. I told him I'd see what we could do. I think the guy wants to confess."

Roxann rested her head against her chair. She had to think. Had to stay focused and not get wrapped up in what this might mean for Michael. *Concentrate on the story and what it means for the* Banner.

"So, is this what Alicia Taylor knew? Does it trail back to Carl or the mayor?"

Phil shook his head. "No. But I'm guessing the money's floating up and Carl and the mayor are getting a piece."

A vision of tomorrow's front page with Leland Wingate's picture on it flashed in her mind. Now they were getting places. "Maybe Carl confided in Alicia about it? Talk about motive. Is it enough to kill someone over?"

"I'm still digging. I need another source."

Roxann put up a hand to high-five him. "Get one other person to confirm it and run that sucker. Front page, maybe even top of the fold. Nice work."

Phil smiled full wattage. "Thanks, Roxann."

"Can you lock it in before deadline?"

"I wrote the story already. If I can find a second source, we're good to go."

She rose and walked him to the door. "Run it by Mitch. I'll call him, but I want the lawyers to check it before it runs." They didn't need a libel suit on a story this big. "I'll reach out to the state's attorney and see if we can get your source a deal."

"I think my source knows someone else who's involved. If we get him a deal, I think he'll give me a name."

"Okay," Roxann said. "I'll see what I can do."

She shut the door behind him and dove to the phone to call Michael. She'd give him the news then call her contact at the state's attorney's office.

If the *Banner* could prove Michael's innocence it would be a win for the paper and for her. She'd be able to establish her worth as a publisher and maybe, just maybe she and Michael could have a fresh start.

While waiting for him to take her call, she yelled to Mrs. Mackey, who poked her head in the door. "Please get me Tim Griffin in the state's attorney's office."

Griff, this could be your lucky day.

"I am loving this," Roxann said, laying the day's newspaper down on Michael's desk. "We broke a major scandal at City Hall."

He flashed a grin that caused an explosion in her chest. Happy to see her? Or was it the story? She didn't care. It had been a wild two days but the *Banner* staff had pulled it off.

"A good story *and* the guy got fired."

Roxann floated to the sofa and dropped onto it. "His problems are bigger than being fired. He's going to jail. The state's attorney raided L&L this morning and found all kinds of funky accounting. It'll be in tomorrow's paper. Three days of huge stories and we got there first."

She rested her head back and giggled. Yes, giggled. *Who knew?* Didn't her first major coup as publisher allow her to be silly?

Feeling the silence in the room, she rolled her head toward Michael who, with his black dress shirt, rumpled hair and five o'clock shadow could have graced the cover of *GQ*. "I called a couple of times and your crabby assistant told me you were in a meeting. That was a few hours ago. And everyone yells at *me* about working too hard." She smacked her hands together. "It's seven o'clock. Pack it up. I want to celebrate."

He grabbed his pen from the desk and tossed it in a drawer. "I just finished signing checks. It's always the last thing on the to-do list."

While Michael organized his desk, she studied the black and white photos of various city buildings lining the walls and realized the office represented its owner. Masculine and tasteful.

"This sofa is a dream." With sprawled legs, she burrowed her leaden body into the sofa, and closed her eyes. She could sleep. For a long time.

"Has the mayor called you?"

"Twice yesterday, three times today. He wanted to know if I knew anyone that could fill the streets and sanitation job." Despite herself, she laughed at her own joke. How could she joke about this? Must be the lack of sleep. "Phil hasn't chipped this iceberg yet. There've been corruption rumors for years. Our esteemed mayor is feeling the pinch."

She opened her eyes, saw Michael staring at her and sat a little straighter.

"Don't do that." He rose from his chair and moved toward her.

"What?"

"Get self-conscious. You can relax in here." He sat next to her and propped his feet on the glass-topped coffee table. "My assistant was nasty to you?"

"I think she's nasty to everyone." She shifted to face him and idly stroked her fingers down his forearm. "You need to do something with her. She's awful. Think about how she must treat your clients."

"I know."

"So, fire her."

"I will, it's..." He shrugged. "She's a single mom with a couple of kids. I feel bad."

He didn't want to put her out of a job. Roxann had to appreciate that. As rough-edged as he seemed, he had a huge, soft heart and she nearly sighed. *Get a grip.*

She patted his leg. "*You're* the one who's been nagging me about my lobby guards. At least they're nice to people."

He focused on her hand resting on his thigh and pointed at his crotch. "Uh-oh." He grinned like an idiot. "Mr. Happy is awake. I'd better lock the door."

Roxann laughed and scooted into the corner of the sofa, but he returned from locking the door and leaned over her.

"Don't you dare." She smacked the top of his head. "Stop it. Mr. Happy needs to go back to sleep."

"Too late." He levered himself over her and kissed her neck, his lips moving up and down, up and down, until her skin tingled.

Yow.

That warm little buzz she felt every time he kissed her made its way into her chest as he ran a hand up her leg and under her dress. The warm buzz turned to raging panic because—heaven help her—they were in his office. She grabbed his wrist. "We can't. Not in your office."

"Everyone's gone. Besides, it's my building and I've never done it in my office."

"But—" The thought trailed off as an involuntary motion forced her to lift her rear so he could slide her dress over her hips.

"There you go," he said.

Oh no. How did she get to being stretched flat on the sofa?

His magic fingers trailed down her legs. "You little tease. You wore this garter to torture me."

"Uh—no—well—maybe?" She whapped herself on the head to clear the fuzz. "What did you say?"

But really, what did it matter what he said when he had just unsnapped the garter? He brushed his fingertips against the inside of her thigh and the combination of gentleness and scorching heat made her gasp.

She wanted him.

She wanted him inside her.

Now.

Apparently, her no-sex-until-he-fesses-up vow took leave. *Bye-bye.*

She pulled him on top of her and kissed him until her body burned. What a fool she was. *Fool. Fool. Fool.*

He backed away and yanked her underwear off just as a knock sounded at the door.

"Go away."

"Mikey, open up."

Roxann's heart seized. Vic. Of all people. "You said everyone was gone."

Michael shrugged. "He must have been in the gym."

He glanced toward the door where Vic jiggled the handle from the outside. "Beat it!"

"What're you doing in there?"

Michael laughed. So did Roxann. She slapped her hand over her mouth.

"Who's in there? Roxann? Open this door before I kick it in."

"You kick in that door and we're going a few rounds. Fuck off. We're busy in here."

She sucked in a breath. "Don't say that. He'll know what we're doing."

Michael grinned. "You think he hasn't figured out what we're doing? Behind a locked door?" He ran a finger down her cheek, his eyes warming her. "You're so funny. Sometimes I can't stand it."

"I'm gonna sit out here until you open this door," Vic shouted.

Michael sat up, rested his elbows on his knees and grunted. "He'll do it. The son of a bitch will sit out there until I open the door."

The devil inside Roxann urged her on. She shouldn't have been surprised. That same devil had been locked away for twelve years and had time to make up for. Damned Vic. The one time she didn't want him around, he showed up.

Well, so what? They were all adults. And adults were allowed to have sex.

She nudged Michael with her toe. "Let him wait."

He raised his eyebrows. "You'll never live it down. He'll terrorize you."

"I'm waiting," Vic shouted.

"He's going to terrorize me anyway. I might as well get *some* pleasure out of it."

After three seconds of thinking about it, Michael stood and removed his pants. "You asked for it."

"I did indeed." She'd even moan a little louder just for Vic.

"You two are *nasty,*" he yelled.

Yes, yes, we are, she thought, but it felt better than anything she'd known in a very long time. This beautiful, generous man who was afraid to fire his assistant made her want more of him than there could ever be, and she knew, without a doubt, she loved him.

Still.

20

IMMERSED IN THAT ODD SEMI-CONSCIOUS STATE WHEN THE brain says wake up, but the body says no, Roxann twitched. A disconnect. Dreaming?

She forced her eyes open and focused on the ceiling fan. *Her* ceiling fan. Her bedroom.

The distant sound of sirens pulled her further awake and she inched her head toward the nightstand clock. Three-oh-eight.

The phone rang. A ringing phone at 3:00 a.m.?

Emergency.

She snatched the handset.

"Roxann? It's Mrs. Martinez. Your car is on fire."

"Huh?"

"Your car is on fire," Mrs. Martinez repeated, throwing some volume into it.

My car is on fire?

Roxann dropped the phone, kicked off the sheet and sprinted to the back bedroom with her heart pounding as fast as her feet moved.

With hands that seemed steeped in molasses, she reached for the window blinds. *Come on, come on.* The blinds finally up, she pressed her hands against the glass.

She sucked in a breath. "No." A bright orange blaze engulfed the interior of her car and spread shadows across the darkened alley. She leapt backward. *This can't be happening. Wake up. Still dreaming.*

She pinched herself. Hard. *Yow.* Definitely awake.

The sirens drew closer. Mrs. Martinez, her elderly neighbor, must have called 9-1-1.

Roxann needed a plan. She peered out the window again. Furious flames lashed at the car's windows and managed to escape out the rear driver's side. Did the fire shatter the window?

She grabbed a robe, slipped into her running shoes and, with her feet barely hitting the stairs, flew to the kitchen. Fire extinguisher. Kitchen pantry. She whipped the pantry door open. On the floor, to the right. *There it is.* She sprinted to the back door, fire extinguisher at the ready.

A flash of red lights bounced off the Martinez house and a fire engine let out a *whoosh* as it came to a stop. A squad car sat idling on the other side of the alley, its headlights facing the truck while two uniformed officers stood watching the blaze.

Firefighters in full gear bounded off the truck and hooked the hose to the fire hydrant a few doors down. Roxann remained on the porch holding the useless fire extinguisher while the heat from the blaze burned her eyes. Bad scene. *Say goodbye to the interior.*

Neighbors had spilled into the alley to watch, but the firemen ushered them out of harm's way while Roxann found herself drawn to the spectacle of it. She watched with a detached fascination as two hundred gallons of water soaked her little BMW.

How had this happened? Gas leak? Electrical fire?

Foul play?

Her shoulders sagged. No. She couldn't get emotional. She had to deal with the situation.

To her amazement, the fire department knocked down the blaze in a little over a minute. A really long minute. Several firemen opened the doors and sprayed the interior while others checked the trunk and under the hood. No flames.

Roxann bolted off the back porch and approached the firemen huddled around the ruined car. Steam rose from the hot metal and the pungent smell of burnt plastic invaded her senses.

"Is this your car, ma'am?" a firefighter asked.

She nodded and her hair drooped in front of her face. *Shoot.* No hair clip. Did she need to look like a sex kitten in front of the fire department? She tied her hair into a knot behind her head. *Control. Maintain control.*

One of the patrolmen wandered over, but remained silent as her body began to quake. She folded her arms to create warmth and willed herself to not fall apart. *Start at the toes. Rebuild.*

"Do you know what happened?" she asked one of the firefighters.

"Yeah. Someone torched your car."

"HOLY SHIT," MICHAEL SAID WHEN HE CAME AROUND THE SIDE of the house and saw the charred wreckage of what used to be Roxann's car. Car bomb. Had to be. His jaw began to throb and he unclenched his teeth.

A band of firefighters worked at packing up the truck while Roxann stood to the side. She spotted him and hot-footed it over. "How did you know about this?"

"Gina called me. Her friend is married to one of these guys. I hauled ass over here. Are you okay?"

She looked okay. Her eyes were sharp. No tears. Of course. Why on earth should she be upset over someone toasting her car?

"I'm fine. They said it was arson."

He grabbed her hand, rubbed his thumb over her knuckles. "I figured."

She stood there, staring at what some dickhead did to her car, but showed no signs of stress. Typical. And she'd been alone when it happened.

Michael rolled his shoulders. *You did this to her.* What if the house had caught fire? She could have been trapped inside. The nerves in his neck flared again and he put his hands on his hips. Either that or he'd pulverize something.

"Mike, how's it goin'?"

Michael turned to see Tom Farrell, dressed in his beat-up fire gear, coming toward him.

"Hey, Tom. Thanks for the heads up."

"Yeah, no problem. I knew you guys—" Tom gestured toward Roxann, "—were friends."

"What the hell happened?"

"Looks like someone broke out the back window and threw a cocktail in there."

"A Molotov cocktail?" she asked.

"Yes, ma'am. We put the fire out before the windows popped, but the back window was broken."

Michael turned to Roxann. "Didn't you hear the glass breaking?"

Her shoulders flew back. Battle stance. *Shit.*

"I was sleeping. On the *other* side of the house. Sometimes people do that at 3:00 a.m."

Their eyes held for a minute. Yeah, his tone had been a little harsh. "Sorry."

Roxann waved him off and, figuring he'd give her a minute, he moved to the car to inspect the damage. The inside was flambéed. Totally gone. All that remained was the charred metal of the seats and the steering column. On the outside, black soot marks spotted the hood and the paint had started to burn off. Michael wrinkled his nose at the acrid smell.

Roxann stepped around him and inventoried the damage. She remained detached, maintaining that ever-important control that sometimes made him nuts, but he knew this was her way of coping. "Have you gotten any threatening calls?"

She shoved her hands into the pockets of her robe. "Nothing specific. A couple of hang ups."

What? "Nothing specific?" The words came out slow, but his blood pressure hit launch. "A couple of hang ups and you didn't think to mention that? After what happened on your run that day? You're shitting me, right?"

"I didn't think it was anything."

Such a liar.

"Yeah, you did. You *chose* to ignore it."

Frustrated, he turned and stalked away. *You did this to her.* He'd never meant for her to be in danger by helping him. All he'd wanted was to clear his name and if she got a great story for her newspaper, it would have been a win-win. This, he hadn't counted on, and rage gripped him. Every nerve in his body crackled and he balled his hands into fists. He pondered making the house his victim, but a broken hand wouldn't help. *Dammit.*

He spun back to Roxann. "Anything else you were ignoring? Hate mail? A brick through your goddamned front window?"

The stone-faced glare she gave him should have shrunk his balls.

"Knock it off with the sarcasm."

"How could you not tell me about those hang ups? We could have had someone check it out."

Okay, he was yelling and she was getting that don't-scream-at-me look. Not good.

"It could have been a wrong number," she said. "I hang up all the time when I dial a wrong number and get voice mail."

Michael held up his hands. Arguing would be pointless. "Right. Perfect. I'm not fighting with you. Won't do me any good because I know how you are. You're *always* right."

She rolled her eyes and opened her mouth, but he cut her off. "Let's get this taken care of." He flicked a thumb to the cop standing with one of the firemen. "You want to file a police report?"

"You bet I do," she snapped, seriously pissed at him.

And yet, as she stood there, arms folded, eyes narrowed, there remained a steadiness to her and he wanted to applaud her for holding it together. Part of him wanted to see her get mad and let that emotion rip, but she'd been taught to handle things without drama. Her way was probably better than the screaming and yelling he knew, but he wanted to see her get wild. The way she'd done in his office hours earlier. Especially if it ended the way it did on the office sofa.

Jee-zus. They had a situation here and he was thinking about getting in her pants. Get it together, man. "You're being an imbecile," he said to himself.

Roxann stepped over, her eyes bigger than Mars. "*Excuse me?*"

Oops. "Not you. Me. I was talking to myself."

She eyeballed him a minute, the color draining from her face. Placing her palms over her eyes she said, "I must be insane."

Michael wrapped his fingers around her wrists and the cold from her skin evaporated under his hand. "I'm sorry. I didn't mean to—" He stopped. What could he say? He went into maintenance mode. "You need to call the insurance company. Have them tow it. I can do that for you while you talk to the cops."

Roxann pulled her hands from her face. "I'm still mad at you."

"Yeah, I got that."

She sighed, glanced at her torched car. "Well, you're irritating, but I could get used to having you around."

He liked the sound of that. Stepping closer, he gave her a peck on the lips. "Careful what you wish for."

Her reaction, even if she had one, remained imperceptible. She didn't shove him away or laugh him off, but she didn't encourage him either. Fine. Maybe they weren't ready to talk about the future, but the disappointment settled on him. *Damn.*

"The number for the insurance company is inside," she said.

He picked up a peanut of a fire extinguisher. "You were going to put out that inferno with this?"

"It's for putting out fires isn't it?"

How could a guy not admire a lone woman willing to fight a fire? "Is there anything you're afraid of?"

"There's one thing."

He smiled, feeling triumphant that she'd admit it to him. "What's that?"

"You breaking my heart."

21

Roxann's mother poured steaming decaf coffee into the delicate cups she loved. Roxann tended to be more of a thick mug coffee drinker, but the pretty floral cups fit her mother. Even dressed in workout clothes, her mother carried the sophistication of a woman who'd been cared for. Tonight, she wore her shoulder length blond hair pulled back at the base of her skull and her eyes, normally a deep, warm green, looked faded, washed-out. Fatigued.

"What's wrong with your car?" Mom asked, setting the carafe in the middle of the table. That often seen habit gave Roxann the feeling of home and safety and a belief that the world had not gone nuts.

Her mother's kitchen stretched across the back half of the house, but the dark oak cabinets and the corner hearth gave it a cozy feel. The house, despite the Stickley furnishings and precious treasures that filled it, seemed empty without her father, but being there helped Roxann feel close to him.

"The car is in the shop." Not a total lie. She left out the part about it being torched by a psychopath. Her mother had enough on her mind without worrying about a destroyed car and what it might mean for her daughter.

Roxann didn't know if the pressmen were responsible, or maybe someone close to Carl, but they had succeeding in terrifying her.

Unfortunately for them, her fear had boiled to anger and she wouldn't quit until she had some answers. Who knew what that meant for her personal safety?

"It'll be good to get your father's car on the road. It's been sitting in the garage since—" Mom broke off.

Since he died. "I know." Roxann forced a breath through her collapsing throat.

Mom fiddled with her cup. "I was thinking I should sell it. It doesn't seem right to have it sit there."

"Really?" Sell it? How could she even think of selling it? Her father cherished that car.

"I'm not sure what to do. What do you think?"

"I don't know." Did they have to talk about this now? "Let's think about it some more. I might keep it for myself."

"Oh." Mom's eyes welled up and she reached for Roxann's hand. "That would have made your father happy."

That tore it. She turned away. Too much pain.

"I'm sorry, honey."

Roxann closed her eyes and counted off ten. "I'm fine." She opened her eyes, breathed deep and sensed her control coming back. "I talked to Max this morning. He didn't have much to say."

"You know Max. I wish he'd find a wife. He's my brother, but he can be a dead bore with that harping."

Roxann clamped a hand over her mouth. Her mother railing on Max was an unexpected pleasure. His freeze-out was still raging. She'd called him to get a read on his mood and was met with single word answers. He'd have to get over it.

"Mother, sometimes you're hysterical. Max is mad about the press coverage. The mayor must be bugging him." She took a sip of her coffee, eyeballed her mother over the rim of the cup. "*You've* never said how you feel about our recent coverage of City Hall."

"Your father left you in charge and I won't question that. I don't disagree with your decision, but the situation bothers me. I know Carl's wife from the club and she is a loyal, loving woman. She deserves better."

"I'm sure she does. That's not our fault though. Max needs to lay off."

Her mother held her hands out. "I'd prefer not to have family problems, but I know you wouldn't have allowed the story to run if it weren't true. It was a business decision. Your father would have run it. Max will adjust."

Roxann nodded. A business decision. Her mother didn't know the half of it. Their bottom line had plummeted—far—due to the cost of off-site printing. At least the single copy sales had spiked on the days an Alicia Taylor or City Hall corruption story ran, but the newspaper's future couldn't rest on newsstand sales.

Roxann needed an influx of cash. Fast. The bank had declined her request for an increase on their credit line and no other bank in the city would touch them right now. She would have to put her personal holdings and newspaper stock up as collateral. It wouldn't come close to bailing them out, but it would buy her time. The presses would be fixed within the week, hopefully, and then they'd get back to business as usual.

"Just so you know, Mom, the story is accurate. I don't

know what it has to do with Alicia Taylor's murder, but we're moving in the right direction."

Mom set her cup back in the saucer. "Would you have pursued this story if you hadn't had a relationship with Michael?"

Knew *that* was coming. "Absolutely. This is big news. My personal feelings have nothing to do with it."

"But no one wants to know they once loved someone capable of such a thing."

Mom sat still and erect, as if they were talking about spring flowers rather than someone's murder. It seemed ridiculous on several levels and Roxann felt a tightening between her shoulders.

"Where's this going, Mom?"

"You never let yourself deal with your feelings about him. You've never talked with me about it, but you can. I hope you know that."

"Thank you." Roxann smiled. She hoped it was a smile. "But there's nothing to talk about. He's helping with the story and we're getting to know each other again."

Liar. She enjoyed having Michael around. Her cheeks went hot as she thought about their nights of lovemaking and the way he simultaneously brought out the best and worst in her. Adventure came back to her life, and his presence freed her from her neurotic tendencies. And wasn't that the most welcoming experience she'd ever had?

Still though, they hadn't reconciled why he'd left her and she couldn't completely give herself over until she had answers. A quiet hum drifted through the air and Mom waited, her eyes unwavering.

Roxann twisted her lips. She was mentally whupped. Again. The constant emotional collisions drained her. "I always thought the hurt would go away and I'd stop

wondering why he left. It never went away. I guess I
compartmentalized. Now the questions are nagging at me
again. I need to find out what happened and put it behind
me. I'm sick of being afraid to love someone."

Mom poured more coffee. "Have you talked to Michael
about it?"

Roxann snorted. "He won't tell me. He says he can't.
Whatever that means. This is part of the problem. He's still
hiding from me. I trust him to protect my business, my
home and even me—" she jabbed her fingers into her chest,
"—my physical being, but when it comes to my heart, I have
a war inside me over whether to trust him."

Mom stiffened.

"What's wrong?"

"Nothing."

"Something is bothering you."

Mom slouched a little, then sat straight again. Steadying
herself. What the heck?

"I think I can help."

O-kay.

Her mother slid her hand back and forth, back and forth
on the table. Nervous. A tingle of alarm crawled up Roxann's
arms.

"What is it?"

Mom closed her eyes, thought for a second then opened
them again. "There's no easy way."

"Mother, you are seriously freaking me out, so you'd
better say whatever it is, and fast."

"I think I know why he left."

Roxann had no words. Nothing. Nada. The tornado
zipping through her had sucked them up.

"The night of your father's fiftieth birthday, he told me

he'd had a talk with Michael." Mom hesitated. "He was trying to help, but it didn't turn out that way."

The ball of panic simmering in Roxann's belly began to expand. "What are you talking about?"

"It started out innocent enough. Your father wanted to see what Michael's intentions, so to speak, were. His employment plans and such. What he expected from his future. We knew you were in love and your father had concerns."

Roxann battled to focus. "What exactly was said during this *talk*?

"As you know, Michael was a bit hot-headed back then. He took exception to your father asking and I guess they had words. I don't know all that was said, but your father was very angry."

"It was none of Daddy's business."

Their eyes met briefly before Mom looked away. "That never stopped your father before. He wanted things for you."

"And he didn't think Michael could give me those things?"

Some irony. Michael's company was now worth more than the *Banner*. This conversation wasn't all that shocking to Roxann because she'd known, down deep, her father had never totally approved, but the idea that her father approached him without her knowing screamed of betrayal.

Michael wasn't a doctor or a senator, and the great Paul Thorgesson couldn't have that for *his* daughter. Damn him. And now, she couldn't even confront him with this. Roxann counted to three. *Rebuild, rebuild, rebuild.* "The military had taken an emotional toll on Michael. He was trying to find a place for himself and Daddy had no right to interfere. It was my life."

Her father had caused the breakup. She'd relied on him. Trusted him. And he'd betrayed her. No. *Start at the toes, tighten, tighten, tighten.* All the way up to her shoulders she went until her body turned to rock.

"Your father wanted to get him a job. A good job."

"He *had* a job. Construction wasn't good enough, I guess? Daddy wanted a doctor or a lawyer, not someone emotionally unbalanced because he'd made a commitment to his country. He deserved a thank you, not to be treated like a loser."

Mom stood and stretched a hand out. "I told your father I thought it was wrong and he should have kept out of it. Obviously, the conversation didn't go as your father expected and Michael used some rather graphic language to tell your father to...well..."

"Shove it?" Roxann offered. "Good for him. I can't believe I'm just hearing this. All those years lost. I could have fixed this."

It was hard to imagine how different things would be if they, including Michael, had been honest with her. Such stupidity.

A deluge of memories hammered at her. *Whap. Whap. Whap.* Over and over again until she thought she'd be sick from the beating. She remembered the party and Michael's sudden irritability. His suppressed anger.

His need to leave.

He'd shrugged off her inquiry as to why his mood had gone south and drove her to her apartment, leaving her to worry about him and his inability to express his rage. The ferocious anger had frightened her back then. And now she knew why. Her father had made it clear to him that he was unwelcome when all Michael wanted was to find a place to belong.

Her father had humiliated him.

After the party, Michael had vanished for three days. Three days of unreturned phone calls and Roxann overanalyzing every conversation, wondering what she'd done wrong. He eventually came back with his car packed.

No explanation, just goodbye.

"You and Daddy let me be miserable, let me wonder why I wasn't good enough and what *Alicia* had that I didn't. You both could have saved me years of heartache. I don't understand." She cleared her throat because—*dammit*—a noose had grabbed hold of her. "I just don't understand. How could you and Daddy have done this to me?"

The color in Mom's face faded, but Roxann felt no remorse for her harsh words. The course of her life had been changed because of her father's haughty attitude and she had a right to be angry.

Running a hand over her forehead, Mom said, "I'm sorry. So was your father. He knew what he'd done, but he was terrified of losing you. It was the only thing he ever feared and he couldn't face it. I should have made him tell you, but I didn't want him to be unhappy. We were worried you'd go after Michael and never come back. I know it was selfish, but as time wore on, we felt it was too late to tell you."

"And to see me happy, rather than as the publisher of the *Banner,* would have been unacceptable? You were right. I'd have given up the newspaper, that's how much I loved him. All my options were taken away."

Roxann covered her face with her hands. Unbelievable. She'd been deceived by her parents. And by Michael. These were the people who loved her?

And suddenly, her chest locked up. She opened her mouth, but nothing came, no air, no words, nothing. She stood in her parent's kitchen wanting to rage at her father's selfishness, but no, he was gone—dead—and she could barely come to terms with that, never mind being mad at him and unable to express it. How had her life gotten so mangled?

Her mother waited in silence, a grieving widow trying to deal with the mess her husband left behind. Then, as quickly as the fierce anger had taken hold, it evaporated. *Poof.* Screaming at her mother wouldn't help.

Quietly, she retrieved her purse and, with cement feet, walked through the mudroom where she lifted her father's keys from the hook before heading into the garage.

"Roxann, you're upset. Please don't drive."

Upset? She was beyond upset. She didn't even know what this was. "I need time alone. I have nothing to say now."

She smacked the button on the garage door opener and slipped into her father's car. The lingering scent of jasmine from his cologne clung to the interior and she drew a scalding breath. He was everywhere. And nowhere. Damn him for interfering. It suddenly occurred to her that no matter how proud he'd been of her, how affectionate and loving, he couldn't stay out of her life. He had always pushed her, guided her decisions on schools, jobs and friends. Molded her to what he thought she should be. Now she couldn't even confront him over an injustice that had changed her life.

Her mother lunged toward the car. "Please don't go."

But Roxann waved her away and backed out of the driveway. She stared at the house and its stately white columns and brick façade. The lawn and bushes expertly manicured. A not so perfect home.

The faultless image she'd conjured of her father had

been shattered. His meddling ways, no matter his intention, had stolen her joy and now she was forced to grieve for the man he was and the man she *thought* he was. Everything had changed.

The last weeks had enlightened her on what an average businessman he'd been. She'd once thought of him as a corporate dynamo, skillfully running his company, but each day the mistakes he'd made, the ones she now cleaned up, chipped away at her vision of him. She, of course, would take responsibility for those mistakes to avoid tarnishing her father's reputation, but she had to find a way to deal with her own naïve illusions about him.

She hit the Kennedy and pushed the accelerator on the beloved Jaguar. This car had always been fun to drive, particularly with the top down, but tonight all she wanted was to get home.

When she found herself on Lake Shore Drive, she had no misconceptions as to where she'd wind up. She reached Oak Street and glanced up at the corner building with the gold tinted windows.

The lights glowed in Michael's apartment, and she pulled into a no parking zone and handed the doorman her keys. He could move it if necessary. The doorman chose not to argue and made a quick phone call to Michael's apartment to let him know he had company.

Only when she was about to ring the doorbell did she hesitate.

Michael opened the door before her finger hit the buzzer.

"Hey," he said. The nasty look she fired must have clued him in to her mood because he reached for her. "What happened?"

She brushed his hand aside and darted into the living

room where Stevie Ray Vaughan complained about being caught in a crossfire. How appropriate. "Nothing good is what happened."

"I see that."

The scent of Michael's soap, clean and woodsy, surrounded her and she breathed it in. She loved that smell.

This whole damn scenario tore a piece out of her.

She went to the sliding glass doors where the gloomy sky over the lake engulfed her in a cold darkness. She turned toward Michael as he lowered himself onto the arm of the sofa. He wore running shorts and a white sleeveless T-shirt that made his arms look like tree trunks.

"Problem?" he asked, knowing full well there was one. A big one.

"I'm mad at you."

"I see that."

She stalked back to him. "Tell me what happened the night of my father's party."

His jaw locked and he motioned for her to sit. Buying time.

"It's old news," he said. "Doesn't matter anymore. You want something to drink?"

"Stop stalling and tell me."

"Seems you already know."

"My mother chose tonight to enlighten me. It appears the people who supposedly loved me the most played with my life. You and my parents lied to me. And here, after all these years, I've taken a risk with you. Based on what I learned tonight, I must be one hell of a fool."

He gave her a look, obviously not happy with her sarcasm. Too bad.

"It's not worth rehashing."

"Tell me what happened."

"We're different people now. This—" he gestured between them, "—can be whatever we want it to be."

"Not until I get some answers it can't. I'll stay here all night if I have to, but I'm not leaving until I understand."

Holding her stare, he shook his head, clearly resigned to the fact that she wouldn't give in. "Why not?" he said. "Let's bang it out and put it behind us."

Now they were getting somewhere, but Michael's fingers twitched at his sides. He so did not want to do this.

"Your father cornered me, wanted to know what I was doing with myself. Hell, Rox, I couldn't get a night's sleep without nightmares of someone's head getting blown away. But your father wanted to know about my stock portfolio. I had two hundred bucks in the bank."

"What did he say to you?"

He ignored her question and slammed both fists against his forehead. "I never wanted to have this conversation."

Roxann watched as he uncurled his fingers and worked them in and out, pulling his temper in check. He brought his gaze to her, and there, in the depths of those dark eyes, she saw that he'd finally tell her.

He marched to the table by the front door, snatched something from his wallet and flicked his finger against it.

"I wouldn't have told you, but if it's that important to you, you win. This is the only time I will talk about this. I'm done having it in the way. Got it?"

She slid to the sofa, not at all sure she got it. "I need to know."

Resembling a man about to be hanged, he dropped into the chair across from her with that slip of paper—*a newspaper article?*—still in his grasp.

"I was not the guy your father had in mind for you."

"Not true."

He held up his hand. "Let me finish. The conversation started out typically enough. You know, concerned father stuff. Where's my life going, that sort of thing. He said you deserved a good life."

Michael grunted. "A better life than I could give you. As if I didn't know I had no right to put my hands on you."

"I always supported you. Always."

Above all, she knew that. *Knew* it. From the night they'd met, he'd often remarked she was too good for him and it would irritate her to the point where they'd argue. And here she was, about to fight that same damned battle.

She drifted back to the first night he'd slept at her apartment. Her roommate had been away for the weekend and she'd asked Michael to stay with her. They'd been inseparable for the better part of a month but, despite several invitations, he'd refused to stay the night. In this instance, his protective instincts had kicked in and, not wanting her to be alone, he'd agreed to stay.

She lurched awake in the middle of the night with Michael thrashing beside her, his arms and elbows flying in all directions. *Nightmare.* He'd briefly mentioned them, but had always changed the subject.

"No," he groaned, kicking one leg against the sheet.

Definitely deep in it. Not knowing what else to do, she poked him hard enough for him to feel it. "Michael, wake up."

Suddenly, he raised his arm, made a fist and—*oh, no*—swung at her. She sucked air as her heart slam, slam, slammed inside her—*move*—and ducked away just before that monster fist connected with her cheek.

She rolled over, off the side of the bed and peeked back at him, now flat on his back, but his arms still flailed, striking out at some unknown predator.

Wake him up before he gets hurt. Jumping away from the bed, her head banging, she ran for a broom. As much as she wanted to help him, she wasn't crazy enough to touch him again.

Gently, she poked him with the stick end. "Michael, wake up."

He smacked at the broom, mumbled something but continued to thrash. Never had she seen him like this, so deep in the throes of terror. Something inside her broke away.

"Michael!" She gave him another solid poke, this time a good solid stick right to the ribs.

After bolting upright, he grabbed the end of the broom and yanked, the force pulling her off balance. She tumbled forward, crashing onto the bed. Well within his reach. *He might still be asleep.* In that brief moment, the merest of seconds, fear took hold, pressed her into the bed, holding her there. *Protect yourself.* She threw her arms in front of her face, squeezed her eyes closed and waited for the blow.

Nothing. The bed went still. No thrashing. No movement at all, only the sound of Michael drawing a breath and holding it. She opened her eyes, found him staring at her huddled on the bed, shielding herself.

From him.

She watched as the realization of what happened hit him and his face transformed into a slack-jawed look of horror.

"Shit," he said, his voice raw and broken as he held his hands up and away from her. "Did I hurt you?"

Launching herself at him, she locked her arms around his neck, holding him close, skin to skin, so he knew she wasn't afraid. "No. Never. I know you'd never hurt me. Not intentionally."

He began to shiver. The shiver grew into full-blown quaking and his breaths came in deep, haunting gulps as he fought against the onslaught. "I'm sorry, I'm so sorry, I'm so sorry."

"Shhh, it's not your fault. You didn't hurt me. I know you wouldn't. I love you. You'd never hurt me."

She loved him. And he was hurting.

They had rocked gently on the bed, back and forth, her stroking his back until his breathing quieted. "I love you," she had said, over and over again.

"I have no right to you."

For the second time that night, her heart had ruptured. He just refused to accept his worth to her.

All these years later, Roxann would never have guessed they'd still be debating this topic. Either way, she was sick of it. Dreadfully sick of it.

"I never felt you weren't good enough for me. You had to know. You could have told me about my dad and I *would* have handled it. We'd been through so much, how could you think otherwise?"

His expression softened. "You couldn't have handled this one, Rox. It was too much of a problem."

"Oh please. It was a conversation. An argument. I could have talked to him."

Michael shook his head. There was more. Had to be. Not much rattled him. He stood, went to the terrace doors and looked out before facing her again. She spread her hands wide in front of her, but when he stayed silent, she stepped over to where he stood. Without a sound, he shoved the article toward her. *Don't take it.*

Somehow, from that empty pit of her stomach, she knew the article had been the flashpoint. Her hand trembled as she reached for it. *Stop. Don't take it.* She didn't want to know. *Rewind. Back button.*

But she couldn't go back. She'd been begging Michael to tell her and now he was finally willing. She curled her toes. *Deep breath. Tighten. Tighten. One, two, three.*

"What is it?" she finally asked.

"It's an article about a robbery."

"Pardon?"

She snatched the article from him, unfolded it and read. One man arrested in a three-man robbery attempt. Skimming the article she saw the name Jerry Foyle. Michael's friend. Oh no...no. Bile curled, hot and nasty and burned up her throat.

"Your Dad gave me that," he said. "He had a background check done. Wanted to make sure I could live up to the Thorgesson standards."

"What does this article have to do with you?"

"A week before I was to report to basic training, Jerry and two other guys held up a convenience store. Jerry got caught. The other two guys bolted, but security videos showed them with masks on. One of the guys was built like me and I went to the top of the suspect list because Jerry and I hung together."

Too much, too much. "Oh, no."

"It wasn't me, Rox, but the P.D. didn't know that. They had no evidence and couldn't build a case, but I left for basic with suspicion hanging on me. And Jerry wasn't talking. I was pissed about that, but he'd have bigger problems if he snitched. With the life he chose, that crowd would have found a way to kill him in prison."

"Everyone thought you were guilty." And here they were again with everyone thinking he committed a crime.

"Yeah. Jerry did his time and kept his mouth shut. They

never caught the other two guys. After my eight years in the army, the robbery was old news and I was able to put it behind me."

Roxann held up the article. "Until my father hit you with this."

"He figured I was guilty, but told me he'd use his influence to help clear me. By that time, the statute of limitations had expired and the P.D. couldn't have charged me, but I still wanted my name cleared. Your dad wanted me gone and, if I went, he'd work the system for me."

"Did you tell him you were innocent?"

"Sure. He didn't believe me and I told him to fuck off. That I loved you and I wanted to marry you. That didn't fly. He threatened to tell you about the robbery and convince you I was guilty."

With the article still in her fingers, Roxann covered her face with her hands. How could her father have done this to them? *To her? Start at the toes. Tighten. Tighten.*

"And you thought I'd believe you were guilty? You didn't think I cared enough to support you?"

Michael gripped her arm. "I knew you cared, but my thinking got whacked. I wanted to get to you first, tell you everything, but he saw it coming and told me you'd probably take my side. I went to find you, but by the time I'd gotten there I realized he'd played me. If I had told you, you'd have fought him, but there would have been a rift between all of us. Plus, I had no way to convince you I was innocent, and I didn't want you to have doubts. Either way, I was screwed because you'd be in the middle. You loved him and it would have destroyed you."

Her father had always—always—controlled her life from behind the scenes. Yes, she loved him, adored him, for all the opportunities and strength he'd instilled in her. For convincing her she had the power to make her dreams come true. And yet, her father's love annihilated the one relationship she had always wished for.

How did she not know about this? Had her mother known about the robbery? She couldn't have known. *Please, let me at least believe that.*

"He should have left us alone."

"Yeah and you'd have told him that. That's the issue."

"Oh, shut up." She was pointing at him now, jabbing her finger. "You and my father played this out and I was clueless. Didn't I deserve to know? When you love someone, you fight for them, and you didn't. My future, *our* future, got tossed away. And then you married someone else and I spent years thinking about it. *Stewing* over it. I'd see pictures of your wife in the society pages and I'd wonder what she had that I didn't. Years, Michael. All wasted."

"Down the road," he said, his voice quiet like the moment after a death. "you'd have resented me for it. Every time I screwed up; he'd have reminded you that you took my side. No way in hell was I living that way."

He puffed his cheeks, let the air out slowly. He'd suffered too. The humiliation alone must have been awful. She had to calm down. Quiet the chaos. *Deep breath.* "You left without giving me an explanation. I had to hear from the grapevine you were in L.A. That wasn't fair."

"I won't argue. I thought it would be better if I left you alone."

"You were wrong."

Michael huffed. "I was wrong about a lot of things. My intention was to get my shit together and come back. Eventually, they arrested one of the other guys on an unrelated charge. He wound up flipping on a bunch of people and one of them was involved in the robbery with Jerry. That at least gave me satisfaction. I came home to prove to your father I was worthy of his daughter, but it was too late. You were already in Philadelphia."

No, she wasn't going for that. She shook her head. "I'd have come home. You never bothered to ask, or to even call."

"I *did* call!"

The niggling feeling that had been with her for so long coiled around her spine. Instinctively she knew, but wanted to hear him say it.

"When did you call me?"

"I tracked you down, got your number and called after work one night. The guy that answered said you didn't want to talk to me. I tried a couple more times, but you never answered and I gave up. I thought you were ignoring me because you were over it. How was I supposed to know whether your dad had told you about the robbery or not?"

She thought back on a phone call she'd always wondered about. The one that would have obliterated the agony. "I'd heard the phone. Joel told me it was a wrong number, but he had acted strange. We'd been dating a few months and he cared for me. That doesn't excuse what he did, but he knew about you and was probably afraid I'd go back to Chicago."

Michael waited and she sensed the question he wanted to ask. It was the same thing she had wondered about Alicia.

"Did you love him?"

"No. He wanted more than I could give. I broke it off and came home. By then, you were with Alicia. I hated you for coming back and being happy with someone when I was still so torn up."

"When you didn't call me back, I thought we were over. That was the only reason I got serious with Alicia. I thought you had moved on."

That didn't make her feel better. "I deserved an explanation. I loved you."

He moved in front of her. "You thought your father walked on water. I didn't know how you'd handle him not being in your life and that's what would have happened. I still believe it. Yes, Roxi, I should have just let him talk, but he pissed me off and I gave him what he wanted. I left."

Roxi. For the first time in all these years, he called her Roxi and it should have been a sixteen-inch knife going through her. She'd dreamed of hearing it and now it seemed so pitiful and sad.

He stroked his fingers down the side of her neck, let them rest on her shoulder. "I was too dumb and scared to know he had manipulated me. By my whacked-out way of thinking, if you had to hate me, it would be because I was an asshole rather than a criminal."

"I didn't hate you. I was confused and hurt."

"I'm sorry. You'll never know how much. I've carried that article in my wallet all these years. I worked my ass off to prove I was a better man than what your father thought of me. Every time exhaustion set in, I pulled the article out and got pissed all over again. When I jumped him on the list of Chicago's wealthiest, well, that was a fucking party. A one-man party. I got so drunk I couldn't see. The real ballbreaker was that it didn't matter. I wanted to show him, and when I finally got there, I was still miserable. I may have been successful, but my wife was a stranger and my marriage was wrecked." He stopped, waved a hand. "For what it's worth, I don't think your mother knew about it. Your dad told me it would stay between us.

This was too much. Roxann's brain refused to absorb it all. Maybe she'd wake up and it would be over. Her father would be alive and she'd still be living in her lonely little utopia of denial.

Denial seemed a lot better than this hell. She'd mourned for Michael by closing herself off, banishing her dreams of love because she'd been unwilling to risk the pain that came with loving someone.

All because of odd circumstances and lies. If her parents had been honest with her, if Joel had given her the damn message, if she'd have tried to call Michael after he'd gotten back to Chicago, her life would be different. The what-ifs tortured her.

He inched closer; his concern evident as his gaze met hers. "You okay?"

"No." She could finally admit that she was not okay. Hadn't been okay in a long time and being here, with him, rehashing all that heartbreak would do her no good. She pushed by him and headed toward the door. "I need to go."

Catching up with her, he clasped her arm. "Rox."

"Please, let me go."

His gaze darted over her face, but she held firm and gently pulled her arm free. Yes, she'd do the running this time.

"It's a lot," he said, "but we'll get through it."

"There's a reason all this happened. I don't know what it is, but I'm worn out. I have to go."

He grabbed his keys. "I'll take you home."

"I have the car downstairs."

He didn't like it. That she could see, because he stood with his hand on the door knob, hesitating to move, probably wondering if it might be the last time she'd be here with him. Finally, he shoved his keys in the pocket of his shorts and opened the door.

"I'll walk you out."

. . .

MICHAEL THOUGHT HE MIGHT JUST BE MAD ENOUGH TO KICK King Kong's ass, but arguing with Roxann wouldn't help, so he'd walk her to her car and figure out what to do on the way.

With everything out in the open now, the opportunity for them to start fresh existed. Maybe the timing was fucked up with Alicia's murder hanging over him, but he knew Roxann believed in his innocence.

Roxann walked beside him in silence. It irritated him when women were silent. It went against the laws of nature because they were supposed to be yapping about every damn thing until a guy thought his head might explode.

They stepped into the elevator and he pushed the lobby button. He couldn't lose her again. Not over the same damn thing. Maybe she needed time to deal with the anger. She deserved that, but if he gave her space it could mean her walking away. He couldn't risk it. Not when they had an opportunity to have a life together.

When the elevator opened, he let her exit first and the doorman handed her a set of keys.

"It's still in front," Hal said.

They stepped into the cool night air and the wind whipping off the lake puckered his skin. Damned cold all around. Michael opened the car door, watched her get in and leaned down.

"I can take you."

"I'm fine." She didn't bother throwing him a glance. He hated fine. Fine always meant far from fucking fine.

"I'll call you tomorrow. We're not done with this." He stepped back and shut the door. No sense giving her the opportunity to disagree with him, which she would do. He watched her pull into traffic and cursed himself for his mistakes.

When she turned off Lake Shore, a crackle of panic fired through him and replaced the chill of moments before.

Would he be that much of a dumbass and let her leave?

No.

He headed inside and took the stairwell to the parking garage because, this time, he'd face the problem.

When he got to Roxann's, he ran up to the door and pounded on it. A few seconds later, she pushed the curtain aside and, with her eyes shooting fire, snatched the door open.

"What?"

He grabbed her face in both hands, hauled her up and kissed her hard enough that she'd get the message he wasn't giving up. If she pushed him away, he'd know she wanted him out of her life. After the incredible night they'd spent, when the uptight Roxann let herself go and allowed him make love to her in his office, he couldn't imagine her pushing him away.

If she did, he would fight harder. He'd wait as long as he had to, but he wouldn't let her get rid of him.

Funny thing, she didn't push him away. She stayed there, kissing him, wrapping herself around him and creating enough heat to roast a city. *Amazing woman.* There would never be enough of her. He'd always crave her. Twelve years of being without her told him so.

He pulled back, searched her face for a hint of what she might be thinking. Good? Bad? Nothing there. *He'd* have to give *her* the answers. Or, at least try.

"We can work this out," he said. "I never thought I'd find it again—what we had—a whole world of our own. I thought I'd had my shot. Now I've got another, and I won't blow it this time. Take a risk, Roxi. You'll see."

No answer. *Dammit.* But he knew that armor of emotional control sustained her. Right now though, he would have preferred to know her thoughts. She bit her lip and those blue-green eyes sparked. Decision time.

She stepped back from the doorway and waved him in.

Score.

"I'm still mad at you," she said when he stepped through the doorway.

"Yeah, but I'm not running."

22

The next night, seated across from Roxann at her kitchen table, Michael stretched in his chair and rubbed his hands over his face. Could he be two days late for a shower? That's how it felt anyway. After combing through an entire box of the investigator's notes, the only thing he knew was Alicia had fucked half the city. He'd seen all of this before but the revisit pissed him off. He had been busting his hump trying to keep her in expensive clothes and all she wanted was to get *out* of them.

"We've been reading this crap for hours," he said. "What am I looking for?"

Roxann, dressed in running shorts and a "Just Do It" T-shirt, clucked her tongue. "Anything that looks...well...odd, I guess."

He had to laugh. "It's all odd. Did you know that my wife had sex with a surgeon in the back of his SUV?"

"I'm sorry," she said. "Go back to reviewing the security tapes."

Tension buzzing under his skin, Michael stood. Sitting

was making him nuts. "I figured another set of eyes on what you were doing would move things along."

Roxann dropped the report she was holding. "You were questioned again today."

Not a question, but a statement. She knew. Phil must have spoken with his P.D. source. Michael moved to the doorway and leaned on the doorjamb.

"An hour. No big deal. They don't have anything. They're so bent on locking me up, they don't realize I've got nothing to give them. Besides, Arnie provides entertainment."

Jesus, he felt pissy. He'd tried to shrug it off as a day in the life of Michael Taylor, but the constant scrutiny wore on him. For everyone's sake, they needed to find Alicia's killer.

"This must be hard for you."

He tapped his hand against the wall. "What?"

"All of it. People staring at you, wondering if you killed her. Reading about your wife's bad behavior. It's tough for me to read and I didn't know her. I wouldn't have liked her."

"You and Alicia were different. She used her body to get what she wanted. You use your brain."

"Did you love her?" Roxann bolted straight and shuffled the pages in front of her. "Forget it. I don't want to know."

More paper shuffling.

"I thought I loved her enough. Then things changed. Being here with you, knowing what I missed. No, I didn't love her. I wanted to believe I did." The shuffling ceased and he stepped to the table, put both hands on it and leaned in.

"She wasn't a good wife to you."

He shrugged. "Maybe I was a shitty husband. After awhile, when my efforts at saving my marriage didn't work and my energy was shot, I mentally checked out. By then I was wondering why some guy hadn't snatched you up."

She walked over and hugged him. Nice. He'd come to

rely on the simple pleasures that Roxann brought. Those pleasures had been missing.

"That," she said, "is the most honest exchange we've had since this whole thing started. Maybe I should have asked sooner."

"Ah, Roxi. I'm sorry." He pulled back, held her at arm's length. "I screwed everything up. If I'd have talked to you back then, none of this would be happening. We could have had a great life together and now, who knows?"

"Don't give up." She waved a hand toward the boxes. "The answer is here. I know it. We just have to find it. I want that life we could have had."

The phone rang. Crappy luck.

"You should answer that," he said. "It could be work."

She scooted down the hall to the living room in search of the cordless. "Hello? Hey Phil...No problem. What's up?"

Phil. Michael wandered to the living room, stood in the archway and she gave him a thumbs up. What did that mean?

"*Really?*" Something Phil said snapped her to attention. "Let me call Griff and float it. Great work. Thank you."

She clicked the phone off. "That was Phil."

"No kidding?"

She walked toward him, stuck her index finger into his belt and pulled him closer. "It's good news." Her eyes wandered to his crotch then back up.

Hello. Rise and shine, Mr. Happy, time to go to work.

"You want to hear what he said?"

"Maybe later. Mr. Happy has an urgent message for you."

She wiggled her eyebrows. "I *love* Mr. Happy."

"Honey, he loves you too."

Fifteen minutes later, to Michael's vast disappointment, Roxann grabbed a blanket off the sofa, pulled it to the floor and wrapped herself in it. "*Now* do you want to hear what Phil had to say?"

Hearing about Phil was probably the last thing he wanted, but hell, he'd humor her. He slipped into his underwear and sat next to her on the floor. "Tell me."

"Our pit bull reporter talked to the recently terminated director of streets and sanitation, who, of course, is facing criminal charges."

"Of course."

"So," she said, enjoying herself. "The not-so-esteemed director has decided to blow the whistle on corruption at City Hall and—" She held up a hand when Michael opened his mouth. "Wait for it." She poked him in the arm. "He wants a deal. He'll talk if the D.A. will lighten his sentence. Yes." She pumped her fist in the air. "We broke this story."

Michael gave her a squeeze. "Good for you, Rox. Great news."

She scoffed, "Don't you get it? We're getting closer. I'm convinced Alicia was murdered because she knew something about Leland Wingate. Add the intern to this new information and I think these little pieces are coming together."

She was riding high and he was a jerk for not sharing in her triumph, but someone had to keep things in perspective. Unless this guy knew something about Alicia's death, there probably wasn't much he could say that would crack the case. The corruption story was big and the *Banner* would get its praise, but the murder hadn't been solved and he didn't want Roxann getting ahead of herself.

"Don't be so negative. Yeesh." She grabbed his T-shirt, slipped it on and walked to the kitchen. "You want a drink?"

A little thrill shot through him at the sight of her in his shirt, but he didn't want to get too comfortable with that. It wouldn't last if his ass landed in prison. "Pop. Thanks," he said from his spot on the floor.

"Hey," he yelled a minute later thinking she was in the kitchen.

"What?" Roxann said from behind him and he jumped about three feet. She handed him a can of pop.

"Jeez, you weren't gone that long."

"I'm fast, remember?"

"Speaking of which, where are your Olympic medals? I figured you'd have them framed or something."

Roxann sat next to him and took a sip of her water. "Shoebox in my closet."

Olympic medals in a shoebox? In the *closet*? "Why?"

She pursed her lips. "I had them out for awhile, but then I put them away. Too many memories of a life I gave up on."

Talk about a showstopper.

She turned to him and patted his cheek. "Sorry. Didn't mean to be a downer."

"What did you mean by that?"

She shrugged. "I was twenty-three and an Olympic medalist. I had dreams of future Olympics, maybe coaching, but I knew my parents, my father mostly, would be disappointed. I was too young to realize I could have done it my way. The medals became a constant reminder. You know me, out of sight, out of mind. Compartmentalize it and it's a non-issue, or so I thought. Instead, I'm dealing with presses that don't work."

Michael tugged lightly on her hair. "You could still coach, couldn't you?"

She screwed up her lips. "I guess."

"Something to think about anyway."

"Yeah, I need something else to think about."

"You can do anything you put your mind to. That's why I

came to you for help. You're the most honorable person I know."

"Keep talking that way and I might have to keep you around awhile."

Michael smiled. "Honey, I'm counting on it."

THE NEXT EVENING, MICHAEL OPENED THE CAR DOOR, BUT held up a hand before Roxann could get out. "Are you sure you're up for this? It'll get ugly."

"Stop it," she huffed. "I can handle this. I'm good with a tough crowd." She shoved his hand aside, got out of the car and stood on the Taylor's tiny front lawn. Mother Nature had gifted them with a seventy degree day, and Roxann absorbed the warmth of waning sun while she contemplated facing a houseful of Michael's family for his father's birthday dinner.

Suddenly feeling overexposed, she ran her hands over her sweater and buttoned two buttons.

Michael held out his hand. "Here we go."

There were aunts, uncles and cousins everywhere. She'd forgotten what a large family Michael had. His mother, Rose, reintroduced her to everyone in the house and then took her to the backyard, where Michael's father, Frank, held court.

Who knew all these people could fit into a fifteen by twenty yard?

"My birthday present is finally here," Michael's father yelled when he saw her. "I told you mopes she'd be here."

After Roxann had shaken hands and kissed every uncle, she made a vow to skin Michael for leaving her. Where had he disappeared to? She spotted Gina across the yard and made a beeline for safety, but was intercepted by the soon-to-be-skinned one. "Where've you been?"

He leaned in and kissed her on the cheek. "Sorry, I got sidetracked. Come with me, I want you to say hi to someone."

Once across the yard, they stopped next to a man Roxann recognized as Michael's friend, Jerry. Max had warned her about Jerry and his rumored criminal connections, but he was Michael's friend and she'd treat him as such.

"Roxi, you remember Jerry, right?"

Jerry, movie star handsome with his dark hair and blue eyes, held his arms wide and gave Roxann a hug. She had to smile. Who could resist such a greeting? It made it hard to believe what people said about him.

"It's nice to see you, Jerry. How've you been?" She prayed he wouldn't mention The *Banner*'s continual coverage of his rumored exploits.

"I can't complain. I hear you're trying to help my friend here. You need anything, you let me know."

Roxann turned to Michael and squeezed his hand. The man had amazing friendships. "I will do that."

"Oh, and listen, Mike tells me you're interested in coaching track."

She cleared the sudden hairball in her throat. "Uh, it was a conversation."

Jerry pursed his lips. "You know that rec center going up on the south side?"

"Sure," she said. "The one for at-risk kids."

"Yeah. My buddy owns part of it and he's looking for volunteers. The center has a huge track, but no one knows what to do with it."

Something flickered inside her. "Really?"

"No pressure or anything, but having an Olympic medalist involved would get some kids in the door and, well, forget about the fundraising opportunities."

Roxann slid a sideways glance at Michael. He smiled, but it wasn't the full throttle Michael smile. *Yeah, buddy, you're in trouble.* Probably. She should be mad at him for not checking with her before he spoke to Jerry, but she couldn't be. Knowing him, he wanted to help her get back some of what she'd let go.

"What do you think?" he asked.

She turned back to Jerry. "Have your friend call me. I'd like to hear more about it."

"Roxann," Gina hollered from the back door. "I need your opinion on something."

Saved by the yell.

"You'd better get in there," Michael said. "See if you can talk to her about those skimpy clothes she wears. She's a mother for God's sake."

Roxann rolled her eyes. "You're an idiot. If I had that figure, I'd wear those clothes too."

"Not in this lifetime, babe," he yelled after her.

WATCHING ROXANN AND HER LONG LEGS MAKE THEIR WAY across the yard would never be a hardship. The legs, they got him every time. Michael turned to Jerry and shuddered. "She's killing me."

Jerry, eyes still on Roxann, said, "What a way to die."

Michael snapped his fingers. "I need a favor."

"Name it."

"Rox has a mess at the paper. You probably read about it. Someone loosened something on the press and the whole thing went to hell. She's trying to figure out if it was one of the union guys."

Michael hesitated. He hated asking Jerry to do this. In fact, he hated having any association at all with Jerry's business, but information was king.

Being one of his oldest friends, Jerry knew Michael wanted a legitimate life and had always respected that. Michael didn't mind stepping outside the lines if the reasons were important, such as keeping an innocent man out of prison, but he wasn't interested in being a career criminal.

"You want me to ask around?"

Michael nodded. "If it's a problem, we'll forget I brought it up."

Jerry lifted a shoulder. "I'll let you know." Something caught his attention. "My wife is giving me the look. I'll call you in a couple of days about the pressroom thing."

23

BLAM. BLAM. BLAM.

What the hell?

Michael sat up in bed, heard the noise again. Someone was pounding on the door. He shot a glance at the clock. 6:00 a.m. *Jesus Christ.*

Roxann, still half asleep, rolled over. "What is it?"

"I don't know."

The sleepy fog crept into his voice and he cleared his throat before slipping on a pair of shorts and the T-shirt he'd tossed on the chair. He headed toward the front door where the pounding continued. *Would you give a guy a minute?* He checked the peep hole. No one there.

"Chicago P.D.," someone shouted. "Open the door!"

Shit.

The gut shredding panic hit him and he doubled over, sucking in deep breaths. Everything spun but he put a hand on the wall and concentrated on the design in the floor tiles. He'd been anticipating this day—the day of his arrest—but how does a guy emotionally prepare for that?

"Michael?"

Still bent over, he turned his head and saw Roxann standing a few feet behind him. *Oh, crap.* This was happening with her here. Could it get any worse?

Her cheeks sagged at the sight of him doubled over. He needed to compose himself. If *he* acted calm, everything would go easier.

He straightened. "This is probably it, Roxi. I have to open the door or they'll break it in."

Without waiting for a response, he flipped the bolt and the door flew open. Loud, demanding voices filled the entry foyer as two uniformed cops shoved through and pushed him against the wall.

Michael's body spasmed with the instinct to fight. *Don't make it worse. Let them do what they have to.*

Roxann, wearing ratty sweatpants and a tank top—*Jesus* —remained frozen in her spot. He'd dragged her into this and now she had to face the humiliation of being with him during his arrest.

"Michael Taylor, you are under arrest..." Hollandsworth, the gray haired, pain-in-the-ass lead detective's mouth was moving, but the words trailed off and Michael didn't hear the rest. His body slipped to an alternate state. Deadened. Someone could have whacked him with a bat and he wouldn't have felt it.

Hollandsworth continued reading him his rights while his younger partner, Dowds, did a quick search of the room looking for who knows what. *Look all you want, fellas. You won't find anything.*

Roxann had backed herself to the sofa, but when one of the uniforms started to pat him down, she lunged forward.

"Michael."

He drilled her with a look, silently pleading with her to stay focused and not panic. "It's okay."

"Stay back," Hollandsworth warned her just before he handcuffed Michael.

But Roxann wore the laser-sharp look of a woman to be dealt with. "Are the handcuffs necessary?"

"Procedure," Dowds said, looking under the sofa.

She whirled on him. "Why behind the back? At least let him be comfortable. He's not going anywhere."

Suddenly, her face blood red, she charged to the doors leading to the balcony, slammed the door open and peered over the rail before storming back inside.

"You leaked it."

Oh fuck. It just got worse. Not only was Roxann here, but so was the press.

"No, ma'am," Hollandsworth said. "There were reporters out there when we got here. Word travels fast."

Prick. Michael turned himself to steel. Had to. These assholes were going to make him walk out bound up like a serial killer. A muscle in his jaw twitched. He turned to Roxann. "Call Vic, tell him to call my lawyer."

Her gaze darted left and right as the cops continued searching. "Rox. Did you hear me?"

"I heard you." She turned to one of the cops. "Do *not* trash this place. Not in front of the publisher of a daily newspaper."

Hollandsworth snorted. *Fucker.*

"Just so we're clear," Michael said. "I want my lawyer."

Hollandsworth grabbed his elbow. "Let's go."

Someone shuffled in behind him and Michael turned to see Roxann moving out the door with them. He halted and she plowed into the back of him. "Where are *you* going?"

"I'm walking out with you."

That was all he needed; her parading in front of the press in rumpled sweats.

"No way, Rox. Stay put."

True to her style of not responding to orders, she continued to follow them out the door. "I'm walking down with you."

One of the detectives snickered and Michael wished he weren't cuffed because he'd risk the assault charge and pop the guy. They stepped onto the elevator.

"Rox, don't do this. Hit three and get off. I don't want you here."

She ignored him and fixed her eyes on the elevator doors. Stubborn. If he wasn't about to vomit, he'd laugh. What a total piece of work.

"Go ahead then," he said. "Go down to the lobby, but stay inside. Once you get to the street, you'll be surrounded and *law enforcement* isn't going to help you."

She shifted toward him, but Dowds held his hand to block her and found himself on the receiving end of her do-you-know-who-I-am look. *Gotta love her.*

She pushed Dowds' hand away and stepped closer. "I'll be okay. Your doorman will help me."

Michael closed his eyes. She would walk out into a sea of reporters, some of whom worked for her, and risk the credibility of the *Banner.* All to support him. Later, he'd tell her what it meant to him, but right now, it was editorial suicide. The muscles in his neck coiled and he opened his eyes to find her staring at him.

"They'll take your picture. You know that. Please, get off this elevator."

The lobby bell clanged.

Damn.

"Too late." With her head high, bedhead and all, she stepped out of the elevator.

The detectives, followed by the uniformed cops, led

Michael off the elevator and he could already see the flash-bulbs snapping. Hal, the doorman, rose from his seat at the lobby desk and his normally cheerful face drooped.

"I'm sorry, Mr. Taylor." As if it were his fault a cop stood guard to prevent him from calling upstairs. Michael actually felt sorry for the guy.

Roxann asked Hal to walk outside with her and Michael turned to see the two of them behind the three uniformed cops. Hal would get a nice Christmas gift this year. It took one hell of a person to walk into that crowd.

"Thanks, Hal," he said, as they walked through the lobby doors into a crush of news media.

NOW ROXANN UNDERSTOOD THE OTHER SIDE. REPORTERS shoved microphones at them and screamed questions while cameramen jockeyed for the spot that would give them a page one photo. Someone plowed into her and Hal pushed the cameraman away. She righted herself. Shook it off by breathing deep, in and out, in and out. She could do this. Risk everything. For Michael.

He had done his job by keeping his head up and his mouth closed as the detectives led him through the throng. She could do the same. *Lock it away, rebuild, concentrate.*

The detective opened the car door and guided Michael into the backseat.

How humiliating for him. She'd give Max a lashing on this one. Particularly if the police had leaked the story. She didn't care what Hollandsworth said, this whole scenario shouted l-e-a-k and it would be easy for her to confirm. She'd simply ask Phil.

None of this made sense. They must have something. Why else would they suddenly arrest him? At his home?

He'd been cooperating these last weeks and they could have allowed him to turn himself in.

That alone infuriated her. Well, Max would get a little surprise of his own. His niece's picture would be plastered all over the morning news as the woman walking out with the accused. He wanted to play dirty, she'd play dirty.

Someone said her name and Roxann turned. A flash popped in her face and white spots saturated her vision. She slammed her eyes shut, let the spots disappear. *Rebuild.* She opened her eyes to Hollandsworth closing the door behind Michael. She stepped to the door and Michael jerked his head toward the building, silently ordering her inside. For added drama, she placed her hand on the window until the car pulled away—oh, she'd play dirty—and left her with ravenous reporters.

"Ms. Thorgesson, what do you think of the charges?"

Roxann, with Hal beside her, angled back to the crush of reporters and ran smack into Phil. Would she, at some point, realize she should be mortified? She honestly didn't know because right now, Michael needed her help. An injustice had been done.

"No comment. At this time."

Once inside the safety of the lobby, Hal locked the doors and Roxann stepped behind a large support column to shield herself from the prying eyes. The sudden quiet surrounded her and the free-fall of adrenaline left a clanging inside her skull. She reached a hand to her head.

Count to ten. She could do this.

"Are you all right?" Hal asked.

"I'm fine. I think I locked myself out of Mr. Taylor's apartment."

Hal pulled a key ring from a locked drawer in the lobby desk. "I can let you in."

They rode the elevator in silence. Hal may have said something, but she wasn't quite sure. Her mind stayed busy with the effort to remain calm. Michael was going to jail. Possibly for the rest of his life. *Helpless.* No. She needed to concentrate on the next step. Contain the anger. *Use* it. The anger would keep her moving.

Hal let her into Michael's apartment and she thanked him. For everything. That scene could have been a lot worse had he not been there. She closed the door and spotted Michael's jacket hanging on the coat hook and something inside her splintered. She brought the jacket to her cheek and the clean, woodsy scent of him tore into her.

Rebuild. But the agony remained, ripping, clawing at her flesh and—*oh no*—the pressure stole her breath and her legs snapped like brittle straw. She hit the floor with enough force to make her hurt later, but the only thing that registered was her heart tearing away. The scream she needed to let out couldn't materialize. These past weeks had tested her and she wondered when it would all end. *Someone please make it stop. Please.*

Get up. He needs you. She shot to a sitting position, placed her palms over her eyes and pressed. *Think. Work the problem.*

Her purse had been dumped over by the cops—*damn them*—and she dove for it. She grabbed her cell phone and dialed.

"This early?" Vic said. "It better be good."

"I'm at Michael's. Michael..." She took a deep breath. *Control.* She needed it. Now.

"What?" Vic sounded instantly alert. "Talk to me, Roxann. What's going on?"

She couldn't do it, couldn't stay calm. The words came fast and jumbled and she hoped they made sense. What had happened to her? When had she become this insane person?

"They took him, banged on the door and he said to call Arnie. He told them he wanted Arnie."

She sifted through the contents of her purse on the floor. Where were the car keys? Throwing the purse aside, she remembered she didn't have her car. She'd have to get a cab or even run home.

"You have to call Arnie."

"Slow down. Please," Vic said, his voice strained with the effort to remain patient.

"They arrested him. He's going to jail."

The sound of it should have made her ears bleed. Michael in jail. Not possible. They had to get him out. Had to help him.

"Roxann, calm down. You need to get your shit together. I gotta help Mike, but I can't do that with you like this."

Rebuild. You can do this. She bobbed her head up and down, forgetting Vic couldn't see her. And then her focus came back because Michael needed her.

"I'm okay. It was hard seeing him in handcuffs. What should we do?"

She could handle paralyzed presses, but this she wasn't ready for.

"I'll call Arnie and then I need to tell the Taylors."

The Taylors. God help them. "The press was outside. It's probably all over the news by now."

"Fuck!"

Roxann jerked the phone from her ear.

A noise from the hallway caught her attention and she turned to see a cop rummaging through the desk in the corner. *God.* She'd had that meltdown with people here. Fabulous.

"I'm assuming you have a warrant," she said to the cop.

"Yep."

"Who's there?" Vic asked.

With her eyes still on the cop, she went back to Vic. "The P.D. is searching the apartment."

Suddenly the competitor in her focused on the task ahead and she became an Olympian, about to run the 400-meter relay. All her energy channeled into the athlete that blocked out emotion and distractions. The gold medalist was back. "You call Arnie, I'll call Gina. She'll help with Mrs. Taylor. I'll go with you to the Taylors'. They'll need to hear he's okay."

"I'll pick you up in ten."

24

"This is a bad idea," Vic said three hours later when he pulled into a visitor's parking space at police headquarters.

Roxann stared straight ahead at the non-descript five story stone building, mentally reviewing her game plan. Oh, yes, she would be ready for anything Max threw at her. "I'm okay. Besides, he knows I'm coming."

To warm her hands, she ran them down her slacks. Even the steaming shower hadn't gotten rid of the chill that gripped her. She snapped open the vanity mirror, checked her hair and lipstick. Everything in place. Not a smudge or errant hair to be found. At least she would *look* in control.

"You think he'll tell you anything?"

"I have no idea."

"Want me to go with you?"

She shook her head. Vic would jump into this snake pit with her, and she was thankful for that, but knew she had to face Max alone. "Thank you, but it'll be better if I'm alone."

Within minutes her heels tap-tap-tapped against the ceramic floor as she made her way down the long, narrow hall to Max's office. The desk sergeant had wordlessly waved her in as Max was expecting her. Most of the offices remained dark, their administrative occupants off enjoying family time on a bright Sunday morning.

"Good morning," Max said before she'd even reached his doorway. Must have heard her coming. And if his grumbling tone were any indication, he was not happy.

She stepped into the doorway, saw him in full uniform—unusual for a Sunday—and his gaze impaled her. Was he tired? Disappointed? Frustrated? All of the above?

Well, that made them a pair because she was disappointed too. Disappointed that he'd turned cold toward her and that she no longer felt able to confide in him. More than that though, he'd chosen to let their relationship crumble while she grieved for her father.

She held her hand toward one of his guest chairs. "May I?"

"Please do."

After counting three breaths, she looked up at him. "As you know, Michael Taylor was arrested this morning."

"I saw it on the news."

"I found it interesting that the press miraculously knew where and when the arrest would happen. I'm not sure I've ever seen such a blatant leak." Max shrugged and she held up two hands. "You want to be mad at me, be *embarrassed* by me, that's fine, but why was he suddenly arrested? Particularly with our former director of streets and sanitation popping off about bribes, ghost payrolling and the litany of other infractions performed by the mayor's staff. Alicia Taylor had some sort of relationship, which I think was a blatant affair, with the mayor's *married* chief of staff. Who knows what he might have told her? Nobody is pursuing *that* angle."

Max picked up a report sitting on his desk and perused it. "That's a police matter. I can't comment."

Roxann dug her heels into the floor. She would not give him the satisfaction of seeing her struggle. "Nice talking to you."

She rose from her chair, swearing to herself it would be a ninety-degree day in January before she gave into his controlling ways.

"What the *hell* is wrong with you?" Max roared.

A glorious buzz raced up her spine. *Yes.* Finally. She slammed the door and spun on him. "What is wrong with *you*? You've been acting like an idiot for weeks."

Max bolted out of his chair and came around the desk.

"Let's talk about idiots. You—" he poked a finger at her, "—have chosen to align yourself with a murderer. Then you go parading around on the news in your pajamas while they're hauling his ass to jail. What were you thinking?"

"There's no solid evidence against him and in order to clear this case the Chicago P.D. will fast track him through a trial. *That's* what I was thinking."

"You think we can't get a conviction on a circumstantial case?"

She snorted in disgust. "It's weak and you know it."

"Not that weak." His tone reeked of sandbagging.

He walked back to his desk and sat. "You are wearing me out, Roxann."

She remained standing and stuffed her hands into her pants pockets. He wasn't the only one worn out.

"So, what is it then? Obviously, you have something you're dying to tell me." She'd call his bluff. If there was anything, Phil would have gotten wind of it.

She hoped.

Max reached into his desk for a file. "I prepared for this meeting."

He held his hand for her to sit, but she waited a moment. Did she even want to hear what he had to say?

She sat.

"Ever heard of a mail cover?" Max asked.

"No."

"We did one on your boyfriend. Had the post office monitor his mail and tell us the return address of all mail received."

A tiny bit of something—fear maybe—rolled in her stomach. "And?"

"He renewed his passport."

Max leaned back in his chair and folded his hands behind his head. So smug.

Roxann scoffed, "Maybe the old one expired. He travels for work."

"Your boy was going to run. As I recall, he's been known to do that."

His words stung like a blast of a hundred tiny pellets. And the triumphant look on his face needed to be slapped off. Just one good *whap*. Damn him for being such a bastard. What she wouldn't do to scream at him, tell him how his attitude sickened her, shattered her already iffy emotional state and then just march out.

But the passport bugged her.

Why hadn't Michael mentioned it? He had to have known it would make him appear guilty. She shook her head.

"There's no proof he was going to run."

"We don't need any. All we have to do is prove there's a possibility we might lose a murder suspect and the D.A. will let us bring him in. He's not going anywhere now."

"So, all you have is the passport and an assumption that he would flee. No DNA? No fingerprints? Nothing else?"

No answer. Just a stone wall of a face. Perfect.

"Stay out of this, Roxann."

She stood and leaned forward on the desk, hovering over it and Max stared at her, his eyes steady on hers. "Not a chance."

She strode passed the desk sergeant, making sure to smile and wave goodbye as if her world was a beautiful place.

Who knew Max's office would make a perfect stage for this actress?

Vic waited in front of the building. A rush of relief filled her, but as she made her way to the car, her body began to crumble and the now familiar squeeze of a bad situation settled in her chest. *Dammit.* The men in her life were tearing her apart. She hoisted herself into the SUV.

"Drive me to the county lock-up."

"No," he said, making no effort to drive anywhere. "You won't see him. They're probably questioning him."

She glared at him, but if it had any effect, he didn't show it. She shifted toward him. "Did Michael renew his passport?"

"How the hell should I know?"

"Don't lie to me. You know everything he does."

Roxann's temper rarely flared so quickly, but this was most definitely one of those times. She needed someone to be honest with her and Vic was the lucky contestant. Badgering him until he gave in would not be out of the question.

"Back off, sister. I don't know anything about his damned passport."

She folded her arms. "He renewed it. They think he's a runner. That's why they arrested him."

Vic snorted. "What a load of manure. You can't believe that. Max is messing with you."

She let out a long breath, stared toward the building where her uncle would be enjoying his victory. "Michael left me before without an explanation, and I have a lot more at stake this time. I've put my newspaper's reputation behind him. He'd bankrupt me by running."

"Mike wouldn't run. Not this time. Not with his responsibilities and not with how he feels about you." He started the car. "Besides, if he was gonna run, I'd know."

"You think?"

"I *know*. You know it too. And I'm gonna cut you some slack because your uncle got into your head, but by the time I drop you off, you'd better know whose side you're on. It's crunch time." He shook his head. "This is one hell of a time to be waffling. I don't fucking get it."

"*You* don't get it? How the hell do you think I feel?"

She spun toward the door, stared out over Lake Michigan and did a mental ten count. Vic continued to drive toward her house and she willed herself to hang on until they got there. She could fall apart in private. But, as she sat in that passenger seat, her body expanded from the pressure. She cracked the window a few inches, sucked in fresh air, but—*dammit*—she couldn't breathe. *Not working.* The pressure. Too much. She bit down, squeezed the door handle until her bicep burned, but still no relief. Insanity. She closed her eyes. *Start at the toes. Rebuild. Rebuild. Rebuild.*

The car stopped and she opened her eyes. Home. Finally. She drew a long, luscious breath and eased her grip on the door handle. Vic shoved the car into park and when she looked at him the disappointment in his eyes turned her rock-hard body doughy. Someone else mad at her. The list continued to grow.

Pushing past opposition had never been an issue before and it wouldn't be now. The Olympic medalist in her wouldn't allow it. No way. "I do believe in him. I do. Lately, I'm always choosing sides. I've lost my father and if I take Michael's side, I'll lose Max, but if I take Max's side, I'll lose Michael."

Vic squeezed her shoulder and it felt soooo gentle and forgiving, as if, for a moment, she hadn't let everyone down.

"Max is a jerk-off," he said. "Who needs family like that? You can talk to Mike about the passport, he'll tell you he wouldn't run and you'll believe him because we've had this conversation. Mike doesn't have to know any of this. We'll just chalk it up to you being overworked, overstressed and temporarily whacked out. We all have shitty moments, right?"

Shitty moments? She was having a lot more than that. This nonsense with Max had to stop. He'd been trying to manipulate her for weeks because his boss wanted to suppress the *Banner*'s content. Well, she now knew where Max's loyalty stood.

A welcome silence filled the car and she glanced at Vic who stared out the windshield. He probably couldn't stand the tension. He wasn't the only one.

She straightened up and focused on the house in front of her. She was back. The controlled, together Roxann had come home.

"Vic, I am losing my mind. This emotional havoc is making me crazy. I have no where left to put everything and eventually it's all going to tumble out."

"So what? Let it tumble. You're entitled."

She jerked her head. "Thank you for setting me straight.

I was angry. Max led me to believe I had been used. I should have known better. Michael warned me about this a couple of weeks ago. He knew Max would continue to manipulate me."

Vic grabbed her hand and squeezed. "Rox, people do crazy shit. Max likes Mike for this murder and he's made you the prize in this pissing match. When this is over, you're gonna have to deal with him on that, but for now, let's work on getting Mike out. Okay?"

She nodded.

"Good," Vic said. "I want to check on Gina and get an update from the lawyer. See what's up. You gonna be all right for awhile?"

Roxann pulled on the door handle. Oh, she'd be all right. She was going to find a way to get Michael out of jail. Whether Max approved or not.

25

Roxann walked by Mrs. Mackey's desk with a feigned, but robust, "Good morning."

What felt like a small mountain of sand had lodged under her eyelids, but that's what a girl got when she stayed up until 3:00 a.m. staring at a computer screen. She hadn't found anything of interest in the files or the tapes, but Roxann wondered if she'd missed something. It wouldn't hurt to go over the notes again.

Mrs. Mackey followed her into the office. "Give it a rest, Sassy. I know you better."

"I figured I'd give cheerful a shot."

"What do you need?"

The list of needs was pretty darn long. No one had enough time for that. Roxann slid off her suit jacket and draped it over the back of her chair before taking her seat. "Screen my calls. If it can wait, let it wait. Only the important stuff today. The meeting with the pressmen will take most of the afternoon and I still need to prepare something."

She stopped and thought about it. How many offers had

she made them over the past month? They'd declined every one. "You know, I have nothing left to give them. Maybe *they* need to offer *me* something."

Mrs. Mackey grinned. "I love the way your mind works."

Roxann smirked. "Anyway, only the important stuff today. Michael's arraignment is this morning and I want to be there."

"Not a good idea," a male voice interrupted.

Roxann glanced up and saw Vic in her doorway. He'd become a regular at the newspaper and no longer required a visitor's pass. Despite the suit he wore, he looked worse than she did. His hair, always stylishly messy, didn't have the style today, but definitely had the mess.

"Excuse me?" she said.

Vic walked into the office, shifted his gaze to Mrs. Mackey and back. No mistaking that hint.

Roxann turned to her. "Will you excuse us?"

Mrs. Mackey inclined her head, obviously not happy about it. "Of course."

Roxann waited until he closed the door. "What's this about me not going? I want to be there."

"Commendable, but dumb-ass. After the show you put on yesterday, the press will be gunning for you."

She pushed back and folded her arms. "I don't care."

"Mike does."

"You talked to him? Is he all right?"

"No, I didn't talk to him. Arnie called and said Mike specifically said you shouldn't go."

Why would Michael shut her out? "Well, I guess if he doesn't *want* me there."

"Oh, please. Don't get all female on me. You know how he feels about you and he doesn't want you putting yourself out there."

"I've not only put myself out there, I've put my news-paper out there. I don't see how any of it matters. After yesterday, this city knows about us."

"Don't bust my balls, Roxann. I'm telling you what he said."

She nodded. "I'll take it under advisement. What else? I know you didn't come here to tell me that."

"I got a call from Jerry Foyle last night. Mike asked him to look into your pressroom problem and he figured I was in the loop. I wasn't, but with Mike being...you know, Jerry called me."

Roxann drove her heels into the floor to steady her quaking legs. Was she about to find out who destroyed her property? "What is it?"

"Jerry made some calls. A friend of a friend type thing."

She propped her elbows on the desk. "Just tell me. Please."

Their eyes met and held for a minute while she braced herself for the news.

"Your production manager has a gambling problem."

Not much shocked her anymore, but the idea of nerdy Craig Rawlins being a degenerate gambler definitely did the job. She scoffed, "You cannot be serious? He's a good man."

"No, he's not."

She waited a beat, her heart hammering.

"He owed Jerry's not-so-nice friends a pile of money. A pile that wouldn't be repaid on *his* salary. The vig alone..."

No need to elaborate on the interest owed. Had to be a lot. Roxann reached down, white knuckled the arms of her chair. "Tell me the rest."

"The guy Craig owed money to had an in with the mayor's office."

An earlier conversation with Phil slammed into her

brain. Phil had made an offhanded comment that Leland Wingate's son had criminal ties. Could this be who Craig owed money to? And was Leland Wingate the in with the mayor's office? Had to be some bizarre coincidence. Couldn't be. Could it?

She shot to her feet, but her head spun and she put a hand on the desk for balance.

"Tell me Leland Wingate's son is the guy Craig owed and the streets and sanitation director was the connection."

"I don't know the exact who and what. Jerry wouldn't tell me, but it's no secret how the mayor feels about the *Banner*. The mob guys, figuring they could score points with the mayor, got word to him that Craig owed them money."

"The mayor made a deal with whoever this person is?"

Vic nodded. "Yeah. If he'd get Craig to disable the presses the mayor would owe him a favor. The guy gave Craig a pass. The mayor owing a favor was worth more. I guess the mayor wanted to teach you a lesson."

Roxann stood motionless, her brain attempting to absorb it. This, she could not believe. Preposterous. Vic opened his mouth, but she jerked a hand at him. "Wait. Stop. I...uh."

She shook her head, then on wobbly knees walked to the window. The sun shone on the building across the street and she realized this sunny day would be remembered as a travesty. She dropped onto the windowsill, one leg swinging, while she dissected the story and put it back together.

This couldn't be true. Craig had worked for the *Banner* for years. Her father had adored him. And this is how he repays that respect? How could he betray them?

She had to face him herself. She swallowed the simmering rage and turned to Vic.

"I need to hear it from Craig. There's no proof."

Vic sat next to her on the sill. "Rox, why would Jerry make this up? He doesn't even want his name brought up. If these guys knew he helped—well, let's not speculate on what would happen."

She narrowed her eyes. "I need to talk to Craig. Give him the opportunity to deny it."

"How are you gonna do that? You can't just hit him with it. We have to protect Jerry. He and Mike have been friends a long time."

Understanding, she nodded. What if it were Janie? What would Roxann be willing to risk for her? Jerry, via Michael, had come through for her.

"I'll say Phil came up with something during his City Hall probe and I put the pieces together. If Craig admits it, it won't matter how we found out. Personally, I hope he denies it. This makes me sick."

"I'm sure. Also, I checked on Mike's passport."

She held up a hand. "I don't care."

Vic smiled. "Fine, but just so you know. His old one expired six months ago. He applied for it, but his application got lost and he had to reapply."

He'd applied long before Alicia was killed. "They're holding him on a coincidence?"

"Pretty much, yeah."

"Another reason to get him out."

Sixty-five minutes later, she sat behind her desk staring out the window. A bird rested on the ledge sunning itself.

Some life.

Craig Rawlins had cried. She'd asked him outright and, without even bothering to deny it, he'd crumpled. He'd owed the mob a hundred-thousand dollars.

A hundred-thousand dollars.

He didn't know anything about Wingate's son. He dealt

with someone else. Probably someone who worked for Wingate's son. The mob was threatening him. His wife had no idea he had a gambling problem and when the mob came to him with a solution, he went for it. With full knowledge of the consequences, he loosened the blanket bar on the press.

After hearing Craig's story, she had called the police and they took him into custody.

Craig wasn't able to give them anything regarding City Hall. He had no idea why he'd been asked to disable the presses. He'd been told it wasn't his concern. Roxann, to protect Michael's friend, chose to keep that element to herself.

She had to speak to the staff immediately. The building was probably already buzzing and the employees were owed an explanation.

The story would be all over the news, but so far, only the *Banner* knew there was a City Hall connection, and Phil had stormed out like a man running from a ticking bomb. By the time he finished, the mayor's office would consider him, rather than her, the most reviled newspaper person in the city.

Good for him.

Mrs. Mackey came into the office, walked to the credenza and turned on the television. She left again, closing the door behind her. On the television, a perky blonde stood outside the criminal courts building as she announced that Michael Taylor had been denied bail.

Denied bail? Roxann began to wonder if the entire universe had a drug addiction. Denied bail. He had no prior offenses and the proof was shaky at best. She'd seen serial killers get bail, but not Michael.

Politics.

It was all politics. She rose, turned the television off and, overwhelmed by the information, collapsed into one of the guest chairs. Life's assault on her system left her numb, and she wondered just how much a girl could take. The rage had been building, and she'd been pushing it back, burying it, sorting it out, filing it away. Now she was done. She had nothing left. No tears to cry, no screams to vent, just a hollow emptiness in her core.

Sunlight glistened off the windows across the street and, fortified by the glow, she started at her toes, and put herself back to together, piece by hollow piece, until she reached the top. She sat straight and took a breath.

Done.

Time to get to work.

She headed to the outer office where Mrs. Mackey sat at her desk. "I'll be in the newsroom. Would you please get me Tim Griffin at the state attorney's office and transfer him to Phil's desk?"

Mrs. Mackey slapped her hands together. "Go get 'em."

"Yep. Time to get Michael out of jail."

MICHAEL SAT ON THE CRACKER-THIN COT STARING AT THE FAR wall of his six by six cell.

His head did a looping spin. Time to lie down.

If this was going to be the view for the rest of his life, he'd rather end it now. Maybe ending it was extreme, but he'd go crazy if he had to stay locked up. Bad enough he'd been denied bail and would have to hope for a quick trial date.

He studied his attire. Dark gray scrubs with Cook County Jail stamped on the left breast.

Shit.

And the damned mattress had that one blasted coil jutting into his back.

What monumental mistake had led him to this place? It wasn't killing Alicia. That he knew for sure.

Marrying Alicia.

Sad, but true. If he'd stuck it out, put up with the bullshit from Roxann's father, he was sure they'd have gotten married. She'd have been a good wife. Strong, supportive and above all, faithful.

He'd fucked that up good.

"Taylor, you got a visitor," the guard, a young kid with a roadmap of a face, said.

Michael sat up thinking it would be Vic.

Roadmap grinned. "She's a hot one too."

That description narrowed it down to Roxann or Gina, and Michael felt the ever present need to pop the guy who talked about his sister that way. As far as Roxann went, he couldn't blame the guy. She *was* hot.

Whichever one it was, Gina or Roxann, she was going to get an earful.

"I have a thing for blondes too."

Mystery solved. "Dream on, dickhead."

That comment risked a beating with the club, but the idea of that maggot near Roxann made Michael sick.

The guard laughed. "Too bad visiting is over in fifteen minutes. I wouldn't mind looking at her awhile."

Michael stepped from the cell and pictured himself putting his fingers in his ears. *Tune him out. Don't listen. La, la, la, la, I can't hear you.* The fucker was trying to rile him. *He wants you to swing at him. Not today, pal. I'm not losing my few privileges.*

Roadmap opened the door to the visiting area consisting

of a long row of thin metal chairs with desks separated by a glass wall.

Roxann had taken the second chair from the door and Michael's heart kicked at the sight of her. He reminded himself he was pissed at her for coming. He'd missed her though. Thirty-three hours without her was too long.

They both picked up their plastic phones, but he turned to watch the guard leave before looking back to Roxann.

Her eyes, shadowed and puffy, stayed focused on him. She wore her hair pulled back and a killer suit that screamed she was too good for this shit hole.

"Why are you here?" he asked.

"Hello to you too."

"Sorry. Hi. Why are you here?"

She sighed. "I was worried about you. Maybe even missed you, but with that greeting, I have no idea why."

He scooted closer to the glass and wished he could reach through and touch her. "I miss you, too, but I hate you being in this place. You don't belong here."

"And you do?"

He shrugged. "They seem to think so."

Ignoring his statement, she said, "I didn't make it to court this morning. Did Vic tell you everything?"

Michael nodded and mouthed, "We're being recorded. Watch what you say."

She smiled in response when the guard's head popped through the door.

"I'm sorry about Craig," Michael said. "I wouldn't have figured on that."

"Me neither, but it's over now. Phil is breaking every rule of political correctness trying to figure out who the link is. I'm sure it's who we were researching."

Wingate.

"Think Phil will figure it out?"

"Yep."

"The mayor's going to be on you."

"And your point is? Besides, he's not nearly as scary as he used to be."

"That's my girl."

She smiled wide and for a minute he almost forgot where they were. Almost. Then her smile vanished and those sparkling blue eyes met his.

"I'm going to get you out of here, Michael. We'll have a life together."

A life together. He and Roxann. Too much to hope for.

"I'd love to believe that, but let's not count on it."

"I *am* counting on it. We've come too far to let it end with you in here. Even if we weren't involved, I'd want to figure out who killed Alicia. Innocent people shouldn't go to jail."

She believed he was innocent. Not much else mattered at the moment. He put his hand against the glass and she did the same.

"Please, don't come back here. I love you, but I don't want you in this place."

She didn't start huffing or pull her hand away. She just sat there.

"I needed to see you. And it's nice to hear you love me. Tell me again when you get out of here. That's the one I want to remember. I'll tell you, too, but not in here."

She loved him. He had hoped for it and now he knew.

He slid his hand away from the glass. "Please don't come here again."

Tears simmered in her eyes and he looked away. *Damn.*

"You won't be here long."

He almost felt sorry for her. "Roxi, I might not get out."

"What am I supposed to do? Leave here? Forget what's happened? Let you go again?"

He jabbed his thumb and index finger into his forehead to quiet the hammering that had started there. "You might have to."

She smacked a hand against the glass. "Stop it."

The guard stuck his head in again and Michael waved him off. *No problem here, sir. You son of a bitch.* He gripped the phone tighter trying to control his temper. "What if I'm convicted and they send me out of state? Will you come every other weekend for a conjugal visit?"

Roxann narrowed her eyes. "Now you're being cruel."

"Maybe, but it could happen. You deserve better."

The door to the visiting area opened and Roadmap yelled, "Five minutes."

"Great," she said. "We've spent the whole time arguing. Well, guess what?"

He stared at her because if he'd learned anything in his lifetime it was not to interrupt Roxann when she was about to rip him one.

"You're not forcing your decision on me. You forced it on me twelve years ago and look how that worked out. If I want to see you, I *will* come here. Get used to it."

She slammed the phone into its cradle, scraped the chair back and strode out without a goodbye. Great visit.

Damn, he loved that woman.

26

"MAYOR IMPLICATED IN MOB SCANDAL. NOW THAT'S A headline." Roxann dropped the newspaper on her kitchen table and reached for the phone to retrieve messages. Every muscle ached and she entertained the idea of crawling into bed. So what if it was only nine o'clock? The phone in her hand grew heavier with each passing second and she contemplated not listening to the messages. She'd been on the phone all day, mostly defending the *Banner*'s editorial content. Even publishers deserved a break.

There had been one call from Rick Turnbull regarding the pressmen. The men, after hearing one of their own had sabotaged the press, decided to review her last offer and wanted to meet again next week to work out an agreement. Finally, after holding her ground, she could put that contract to rest.

She dialed her voice mail. Why not? When it came to the *Banner*, she always had a little fight left. Besides, the only call she was interested in would be her mother's. They'd been phone tagging all day and Roxann wanted to update her.

Yesterday, Vic had told Roxann about Craig's gambling problem and, after Phil's hard work, the story was now on page one.

Wingate's son was part of a south side crew that ran the mob's illegal gambling operation in Chicago. Phil took that information to the former director of streets and sanitation and, after Roxann tapped her friends at the state attorney's office to get him immunity, he admitted he set up a meeting between Wingate's son and the mayor. Carl Biehl also attended the meeting.

At that meeting, Wingate's son told the mayor about Craig's gambling problem and offered to help with the *Banner* issue. Helping the mayor meant forgiving Craig's gambling debt if he'd disable the presses.

Roxann now had answers to her pressroom problem. Alicia's murderer was still out there, but they were getting close. Now, more than ever, she was sure someone in the mayor's office had killed Alicia. She just didn't know why.

It had been a whirlwind day. They'd printed an extra fifty-thousand copies to increase the draw, but even with those extra rack copies, it still wasn't enough. The *Banner* was a hit.

The mayor was not. Roxann never would have believed him capable of such treachery, but she supposed power could transform a person.

Damn him.

It was business and the mayor made it personal. Roxann balled her fists and her nails pricked her palms. And what about Carl's involvement? He and the mayor should rot in prison.

The doorbell rang and she grunted. *Please, leave me alone.*

She walked to the front door, peeked out the peep-hole. Her breath clogged. This, she could not believe. *Breathe.*

With the chain still on the door, she opened it an inch. "Good evening, Mr. Mayor."

This man, his clothes and hair a rumpled mess, could not be the mayor she knew. His bloodshot, menacing eyes were the worst. She thought about shutting the door.

"Need to talk to you." His voice held the low growl of fatigue and something else...what?

Intoxication.

Oh, bad, bad, bad. She stole a look behind him. Where was his driver? His security detail? Could he be alone?

"Give me a minute."

Roxann closed the door, leaned into it. Fear licked at her and she swallowed. She should tell him to leave. Being alone with an intoxicated man whose career her newspaper had ruined would not be a wise choice.

But maybe he wanted to clear his conscience and if she sent him away, she'd lose the opportunity.

She reached for the phone on the end table and dialed the only person she thought could help. Hopefully, Max would put their differences aside for one evening and help her deal with his boss.

"It's Roxann. I need help. The mayor is at my door. He looks drunk and, well, I'm scared."

She'd never spoken those words. She wouldn't have allowed herself to admit it, but sometimes pride had no business horning in.

"I'll be right over," Max said. No argument, no gloating. *Thank you.*

She wasted a few minutes to give Max time. The mayor pounded on the door and, for a moment, she thought about not speaking to him at all.

The nagging began. He came to her house for a reason. If he wanted to yell at her, he'd have done it over the phone. The mayor had something on his mind and, with any luck, it had to do with Alicia Taylor.

Time to find out. She'd talk to him on the porch. Safer outside. Her neighbors could hear her scream. She'd take the cordless with her though.

Unwilling to risk opening the front door and have him push through, Roxann walked to the kitchen, pulled her running shoes from the closet and slipped them on.

She strode out the back door and through the alley with her hands twitching. *Be still.*

The mayor spotted her on the sidewalk and stepped off the porch, his stride fast, but not aggressive. He halted a few feet in front of her, his suit wrinkled and eyes hollow. To her, he appeared worn and battered. She refused to feel sorry for him. Not after what he'd done. He'd been a good mayor once, a great mayor, and now he was a criminal.

"Mr. Mayor, what are you doing here?"

He glared at her with those dead eyes. "I made my choices. I did. I got greedy, but I've done a good job for this city."

Stall. *Don't agitate him.* "I know you have."

"Everything I worked for in my life has been destroyed by two women who've been fucked by Mike Taylor."

Whoa. The venom in his voice smacked at Roxann's nerves and she retreated a step. "Excuse me?"

"You insulted?"

"I'm insulted that your way of dealing with my news-paper was to disable my press. And what does taking bribes have to do with Michael Taylor?"

He stalked the walkway. "That crazy bitch. I told Carl to take care of it. And what did she do? She used it against us."

Roxann waited. This was it. And she was alone. Didn't that figure? It'd be her word against his and who knew what the public would believe?

"Used it against you how?" She had to get him to say it. "You know I can help you. Tell me about Alicia Taylor. Make this right."

He turned toward her again, their eyes meeting. His breathing quieted and he dragged his hand over his mouth. Three times. "She was blackmailing me. Threatened to go to the press over Wingate's payoffs. I could have denied any knowledge of it and fired anyone involved. We would have gotten away with it, but Carl was nervous. Kept trying to convince her to stop."

Roxann listened and waited for the telling sign of his involvement with Alicia Taylor's death, but the information came too fast for her to analyze.

Somehow, probably through her relationship with Carl, Alicia had known about the corruption and had foolishly tried to blackmail the mayor. This man was a political powerhouse. She should have known, one way or another, he'd destroy her.

Where was Max? The mayor's anger escalated again and she hoped her uncle would arrive before it spilled over. Max could calm him. The man was his boss and Max knew the intricacies of his temper.

"Mr. Mayor, what are you trying to tell me?"

"Roxann!"

She spun to see Max charging around the corner of the house. Relief surged. He stopped and did a quick survey of the mayor's appearance.

"Doug, what the hell are you doing here?"

The mayor shrugged. "It's over, Max."

"Get in the house, Roxann." Max didn't take his eyes from the mayor.

"Max—"

He turned toward her with gritted teeth. "In the house."

No way. Not with Michael's life on the line. But Max had that determined look to him.

"Fine. Talk to him, but I want to hear his side of this mess. He knows something about Alicia Taylor. He's already told me most of it and I'm going inside to call Phil. I'd better get the rest or it'll be a half-told story and the first half isn't good."

She turned to leave, but the mayor lunged at her, grabbed her throat. She tried to step back, slapped at his arms, but he squeezed harder and she gagged, felt the bulge of her eyes. Her pulse pounded against his thumb. He'd kill her. She saw it in his eyes.

A murderer.

"Bitch."

Max hauled the mayor off and, with the speed of a well-trained black belt, rammed a brutal strike into the man's nose. A horrid crunch followed and Roxann reeled backward into the brick steps. Off balance, she landed on her butt.

The mayor hit the ground, his body limp and still against the concrete. *Dammit. Wake him up. Get answers.*

Max dropped to his knees and checked for a pulse. "Shit, Doug."

"Help him!" She needed to call 9-1-1. Where was the phone?

Max, lost in his thoughts, stared down at his unconscious boss. He finally glanced at Roxann but made no movement to help. Shock? Had to be.

"Call for help," she said.

Max finally jumped from the ground, folded his arms over his head and paced. "Fuck."

"Call someone."

"He's dead."

"*Dead*?" She ignored the ache in her tailbone and stood. "He can't be."

He may have been a corrupt politician, but he didn't deserve to die.

Max scrubbed his hands over his face. "Shit."

Roxann glanced back at the mayor's blood-soaked face and swallowed hard. *Don't look at him. Don't look at him.* Sickness filled her and she tilted her head skyward, inhaling and exhaling. She turned to Max, who had lowered himself to the steps and covered his face with his hands. The superintendent of police, a man that had spent his life protecting the community, had just killed his boss.

She walked to him, grabbed his wrists and pulled. "It was an accident. You thought he was going to hurt me."

And now the man was dead on her front walk. The ground suddenly shifted under three of Max's feet. Three? Then her knees buckled and the blackness came.

27

"You're all right, Rox. You passed out."

The voice, familiar, but distant penetrated her mind. A tunnel maybe? She opened her eyes and saw Max's face above her. Turning her head, she saw the stairs leading to her second floor and surmised she was on the couch in her own living room. Safe. She took a breath, reached a hand to Max and he guided her to a sitting position.

"Take it slow." He jerked his chin toward a uniformed officer. "Get her some water."

The horror of the situation began to settle and she shuddered with a violence that nearly broke her. She curled her knees into her chest, rested her forehead on them and counted to three. Hold on. *Just hold on.*

Max knelt beside her. "Janie is coming over. Your mother doesn't know. I didn't want to upset her. I'll tell her later."

"We should do it together. It involves both of us."

He placed his big hand on top of her head and gently rubbed. "We'll do it together."

She sucked in a long breath and let it out slow. Her body warmed and a sudden quiet filled her system.

"Thank you for being here. I don't know what he'd have done."

"I'll always take care of you, Rox."

The sound of the back door crashing open prompted them, including the uniformed officer, to peer down the long corridor toward a charging Janie.

"Here we go," she said, anticipating the wrath of Hurricane Janie.

Thirty minutes later, after hearing Roxann's version of the story, Janie said, "You need sleep. You're coming to my house. The cop outside says you can't stay here. They need to work."

Janie propped her hands on her hips, and Roxann thought it would be nice to evaporate into the couch rather than deal with Janie in school marm mode.

"Not yet," Roxann said. "I want some answers on whether they're going to release Michael."

"Michael, Schmicheal. It's late and, if I know you, you'll be getting up at six for a run and then off to work. Besides, the cops won't have this sorted out until morning. And Rox, the mayor is dead. D-e-a-d. Max said something about bone fragments into the brain and a hemorrhage. I don't think Michael is going to be top priority."

"I know he's d-e-a-d. I saw him die. On my front walk. At my uncle's hands." A wave of nausea crept its way up and burrowed into her throat. "I'm going to be sick."

Janie shoved Roxann's head between her knees and bolted to the kitchen.

"Here." She handed Roxann a plastic bag while sliding next to her.

Roxann stuck her face in the bag, but nothing came. The story of her life lately. Nothing went as planned. Her entire body was an abandoned building about to crumble.

She'd run through her emotional reserves over the past six weeks and was beaten and tired and scared. Rolling herself to the side, she settled her head on Janie's lap as her battered existence played over and over inside her head.

"Come to my house, Rox. Just sleep for awhile. It'll be better in the morning."

"I love him."

Janie sighed and brushed a hand over Roxann's head. "I know you do, honey."

A DULL BUMPING IRRITATED HER AND ROXANN SLAPPED AT THE invader. Finally asleep and someone had the nerve to wake her up.

"Don't be smacking at me," Janie said. "You've got company."

Roxann flipped to her other side. "Go away."

"I'm not the one insisting on seeing you."

"Then tell *them* to go away."

Janie laughed.

"You might want to talk to this person."

"Ugh." Roxann peeled her eyes open, felt the soft material of Janie's couch against her nose. "What time is it?"

"Seven-thirty. And, by the way, you missed your run. I'll tell your guest to come in."

"Wait." Roxann hoped to get cleaned up for what she assumed would be a detective questioning her again. Too late. Janie had already told them to come on in. *Thanks so much.*

With practiced hands, she tied her hair into a ponytail. It would have to do, but brushing her hairy teeth had to happen pronto.

She missed her run. Again. For the five-hundredth time.

At least now, she didn't get upset anymore. She had bigger things to worry about.

"Good morning."

That deep toned voice snapped her head sideways. She had to be dreaming. She blinked and focused, and Michael appeared in front of her. Her heart tripped like a jackhammer and she leaped off the couch and into his arms.

She kissed every inch of his face, hairy teeth and all, just to be sure he was really there. His cheeks bunched into a smile and she kissed harder.

Finally, she stepped back and took in the wrinkled shorts and T-shirt he'd been wearing when arrested. "When did they let you out? What happened?" She punched her fist into her other hand. "I knew I shouldn't have slept."

"They released me about half an hour ago. Reporters were everywhere. Arnie snuck me out through the underground garage at the jail."

"Did they tell you what happened?"

He closed his eyes, pulled her close. "Yeah. You must have been terrified."

She thought about it a minute and hugged Michael closer. "It happened so fast. Max helped me."

"He can be a son of a bitch, but I'm glad he was there for you."

She rested her head against Michael's chest, ran her fingers over his shirt just for the comfort of being near him. "They think the mayor killed Alicia. He admitted she was blackmailing him."

"Did he say he did it?"

"No and it's bugging me. He was about to say something about the murder when Max showed up."

"According to my lawyer, Carl backed the story. Said he didn't know anything about the murder, but that the mayor was adamant Alicia needed to be dealt with. With Max's help, they got me released in a hurry."

"Well, sure. The mayor's dead now. Carl can blame everything on him. Maybe Carl was involved and he's using the mayor to save himself."

Michael pushed her to arm's length and drilled her with a look. "Let it go. It's not perfect, but they got the bad guy. And without you, it wouldn't have happened."

They got the bad guy. Michael had won his freedom. Why analyze it? "I'm sorry."

"What are you sorry for?"

"All of it. You didn't deserve to be humiliated."

"Yeah, well, sometimes life sucks."

"Yep."

"I missed you, Roxi. I could have given everything else up, but I couldn't think about never being able to touch you again. That drove me nuts."

He leaned down to kiss her and she slapped her hand over her mouth.

"Hairy teeth. I have to brush. Then I'll suck your face off."

He waited for her. He would have preferred to follow her up and find a bedroom, but this was Janie's house and he'd never disrespect her that way. Suddenly, all he could think about was getting Roxann into bed. He'd only been in jail a few days, but it could have been five hundred.

He had slept on the pitiful excuse for a cot making all kinds of deals with God, begging for freedom. He'd never been a deal maker when it came to God. He typically just trusted the plan, no matter how screwed up it seemed, but this time things had changed. He'd spent half his adult life wishing to have Roxann back and it had finally happened.

Until he got locked up. Life in a cage would not do. That's when he started making deals.

Roxann came downstairs and grinned at him. She'd washed up and her hair hung loose around her shoulders. The way he liked it. What a kicker.

"You've had a rough night," he said. "Why not take a day off? Go back to bed. With me."

Without taking her eyes from his, she grabbed her cell phone from the end table. "It's me," she said into the phone. "I won't be in today. If there's an emergency you can call me, otherwise, do your Stonewall thing. Thank you."

She hung up and sat on the couch.

"You really should get some sleep."

Roxann shrugged. "I need a run."

"Forget it. You've got a herd of press looking for you. Come home with me. I've got my guys there holding off reporters. I'll sneak you in and you can use the gym in my building."

"You don't have to stay with me. I'll be okay. Your parents are probably wondering where you are."

He shook his head. "I called them. Told them I'd be over in awhile. I want to go home first. Shower in my own bathroom. You really look beat, Roxi."

"I am beat. Maybe I'll take a nap at your place."

"Good idea. I'll have Vic come over when I leave to see my folks."

"I don't think that's necessary. It's over now and Vic has better things to do than babysit me. I'll keep everything locked up."

"Humor me."

He wasn't leaving her alone. Even if he did live in a secure building.

Roxann shrugged. "For once, I'm not going to argue."

"Good." The tingling up his spine told him she'd given up *way* too easily.

28

AFTER A LONG NAP, ROXANN SAT ON MICHAEL'S COUCH WITH Vic across from her and decided having him around might be a good idea. She could bounce ideas off him about the mayor being a murderer and he'd be more objective than Michael.

She had questions. Big ones. "How would the mayor even know how to snap Alicia's neck? He'd never served in the military or had any training where he might learn that."

"Couldn't tell ya."

"And what time did he leave the PBA function the night Alicia was killed? Did he stay late or leave early? Has anyone bothered to check the timeline?"

"Couldn't tell ya."

So much for bouncing ideas off him. The man was useless right now. "I need to talk to my uncle."

"I'll go with you."

She held her hand out. "I need to talk to him alone."

No response. Probably thinking about how to handle her. He had to be bored stiff from an entire afternoon of small talk.

"I'll drive you then."

Rolling her eyes, she pulled her purse from the closet. "Fine. Just drop me off and leave. Max will drive me home."

She didn't want Vic sitting out in the car waiting, in case her meeting with Max ran long.

He pulled his cell phone. "Who're you calling?"

"Mike."

Roxann slipped her bag over her shoulder and threw her hands in the air. "Now I have to report in every time I want to go somewhere? This is stupid."

Ignoring her, he spoke briefly to Michael, ended the call and grinned. "Ready, darlin'?"

She pushed by him. "Whatever."

When she arrived at Max's office, she was told she'd find him working out in the basement. The taxpayers had provided a professionally designed gym, including top of the line cardio equipment, heavy bags and a steam room. The *Banner* had covered that story and Roxann found it ironic that it was the catalyst to the problems with City Hall. After the story broke, the mayor hounded her and her father regarding their coverage of his office.

The desk sergeant waved Roxann through the swinging gate that allowed access to the administrative offices and the stairwell to the basement. Along the way, she wondered how to get a city job because at five-thirty the offices were barren.

She opened the door to the gym, expecting to hear a blast of weights clanging, stereos blaring and people grunting, but the room offered little of that. Several men worked out with free weights, a couple more on cardio machines and a television was on, but the volume had been turned down. The only noise in the room came from the clink of a weight being shifted onto a bar.

Max, dressed in a black karate gi, his black belt tied

securely at his waist, sparred with another man in the far corner of the oversized room and Roxann stood back for a moment, watching as they kicked, retreated, kicked again. The *pfft-pfft-pfft* of feet connecting with clothing proved Max could move when he needed to.

Another man, also dressed in karate garb, stood with his back to the door and she stepped beside him. When he turned to her, recognition sparked and she thought back to where she might have met him. His sandy hair and long, angular face brought images of a man more pretty than handsome and she smiled.

"Ma'am." He turned back to the action.

"The desk sergeant told me Max was here."

"I think he's almost done."

She nodded and stuck her hand out. "I'm sorry. I can't remember your name. I'm Roxann."

Looking down at her hand, he pursed his lips, hesitated, then held his hand to her. "I'm Adam. I work for Max."

Not the friendliest guy on staff, but she wasn't here to see him anyway. She turned her attention back to Max who remained so focused on his opponent he failed to notice her standing there. He let a roundhouse kick fly and sent the enemy to the mat.

Roxann smiled. "I forget how good he is."

"He could do some damage."

Unfortunately, Roxann had seen that firsthand. She turned toward a smiling Adam and froze.

Adam, who worked for Max, had a crooked front tooth.

A clawing darkness swallowed her and she held her breath, let it out slow. She'd never forget that tooth. Not when its owner had threatened her.

He tilted his head. "Are you okay?"

Pull it together. Shake it off. He doesn't think you recognize him.

"I just remembered a call I forgot to make. Will you tell Max I'll see him later?"

She turned and strode to the door. *Don't run. Don't run. Don't run.*

"Roxann, wait," Adam yelled.

She glanced back and saw Max stop his workout. He looked at Adam, then back to her.

Run.

She bolted through the door, taking the steps two at a time and thanking the little voice that had told her to stay in her jeans and sneakers. None of them could catch her when she wore running shoes.

She shot through the stairwell door expecting to see someone, but the corridor remained empty. She heard Max yell before the door closed and, sickly fear penetrating, she ran past the desk sergeant and out the main entrance.

Once on the sidewalk, she sprinted through an alley and zipped across a side street. She wanted to stop and dig her cell phone from her purse, but the loud thumping in her ears signaled her to keep going.

Why did she tell Vic to leave?

Think. Think. Think. She darted around evening rush-hour pedestrians and cut across another alley. Three more blocks and she'd reach the *Banner*. The busy streets would keep her safe until she reached the newspaper. She hoped.

Her thoughts bounced with wild assumptions. Maybe Adam was asked by the mayor to threaten her? He said he worked for Max though. Could Max have asked him to do it? No.

A painful sob broke free and she urged herself not to get

dramatic. *Rebuild. Rebuild. Start at the toes.* There had to be an explanation. Had to be.

A police cruiser came to a screaming halt in front of the *Banner* just as Roxann pushed through the lobby doors. She ran by the stunned security guards at the lobby desk and yelled not to let anyone up. No one.

Taking the stairs that would lead her to the executive suite, she dug out her keys as she made her way up. She hoped some of the executives were still working, but didn't count on it. She'd heard something about drinks after work to celebrate the paper's ace reporting.

After bolting the executive suite door, she locked herself in her office.

Michael.

Had to call him. Diving for the phone with trembling hands, she dialed and waited. *Come on. Come on. Answer.*

BEHIND THE WHEEL OF HIS SUV, MICHAEL GLANCED DOWN AT the ID on his phone and smiled. Roxann calling from the office. "Hey, I thought you were going to see Max."

"Michael." Her voice squealed and his body tensed.

"What's wrong?"

He turned down an alley and shot through, knocking over a couple of garbage cans on his way to the *Banner*.

"Something's happened. I think Max is involved. I don't know."

What the hell?

"The guy with the crooked tooth works for Max. I saw him at the station. "

Son of a bitch.

"Rox, lock yourself in."

"I am locked in. Someone's here though. I saw a police

cruiser pull up when I ran through the lobby. I told security not to let anyone up."

"Good."

Two blocks from the newspaper and he was stuck in traffic. *Damn.* "Just stay on the line with me. I'm in traffic, but I'll be there in a few."

"Security is on my other line. Hold on."

He waited an endless minute for her to pick up again, but reached another alley that stretched two blocks and would get him to the newspaper. Bingo.

"Sorry," she said, her voice littered with tension. "Max is on his way up. I told them not to let anyone up. *Dammit!*"

Michael nearly crushed the phone in his hand. "Don't let him in. I'm about to pull around the corner."

"There he is," Rox said. "He's knocking on the outside door."

"Don't let him in."

She didn't answer. Bad sign. "Roxi, whatever you're thinking, stop."

"I can get it out of him. Whatever his involvement, I'll get him to tell me."

"No."

"I have to go." The phone clicked.

Roxann stood staring at Max through the glass doors. He held his hands out. "What the hell's going on? Why'd you tear out of there?"

This was it. She had to open the door. It struck her as odd that last night she'd called on her uncle for help, but now he brought terror.

Taking a deep breath, she flipped the lock and opened the door. Still wearing his workout gear, he stepped forward and hugged her. Roxann kept her hands at her sides until he released her.

When had he become someone she didn't know?

"Who is Adam?"

"He works for me."

"What does he do?"

He held his hands wide. "What the hell is this about?"

"Did you send him to scare me that day? On my run?"

"He's a police officer. He protects people."

"Not all do, Max. You know that. Cops are corruptible."

"Right." He waved his arms. "Is this the kind of crap Taylor feeds you?"

"Don't bring him into it. This is me talking and I think you know something about Alicia's murder. I think you didn't want me involved and you sent Adam to scare me."

Max moved to one of the sofas in the reception area, sat down and leaned forward on his elbows, the weight of his body pressing him down. For the first time, she noticed his exhaustion. She knew that feeling.

"I knew Richmond did it."

"You covered it up?"

"Absolutely not. There was no proof. I had a feeling."

"And you were willing to let an innocent man go to jail?"

"The evidence said it was Taylor. We had to go with what we had."

"Bull, Max. You could have done something."

"HE DID DO SOMETHING," MICHAEL SAID.

Roxann spun toward him and Max's head shot up. Michael had been standing in the doorway listening and a thought too preposterous to believe struck him.

"Michael," she said. "I didn't hear you come in."

Max stood and faced him. "This is a private conversation."

The look of hatred only gave more merit to Michael's thoughts.

"I want him here," Rox said then shifted back to Michael. "What did he do?"

Michael stepped into the room, placed a hand on her forearm and squeezed. "He killed Alicia."

"*What?*"

Max laughed. "This is brilliant. Cut the crap. You're scaring her."

Rox remained silent while she absorbed what he'd said, but her arm tensed under his hand. The idea that she'd take Max's side never occurred to Michael, but her silence made him wonder if he should have considered it.

"Why would you say that?" she asked.

"It's true, Roxi. Your uncle is a stone cold killer."

STILL STANDING BETWEEN THEM, ROXANN BROUGHT HER PALMS to her forehead. Maybe holding them there would stop the unruly battering to her brain. "Where is this coming from?"

Michael kept his eyes fixed on Max. Two gladiators about to engage. "Max has been trying to get you off this case. He's manipulated you, rejected your theories, and any leads you've given him have not been investigated. He's hiding something. At first, I thought he was covering for the mayor or Carl, but Carl doesn't have the balls and the mayor wouldn't have gotten his hands dirty."

"That's a wild assumption," Max said.

"Yeah? Why don't you explain why you hit Richmond with a lethal blow when you could have incapacitated him? I'm no black belt and even I know you can do a palm strike to the nose without killing someone. You chose to aim up rather than straight on which would have only broken his nose. You *chose* to kill him."

"Shut your mouth," Max roared.

Roxann faced her uncle. "Tell me what you did."

Her control tight-roped along the edge of hysteria, but she refused to break down. She needed to focus on getting the answers they needed.

Max's stormy eyes snapped at her. "You cannot believe this garbage?"

With Michael standing behind her, she raised her chin. "I wouldn't have believed my father would drop dead in his office. I wouldn't have believed Craig Rawlins could destroy our press, and I certainly wouldn't have believed you could murder someone. But I don't hear you denying it. The mayor never told me he killed Alicia. All he said was he told Carl to handle Alicia blackmailing him. That's it, Max. Tell me what you did."

Silence.

That shattered her. If he didn't do it, he should be denying it. And suddenly it all made sense. "When I called you last night asking for help with the mayor, you knew I was getting close to figuring it out. After the *Banner* ran the story on the mayor being involved with the pressroom damage, you knew he was coming undone. You *knew* he wouldn't let himself be blamed for Alicia's murder. He came to see me to save himself, and what better way for you to protect yourself than eliminate the threat? With all the corruption and payoffs, who wouldn't believe he was a murderer? You were going to manipulate me, just as you've always done, into believing the mayor did it."

"Roxann—"

"And you sent your staffer to scare me. You torched my

car! All to get me running to you for help. You terrorized me, Max. How could you do that?"

"You son of a bitch," Michael said.

A groan came from Max and his face morphed into something hard and dark and evil. "Just so you know," he said to Michael. "Your wife was a great fuck."

Roxann let out a gush of air. Sucker punched. "It was you? *You* had the affair with Alicia?"

Her uncle lunged forward and Michael shoved her aside the second before Max's fist connected with his jaw. He stumbled backward, recovered quickly and blocked the second punch.

Roxann ran to the phone on Mrs. Mackey's desk, dialed security first and then, with furious fingers, called 9-1-1.

A *whoosh* came from behind her and she turned to see Michael ramming his shoulder into Max's midsection. The two men went down. Max, with his martial arts expertise, kicked Michael off and bounced up.

Michael, back on his feet and anticipating the round-house kick Max leveled on him, jumped clear.

Roxann couldn't stand it anymore. Too much. The chaos had to stop. She needed to end this insanity. She picked up one of the marble bookends on Mrs. Mackey's desk—an excellent weapon—but the glint of metal caught her attention.

Gun.

Max had pulled his service revolver from somewhere. *No.* Roxann dove for it. A loud bang sounded from somewhere and a searing heat flooded her shoulder.

How odd.

And the pain. Oh, how it ripped through her. Her legs buckled and she went down.

"Rox," Michael yelled.

But she saw Max staring at her, the shock of his actions paralyzing him. He was no one she knew. "Did you shoot me?" she asked, too stunned to actually believe it.

Michael knocked the weapon from Max's hand and began pounding on him. Punching, punching, punching. She turned away. He too, in this violent tirade, had become unrecognizable to her.

Max's face became a bloody mess and when he fell to the ground Michael began kicking him. Roxann, still on the floor with her hand on her bleeding shoulder said, "Stop. Please."

Two security guards barreled through the door and pulled Michael from Max. Exhausted, she curled into a ball and her body shook, every bone coming unhinged from its joint.

Within seconds Michael was on his knees in front of her examining the wound.

He pulled his phone from his pocket and dialed. "You'll be okay. An ambulance will be here soon."

Michael turned into triplets and she blinked a couple of times. "Is it over?"

Her fingertips tingled and her eyes drooped. *Heaven.* "I'm going to heaven. To see my dad. Not ready though."

Michael made a snorting noise that Roxann found quite irritating. "Actually, you're passing out."

"Oh."

"I really thought I was dying." Roxann laughed at herself and flopped her head back on her hospital bed.

The surgery had left her groggy, but at least she no longer had a bullet lodged inside her. Her hands and feet had swelled from the anesthesia and, although she didn't have a mirror, she could feel the puffiness in her cheeks. She felt like a five-foot-ten version of Shirley Temple.

Michael sat in one of those awful metal armchairs next to her bed and scooted closer to hold her hand.

"I knew you weren't dying. I fixed a few of those injuries in my army days."

Her eyes began to droop. So tired. "Hmmm, lucky you were available."

"Yeah, well, it scared the crap out of me. We're reassigning your lobby guards and that's the end of it. My guys would never have let Max through."

He'd been after her to replace the security guards and now she understood why. At least he didn't say she had to fire them. She'd find a spot for them somewhere.

The door to her room opened and a nurse stepped in. "Ms. Thorgesson, there's an officer outside. He has a man with him who says he's your uncle and he's asking to see you."

Michael stepped toward the door. "No way."

"I'll see him."

He spun on her, his eyes hard and so clearly out of patience. "*What?*"

The nurse's gaze ping-ponged between them and Roxann held up a hand. "Would you please give us a moment?" The nurse darted out and Roxann turned back to Michael. "I need to hear from him and then I'll be done. I may not achieve any sort of understanding, but at least I'll have heard his side."

"Not that you owe him that."

"I owe it to myself. And..." *How to say this?* "You need to leave me alone with him. He won't talk to me in front of you."

Michael set his hands on his hips and stared up at the

ceiling. She half expected him to pop off at her, but he remained quiet and thoughtful. Maybe he could find it in himself to understand.

"I'll leave, but the cop comes in. You can't be alone with him. He *shot* you."

No arguing that point. "The officer can stay." She smiled. "But you have to go."

Two minutes later, with Michael in the hall, Max stepped through the door in handcuffs, his right eye battered and stitched. Michael had done some damage. Another man entered behind him. Not the police officer, but Max's lawyer. Max had refused to speak to her with the officer in the room and Roxann agreed to let his lawyer stand in. The officer remained outside the door. She never imagined she would need protecting from her uncle, but she'd also never imagined him capable of murder.

Max stood next to the bed and she motioned to the chair. "I'll give you time, but I don't want excuses. I've been through hell, apparently at your hands, and I deserve the truth."

He dropped his head, shook it a few times and when he looked up at her, his eyes glistened. Max crying? Had she ever seen that? Now she knew her life would never be the same. Either way, she couldn't be sure if he was crying because he got caught or because he was sorry.

"You were sleeping with Alicia Taylor?"

He nodded. "It was a few months."

"Did you care for her?" Why on earth would she even want to know?

"I don't know. You wouldn't understand, but she had a way about her. Exciting. Wild."

What was it with these men wanting excitement? At

least Michael had grown out of it. "I don't need the details. You're a single man and entitled to companionship."

"I made mistakes. Got sloppy. I was infatuated and shared some things I shouldn't have."

"Oh, Max."

"I was stupid. Then she started to pressure me about moving the relationship forward. As if I'd get married at this point in my life. She wanted the status that came with my job. By that time, I realized I may have wanted her body, but I had career aspirations that wouldn't tolerate a slut on my arm."

Max had always said he wanted a federal job. Something in D.C. Alicia must have known it too.

"So, you tried to end it?"

"Yeah. She went nuts. That's when she approached the mayor and threatened to go to the press. When I couldn't talk her out of it, the mayor told Carl to deal with her. That's why he was visiting her. He wasn't screwing her; he was trying to convince her to stop threatening Richmond. The night of the PBA function, Carl came to me because Alicia wouldn't budge. He told me I needed to fix my mess before she blew us all to hell. I went to her house to talk. We argued for a long time. It got out of control."

"And killing her was the answer?"

Max eyeballed her. Could he be offended? Really?

"I had worked years to establish my career. I couldn't let her destroy it all. It wasn't just me, Rox. The mayor, Carl. We were all at stake."

"You can't believe I'd feel sorry for any of you. Not after all this. Whatever her mistakes were, she didn't deserve to die."

None of them counted on Alicia Taylor destroying their careers and then they had the gall to blame her for their erroneous ways. They were all criminals, but Max had been stupid enough to tell his lover too many secrets. Max and Carl would go to prison and the mayor was dead. Stupid, stupid men.

The now familiar ache of emotional warfare sparked inside Roxann. Her body had been pummeled by life. How would she ever get over this? She'd adored Max and now had to live with the devastation he'd inflicted upon her.

"I'm sorry, Rox. For all of it."

She stared into his eyes, wondering if the sadness she saw could be meant for her. Probably not. "Well, it's over now," she said. "You'll have to live with it."

The officer from the hallway stuck his head in. "Time is up."

Michael pushed through behind the officer, spared Max a scowl and jerked a thumb toward the hall. "Get out."

When Max stood, he leaned toward her—could he actually mean to kiss her cheek? She held up her good hand. "Don't."

"Out," Michael said again in a voice thick with simmering anger.

Who could blame him after what Max had done?

Max left without a glance at her and she shook her head. "I can't believe this." She knew it was true. Max had told her himself. "What prison could they possibly send him to? He'll spend the rest of his life in solitary confinement because a police superintendent doesn't have a very good life expectancy when he's locked up with murderers."

Michael raised his eyebrows.

"Don't say it. *He's* a murderer. I know it. I just can't get my heart to accept it."

Michael sat on the edge of the bed, wrapped his hand around hers and squeezed. "Your heart may never accept it.

Maybe it's good enough if only your head does. You'll probably always love him."

"It's not reality. I'd be fooling myself."

"Yeah, but reality sucks."

That shut her up, but she still grinned. Michael was
here. With her. Really with her. She'd waited years for this
and although she was happy, she couldn't be overjoyed.
There'd been too much loss in getting him back.

"In six weeks, I've lost two men that I loved—"

He nodded. "I'm sor—"

"But I also got one back."

His shoulders dropped and he leaned forward to press a
kiss on her lips before pulling back. "I owe you so much. You
put everything on the line for me, and I could say thank you
for the rest of my life, but it wouldn't be enough. I was in jail
and you still fought for me."

"We did this together. It wasn't just me."

"Yeah, but you had the spine to go for it. I'm not sure
anyone else would have. You didn't totally trust me, but you
had faith. You've *always* had faith in me, Roxi. Even when I
didn't have it in myself. And if there's a woman who should
have punted, it's you." He looked up at the ceiling, bit his
bottom lip and brought his gaze back to her. "I screwed up
by leaving you, I screwed up by not trying harder and I
screwed up by not being the man I should have been for
you. The thing I want you to know is that, from now on, I'll
always be here for you. Nobody will ever love you the way I
do. Ever."

A rush of tears submerged her. Such emotional
upheaval today. No more. She needed to enjoy this bit of
happiness. She eased out a teasing, heavy sigh. "Well, I'm
glad *that's* cleared up. There aren't many men who enjoy
sparring with me." She tightened her grip on his hand.

"We're competitors, Michael. We play to win. I think we just won big."

He fired off a lightening quick smile that she hadn't seen in twelve years. The old Michael was definitely back. And she'd keep him.

Forever.

Want more of the Private Protectors series? Read on to enjoy an excerpt from *Man Law*.

MAN LAW

BY ADRIENNE GIORDANO

Enjoy an excerpt from *Man Law*, book two in the Private Protectors Series:

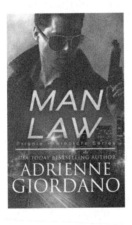

Man Law: Never mess with your best friend's sister.

"Ah, shit." Vic Andrews, butthead supreme, listened to the churn of the ocean's waves. Or was it his life skittering off its axis?

Gina laughed that belly laugh of hers and he couldn't

help smiling. He extracted himself from her lush little body and rolled off. The St. Barth sand stuck to his back. Yep, they'd worked up a sweat. Salty sea air invaded his nostrils and he inhaled, letting the moisture flood his system.

Jesus Hotel Christ.

What had he been thinking? He'd been heading back to his room after closing down the resort's bar and there she was, the girl—er, woman—of his dreams, crying on the beach. No condition for her to be in after witnessing her brother's marriage to the love of his life.

Vic didn't mention the fact it was 3:00 a.m. and she was alone on a secluded beach where any drunken asshole, like him, could have at her. Although technically he wasn't drunk. Buzzed maybe. Big difference. Besides, they'd been at a wedding. Buzzed was allowed.

Gina moved and he finally turned toward her. "I'm—"

"No, absolutely not," she said. She swiped at her curly mane of dark hair. Her face gave away nothing, but that meant squat. Gina knew how to hide bad moods.

The whoosh of the ocean lapping against the shore distracted him and he stared into the blackness.

"What did I say?" he asked.

"You were going to apologize. I don't want to hear it."

Apologize? Him? "I'm not sorry." He touched her arm. "Are you?"

Please don't say you're sorry. Please.

That would be all he needed. He'd just freakin' obliterated the sister rule Mike had invoked nearly a million—maybe two million—times. The sister rule was Man Law, and Man Laws were about the only rules Vic followed.

He only wanted to check on her, and before he knew it, voila, the clothes were off, the condom was on and they were humping like bunnies right there on the beach. At least no one saw them. All the well-meaning people were asleep.

Gina brushed sand from her legs and stood to straighten the slip like dress he'd shoved up over her hips. The silky fabric glided over her curves, and the activity in Vic's lower region made him groan. A thirty-five-year-old mother of three, and she was killing him. He should be ashamed.

Screw that.

She was right there. Right there. And, because he'd probably never get the opportunity again, he should grab her and—

"I'm not sorry," Gina said. "Not about the sex. I'm sorry about other things, but this, I loved."

Vic retrieved his pants and stood. Gina and her honesty. Good or bad, she just put it out there and didn't worry about the repercussions. He guessed it came from losing her husband at the age of thirty-one. She had nothing to lose.

"I need to go," she said, watching him with her big brown eyes as the moonlight drenched her face. He put his shirt on. Did she have to look at him that way? Particularly when he wanted a replay.

"Aren't the kids bunking with your folks?"

"They are, but you know how Matthew is. He might search for me."

Fifteen-year-old Matt, her eldest son, took his job as man of the family seriously.

"Right. Okay." Vic motioned toward the resort. "I'll walk you."

Gina held up a hand. "I'll be fine."

Nuh-uh. No way. "I *am* going to walk you. It's late and you shouldn't go by yourself."

Hell, she shouldn't have been out here alone in the first

place, but he knew she'd tear him a few new ones if he said it.

She stood there, peering up at him and—*God*—she was fantastic. She had a classic oval face with high cheekbones and a nose he knew she hated. For over two years now he'd imagined running his finger over the little bump in it, but never dared. Every inch of her seemed perfectly imperfect.

Blown sister rule.

Gina shoved her fingers through her curls. "We screwed up. I can't believe it. We've been so good."

"We didn't screw up. We had a simultaneous brain fart. Again."

She laughed and shook her head.

"Anyway, walk me to the edge of the beach. You can see my room from there and can watch me go up."

"Gina, what's the big deal? Nobody will know we just—" he waved his hand, "—you know."

"It'll be better if you don't walk me. With his mental radar, Michael is probably waiting by the door. On his damned wedding night. I swear he's a freak. He should stay out of it."

Oh, boy. She was getting fired up. *Maintenance mode.* His friend needed protection. They were both ex-special ops, but they didn't stand a chance against all five foot three of Gina.

"Mike loves you. He's trying to protect you."

"From you? You're his best friend."

Vic ran his hands over her shoulders. "Yeah, but I'm not right for you."

"The circumstances aren't right. That's true, but he doesn't have to keep reminding me."

"He does it to me too."

They strolled to the edge of the beach, and he squeezed

her hand. *Don't go. Just stay for a while.* All he wanted was more time with her. Not a lot to ask.

On tiptoes, she brushed a kiss over his lips. A little hum escaped his throat. What the hell was that?

"I had a great time," she said. "You were just what I needed."

"I think a 'but' is coming."

"We can't do this again."

Yep. Not good. "I know."

She pulled her hand from his and hauled ass toward her room. Away from him.

He waited while she went up the stairs and she stopped in front of the window of the room next to hers. A minute later the door opened and Matt came out. He turned and, apparently using his Spidey sense, looked straight at Vic.

And we're busted.

ALSO BY ADRIENNE GIORDANO

PRIVATE PROTECTORS SERIES

Risking Trust

Man Law

Negotiating Point

A Just Deception

Relentless Pursuit

Opposing Forces

THE LUCIE RIZZO MYSTERY SERIES

Dog Collar Crime

Knocked Off

Limbo (novella)

Boosted

Whacked

Cooked

Incognito

The Lucie Rizzo Mystery Series Box Set 1

The Lucie Rizzo Mystery Series Box Set 2

The Lucie Rizzo Mystery Series Box Set 3

THE ROSE TRUDEAU MYSTERY SERIES

Into The Fire

HARLEQUIN INTRIGUES

The Prosecutor

The Defender

The Marshal

The Detective

The Rebel

JUSTIFIABLE CAUSE SERIES

The Chase

The Evasion

The Capture

CASINO FORTUNA SERIES

Deadly Odds

JUSTICE SERIES w/MISTY EVANS

Stealing Justice

Cheating Justice

Holiday Justice

Exposing Justice

Undercover Justice

Protecting Justice

Missing Justice

Defending Justice

SCHOCK SISTERS MYSTERY SERIES w/MISTY EVANS

1st Shock

2nd Strike

3rd Tango

STEELE RIDGE SERIES w/KELSEY BROWNING

& TRACEY DEVLYN

Steele Ridge: The Beginning

Going Hard (Kelsey Browning)

Living Fast (Adrienne Giordano)

Loving Deep (Tracey Devlyn)

Breaking Free (Adrienne Giordano)

Roaming Wild (Tracey Devlyn)

Stripping Bare (Kelsey Browning)

Enduring Love (Browning, Devlyn, Giordano)

Vowing Love (Adrienne Giordano)

STEELE RIDGE SERIES: The Kingstons w/KELSEY BROWNING

& TRACEY DEVLYN

Craving HEAT (Adrienne Giordano)

Tasting FIRE (Kelsey Browning)

Searing NEED (Tracey Devlyn)

Striking EDGE (Kelsey Browning)

Burning ACHE (Adrienne Giordano)

ACKNOWLEDGMENTS

Thank you to my husband who, during the course of this manuscript's journey, offered ongoing emotional support and his vast newspaper knowledge. Also for putting up with me constantly saying "I have a question." You can relax now. I'm done asking questions.

To my dynamic duo, John and Mara, I'm running out of ways to thank you. John, I drive you crazy with my law enforcement questions, but you always respond. You're the best. Theresa Stevens, you were the first to read this story in its entirety, and I'm thrilled you get to join the fun of seeing it published.

To Lieutenant Josh Flanders, thank you for sharing your firefighting knowledge. I'd be terrified to do your job and am thankful there are people like you to answer the call.

Paul Seveska, thank you for getting into the nitty-gritty of newspaper operations with me. Hopefully, I've gotten it right. John Kocoras, you gave me great ideas regarding circumstantial evidence and I had a blast working out the various scenarios.

To my critique partners, Kelsey Browning, Tracey

Devlyn and Lucie J. Charles, thank you for responding to all those last-minute emails begging for help. You're an awesome team.

To Gina Bernal, this is the book of my heart and I'm grateful for your assistance in getting it ready for publication. As always, thanks to the team at Carina Press for all the support.

Finally, to my son, the junior alpha male in my life, thank you for supplying never-ending entertainment (even when you interrupt my writing time to ask me if I saw the 1993 All-Star game). I love you.

A NOTE TO READERS

Dear reader,

Thank you for reading *Risking Trust*. I hope you enjoyed it. If you did, please help others find it by sharing it with friends on social media and writing a review.

Sharing the book with your friends and leaving a review helps other readers decide to take the plunge into the world of the Private Protectors. I would appreciate it if you would consider taking a moment to tell your friends how much you enjoyed the story. Even a few words is a huge help. Thank you!

Happy reading!
Adrienne

ABOUT THE AUTHOR

 Adrienne Giordano is a *USA Today* bestselling author of over forty romantic suspense and mystery novels. She is a Jersey girl at heart, but now lives in the Midwest with her ultimate supporter of a husband, sports-obsessed son and Elliot, a snuggle-happy rescue. Having grown up near the ocean, Adrienne enjoys paddle-boarding, a nice float in a kayak and lounging on the beach with a good book.

For more information on Adrienne's books, please visit www.AdrienneGiordano.com. Adrienne can also be found on Facebook at http://www.facebook.com/AdrienneGiordanoAuthor, Twitter at http://twitter.com/AdriennGiordano and Goodreads at http://www.goodreads.com/AdrienneGiordano.

Don't miss a new release! Sign up for Adrienne's new release newsletter!

Made in the USA
Middletown, DE
20 May 2023